# AHRIMAN:
## The Spirit of Destruction

By
**Puja Guha**

**Book I of the Ahriman Legacy**

Ahriman: The Spirit of Destruction
© 2014 Puja Guha
ISBN: 9781730889950

Find out more by joining Puja's mailing list at:
http://smarturl.it/PujaList
www.pujaguha.com
pujaguha@pujaguha.com
Printed in the United States of America

## Also by Puja Guha
## Spy Thriller Suspense Series:

The Ahriman Legacy Book I —
*Ahriman: The Spirit of Destruction*

The Ahriman Legacy Book II —
*Road to Redemption*

The Ahriman Legacy Book III —
*Resurgence of the Hunt*

## Contemporary Indian Family Drama / Woman's Fiction:
*The Confluence*

**Find out more by joining Puja's mailing list at:**
http://smarturl.it/PujaList

# Dedication

*For my father, who helped give me the vision;*

*For my mother, who helped give me the discipline;*

*and*

*For my husband, who gave me the motivation to begin.*

# Table of Contents

# Map of Kuwait

Source: ESRI Online

# Prologue

## *Tehran, Iran – May 28, 2018*

"Is this Kasem Ismaili?"

"Yes," he said as he groggily rubbed his eyes. "Who is this?"

"It's Nurah Bahar. Do you remember me?"

Kasem sat up abruptly and frowned. "Yes, of course. You're that friend of Lila's. Is everything all right?"

"I have a message from her."

Kasem's heart started to race. "What is it?"

"We can't talk about this over the phone. Can you meet me in an hour?"

He reached over to his bedside table to grab his digital alarm clock. He blinked twice in astonishment at the bright red numerals that read 2:04. "In an hour? You mean meet you at three in the morning? Are you crazy?"

"You're both in danger. Do you want to hear the message or not?"

"Yes, of course! But I have to get to work in a few hours."

"I'm already breaking the rules by trying to get this message to you. It will all be irrelevant in twenty-four hours."

"Oh, come on! You have to give me more than that to go on. How do I even know that you've spoken to Lila?"

"I have the locket that Lila wore. Will it be proof enough?"

"The locket?" he said and took a deep breath. *Lila said that would be the signal.* His thoughts began to run toward dark places. "I guess another sleepless night won't do me any harm," he finally conceded. "Where should I meet you?"

"The place where we first met. I'll see you in an hour. Don't be late."

The line went dead. *Where we first met? It'll take almost an entire hour to drive there.* Kasem groaned as he fumbled around the room to get dressed.

He was en route to his car when he remembered that his friend Jamal was huddled on the couch after locking himself out of his apartment down the hall. *He just had to forget his keys tonight.* He pulled out his cell phone and typed a hurried text message while stopped at a traffic light.

*"Running urgent errand for L on other side of town. See you in few hours."*

Forty minutes later, Kasem pulled up in front of the empty lot where he and Lila had parked the last time they visited this flat on the other side of the city. Choosing the safety of the garage next door instead, he parked his car and walked over to the building.

It was eerily quiet at close to three in the morning. Cars passing by on the nearby highway were few and far between. Kasem shuddered. *This had better be an emergency.* His thoughts drifted back to Lila and he could feel his stomach tying in knots. He tried to push his mind away from the worst-case scenario to no avail and shuddered once again.

Kasem entered the lobby quietly and walked toward the elevator, which still had a large worn-out sign on it written in Farsi that read, "Elevator out of order." He pushed open the door to the stairwell and rushed up to the third floor.

He knocked softly when he reached the apartment door. A few moments later, Nurah opened the door a crack.

"Did you come alone?"

"Are you fucking kidding me? Who would I bring with me? It's three in the morning!"

"I had to be sure. Come in," she said while opening the door to let him inside the dimly lit apartment.

He stepped past her into the living room and felt something sharp jab him in the neck. "What the h—?" he cried out.

Kasem's eyes widened as he fought to maintain his vision. In his peripheral vision, he could see two burly men appear from the shadows of the dark room and grab his arms. He tried to lash out, but his muscles refused to respond. His legs started to sway and the room grew even hazier. "Nurah, what are you doing? Who are these men?" He tried to shout, but he could barely hear the whisper that escaped from his throat.

His legs buckled and he fell, first to his knees and then over onto his right side, landing hard on the side of the small couch near the entryway. Without realizing it, his phone slipped out of his pocket.

"I'm so sorry, Kasem. They already knew everything. I have to protect my family."

In the back of his mind, he could hear the echo of Nurah's voice.

The room faded as they thrust a dark sack over his head. "Where are you taking me? What do you want with me?" he tried once again to shout.

Then everything went black.

****

# Book I
# 2021

# Chapter 1
# Three Years Later

*Shuwaikh, Kuwait – May 15, 2021*

"Salaam alaikum."

"Alaikum salaam." The old gatekeeper paused, surveying the young man as he entered the building. "Come in, my son. What brings you to our chambers? To whom are you here to speak?"

"Your malik has requested my presence."

The gatekeeper nodded slowly. "Very well. Take the elevator to the fifth floor and follow the corridor to the right. Knock on the last door and wait for a response before you enter."

"Shukran ya sayeedi." *Thank you, sir.*

The young man walked away from the old gatekeeper. The elevator doors creaked as they opened, and he stepped inside. It reached the fifth floor a moment later and he stepped out into the hallway. The air felt dank in the old building and a dim light cast a strange glow across the different doors he passed. The door at the end of the hallway looked more like a plain black panel, similar to an odd piece of modern art he once saw at the San Francisco Museum of Modern Art.

He reached the door and knocked slowly.

"Come in."

The door swung open with a loud screech.

\*\*\*\*

Marzouk Fayed was staring at the file on his desk when his senior aide, Khaled, knocked on the door of the makeshift office that they had created as a front for certain illicit activities. The office building was older and shabbier than the one that housed his real office only a short drive away, but at least he did not have to entertain dignitaries while worrying that someone would notice an incriminating file mistakenly left out in the open.

"Sayeedi, he is here."

"Show him in."

Khaled led the young man into the office. The dark room smelled faintly of apple-flavored *sheesha* and burned incense. Fayed sat at a desk in front of two windows with shutters that almost completely blocked out the intense sun. He was dressed in traditional garb—a long white *dishdasha* and checked *gutra* headpiece marked with bright red. The large desk dwarfed the small, portly man sitting behind it.

The young man held back a smirk as he approached the desk.

"Salaam alaikum."

"Alaikum salaam."

"Aren't you a little young to be one of the world's best?"

The young man ignored the biting remark and looked squarely into Fayed's eyes.

"I see that you didn't even bother to make yourself look presentable after your arrival yesterday," Fayed continued.

"If I were wearing a suit instead of these old jeans, would that make you more confident in my abilities?"

"Most real men would wear a suit to a job interview."

"Oh, I see. Is this a job interview then?" The young man snickered. A moment later, an out-the-front switchblade was wedged upright in the center of Fayed's desk; the cherry-colored wood cracked sharply.

"Would you like any further demonstrations of my skills?"

Fayed's face turned ashen. "No, that will not be necessary."

"I think we both know that this is no job interview."

"Er, yes, indeed. Your reputation precedes you." Fayed's hands began to tremble uncontrollably and he barely maintained the false bravado in his voice.

"So let's not waste any more time," the young man said curtly. "Why the hell did you ask me to come here?"

"Well, as I said, your reputation precedes you. We have summoned you here for an important task given what you've done for our mutual acquaintances."

"Indeed. Do you want to give me any details then? Or would you like me to pick my own targets?" The young man reached over on to the desk, retrieved the blade, and then holstered it.

Fayed slid the file across the table and forced himself to make eye contact. "The t-t-task is explained in there. We would, we would like you to make it look like an accident."

"And the money?"

"The first half will be wired to your account within twenty-four hours. You'll get the second half upon completion."

"Completion in…?"

Fayed straightened up in his chair. "Please read the file before you ask me any more questions. We, we expect completion by a specific date. The details are in the file."

"You could have had this file delivered to my hotel. Don't you want to make certain that everything is absolutely clear?"

"You may go now." Fayed's voice faltered as he spoke.

The young man bowed his head slightly as he backed out of the room. *Who's the target?*

Twenty minutes later, he exited his car and walked into a hotel lobby in Salmiya, the so-called bustling center for Kuwait's youth. Even though it was officially a completely different city, the distance between Kuwaiti cities always astounded him. With less than a thirty-minute drive, the Shuwaikh industrial desert turned into the blue Salmiya seafront.

"Good afternoon, Mr. Mubarak," the concierge said with a smile.

"Hello, Imran. Any messages for me?"

"No, sir. Do you need anything for your room?"

"No, everything's fine. I just need a nap. This heat is exhausting."

"You've been in England too long, sir. Summer hasn't even started."

"Isn't that a comforting thought?" The young man shook his head and smiled sheepishly, then turned and headed toward the elevator. If only he actually had been away for the past two years as the concierge thought. Perhaps someday, he could finally escape the region's sweltering heat, which once had welcomed him but now made it difficult to draw even a single breath.

When the door to his room clicked shut, he locked the dead bolt and slid open the file. The first sheet outlined the timeline of the assignment. *Another kill.* He sighed as he dumped the rest of the envelope out onto the bed. A single photo floated down onto the comforter.

The man known as the Ahriman, named for the Persian spirit of destruction, tried to sit down slowly. His muscles stiffened and he slid off the bed onto the floor, grasping the picture in his right hand.

He had seen that picture on billboards all over Kuwait.

## New York City, United States – May 15, 2021

Petra Shirazi was still in bed when the phone rang, jerking her from a slew of early morning dreams. The man at her side stirred and said, "It's Saturday. Who the hell is calling you at eight thirty in the morning?"

She gave him a bemused smile. "Who do you think?"

"Tell them to go to hell. It's Saturday!"

"That would be great for us wouldn't it? Both out of a job in one morning." She reached for her purse, rummaging to find the ringing cell phone.

"But…"

"Shh, go back to sleep," she whispered as she retrieved it. "Hello, this is Petra Shirazi."

"Petra, we need you here immediately. We've received some new intel from the Middle East. It's urgent."

"I'll be there in an hour."

Petra groaned as the call ended. *And I was supposed to be on vacation this week.*

"Honey, I have to go in to the office. I'll see you tonight," she said as she hastily pulled on a pair of jeans and a T-shirt.

"Okay, babe," Grant muttered in a sleepy haze. She gave him a peck on the cheek and headed straight out the door.

## Kuwait City, Kuwait – May 15, 2021

The oppressive Kuwaiti sun streamed in through the windows of Bayan Palace as one of the Emir's aides exited his office. Once the door shut, the monarch sighed.

Three weeks ago, he had been extremely displeased when he once again had to disband Parliament for the thirteenth time in the past fifteen years. His actions had seemed warranted at the time, but the situation had only worsened since then and showed no signs of improvement.

A knock at the door pulled him away from his thoughts. "Come in."

His aide entered. "The prime minister is here to see you, sir." "Show him in."

Sheikh Mohammed entered a moment later. "Sabah al-khair."

The Emir smiled as he stood and the two men kissed on both cheeks, as is the Arab custom. "Now, tell me Mohammed. What is it?"

"I am very sad to say that I am here to tender my resignation."

"But why? That isn't necessary! By the time the next election occurs, it will be too late for the Assembly to investigate you."

"And then in another two months, they will find another reason to blame this entire crisis on me, and through me, on you. Or they'll start another rumor—a secret lover, a new private plane, an illegitimate child. What difference does it make? It's all the same in the end. They will find a reason to grill me in public and then even you will be forced to accept my resignation. Why go through all that pain? My wife and children have suffered enough."

"But your dealings with Global Petrol were completely legal. And innocent, damn it!" the Emir protested. "There was no way you could have known that they had no real interest in investing."

"My friend, you know that the Assembly does not see it that way. Besides, I should have been more careful. The members who pushed for my questioning will just be reelected in a few months and they will not forget my weakness."

Their gazes locked, neither willing to concede.

"We both know that I am only doing what's necessary."

They stared at each other in silence before the Emir finally gave in to him. "Very well, Mohammed. Your mind is made up then?"

"Yes," he nodded. "May I leave you with two pieces of advice?"

"Of course."

"Finalize the contract for mining the new oil fields before Parliament is reelected. I don't know if you're planning to give it to the Americans, but whatever you decide, we cannot afford to waste any more time on this. That contract will inject more money into this economy than the entire stimulus package."

"I agree. Which company do you think we should give it to? Under normal circumstances, I would need your sign-off to proceed."

"The offers are similar enough," Mohammed said and then shrugged. "We owe the most to the Americans. I would give it to them."

"I'm leaning toward that as well."

"Glad to hear it. I'll take your leave then," Mohammed said before turning toward the door.

"You said you had two pieces of advice. What is the other one?"

The prime minister turned back to face the Emir. "Appoint the Crown Prince as your next prime minister. There is too much at stake to keep this cycle up with the Islamists. You must set your own rhythm. Without that, you will never be able to get any productive legislation through, including your financial stimulus plan."

"The stimulus is necessary to bring capital back into the economy," the Emir said emphatically.

"When has that ever convinced them?"

The Emir nodded. "But what if appointing him just adds more fuel to the fire? We would be giving their words more credence. They could become even more powerful. And what if it instigates something like Bahrain in 2011? We will lose whatever footholds we still have."

"You are still the Emir. You must be able to exert some power other than simply delaying the onset of Islamic law. And the situation in Bahrain was completely different."

"No one is calling for Sharia law." The Emir threw his arms out at his sides. "That would be far too extreme, even for the Islamists. Most of them enjoy a drink or two under the table and a woman on the side. Would they really be willing to give that up?"

"Why would they have to? They enjoy those things outside the public eye. There's no reason that wouldn't continue. They have nothing to lose by calling for traditional law. They might even be able to appeal to a larger part of the population—the part that thinks of them as a bunch of religious phonies. Don't you see? You have to strike back."

The Emir looked at him intently, slowly grasping the prime minister's meaning. "We cannot allow that to happen."

"Exactly. If they had their way, they would blanket every woman in a burka and forbid them to drive. Forget about running for office and having a vote. The monarchy is the only thing standing in their way!"

The Emir's shoulders slumped. "I will consider what you have said."

The prime minister gave him a halfhearted smile. "You will have my official resignation within the hour."

"As you wish."

The two men repeated their customary greeting as they said goodbye. "At the dewaniya tonight, we will greet each other as brothers."

The door shut slowly behind Sheikh Mohammed.

The Emir called out to his aide. "Please summon the Crown Prince. We have important matters to discuss."

### *New York City, United States – May 15, 2021*

An hour after receiving the phone call, Petra Shirazi walked from Grand Central Terminal toward a midtown Manhattan office building. The station once again bustled as it had prior to the attacks two years earlier. While the presence of security certainly had been increased, many security personnel were plainclothes operatives designed to blend in with the crowd. Anyone trained in field ops could spot them from a mile away, so their effectiveness was likely quite limited, though. She shuddered at the thought of what another attack might do to the city.

On the way to the office, she stopped at a food truck and picked up an extra-large fruit smoothie. "I'm surprised to see you here on a Saturday," the vendor said with a grin.

"Very funny, Eric."

"You weren't here last week so I thought things might be changing."

She shrugged. "I just can't get away from it."

"I hope your company pays for all of these weekend smoothies."

"Don't worry. I've got that covered," Petra winked as she walked away.

Fifteen minutes later, she entered her boss's office on the fifth floor. Chris McLaughry sat behind his desk wearing a button-down green shirt and jeans, which contrasted dramatically with his dark Kenyan skin tone. "Morning, Chris. Aren't we all up early for a Saturday?"

"Petra, thanks for coming in. Follow me," he said in a round Scottish accent. Chris grabbed the blazer hanging on the back of his office door and they started down the hall.

"Care to tell me what's going on?"

"You'll see in a second. One thing, though. The intel we just received came from the CIA. I'm not going to mention it at the meeting, but I wanted you to know before we went in."

"But why n—?"

He shook his head. "I can't explain now, but I will later."

She followed him to the main conference room on the secured section of the floor. Two of the other regional research leads were already there, along with one of their intelligence gathering heads and a few analysts. Even though she had met each of them a number of times, the numerous ethnicities and nationalities brought a smile to her face. The eight individuals in the room covered as many countries, each with their own unique ethnic and racial backgrounds.

"Morning, Petra. Thanks for coming in during your vacation," said Brian, the North American Domestic Protection Division chief. "We were hoping to let you have the rest of your time off, but we really need your expertise on the Middle East."

"That's what I get for staying in town. I should have been off on some beach with no cell service."

Several of them were still laughing as the briefing started. "We've received some new intelligence from Kuwait. We suspect that a new Al-Qaeda cell may have been planted there," Chris began.

"In Kuwait?" Petra paused, frowning. "Really? The general population has always been fairly moderate, although the Islamists have gained more popularity in the past few years."

"The intelligence suggests that they may be planning some kind of attack," he continued.

"Hmm…What's the intel? And who's the source?" Veronica, their European expert, asked in a strong, excessively posh British accent.

Chris's hand moved to the button on his blazer, which he proceeded to fasten and then unfasten as he responded. "We intercepted a phone call through an agent in the field. Petra, I assume you can supplement the translation provided by our agent?"

"Of course." Petra held back a frown. *Why is he avoiding her question? What's the big deal?*

"Great. Before we get to that, can you give us a brief summary on Kuwait?" Brian asked. "We haven't really seen it on the intelligence radar."

She nodded. "As I'm sure all of you know, Kuwait is a major oil exporter and historically has been one of the richest countries in the Middle East. Before the first crisis in 2008, the country was booming along with Abu Dhabi and Dubai. When things here went south in 2008, oil prices dropped and there was a major squeeze on the local economy. It was just starting to recover when the June attacks occurred in 2019 and sent economies back into recession globally. Most of the workforce is foreign. The population is about three million, but there are only about six hundred thousand Kuwaitis."

"Was that affected by the backlash from the June attacks?"

Petra sighed. "Kuwait was impacted pretty badly. It's become much harder to entice expatriates to go there or anywhere else in the region. Tax-free income and a low cost of living aren't enough of a draw anymore."

"What about before that? Were they impacted by the Arab Spring at all?"

"Not really."

"Sorry about all these questions. I want to make sure that we all have the basics since most of us work on other regions," Brian apologized.

"Not a problem. Kuwait is actually more democratic than many other Arab countries. It's a constitutional monarchy and the king—the Emir—doesn't have legislative powers while Parliament, formally the National Assembly, is in session. He is able to disband it under extreme circumstances, but most of the time Parliament members hold the strings. What's particularly interesting about Kuwait, though, is that the monarchy is much more progressive than the democratically elected Assembly is. It took five years for the Emir to push the bill through Parliament that gave women the right to vote and run for office."

"Are there any female members?"

"In Parliament? Yes. That law passed in 2005 and women have held several posts since the elections in 2009."

"What's the general stance of the Assembly?"

"It is hugely fragmented. The Islamist and liberal factions can't seem to agree on anything and it's only gotten worse in the last decade. My dad sent me a video from one of their sessions because it was so funny. They couldn't even agree on increasing the number of traffic lights on one of the main roads."

"Sounds like Congress."

Petra held back a laugh. "Exactly, so forget trying to get more controversial legislation passed. The Islamists have gained more and more power in the Assembly as the economy there has gotten worse. The older segment of the population is disillusioned with the Western slant of the royal family, and politicians have used that to garner support for more Islamic legislation. The youth population hasn't taken kindly to this. Protests calling for change happen at least once a month at local universities—part of what they call the Orange Movement."

"What's the split in Parliament now between the two factions?" Brian asked.

"I don't know the exact numbers off the top of my head, but I would say the Islamists hold about half of the parliamentary seats, even including all of the more moderate cabinet members."

"And what is—?"

"Let's hold off on asking any more questions until after we listen to the phone conversation," Chris interjected sharply to give Petra a break from Brian's inquiry. He hit play on the holographic screen that projected a foot above the center of the desk in front of him and some initial static filled the room. The screen displayed a straight green line that flickered as the conversation began.

Petra's eyes widened as the thirty-second conversation ended with another burst of static.

"Petra, what's your first impression of the recording?" Brian asked.

"The intercepted call is a conversation between an official and what sounds like one of his aides. Chris, can you pull up our agent's written translation?"

"Sure, Petra."

Chris pressed a few buttons on his tablet keypad and the written script appeared on the projected screen.

*"Malik, I have requested the presence of our visitor."*

*"You have done well. When does he arrive?"*

*"Tomorrow morning."*

*"How much did you agree to pay him?"*

*"Thirty million euros."*

*"The maximum that we agreed upon? Very well. It is a necessary expense."*

*"Thank you for your trust in my judgment."*

*"You have grown quite a bit in the time we've worked together. You have earned my trust. All your efforts are an important part of our upcoming journey."*

Once she had read the translation, Petra interjected. "There are a couple of nuances that I want to point out. They use the word *malik*, which essentially denotes 'sir,' so as I said before, this is some sort of official talking to one of his aides. They also use the word *rehla*, which I want to emphasize—as the translation says—means 'journey' and not 'jihad.' Based on what I've just heard, I'm not sure that this call has anything to do with terrorism."

"But thirty million euros?" Veronica asked. "He's a lower-level politician. What could possibly cost that much? And where are they getting it?"

"We'll have to figure that out. *Rehla* can denote some kind of endeavor, which could potentially mean an attack, especially with that kind of money at play," Petra replied. "But it could also mean something else, so we should consider other possibilities. Do we have any additional context on the recording?"

"According to our agent, the call was intercepted from the home of Marzouk Fayed, a conservative member of the Kuwaiti National Assembly," Brian said as he read from a small screen embedded in the table. "Former member, I should say, given that the Emir dissolved the Assembly earlier this month. We haven't been able to trace the other end of the call."

"Fayed was reelected to Parliament after the Emir dissolved the Assembly last year and will probably be reelected in two months with the new Assembly," Chris added. "He is an ultraconservative. He was one of the main proponents for the whole stream of Islamist legislation, including heightened school segregation."

Petra nodded. "I agree that he would be a proponent of Islamic law, but that wouldn't necessarily make him anti-American. Kuwait has never been a stronghold for Al-Qaeda."

"That's true," Veronica acknowledged. "But that kind of money definitely merits an investigation."

"Yes, you certainly are right about that," Petra agreed. "Brian, can you give me access to all the files? I'm going to do some more research on this. Chris, I need your authorization to call in two of my analysts to work with me on this."

"You have it."

"Okay then. Please let me know if anything else comes up on the grid." Petra stood up, ready to leave.

"Will do," Chris said when he stood to leave. "Also, Veronica can you liaise with some of your operatives to see if we might be able to trace the money to somewhere in Europe?"

"I need to contact Swiss intel to get some real leads," Veronica responded.

"That's fine," Chris said. "Do what you have to do. You know the drill—keep things quiet."

"I will."

Chris gave them a tight nod. "Let's get to work. Meeting adjourned."

****

It was May 15, 2021.

It was the year when global economies continued to plummet despite analysts' predictions of a turnaround.

It was the year when the Kuwaiti National Assembly consisted of the largest Islamic contingent in more than two decades.

It was the month when the price of oil plunged to twenty dollars a barrel.

It was the month when the Emir of Kuwait dissolved the National Assembly for the thirteenth time in fifteen years.

It was the day when the head of the Islamic majority of the Assembly hired an assassin and the CIA intercepted intelligence about a new wave of terrorist attacks.

It was the day that would change the face of the Middle East forever.

****

# Chapter 2
# The New Prime Minister

## *Kuwait City, Kuwait – May, 2021*

When the Emir summoned the Crown Prince, he was sunning himself at a Red Sea resort in Aqaba, Jordan. On a whim, the Crown Prince had decided that he and his wife and children deserved a vacation. In reality, he was trying to escape the tense and precarious atmosphere mounting within his family and government back in Kuwait. The Emir's push for increased civil liberties and women's rights resulted in continuous friction with the more conservative members of the democratically elected Parliament. Upon the Emir's summons, he cut short his vacation and took one of the royal family's planes back the next morning, leaving his family to enjoy the sun and sea for another week.

Having just returned to Kuwait that morning, he was severely displeased that the Emir had kept him waiting alone in his office at Bayan Palace for the past thirty minutes. Because there is far less air traffic in Kuwait than most major metropolitan airports, his flight had arrived thirty minutes ahead of time. He had informed the Emir of this while en route from the airport, yet, for whatever reason, the Emir was still in the process of emerging from his chambers.

After another twenty minutes of staring at the clock on the wall while sipping Turkish coffee to prevent himself from falling asleep, the Crown Prince had reached the end of his patience. Using the phone on the Emir's desk, he buzzed for an office aide.

"You called, malik?" the aide said as he opened the office door and peeked inside the room.

"Yes, Omar. Do you have any word on the Emir's arrival?"

"I believe he is on his way, sir."

"Could you check? I've been waiting for thirty minutes already. If he is not on his way, then I would rather come back later."

Omar raised his eyebrows. "I will check for you, sir."

"Thank you."

On his way out, Omar asked, "Would you like anything else, sir? While you wait?"

"Another Turkish coffee would be nice. Hopefully I won't have enough time to finish it before my uncle arrives."

"Turkish coffee sweet?"

"Yes, same as this one."

"Very well, sir."

Omar walked out of the Emir's office and over to the next room. Using the intercom, he buzzed for one of the servants in charge of the Emir's chambers.

"Sabah al-khair."

"Sabah al-noor. I'm calling to ask about his highness the Emir. His highness the Crown Prince is waiting for him in the office."

"Yes. His highness just left. He should be there in the next five minutes."

"Thank you."

Hanging up, Omar went over to the kitchen. "Two Turkish coffees sweet, as quickly as you can," he barked at a member of the kitchen staff. Omar knew that the Emir would want his morning coffee to start the day.

"*Shway shway,*" one of the kitchen attendants said, cupping his fingers and thumb in a gesture that conveyed his meaning—*all in good time.* This cultural phrase, commonly used in Kuwait, infuriated foreigners and exacerbated their impatience in spite of its calming intent.

When Omar was about to reenter the office with the coffee, the Emir had just presented himself to the Crown Prince. The two men exchanged two brief kisses on the cheeks. "Sorry to keep you waiting."

"No problem, Uncle. What was so urgent?"

"I trust you had a good trip?"

"Yes. My wife loves the Red Sea."

Smiling, the Emir responded. "It always surprises me that you prefer the Jordanian side to the Egyptian one. The Sharm el-Sheikh resort is usually the place to go."

"She prefers it—slightly less crowded, I guess. I don't know. Who can really understand women anyway?" the Crown Prince said with a chuckle that was joined by a deep guffaw from the Emir.

"So what is it, Uncle? Why did you summon me so urgently?"

"Mohammed resigned his post as prime minister yesterday."

"What? I thought everything was under control since you disbanded the Assembly."

The Emir shook his head. "I thought so too."

"Then—"

"Mohammed took it upon himself. He believes that when Parliament is back in session, they will just find another reason to investigate him."

"I see…"

"I do understand his point. The allegations were completely made up. His dealings with the oil company were justified and legal, but they only had to twist the context and release a couple of pictures showing that Mohammed met with the company."

"They could easily do something like that again." The Crown Prince turned away from his uncle to look out the window and sighed.

"Yes, indeed. They could just create a new rumor. That's what drove out my last prime minister."

"Yes—"

"Abdul Aziz, I would like you to take on the post."

"Uncle, you know my opinion on this. Appointing the future emir as prime minister will anger Parliament even more!"

"What choice do I have? I cannot have another prime minister forced out as part of their power games."

"But don't you see? You'll be feeding right into their allegations."

"What do you mean?" The Emir raised his eyebrows and looked intently at his nephew.

"The Islamists in Parliament have been feeding the media lies about how you have split from the ways of Islam, how you are moving away from their wishes and from what is best for everyone."

"But won't the economic stimulus package I'm going to implement speak for itself? How could they call that anything but beneficial?"

"The Islamists will manage to twist it. Or they will distract the public from any good you are doing by pointing out how you have undermined the democratic process, which is what first brought our family to power."

"Do you really think they would go that far? It is our system of government that puts them in power too."

"Being able to discharge Parliament is one thing, but if you believe that appointing me as prime minister will stop their desire for blood, you are 100 percent mistaken. They will come after you with even more force. They will tear you apart for appointing the future emir when you are entrusted to appoint a mutually acceptable party. You may have the power to make this decision, but they are an important part of the process."

The Emir frowned as he considered his nephew's point. "Why don't we discuss this with Mohammed as well?"

"Certainly, Uncle."

Reaching for his phone, he buzzed for Omar once again. Neither of them realized that Omar had been standing outside the door listening to the entire conversation. Hastily setting down the tray of now cold Turkish coffees, he opened the office door.

"Yes, sir?"

"Summon the prime minister please. Feel free to wake him. We need to speak with him urgently."

"Very well, sir."

"And Omar?"

"Yes, sir?"

"Could you bring us some Turkish coffee, sweet, please?"

"Of course, sir."

The Crown Prince looked quizzically at Omar, wondering what had happened to the coffee he had requested earlier.

For the next half hour, both the Emir and Crown Prince attempted to relax. They sipped their coffees slowly and discussed the Crown Prince's young children, both of whom were happily running around on the beach at Aqaba. When Sheikh Mohammed finally arrived, both were pretending to be in better spirits. In reality, neither was willing to concede his respective point and both were apprehensive about the outcome of the discussion.

Amid his own thoughts, the Crown Prince attempted to think of an alternative for the position of prime minister who Parliament would find difficult to discredit. Given that the National Assembly appeared to have no qualms about making up rumors, picking someone outside of the royal bloodline was almost impossible.

Within five minutes of his arrival, Sheikh Mohammed made his views clear. "As I said previously, we cannot continue to dance to the tunes chosen by Parliament. You are the monarch. You stand for progress. You must set your own tune. Make them conform to *your* wishes."

"If you are both in agreement, then I cannot convince you," said the Crown Prince. "The Assembly will not react well to us pushing back on their power play. But if it is what you desire, Uncle, I will take the post."

"It is."

"I hope this doesn't backfire."

"In sha'allah." *May God be willing.*

## New York City, United States – May, 2021

Petra had spent the past two days pouring over any information available on Marzouk Fayed. She sifted through conversation records with the department and scoured through research documents. Most of the literature indicated that he was an extreme conservative Islamist, but little seemed to suggest that he would have any desire to target the United States or any Western country for an attack. None of his past legislative efforts had anything to do with Kuwaiti defense budgets, the military, or Kuwait's relationship with the US.

She was studying a research document provided by one of her analysts on Fayed's family and lineage. The document was projected onto the left side of a large evaluation monitor. She was using the other side as a white board and attempting to draw an annotated family tree when a knock at the door pulled her back to reality.

"Hi, Petra. Sorry to break your concentration," Chris said from the doorway.

"Computer, save all on-screen images," she said hastily. "It's okay. I was just lost in the paperwork again."

"It's okay. I'm used to how you operate in research mode by now," he said with a smile. "I just have a couple of things to go over with you, Petra. I had asked my assistant to put together a background report on Kuwait to help me get up to speed. I'm sure you already know most of it, but I thought I would drop it off anyway." He handed her a slim file.

"Thanks. I'll have my team take a look at it."

He looked at her intently with his dark brown, almost black eyes. "I also wanted to check on how things were going. I see you sent your analysts home."

She shrugged. "It's Sunday afternoon. They'll be better tomorrow because of it."

"How are things going?"

"I'm still looking through our reports. I did have one question though. Why didn't you mention that this intel was forwarded to us by the CIA at the briefing yesterday? I don't get it. Langley forwards intel to us all the time." She tilted her head. "Unless they are actually handing this off completely?"

He nodded.

Petra looked at him, taken aback. "Why would Langley hand off this investigation to us? I understand asking for supplemental input, but just taking it off their plate? That doesn't make sense. They have more boots on the ground than we do."

"You know the drill. We can bypass government protocols."

"But what government protocols would they need to bypass for this? It's an obvious flag for investigation."

Chris glanced around to make sure that no one was nearby and closed the door to her office. She looked at him with eyebrows raised, waiting for an explanation.

"Keep this between us, okay?"

"Of course."

"Langley wants to keep their distance from anything to do with Kuwait."

Petra frowned. "Obviously, but why?"

"Well, you remember the new oil field Kuwait discovered last year?"

"Yeah, of course. They're still deciding who will get the contract."

"Exactly."

She stared at him until the realization came. "Of course," she said, shaking her head. "One of the bidding companies is Textron. Shit."

"So now you get it? Just don't mention it to anybody."

"This is bullshit. The CIA wants us to manage its risk so that the president's best friend can pocket a boatload of cash."

Chris nodded again. "Yup, and there's nothing we can do about that. So other than that, how are things?"

"I can't seem to find anything to indicate that the conversation was about an attack on the West, but I haven't seen anything to counter that either. We're missing something, probably something that's staring us in the face."

"If anyone can find it, it's you. Remember to trust that gut instinct. That's why we had to keep you around."

She grinned.

"What are you smiling about? It's true!"

Petra looked away and he continued, frowning.

"Well, thanks for coming in during your vacation time. I know you enjoy being in New York without work. And, Petra, I was asking about you, not the research. How are *you* doing?"

"Things with the family are tough. Hopefully, I'll get out of here in time to go see my dad."

"The hospital is only a few blocks away. Take a break and go see him."

"That's a good idea. Okay, I'll do that." She reached for her purse.

"Before you go, I also wanted to make sure that you're still coming to the Canadian Consulate Spring Ball next month."

"Isn't it a requirement?" Petra scoffed.

"Well, yeah, they're one of our key funders. I'm just reminding everyone. I'll be showing off my newest swing dancing moves."

"Can't wait to see that. Maybe I'll even steal you away from Jenna for a dance."

"Only if Grant is okay with it."

She raised her eyebrows sharply. "Not everyone knows, remember? But, yes, he had better be. If that's all for now, Chris, I'm going to head out."

"Send my regards to your dad."

"I will. He'll probably ask about you before I get the chance, though. You were so kind to him while dodging his questions about work when I was in Paris. And now he's always hinting for me to bring you along when I go to their house for lunch. If they didn't know you were married I bet they'd want us to date. You make a good impression, McLaughry."

She grabbed her purse and headed out of the building. During the ten-block walk to the NYU Medical Center, she sorted through the chaotic mess in her head. Chris was one of the agents who first trained her. He was the only one at the Agency that knew about her relationship with Grant, at least officially. When her parents had put pressure on her about her love life after college (or lack thereof), he had been her confidant, a rare find within the Agency. They'd always had a fun, "buddy" relationship, and he had protected her when things in the field went sour.

Her relationship with her father was much more complex. She was still unable to share details with him about her chosen career path. In some ways, she believed he was still disappointed in her for not following her mother's footsteps into the field of medicine. Perhaps she had simply rebelled against it because her parents had always wanted her to be a doctor.

She walked through the automatic doors of the medical center and headed to the Neurology Department.

"Hi, Emily, how are you?" Petra greeted the department assistant.

"Petra, it's great to see you. How are things in the consulting business? Are you traveling the world again?"

"No, I'm finally getting a chance to relax at home. Is my dad in his office?"

"Yeah, he should be. I think he just finished installing some fancy machine in the new surgical suite."

"Sounds great. I can't wait to hear about it."

"You should come by more often now that you're home."

"I will," Petra said as she turned to walk down the hall to her father's office.

*The consulting business.* After graduating from college, she had considered joining a consulting firm. The people were smart and friendly, the job would have paid better, and she could have been more open about her work. The irony was that the life she had once rejected had become her public identity. No wonder they encouraged dating within the Agency; how else could people build some form of an honest relationship?

She knocked on the door to her dad's office. "Who is it?" he bellowed in a gruff voice with hints of both Irish and Iranian accents.

"It's Petra, Dad."

He opened the door beaming. "My dear Jaleela!" he said in Farsi, using her middle name meaning "exalted one" in Arabic, and gave her a kiss on the cheek. "So how's my favorite financial consultant? Are you back from saving the King of Siam's riches?"

"I'm back in New York for a little while," she replied, also in Farsi. Whenever work became especially busy, she told her family that she was going out of town on a project. Luckily, Grant was with the Agency, so she could be more honest with him about where she was, even if she couldn't tell him details about her work.

"Well, when are you coming to see us? Queens isn't that far, and your mother would be happy to see you." He looked her up and down and shook his head. "You've gotten even thinner, my dear. She's going to flip out."

Petra crossed her arms across her chest. "You and Mom make it sound like you think I'm anorexic. I've just been exercising a lot, like usual. It's just normal weight fluctuation." *Why do they always worry about that?* At five foot seven, she was of medium build. Although her weight did fluctuate from time to time, Petra was in great shape and body image was the least of her concerns.

"I'll come by this week. Things at work are still really busy, even if I am back here."

He nodded. "And how are things with Grant?"

"Things are good. He's sweet and nice and," she hesitated, "and he takes good care of me."

"What does he do again? I think you told me on the phone, but I can't remember."

"He manages the IT Department."

"And how old is he? He's older than you, right?"

"He's thirty-four." Petra's shoulders stiffened as she waited for her father's response.

She watched him raise his eyebrows slowly and deliberately. "That's a big age difference. He's probably ready to settle down."

"We're just taking things slow, Dad."

He shook his head. "But how do you feel? Do you love him?"

"Dad! We just started seeing each other three months ago. Things are good. We're happy."

"I can always rile you up, can't I?"

Petra rolled her eyes and tried hard not to smile. He laughed and threw his arm over her shoulder in a half hug. The contact reminded her again of how much she really did miss her parents. She blinked quickly and changed the subject. "I'll call Mom later about coming over to Queens for lunch next weekend."

"Come see us anytime, Jaleela. And since you won't let us meet Grant yet, bring that Chris along. If we can't hear about your love life maybe he can tell us something about your job." He gave her shoulder a brief squeeze. "Well, I have to get to a consult in a few minutes, but you go back and save the sheikh's money, okay? I'll see you later this week?"

"You will." She gave him a kiss on the cheek. "Love you, Dad."

On the walk back to the office, she sighed as she thought about her parents. She hated lying to her family, which was probably why she tended to distance herself from them when her classified work was particularly stressful or dangerous. It certainly made her happy to see them, though. As an only child, she had always been very close to her parents.

Thirty minutes later, she walked back into the office after picking up a coffee from a local family-owned coffee shop. She sat back down at her desk and began pouring over the information with fresh eyes. The first thing she started to read was the report that Chris had left on her desk.

*When the current emir took power in 2006, the Kuwaiti economy was at its height. The ever-rising price of oil had pushed the economy upward and the Middle East was in the middle of an economic boom. Foreign investment was blossoming, especially driven by new developments in Qatar, Abu Dhabi, and seemingly exciting investments in Dubai. Women had just achieved the right to vote and there was a strong momentum for continued increases in civil liberties.*

*The Al-Sabah family originally came to power through agreements between regional sea traders in the 1750s with the unanimous election of the first emir. In an effort to protect the country from the Ottomans, the royal family agreed to British protection. With the end of British rule in 1961, the Kuwaiti royal family established an assembly to draft a constitution for the new nation. As part of the constitutional movement, a democratically elected National Assembly (or Parliament) was created in January 1963. The written constitution severely limited the emir's ability to rule by decree, despite the fact that Parliament was headed by a prime minister appointed by the royal family.*

*The constitution designated the National Assembly with primary legislative powers. They had the ability to set the emir's salary and investigate the prime minister, among numerous other privileges, many of which rarely were exercised. Although the majority of legislative power rested with Parliament, the emir was able to dissolve the assembly if he felt that their decrees fell outside of the best interests of the nation. In a region dominated by different forms of monarchy and tyrannical governments, Kuwait seemed far ahead of its fellow Arab neighbors in the movement toward democracy and greater civil liberties. Their political system was identified as a beacon for progress in the Arab world.*

*Even the most gifted analyst or fortune-teller would not have been able to predict how fragmented and divided the Kuwaiti National Assembly would become. Factions of Islamists and liberals, among others, seemed incapable of even agreeing to increase the number of traffic lights on a particular main road. Barely contested legislation would stall when it reached the Assembly—certain members of Parliament were simply too offended to stoop to accepting anything proposed by a member of an opposing faction. The system has become akin to desperate clans vying for the top of the pyramid.*

After the first few paragraphs, she switched her attention back to the man from the recording, Marzouk Fayed. Three hours later, she found something that seemed somewhat promising.

She picked up the phone and dialed the number for the secured line of their field research coordinator in Istanbul.

"Alex Mittal," his voice crackled through the rough connection.

"Alex, it's Petra Shirazi. How are you doing?"

"You know me. I'm always suffering bec—"

"Because you are understaffed, underfunded, and don't have enough resources. I know, I know," she said with a chuckle.

"I mean it! It's difficult," he replied. "Enough of that, though, because I doubt I could convince you to get me more agents since I couldn't even get you to come back as a field agent. By the way, how come you don't want me to use your nickname anymore?"

"Alex, it's been years since I stopped using it. Nobody has called me that since Paris."

"Okay, okay. Anyway, you didn't call just to say hi. I take it you need some more work from me?"

"Guilty as charged."

Alex sighed. "So what can I help you with?"

"I'm going through some of the reports and research we have on Marzouk Fayed."

"Ah, okay. Based on that recording, right? How is that going?"

"I need more information on one of Fayed's aides—a man named Khaled Majed. Iranian descent, tall, dark, and handsome. He's the nephew of an Iranian general killed in the Brits' raid three years ago."

"The Big Botch?"

"Yeah."

"Great, more fallout."

"Let's not get off track," she interjected. "I need more information on him. His background, what he's doing in Kuwait, why he's working for Fayed, how much he might know about the raid and who was involved, everywhere he's lived in the past five years. You know the drill."

"I'll keep you posted on what we find."

"Thanks, Alex."

After hanging up, Petra called Russell, one of her analysts, into the office.

"I want you to dig up anything you can on Khaled Majed, one of Marzouk Fayed's aides. I've already asked Alex to liaise with us on this, but we need to do our own desk research."

"Sure, but why this particular aide? Fayed has several."

"Khaled Majed is the nephew of General Majed."

"General Majed?"

Petra pursed her lips. "He's an Iranian general who was killed in the Brits' raid."

"Is that what you guys call the 'Big Botch'?"

"Yes."

"What actually happened there?"

Her eyes widened. "A couple of years ago we got some intel that identified what we thought was a site used for manufacturing nuclear weapons in Iran. The Brits led a covert ops raid on the facility, and fifty-five people were killed, including the general. Afterward, we found that there hadn't been nuclear material anywhere near it for over a decade. We managed to keep it all out of the media, but it was a huge scandal. The source was bogus and the head of this department actually got reassigned because he had pushed so hard to move forward with the strike based on bad intel."

Russell exhaled loudly. "So if Khaled Majed found out about how his uncle died, that might be motivation for an attack."

"Exactly."

****

When Petra got home that night, she lay in bed smiling as she recalled the few precious moments that she had spent with her dad. She reached for her phone and called her mother's cell phone number. She was waiting for the first ring when she realized how late it was and hung up promptly. Instead, she called her grandfather's number, since it was still early on the West Coast. The phone rang four times before connecting to his voicemail. "Baba bozorg, it's Petra. Call me when you wake up tomorrow," she said in Farsi.

She hung up the phone and thought back to one of the stories her grandpa would tell at family dinners. The last one that she'd attended was almost two years ago. She was still thinking about him and the rest of her family when she fell asleep a half hour later.

# Chapter 3
## Burn in the Heat

*New York City, United States – May, 2021*

Petra walked out of Grand Central station wrestling with frustration. She had been pouring over records from their field offices for almost a week trying to find something to shed light on the recording they had intercepted the previous weekend. Since leaving the field three years ago, she had decided to never let her work life influence her personal life. She had even begun to pride herself on this over the past three years. The recent bit of intelligence, however, had brought up a stream of concerns that she had been unable to quell or leave behind at the office.

She gathered her thoughts as she navigated around bustling commuters on her walk toward Sixth Avenue. The office was a few blocks north of Bryant Park. In the summer, she and Grant occasionally would sneak out to the park for a quick lunch before returning to the mass of work that had piled up on their desks. She envied Grant for his work—he was a senior technology manager at the Agency. Since he liaised with multiple departments on a daily basis, he was officially kept in the dark about operations. This ensured that he never had to worry about bringing work home, but also had one of the best understandings of the Agency as a whole. Even as a senior intelligence officer, Petra knew little of what happened outside of her department. Her boss, Chris, knew slightly more, but the Agency really did operate under the "need to know" principle.

When she walked into her office ten minutes later, she saw the red light blinking on her phone indicating that she had a message. "Computer, play messages," she said, and then sat down and kicked off her shoes under her desk as she waited for the message to play.

"Hey, Petra. It's Alex. I just sent you the information you asked for about Khaled Majed. I can run you through it if you can call me back. We can figure out the next step after that. Talk to you shortly. Thanks."

She logged on to her computer and the large translucent monitor darkened as she pulled up the sizeable document that Alex had sent over compiling the information he had managed to find. Once it opened, she hit the call back button.

"Hello, Alex Mittal speaking."

"Alex, it's Petra. Just got your message."

"Great. Have you looked at the file yet?" A hologram appeared projected from a sidelight on her computer monitor that displayed a full-size image of Alex from the shoulders up. The image sharpened so that she could see his curly brown hair and scruffy beard. On the other end of the call, Petra's face appeared on a projection in front of Alex.

"I just opened it."

"Okay, so here are the basics. Khaled Majed is the son of General Majed's brother, a Yasser Majed. We don't really have any intel on Yasser Majed. He died when Khaled was in his midteens. Khaled moved to Kuwait shortly after General Majed died in the Big Botch."

"Did he visit Kuwait prior to moving there?" Petra asked.

"Our info isn't complete, but we know he visited Kuwait just before the start of the Iran-Iraq war when he was in his midtwenties."

"Do we have anything that indicates why? What was he doing in Kuwait?"

Alex shrugged his shoulders. "It looks like it was some sort of family business, but we don't know much."

"Hmm, maybe he was trying to shore up support for Iran in Kuwait when the war was looming?"

"It's possible, but we both know that Kuwait was never going to side with Iran."

She drummed her fingers on the desk quietly. "True. Did he return to Kuwait after that?"

"He went back on another trip right after the Gulf War. We have some more information on that trip—he met with a few people in the Islamist contingent from Parliament. It was a lot smaller back then."

"Yeah, they've grown much more powerful. Still, that's interesting. I wouldn't have suspected there were any ties between the Iranian government and the Kuwaiti Parliament."

"Yeah, it does strike me as a bit odd."

"Was Khaled ever in the military?"

"We know that he acted as some kind of military liaison when he lived in Tehran."

She tilted her head to the side. "But not in the actual military?"

"Not that I could find, but if he were involved in anything remotely restricted, we might not have access to it."

Petra nodded. "Fair enough. I see that in the past few years he lived in Tehran, Ahwaz, and then, of course, Kuwait. Anything in particular about Ahwaz that seems strange?"

"No. He worked on the Iraqi border, looks like some kind of government support position."

"Government support?" She frowned. "Do you think he was intelligence?"

Alex shrugged his shoulders. "Maybe. The information would certainly add up that way. But based on what we've got, I can't say for sure."

Petra paused and studied her computer monitor. "What do we have on his time in Kuwait? Did he always work for Fayed?"

"No, he spent a month at the Iranian embassy and then started working with Fayed."

"How do you think he got the position?"

"Ties between their families maybe?" Alex speculated as he started flipping through files and paperwork.

"That seems pretty weak. Would a simple tie between their families really be enough to get him such a prominent position?"

"There's probably something else." Alex continued to flip through documents, pausing to skim.

"Yeah, maybe he knew some information that Fayed needed. I don't know, but we've got to figure it out," Petra said as she scribbled notes on a legal pad on her desk.

"He might have proven himself worthy of the job."

"That's possible."

"Or maybe their family ties really are that strong."

"Maybe...The whole thing is pretty strange." She began absentmindedly tapping the end of her pen on the notepad. "I mean, ties between Fayed and the Iranian government are hardly conclusive evidence of a terrorist plot."

"Definitely true, but we can't just brush aside the investigation."

"No, not with that kind of money at stake. Alex, you don't think this has anything to do with the Textron contract do you?"

"I don't know. It might, but neither Fayed nor Majed is really big in the oil business."

"Yeah, I don't think so either."

"So what's your next step, Petra?"

"I'll take a deeper look at this with my team and get back to you."

"Okay, sounds good."

"Thanks, Alex." He blinked and then disappeared as the phone clicked to hang up the call. Petra snuck a look at her watch. *12:30 p.m.* Maybe she and Grant could steal a quick lunch date. *I really need a break at Bryant Park today.*

She logged on to the office messaging service to send Grant a simple question. *"BP?"*

Grant answered quickly. *"Yes."*

Petra replied that she'd be ready in fifteen minutes and then smiled broadly as she stood and grabbed her purse. The Agency unofficially encouraged dating among employees because it was easier for an agent, rather than constantly abiding by the rules of the Agency's confidentiality agreement while in a relationship with a civilian. She and Grant had decided to keep things quiet for a while, though, because he was up for a promotion, and they did not want their relationship to get in the way. They hoped to "go public" with their relationship after another month, but not until then.

### Salmiya, Kuwait – May, 2021

The Ahriman lay on his back, splayed out on his bed in only his boxers as he fervently wished for increased airflow. At just over six feet tall, his body stretched to encompass the entire double bed. He sat up and downed most of the half-liter bottle of water at his bedside. He poured the last bit over his tanned, muscular torso and relished the momentary reprieve from the heat.

His hotel room had become disgustingly hot as the sun streamed in from the windows and baked it in a typical greenhouse effect. In an attempt to circulate the air, he had left the windows open after giving up on the air conditioning and netted drapes, which actually seemed to raise the temperature in the room rather than cooling it. Since he had chosen a hotel off the beaten path in Salmiya, the air conditioning was remarkably worse than it would have been in any other hotel. *I thought I could at least trust Kuwait for the world's best air conditioning service.*

The hotel was top notch for his work in other ways. At check-in, they required minimal paperwork and allowed him to pay in cash. Each room was a small suite with a separate kitchen in addition to the main bedroom and bathroom. The hotel staff employed minimal service standards and left him alone in his room. They were happy to believe that he spent many late nights at his girlfriend's place.

In Kuwait, as in many other Islamic countries, unmarried couples were not allowed to live together. Officially, the rule was strictly enforced, although in practice many people were able to effectively live together with little interference. The Ahriman used this to his advantage, allowing the hotel staff to think his only illicit activity was spending most of his nights with a girlfriend. By revealing this scandalous detail, he had provided the hotel staff with a source of gossip, but nothing that would prompt them to try to meddle in his affairs.

Over the past several days, the Ahriman had attempted in vain to come to terms with the assignment he'd received. He had done many terrible things in his life, especially over the past three years, but nothing equaled what he was being asked to do now. He had never killed a national leader in cold blood, and certainly not one whose position he secretly found sympathetic.

Somehow, he would have to gather information on how, when, and where he would be able to conduct his attack. He would also have to spend a considerable amount of time developing escape route possibilities. While he did not expect anything on the same level as the US Secret Service, he knew that if he were to carry out the assignment, he must prepare for all possible contingencies.

The Ahriman distracted himself from the outcome by focusing on the setup. He turned on his tablet and spoke to it directly. "Computer, set automatic level-three encryption for all notes."

"Automatic encryption is in place," the computer replied in a halting female voice.

In the notebook application, he scribbled some initial thoughts with his stylus to try to break down the steps necessary to accomplish his mission.

1.  *Infiltrate the inner circle.*

2.  *Access the calendar for the Amiri Diwan.*

### 3. *Identify strike date.*

He circled the first step and pondered it for a moment before jotting down the words "social circle" and connecting it with an arrow. He had spent some time researching general Kuwaiti social customs prior to this assignment. They were similar enough to Iranian customs that he could catch on quickly, especially with the knowledge he acquired during previous assignments in other Arab countries. When he felt as if he had a reasonable handle on the nuances of Kuwaiti customs, he walked over to his closet and looked at his clothing options. The hotel phone rang as he surveyed his two suits and three pairs of jeans hanging in the closet.

"Mustafa Mubarak speaking," the Ahriman said as he picked up the receiver.

"Hey, Mustafa. It's John Matheson."

"Hey, John. How are you doing?"

"Pretty good. How are you settling in?"

"Doing fine. I'm getting ready to come into the office next week."

"Glad to hear it. I told you a week would be enough for you to settle in."

"I guess so." The Ahriman shrugged as his mind shifted back to planning the operation.

"Have you had a chance to do anything fun?" John asked.

"Not yet."

"Well, I don't know if you remember, but I'm going over to this guy's dewaniya on Thursday night if you want to join me. It won't be anything like the crazy partying you probably did in London, but it's usually a good time. We smoke some sheesha, drink a bit, and chill out with a bunch of guys."

"That sounds fun. Do I need to bring anything? Should I wear a suit?"

"Definitely not a suit. Since you're going to be here for a few months, you should go ahead and pick up one of those nightgown things."

The Ahriman chuckled. "Nightgown things?"

"Yeah, I can't really pronounce it. Dis, dish, dishdata or something like that?" John's Texan drawl struggled to pronounce the Arabic word.

"Dishdasha actually."

"Yeah, that thing. You can pick it up at one of the malls. Sharq mall is probably the nicest. Shouldn't be an issue."

31

"Okay, great. And should I bring anything?" the Ahriman asked, playing along with his cover identity.

"You don't need to bring anything, unless you have any of the finer stuff, something in a smaller bottle or a flask. Did you get one through airport security like I told you?"

"Yeah, I got the cork one you told me to get."

"Isn't it amazing? It doesn't show up on the detectors at all. One of the Frenchies at the office told me about that trick." John sounded quite pleased with himself.

"I was surprised it worked out. Thanks for the recommendation."

"Awesome. Fill that up and bring it over."

"John, you sure I can walk around with that?"

"Now that is the beauty of wearing a nightgown. You can hide anything in there. I bet you could probably hide a musket inside it and no one would ever know."

"Maybe I should try?"

John chortled at the idea. "Okay, Mustafa, I have to go, but I'll see you on Thursday. I'll text you the information about where exactly it is."

"Sounds good. I'm off to buy a nightgown then."

"Sweet!"

The phone clicked as John ended the call and the Ahriman grabbed his shoes and finished getting ready to leave the hotel room after several days of cabin fever. When he exited the lobby, the first rays of direct sunlight hit him and he groaned before putting on his sunglasses. He cried out as he touched the hot metal door handle of his car with bare hands. Using his shirttail, he managed to open the car door. He eased onto the scorching seat, placed the key in the ignition, and turned on the engine. Immediately, he blasted the air conditioning, all the while making sure only to touch the car with his hands protected by his shirttails. After a minute with the air conditioning on and the door still open, he gingerly touched the steering wheel. It was still hot, but not burning to the touch. He closed the door and backed the car out of the parking space. Before exiting the parking lot, he managed to fasten his seat belt, but not without first searing the tips of his fingers on the hot metal buckle as he maneuvered his way out of the lot toward the mall.

Souq Sharq was one of the first malls built in Kuwait, and it was right on the water. It was part of a large number of seaside developments built during the height of the economy's boom. The

Ahriman did not often brave traffic to get to any of Kuwait's malls, but he enjoyed having a cup of coffee while sitting beside the marina in the shade. From there, he had a viewpoint of Kuwait Towers and other monuments cradled by the deep blue of the Gulf.

*And now I have to buy a nightgown!*

## Surra, Kuwait – May, 2021

Marzouk Fayed shrieked at the combined computer monitor and television as he watched the national Kuwaiti news.

"I am honored to appoint Sheikh Abdul Aziz Ibn Al-Sabah, the Crown Prince, to be the new prime minister to head this government," the Emir touted on screen.

Fayed grabbed the remote and hurled it at the wall toward the eighty-five-inch flat screen TV that sat center stage in his home's study. Khaled Majed and one of the servants rushed in from the next room after hearing the remote hit the wall next to the TV and fall to the ground.

Khaled rushed over to the TV and tapped a button that released a protective screen over the monitor. He grabbed the remote to keep it well out of his superior's reach, thankful for his boss's poor aim. "Sir, are you all right?"

"The Emir thinks he can just do whatever the fuck he wants? If he thinks that appointing the Crown Prince as prime minister will stop us, he is wrong!"

"Yes, sir."

The Emir continued to speak on the news broadcast. "Given this new development in the government, we believe that it is best for the National Assembly's election to be moved forward. It will be held on July fifth."

"Look at him on that screen, exuding pride. He thinks this solves all of his problems. He doesn't even think he has to worry about Parliament anymore."

"Yes, sir," Khaled said, forcing himself to appear calm and collected without criticizing his superior's crazy behavior.

"Tanya! Come here!" Fayed shouted, summoning his housekeeper. "Tanya!"

"Yes, sir!" she responded as she rushed in from the kitchen.

"Some mint tea, please. Now! And some biscuits."

"Yes, sir. Right away, sir." She hurried out of the room back toward the kitchen.

A few minutes later, she walked back in unsteadily, carrying a large pot of tea, two cups, and a plate of traditional Arabic biscuits. By this time, Fayed had calmed down slightly, but his breathing remained heavy as he fumed to himself.

Khaled reached for the teapot, poured two cups, and handed one to Fayed. "Drink this and you will feel better."

"I would feel better if it were laced with whiskey," Fayed grumbled, shaking his head. "My liquor cabinet needs to be replenished."

"Just be careful, sir."

He grunted derisively. "I'm not the only one who enjoys a drink."

"Of course not."

As Fayed sipped his tea slowly and wolfed down four of the biscuits, he calmed down further. "I guess you're right," he mumbled.

Khaled smiled and drank his tea quietly. He listened attentively as Fayed vented about his anger and frustration with the Kuwaiti royal family. "They were appointed to power by the people! But these Al-Sabahs, they have become puppets of the West. They have neglected the people and our Islamic roots. It must not be allowed to continue."

After letting Fayed vent for almost thirty minutes, Khaled excused himself and returned to his own office, a small room allocated to him as one of Fayed's senior aides. After checking to make sure that no one was nearby, he closed the door firmly. Always concerned with appearances, Fayed constantly updated his home to impress visitors. When Khaled supervised the most recent renovations, he used the opportunity to install soundproof padding beneath the garish wallpaper chosen for his office. Khaled paid for it out-of-pocket, explaining to the contractor that he didn't want to offend his rather loud boss. Luckily, the contractor had managed to procure padding that blended well into the wallpaper. Khaled made sure that the soundproof padding around the doorway was still very much in place and logged on to his anonymous messaging service and pushed the call button.

"Khaled," he heard a moment later.

"Yes," he answered. "I'm here."

"Good," the voice responded. "Can you speak freely?"

"I can."

"Update me then." A webcam video link with Khaled's handler appeared on the screen.

"The Ahriman has begun preparations."

"And Fayed? Does he suspect anything related to the Textron deal?"

"Not at all. He doesn't realize who the real target is."

"Is he behaving as you expected?"

"Even better. We'd already heard that the Crown Prince was going to be appointed prime minister. It was never a surprise, but he still went ballistic."

"Fayed is an emotional man. I'm glad we're making use of that."

Khaled smiled.

## New York City, United States – May, 2021

Petra forced down her sixth cup of coffee for the day in an effort to stay alert. Instead of delving back into her notes on Marzouk Fayed and Khaled Majed, she glanced through the rest of the report about Kuwait that Chris had given her a few days earlier.

Since assuming power, the current emir has dissolved the National Assembly for a variety of reasons, including threats to publicly grill the prime minister and push forward ultraconservative legislation. Such threats generally originated in the Islamist faction of Parliament. They often voice huge discontentment with the level of the royal family's commitment to Islam and religious law, accusing the monarchs of turning their backs on the Qur'an.

A wave of hope seemed to appear in 2011 when a flame of revolutions ignited in Tunisia and then swept across North Africa and the Arabian Peninsula. As Hosni Mubarak stepped down after almost thirty years as president of Egypt and opposition forces fought the Bahraini and Jordanian monarchies for prodemocratic legislation, Kuwait remained largely unscathed. However, the success of these revolutions did lend credence for increased democracy in Kuwait and the Islamists seized the opportunity to gain further prominence within the National Assembly.

In December 2011, protesters finally forced the resignation of Prime Minister Sheikh Nasser Mohammed. It was Sheikh Nasser's fifth attempt at resignation, and finally, in an effort to calm the accusations running amuck from the Assembly, the emir was coerced into accepting it. Sheikh Nasser's deputy replaced him, and after another shuffle in Parliament in early 2012, the political waters appeared to turn calm. The scandals returned in 2015 when a joke blown out of proportion led Parliament to force out another prime minister with false accusations of having an illegitimate child living in Europe.

These accusations seem trivial when compared to the impact of the global economic crisis on the political situation in Kuwait. The collapse of the American economy, which began in 2008, pushed oil prices downward, resulting in economic downturn around the Middle East. The catastrophic attacks in June 2019 have only worsened the situation.

In the wake of the global economic crisis, the Kuwaiti public became increasingly divided. With each successive fall in the price of oil, public unrest has worsened. Islamists in Parliament have gathered even more traction for extreme policies by blaming the current economic situation on the monarchy's departure away from traditional Islamic (or Sharia) law. Though many of them have been educated in prominent Western institutions, they have directed support toward a more anti-Western stance in the National Assembly.

Over the past twelve years, the Islamists gradually have gained more of a majority within the Assembly. Voting rates tend to be much higher among the older population. Many of the most vocal Kuwaiti youth, who would have pushed for a more moderate Parliament, were unable to vote due to voting age requirements.

After the most recent election, the Islamist faction had managed to secure thirty-five of the fifty seats in Parliament. Given that cabinet ministers automatically hold seats in the Assembly, the Islamist faction was reduced to about 50 percent. This Assembly composition has prevented the emir from passing a number of bills.

These include an economic stimulus package targeted at sectors with declining foreign investment and a new regulation that would reduce Ministry-enforced controls upon school curriculums and activities. In all likelihood, one of the emir's goals is to push the stimulus forward during the current suspension of Parliament prior to the next elections.

Petra closed the file, sighed, and then stared at the manila folder as she tried to focus her thoughts. In a moment of inspiration, she gulped down the remainder of her coffee. She then took the mug and a bottle of scotch from her bottom desk drawer to the conference room next door. There, her two analysts scrutinized computer files and hard copies of documents on Kuwaiti politicians, Iranian military men, and their every possible financial connection. Two coffee mugs and an array of empty chip bags and candy wrappers were strewn around the table.

"Okay, guys, it's past eleven. We have to take a break. Finish your coffee and I'll pour you a real drink."

Russell and Ben looked up from their monitors and did as instructed. They both completely drained their mugs, with Ben guzzling down a recent refill. Petra poured them each two fingers of scotch. "Let's have a toast to figuring out these bastards," she said, raising her cup. "And to both of you. Thanks for sticking around, Russell and Ben. I know there are places you'd rather be."

"We'll get them," Ben said, raising his cup as well.

"We'd better." She took a swig from her mug and squeezed her eyes shut in a dramatic wince as she gulped it down. "Ugh."

"Are you kidding me?" Russell said. "Petra, this is great scotch."

Ben looked at her, smirking and obviously holding back a laugh. "If you don't like scotch, why do you keep it in your office? Glenkinchie is a pretty high-end brand for someone who hates scotch."

Petra smiled wistfully. "I don't know. I never could develop a taste for scotch. My ex-boyfriend was the one who loved it. This was his favorite brand."

The two men exchanged awkward glances and rapidly changed the subject.

"Can I ask you something, Petra?" Ben tapped his fingers on the table as he spoke.

"Of course."

"Why did you stay in this business? It seems like a tough life to handle long term. I've only been here a year, but I don't know how long I can stomach all the secrecy and the craziness."

"There have been a lot of times when I was close to leaving, but most recently I think I decided to stay because of everything that happened with the June attacks. I just felt like I couldn't walk away when I might be able to make a difference, might be able to stop something like that from happening again. What made you both join?"

Russell shifted nervously in his seat. "I think I read too many spy novels growing up. I've known this was what I wanted to do for a while, just wasn't sure I'd be able to. I applied to Langley, but before I heard anything, someone from here approached me."

"I was recruited at a college fair," Ben said. Then his voice turned somber. "It was right after the June attacks. I hadn't seen anything like that since 9/11. After they pitched it to me, I felt like I owed it to myself to try to stop something like that from happening."

"Where were you when it happened?" Petra asked, shuddering as she gulped down some more scotch.

"I was back home in Vancouver when it started. I couldn't believe all the news reports. At first the Suez Canal seemed so far away, but then London, then Paris, then here." He shook his head. "It was so awful."

"I was sheltered from a lot of it. I was studying abroad in Venezuela, but I watched it on the news," Russell said.

"What about you, Petra?"

Her eyes suddenly welled up with the memory, but she quickly blinked back her tears and took a deep breath. "I was actually in Paris when the first attacks on the metro started. I've never been so scared. They train us for so many things, but it didn't even come close to preparing me for that. And then when I came back here to New York, the attacks at Grand Central began. I don't know if I've ever fully recovered." She closed her eyes softly. "But none of that was as bad as what happened afterward."

Russell cocked his head to the side. "What do you mean?"

"After all the attacks, the economy got worse and worse. The recession returned and tons of unemployed people were back on the streets. Everything around here became so tense. There was backlash everywhere. If you had brown skin, it wasn't safe to walk around. Lynch mobs went through every big city all over the world.

In response, Arab youth formed gangs to protect themselves and then the gang wars started."

She stood and glanced at Ben. "Canada was a bit more insulated, but it was awful here in New York." Her shoulders drooped. "That's when I knew that Al-Qaeda had won. They made people too scared to go about their daily lives. It's the same as driving a stake into someone's soul, but multiplied by a billion for every person who felt threatened and unsafe. That's why I decided to stick around here."

The men only nodded in response and the group finished their scotch in silence.

Petra tilted her head back to drain the last drop and thumped her mug onto the table. "Let's make sure it doesn't happen again."

\*\*\*\*

"Can you give me an update?" Chris asked, stopping by the table in the conference room where Petra and two research team members had scattered a slew of files in their attempt to figure out the best course of action.

Petra sat alone at the end of the table and shook her head in frustration. "We haven't found anything new since Alex sent over the information on Majed's background. After three days of digging, my team's been able to confirm the relationship between Fayed's family and Majed's, but that's about it."

"So no smoking gun," Chris paused while tapping his fingers on the table for a moment, then turned his gaze back to her. "What are you going to recommend?"

"I don't know yet."

"With that kind of money involved, we need to send in an agent to investigate either way, right?"

"Yes, but we have to decide which way to do it."

He frowned. "Your team's gone home for the night?"

"Yeah, they left fifteen minutes ago."

"Just confirming," he responded. "So you're considering an off-book mission?"

"I think that we have to. Trust me, I don't like it any more than you do. At least with normal Agency Watch List missions, the head operative goes in with some support in the vicinity."

Chris nodded in agreement. "Why don't you talk me through the options? That might help us figure it out." He pulled out a chair near Petra and sat down.

"Well, we still don't have enough information to conclusively go with any of the options," she said and then sighed. "But talking through them would not be a bad idea, especially since you didn't give me clearance to talk about that stuff with my team."

"You know that there's no way I could give that clearance," he said, rolling his eyes at her.

"Fine."

"Let's start with this. What does your gut tell you to do?"

"We can't go with what my gut says this time. If I were to rely just on my intuition, I would put Fayed on the Interpol Watch List and try to track down his funding. Fayed doesn't strike me as a member of Al-Qaeda or Hamas. He's an Islamist, but I don't think he fits the profile of a jihadist." Her jaw set in annoyance, wishing that she could give her boss a better answer.

"What about Majed?"

"Khaled Majed is a total enigma to me. He seems harmless on the surface, other than the fact that he is General Majed's nephew. Is it possible for someone related to General Majed to be anything but dangerous? I just don't know." She shook her head. "Regardless, this isn't worth discussing. There's no way that we could only recommend the Interpol Watch List. That wouldn't be enough given all the intel that we have. We can't just put them on a global registry of people with suspected ties to terrorist organizations. There has to be continuous monitoring."

"Yeah, there's too much money at play for anything that simple. Plus that would deprioritize the whole investigation, and we can't risk doing that."

"Agreed."

Chris rubbed his chin briefly. "So what about putting Majed and Fayed on the Agency Watch List. That's the first viable option that we have, right?"

"Yes, but I don't know if we really have time to try to install someone within Fayed's inner circle. That kind of op can take months. Besides, we barely have any diplomats or national politicians on the list since it's so hard to establish a half-decent cover story for agents. And we don't even have any active agents in the area that could serve as backup for the new agent that we would send in. I don't see how we could possibly design a normal mission that has any chance of success under these circumstances, forget our normal fifty-fifty odds."

"Yeah, and designing a regular Agency Watch List mission would require a lot of extra clearance time." Chris paused and began drumming his fingers on the edge of the table again. "What about trying to turn someone who's already in Fayed's inner circle?"

"We'd still have to send someone in to try to meet with the asset, and we don't have much information on the people in his inner circle. We'd need to do a ton of research and prep work to identify the target asset, and there isn't any assurance that we'd succeed."

"But it would probably yield the most credible results since we would actually have someone inside the building."

Petra nodded. "I just wish we had more time. I don't know if I can make that a viable option. We don't have a station there and we can't use Langley since they've decided to off-load this whole thing because Reynolds needs to keep his hands clean." She glared at the ceiling as she thought about Tom Raver, the spineless director of the CIA.

"And then there's the option of an off-book mission."

"I know most of the other department heads would order that in a heartbeat, but they've never actually spent any time on the ground. It's hard enough being an operative with all of the support of a normal mission. I'm not going to send in one of our agents blind unless we have no other choice." *Maybe not even then.* She gritted her teeth, waiting for him to challenge her.

"Off-book missions don't necessarily mean that the agent goes in blind."

"Fine, but how many off-book missions do you know about that are successful? I know of at least four that exist, but I don't know if things went well or completely to shit. And why is that? Because there are no records for us to review. If we don't even know if that kind of mission can work, then why send in an operative facing so much risk? When agents are caught in the field, we can't even claim them. As I said, it's hard enough being out there. Forget having to worry about how you are going to exfiltrate yourself without any support if things go poorly!"

Chris frowned. "Come on, Petra. We don't recommend off-book missions unless we actually need to move forward at a moment's notice. I know that not all of my department heads have your experience in the field, but no one wants our agents coming back in body bags. The only way that this goes out as an off-book mission is if you and I recommend it. Try not to worry so much."

"Okay," she conceded. "Thanks, Chris."

"No problem. Just let me know what you decide before the meeting tomorrow."

"I will."

"And Petra, official missions go wrong as often as off-book ones do."

She gave him a forced half smile as he walked away, turning her attention back to the dilemma at hand. *It's going to be a long night,* she thought as she drank some more coffee.

*I just have to decide.*

The next internal department head meeting was in less than twenty-four hours.

**\*\*\*\***

# Book II
# Six Years Earlier
# 2015 – 2016

# Chapter 4
## The Beginning
## Six Years Earlier

*London, United Kingdom – January, 2015*

Kasem Ismaili was beaming as he made his way to one of his favorite Saturday night hangout spots in London. He was dressed in light brown khakis, a slim fit white collared shirt, and a custom cut dark blue overcoat that probably cost more than the average monthly salary in the UK. *Maybe I'll get lucky tonight.* He walked toward a group of friends huddled together outside in the nippy January air. They were standing in the entrance line, which was now starting to wrap along the neighboring block.

"Kasem! Over here," one of them hollered. "Can you get us past this line?"

"No problem," Kasem answered. "Come with me."

The group followed him up to the bouncer standing at the door.

"Hey, Barry," Kasem called out.

"Hey, Kasey. You coming in tonight?"

"Yeah. Can you let me and my friends in past the line?" Kasem shook the bouncer's hand and handed over a twenty-pound note in the process.

"Go on in, but you'll have to fend for yourself to get a table."

"Will do."

"Talk to Jazmine, the new hostess. She might hook you up."

Kasem grinned. "Come on, this way," he said, gesturing to his friends. "Thanks, Barry," he called out to the bouncer as he walked inside the club.

A cacophony of techno music greeted them as they walked into the lounge. "Welcome to the Book Club," they heard one of the hostesses say.

Kasem gave her a once over quickly and could barely stop himself from whistling. "Did you just start working here?" he asked, making firm eye contact with her. "I come here regularly, but I haven't had the fortune of meeting you until now."

"Yeah, this is my second day," she said tightly. "I'll set you guys up at a table." They followed her into the main lounge area.

"Will you at least tell me your name?" Kasem asked, touching her arm softly. His hazel eyes peered at her intensely.

"It's Jazmine. Can I take your order now?" she asked as they sat down.

"We'll have two bottles of Grey Goose with some Sprite and orange juice."

"I'll have that brought out to you right away." She turned away and Kasem followed her toward the bar.

"Where are you from, Jazmine?" He could barely keep his attention on her voice because he was so busy eyeing her hourglass figure emphasized by a short dress and skin-tight leggings.

"I'm from Stanton. What about you?"

"I grew up in New York, but my family's Persian."

"Oh, really," she said, blinking rapidly. "So is mine. Where did you grow up?"

"Just outside of New York, in Brooklyn."

"What's a New Yorker doing in London?"

His eyes twinkled. "I took a job here a couple of years ago."

"Let me guess. You work in finance?" Her tone turned tight once again.

"Yes, I do, but all finance people aren't the same."

"I'm sure."

"Would you just have a drink with me so that I can at least try to prove you wrong?" He gestured widely with his hands. *Good thing she's Persian too. That's my only shot here.*

The bartender appeared, and Jazmine put in the group's order. Kasem continued to watch her and waited until she looked his way again.

"Come on, Jazmine. You know you can't resist me," he said, grinning sheepishly.

She rolled her eyes. "Fine. My shift's over in an hour. I'll be at the bar, but I won't wait more than five minutes."

****

Later that night after the lounge had quieted, Kasem sought her out and they took a seat at a nearby table with a bottle of Nero d'Avola Italian wine.

"By the way, I forgot to introduce myself. I'm Kasem."

She nodded. "So how did your family end up in Brooklyn, Kasem?"

"My parents immigrated in the seventies."

"Before the revolution?"

"Yeah. My mom is Armenian Christian, so after my parents got married, they decided to leave Tehran. Their immigration papers took a couple of years to process, but they finally left with my grandma."

"Did they leave a lot of family behind?" Jazmine asked.

"My dad's parents stayed behind. They were supposed to process immigration paperwork shortly after that, but it never happened."

"Are they still in Tehran?"

His eyes darted across the room before he returned her gaze. "In a manner of speaking. They died there during the revolution before I was born."

"Do your parents talk about it much?" she probed.

"Tehran? Or how they left?"

"Both. Tehran…how they left, what they remember, anything else about Iran."

He shrugged. "We only speak in Farsi and they've definitely exposed me to the culture. We listen to the music all the time. I grew up hearing my mom sing songs in Farsi. That said, they don't actually talk much about how things were when they left."

"My family's the same. I just wish my parents would talk about Tehran more. When I was a kid, I walked in on my mom looking through an old photo album. She was crying, and I could tell how much she missed it. They love London, but it isn't home for them."

Kasem looked at her pensively. "I hadn't thought about it much, but yeah it must be really hard on them to know that they can't go back there."

Jazmine raised her eyebrows. "They can go back, but it isn't the same. I wish I had the chance to go."

"Really?"

"Why not? There's so much history there and you could learn a lot about your family. I know that I'd have to be careful, but I'm sure that it would still be amazing."

"I was there a couple of months ago for work."

Her eyes lit up. "You were there? Oh my God, tell me everything. What was it like?" For the first time during the conversation, Kasem felt like he had really captured her attention.

"It was amazing, but kind of sad. There were so many big contrasts."

"What do you mean?"

"There are wonderful things everywhere you look—beautiful hotels, historic sites, monuments. The people are so friendly, and the food is amazing, but there's this haze that covers everything." He sighed and continued, "The ambiance is tense, and this sense of despair and fear cloaks the whole city. The pain that the city went through is palpable on every street corner, in every café or marketplace. It felt like Tehran was yearning to go back to a time when things were simpler—you know, before the shah, the hostage crisis, and the revolution."

"Was there a lot of anti-Western or anti-American sentiment?"

"Not really. People were just going about their daily lives. They warned me not to wander around at night in certain areas because there are a lot of muggings, but that could happen anywhere. It's definitely not ready for tourists, but there's so much to see. I wish there weren't such strong prejudices against it."

"Yeah."

Jazmine then leaned over and kissed him, surprising Kasem, although he took only seconds to respond to her kiss. Twenty minutes later, they left the bar and spent a passionate night together back at Kasem's loft. The next morning they were lounging on his bed when he opened up further.

"I haven't told anyone yet, but I actually just got offered a job there," he said quietly.

"Where?"

"In Tehran."

Jazmine sat up and turned back to face him. "Seriously?"

"Yeah. When I was there a couple of months ago, I met with the national securities exchange about a deal we were working on. Apparently they just received a directive to make their staff more international, so they called yesterday to offer me a job."

"That's amazing. What are you going to do?"

He sighed and shook his head. "I don't know."

"Well, do you like the position?"

"It looks like a good opportunity. The salary and benefits are great for that kind of work. I've never worked with a regulator, but I think it would be interesting. The hours would be a lot better, and I have been thinking that it might be time to move out of my current job. The lifestyle is starting to get to me."

"You mean you don't like going out every night and hooking up with every girl on the planet?" She giggled and planted a kiss on his cheek.

He rolled his eyes. "Of course I enjoy partying sometimes, but it's starting to feel a bit hollow. Maybe I'm ready for a change."

"So what's holding you back?" She traced her finger down the creases of his well-defined abs.

"Living in Tehran. I don't think I can seriously consider this job because of everything that I would have to give up to move there."

"What do you mean?"

His body tensed up as her hand moved further down his chest. "Err, basic freedoms. To drink, uh, meet people, walk around and err not be afraid I'd wind up somewhere I shouldn't be. All of that stuff."

She bit her lip and moved her hands back to his abs. "You would probably have more freedom than you think. I'm sure you would learn where you should and shouldn't go once you've lived there for a little while, just like any other city. People who grew up there aren't any less than either of us. They've just had different opportunities and a few more struggles. I'm sure they have plenty of interesting things to say. And, come on, there must be a huge black market for you to get as much booze as you like."

"But you never know who's listening. I asked the guy who would be my supervisor about life in Tehran and having access to all that stuff when he called with the job offer. And get this—he answered me in French."

"Who cares? This could be a big adventure." She sat up and threw her arms out to the sides with wide eyes.

"Are you saying that I should go?"

"If it were me, I would consider it."

He sighed. "I just don't know."

"Flip a coin."

"What? Flip a coin to decide if I should move to Tehran?"

Jazmine tossed a pillow at his head. "No, dumbass. Flip a coin to decide if you should even consider it."

He frowned as she took out a ten pence coin. "Heads or tails?"

"Heads."

"Heads you consider it and tails you don't."

He nodded and she tossed it. Once she caught it, she placed it on the back of her hand and glanced at it without showing him. The head of the queen looked back at her. "Tails."

"Oh," he said, feeling his stomach sink. He lowered his head. "Maybe we should do best out of three?"

"Actually, it was heads," she said, laughing. "I wanted to see how you would react. It's a trick my brother uses." She shrugged. "I think it's pretty obvious how you feel, even if your head hasn't caught up yet."

He gave her a sheepish smile. "Maybe you're right."

## *Tehran, Iran – Three months later, April, 2015*

Kasem knocked loudly on the door of his neighbor Jamal Soroush's flat. "Come in!" he heard from inside and pushed the door open.

"Kasem, my friend, come in. How are you?"

"Great. I brought this for you." Kasem handed him a large flask.

"Thank you! What did you bring?"

"Nothing special, just some vodka."

"Any alcohol will do the trick here, my friend." Jamal filled two tall glasses three-quarters full with vodka and then topped them off with a splash of tonic water. "Even for big guys like us, these drinks should keep us going for a while."

Kasem grinned as they raised their glasses. Both men boasted traditional Iranian features—tanned olive brown skin, moderately sharp features, and hazel eyes. At over six feet tall with wide shoulders honed from years of weight lifting, they were considered freakishly tall and built by local standards. One of the first things they had bonded over was their shared obsession with the gym.

"Cheers, Jamal."

"Cheers. Have a seat," Jamal said, taking a seat at the dining table in front of them and motioning to the chair in front of him. "So Kasem, how do you like your job? It's been a couple of weeks now. Last time we talked you were still in training."

"It's fun. I do a lot of research on potential investors and how other countries have managed to attract investors."

"Do those methods really apply? Iran is so fucked up, so we must be a special case."

"In some ways. But I still have to keep up with everything that's going on. I talk to a lot of different firms and contacts that I used to work with in London."

"How does it work? What exactly do you do?"

Kasem chuckled. "I've been trying to explain it to my mother for years. Basically, I call people, companies, or organizations with money and try to get them to give us some of it."

"Their money gets committed to particular projects?"

"Yeah. Most of it is infrastructure. So XYZ company can send us money to help build a new road and two hotels and they own part of the project. Once it's built, they get some of the profits of whatever was built."

"Makes sense. How do you get them to invest in Iran?"

"There is the possibility of making money, so that helps. The issue is all the history, and, of course, the government." Kasem gulped down the last of his drink and Jamal poured him another one. Kasem took a sip, and grimaced. "Is this even stronger than the first one?"

"Oh, come on. Live a little. Now, you were saying?"

Kasem shrugged. "Just that the government has done a lot of harm. That makes it hard to get people to commit money."

"Naturally. We all know that the elections have been a complete sham. Every time one president steps down he sets up one of his puppets to take his place. No one can stand any of them. The media and press are in his pocket. After the last election, there were so many protests, but then the police just fired tear gas into the crowd and it was over. People are too scared to push for anything else."

"Indeed," Kasem said with a sigh.

"I'm getting out of here as soon as I can. Nothing will ever change." Jamal poured himself another drink and topped off Kasem's glass with some more vodka.

"Come on, my friend. Look what's happened all over the world. India, China, Brazil, they've all developed so fast."

Jamal grunted, "India? China? This is Iran. We've never been poor—that was never the problem—but we still don't have any decent roads outside the big cities. You know that my village is only a hundred kilometers away from here? Guess how long it takes to get there because of the horrible roads." He paused for an answer, but Kasem just looked at him in silence. "Not two, not three, not even four, but six hours once I get outside Tehran. We have power cuts all the fucking time, even in the cities. And then there is all the sewage that is dumped into the Gulf. The best part of it is that the government thinks they can pull the wool over our eyes. Did you know that six of the largest sewage pumps broke down last year?"

Kasem shook his head.

"Exactly. But everyone here knew. We switched to river fish instead of fish caught in the Gulf. The president only thinks he can keep us in the dark. The Republic News Agency is such a piece of crap."

"Oh, I have to tell you this story," Kasem exclaimed. "Yesterday, I was in the office and someone came by my desk to show me that ridiculous article they published on Tuesday."

"Which article?"

"The headline was 'Americans Worry a Lot.' A whole article about Americans worrying and they asked me if it was true. I could have died from laughing."

Jamal leaned forward with an arm wrapped around his stomach because he was laughing so hard. "That's nothing. They showed me something like that last month. About the Brits. They were like, 'You went to school in London, is it true? Do the British really drink beer every night because they are totally depressed?' And last year, there was one about the French. It said that the only way to be French was to be either unhappy or bored!"

Kasem's stomach was convulsing so much from laughter that he barely gulped down the swallow he'd just taken of his drink. When their laughter finally subsided, Jamal raised his glass once again. "I am glad that you came here my friend."

Kasem smiled. "So am I, so am I." He felt his phone buzz in his pocket and checked it quickly, then rolled his eyes.

"What happened?"

"A friend from school just sent me an e-mail. He just got engaged."

"Ah, yes. Will you be next? Do you have a girlfriend back home?"

"No. The last girl I seriously dated cheated on me, and I haven't really been with anyone since," Kasem scoffed. "That's something my mother bugs me about constantly. Dad tries to keep her in check, but I know he feels the same way, just knows how to hide it."

"That's part of their job. My girlfriend left me when I decided to come back here and my parents have not stopped trying to set me up since."

"What made you decide? You've never told me much about your job."

"It's the Ministry of Education. Bullshit government job. What more is there to say?"

Kasem tilted his head to the side. "Dude, it can't be that bad."

"I joined the government because I wanted to make a difference. I thought what better way to reach people, what better way to ensure future reforms and growth than education. But in the end, what I do is complete shit."

"What do you mean? It can't all be complete shit."

Jamal glared at the table. "I process paperwork that schools are required to submit. Every month the government forces them to waste time and effort to fill out a report that states how they are compliant with the latest set of Islamic guidelines circulated by the ministry."

"Is there anything useful in the reports?"

"There should be. We should be checking for the quality of teaching, the accessibility of student activities, and the size of the classes, and then make decisions, make changes based on that. But all we do is check for how close the schools are to being Sharia compliant."

Kasem nodded. He was unsure of what to say to cheer up his friend.

"Don't worry. I've come to terms with it. I'm going to get out of here as soon as I can. Actually, it's encouraging that the securities exchange got someone like you to come over here. Maybe change will come after all."

"And to that, we should have another drink."

The two men then filled their glasses from a bottle of single malt scotch that Jamal had procured off the black market. Kasem examined the bottle of Glenkinchie as he took a sip. "Jamal, this is some really good scotch. How much did you pay for it?"

"Don't ask such terrible questions. I paid far too much, but don't worry about it. Just enjoy it." Together they downed another glass and then helped themselves to yet another as the night slipped by them.

"You know what we need to do?"

"What?"

"We need a vacation! Let's call in sick and take the morning flight to London. We can be back by the start of next week." Kasem looked at the glass in his hand. "We can meet some women, go to the club and dance...and have some more scotch." Kasem leaned back, envisioning a fully outfitted whiskey and cigar bar. It only needed a few stripper poles and the image would be perfect. "Jamal, my friend, it will be legendary."

"London?" Jamal scoffed. "We can meet more beautiful girls at the underground clubs here. We just don't have any connections to get in." His face looked crestfallen. "We should go somewhere with beaches. With even hotter women!" Jamal jumped up from his chair and spilled scotch all over his shirt.

Three hours later, Kasem stumbled down the hall unable to steady himself. *Going to the office tomorrow is going to be murder.* Once inside his apartment, he collapsed face down on the bed. *I should get up and drink some wat—*

Before even completing the thought, he fell into a deep, drunken sleep.

At eight in the morning, Kasem woke to sunlight streaming into his east-facing bedroom window. "Oh," he groaned. His head was pounding and the light hurt his eyes. He could barely resist the temptation to draw the curtains and collapse back into bed. He looked down at himself as he managed to sit up and get out of bed. In his inebriated state, he had collapsed on his stomach fully clothed without even taking off his shoes. *We are never doing that again.* He dragged his sluggish form into the shower to get ready for work.

## *Philadelphia, United States – April, 2015*

Petra was excited as the week ended. The second semester of her junior year at the University of Pennsylvania had been one stressful experience after another. She enjoyed her coursework in international studies and business, but wished fervently that she could take a vacation on an island somewhere without recruiting, grading curves, or group work of any kind.

Lea, her advisor, was sitting just inside the Huntsman Program office across from the main Wharton building, Huntsman Hall. "Petra! Hi, how are you?" she said.

"Exhausted, but I'm really looking forward to this weekend. I can't believe we're finally done with classes."

"I know, and it's Spring Fling. Believe me, you've earned it after the semester you've had."

"Thanks," Petra beamed. Lea had heard all about the hellish time she'd had with internship recruiting and a bad breakup. She had never been so glad for a semester to be almost over. "I hope so."

"Congrats on the internship offers. Have you decided what you're going to do?"

"Thank you. I'm going to take the one in New York."

"You don't sound very excited. Is everything okay?"

"Yeah, of course. I'm excited about the job. It was such an exhausting recruiting process, though. I didn't realize how competitive things would get or how much class I would miss for interviews."

"It happens. I wouldn't worry about it too much. I'm sure you'll do fine."

"Thanks, Lea. I hope so."

"So I have some news."

Petra looked at Lea expectantly. Smiling, Lea held up her left hand.

"Congratulations!" Petra exclaimed. "I'm so excited for you."

"Thank you!"

"So when is the big day?"

"Probably not until next year. There are just too many things to plan."

"I hope I get to meet your fiancé sometime soon."

"Actually, why don't you come over for dinner the week after next? James's parents are coming over for a casual meal and I've been raving about you. I'm sure they'd love to meet you. His father actually spent some time in Kuwait, I think, so I'm sure that you both will have a lot to talk about."

"Are you sure? I wouldn't want to impose."

"Oh, definitely not. So, dinner on Tuesday, which might mean you have to do a little bit of work the next couple of weekends so you can make it."

Petra smiled. "I need to do a little work regardless. I'll make it—don't worry. Should I just plan on leaving from here with you?"

"Sure, that sounds great."

Thirty minutes later, Petra disappeared into the haze of the exhilarating Spring Fling weekend.

\*\*\*\*

# Chapter 5
# Black Market Liquor

*Tehran, Iran – May, 2015*

"Hey, dude," Kasem said as Jamal opened the door to greet him.

"Hey. Guess what? I brought some more stock." Jamal gestured towards a plastic bag on the sideboard that contained two bottles.

"Jamal, you have to be careful! This shit is expensive."

"Don't worry about it. What else do I have to spend money on here?"

Kasem raised his eyebrows as he surveyed his friend's unsteadiness. "How much have you already had to drink?"

"Just a couple of gin and tonics. I'm fine, don't worry."

"Sure," Kasem nodded. *As long as we don't have to drive anywhere.*

The two of them sat down at the table where Jamal had laid out an assortment of kebabs. "Eat before they get cold. They just got here. I'll make you a drink."

"Sorry I was late. I wasted so much time this morning that I couldn't get out on time. I don't know how you guys do this six-day workweek. It's killing me!"

"You'll get used to it." Jamal handed him the drink and raised his glass.

"Cheers to another boys' night," Kasem said with a wistful grin.

"So what's happening in your office? Did you finally decide which projects you want to focus on?"

"Yeah, I think I'll ask to work exclusively on two projects."

"Which ones?"

"Did I tell you about the Flower of Eden?"

Jamal tilted his head to the side. "I don't think so, but it sounds familiar. Is that some kind of hotel chain?"

56

"Not a chain, but a hotel and tourism program for Kish Island."

"That's awesome. Can we go out there for an on-site visit? I'll happily pay for my own ticket, but I'm crashing in your hotel room. I might have to put a sock on the door one night! Kish Island has amazing clubs and even hotter women. And we can drink in public there."

Kasem leaned his head back and imagined the scene. "Yeah, it would be awesome to go out there. I hope we can resuscitate that project. You probably heard about how it was suspended when they couldn't find enough investors. Basically, we are trying to bring it back now. If it gets built, we would try to even get international tourists to go out there."

"Sweet. Keep me posted. I don't need any other excuse to go out there."

"We should go anyway. It's so close and we don't even need to take a passport."

"We can't, dude. We work for the government, remember? They monitor that shit. It would be better if at least one of us had a real reason to go out there."

Kasem's shoulders slumped and he nodded.

"What about your other project?" Jamal asked. "I thought you did more traditional infrastructure stuff."

"The other one is like that. We call it the Basra Project. The plan is to develop the roads along that part of the Iraqi border and set up a new hospital. It's part of the new 'Iran and Iraq are friends' initiative. The idea is to have companies invest in businesses all along the roads so that the costs can be recouped in their returns."

"Are the Iraqis raising money as well?"

"Yes. We're both supposed to raise half, but we're nowhere near the target. That's actually why I'm late—I was working on it this evening. We have a potential investor from Kuwait and I finally managed to nail down a meeting with him and his senior aide. I called them to confirm it today and they almost canceled." Kasem let out a long sigh and stretched out his legs.

"Did they?" Jamal asked.

"No, but I had to push hard on the teasers that I sent over to them. It's all set up now for next week."

"So you'll be going to Kuwait then?"

"Yeah," Kasem responded.

"Too bad the meeting's not in Doha or somewhere else. You could bring me some booze to replenish my stock."

"I'll have to find another way."

They raised their glasses again and the evening passed in a blur much like all of their boys' nights.

## *Philadelphia, United States – May, 2015*

After finishing her first exam of the week, Petra walked over to the Huntsman Program office to meet Lea. Together they would head to Lea's house in the suburbs just outside of Philadelphia.

Penn's campus was stunning when spring came around. Locust Walk, the main street that stretched through campus, was lit by the sun catching on the buildings' red brick facades. The trees on either side glittered as sunlight danced on their newly sprouted bright green leaves. The contrast of buildings, ranging from the modern design of Huntsman Hall to the majestic arches of Fisher Fine Arts Library, gave the campus even more personality in pleasant weather. As Petra took in the scenery, she knew she would miss the campus while she interned in New York over the summer.

Five minutes later, she entered the Huntsman Program office on Locust Walk and quickly stopped at the bathroom to check her reflection. Satisfied, she headed to Lea's office and knocked on the door.

"Petra! I'm so glad you are still coming to dinner. I was starting to get worried."

"I'm so sorry. My exam ended a bit late and I wasn't paying attention to the time."

"No problem. I'll grab my bag and then we can head out. Are you ready?"

"Yes, definitely."

They cut across the Penn and Drexel campuses to reach 30th Street Station just barely in time to catch the 6:21 p.m. SEPTA train. Forty minutes later, they arrived at Lea's home.

Before Lea could rummage through her bag to find her house keys, the front door opened. "Hello, ladies," James Collins said, greeting Lea with a peck on the lips. Turning toward Petra, he said, "And you must be Petra. I'm James, Lea's fiancé. I've heard so much about you. I'm glad to finally meet you."

"It's good to finally meet you as well. Congratulations on your engagement."

"Oh, thank you. Come in both of you."

James was a pleasant-looking, well-built man about six feet tall. He had bright green eyes that sparkled in the living room light. Petra could not help but find him attractive. She smiled, taking in the mutual love and respect in his and Lea's eyes when they glanced at each other.

He directed them into the dining room where the oak dining table was already set. "Mom, Dad, this is Petra, the student Lea has been telling us about."

"Oh, how wonderful to finally meet you. I'm Elizabeth." James's mother said, grabbing Petra's hand with enthusiasm.

"Thank you so much for having me. I brought this as a little token of appreciation." Petra said, handing over the nicely wrapped Godiva box.

"Why, thank you! How sweet of you."

Tony Collins emerged from the kitchen. "Petra, so glad to meet you. I'm Tony, Lea's proud father-in-law-to-be, who can't wait for these kids to get married so that I can drop the 'to-be.' She's quite the catch for the family. My son's a great guy, but I still can't figure out how he convinced her to marry him." Everyone chuckled as they all took their seats at the dining table.

As soon as they were seated, Petra began munching on the dinner salad already set out for them—she hadn't realized that she would be starving by the time she got to Lea's house. *I hope they serve something other than salad soon,* she thought while stuffing her face as politely as possible.

Petra attempted to pay attention to the conversation over the sound in her ears of lettuce crunching as she devoured the salad. Elizabeth and Lea were discussing the wedding while the men looked at each other uncomfortably. Both of them glanced at Petra occasionally, likely to make sure she was not dying of boredom.

When Elizabeth brought out a delicious beef stew to serve immediately after the salad, Petra was content to remain silent. She had minimal interest in the size of the wedding hall and the colors of the bridesmaid dresses.

After another thirty minutes of wedding planning, James brought out dessert—a raspberry sorbet. Having finally satisfied her hunger, Petra sat back as he served it, hoping to join the conversation if it happened to drift away from wedding decorations and floral arrangements.

"All right, my dear ladies," James said. "Enough wedding talk for tonight. Why don't we get to know our young guest a bit better?"

Petra looked back at him expectantly.

"Lea has told us a lot about you, but I'm sure we'd much rather hear it from the horse's mouth."

Tony also jumped into the conversation. "So Lea tells us you grew up in the Middle East?"

"Mainly," she responded. "I've spent a bit of time in San Francisco, but I grew up mostly in Kuwait."

"I spent some time in that neck of the woods before I retired from the Air Force."

"Oh, wow. Did you serve in the Gulf War?"

"Briefly. I commanded a team that went over the border into Kuwait from Saudi Arabia. When the Iraqis pulled out, I would have liked to follow them to Baghdad, but finally we elected not to go."

Petra nodded.

"So what are things like there now? I haven't been back since," Tony asked.

"Honestly, you wouldn't really think the war had happened from looking around. A ton of new buildings have sprouted up all over the place, although things have slowed down since the economic crisis."

"Do most people speak English there?" Elizabeth asked.

"Most people do in offices, schools, big stores. People working in some of the smaller restaurants often don't speak English, but other than that it is quite easy to get around."

"So do a lot of people speak Arabic?"

"Well, Kuwait is actually full of expatriates. Kuwait's population is about three million, but there are only about seven hundred thousand actual Kuwaiti citizens. Expatriates from all over the world make up the rest of the population, and within the expat community, probably about half speak Arabic."

"I'm glad it's gone back to being that way. When we pulled out after the Gulf War, there was some speculation as to whether or not the expats would return," Tony said with a slight frown on his face.

"Petra, do you speak Arabic?" James asked.

"I do. I learned to read and write in school, but really, I learned it from a family living in our apartment building. My friend Rana and I—she's Egyptian—we grew up together and I learned Arabic from her."

"Where is your family from originally?" asked Elizabeth.

"My dad is Iranian and my mom's American."

"Iranian and American, that's interesting. How did your parents meet?" Elizabeth continued.

"They met when they were both working in Kuwait."

Tony smiled and exchanged a glance with his wife. "Well, then it was meant to be. How did they both end up there?"

"It's a long story. My mom is a doctor and she worked there for a while. Expats have a pretty good lifestyle and she took the job there to save money and pay back her student debt."

"Is that how she met your dad? Did he move there for work as well?"

Petra shook her head. "No. My dad's family fled Iran in the seventies during the revolution. My grandpa actually told me the story the last time I visited. My dad was about eighteen when the protests against the shah started in 1977." A faraway look passed over her face as she remembered the story her grandfather had relayed to her. "Everyone was so scared of him, but the shah had already killed so many people. My dad even participated in the initial protests, but my grandparents started to talk about leaving when more people started dying in the name of the revolution. My grandfather had a good friend who worked at the Ministry of Education and he was killed just because he worked for the government. When they went to his funeral, his wife was killed by a car bomb and my grandma was badly injured. As soon as she was well enough to move, they packed up and left."

"What did your grandpa do?" Lea interjected as she stood in the doorway to the kitchen.

"He worked for the national bank."

"So they fled to Kuwait?"

"No, actually, they drove across the border to Iraq. That's where most of the Iranian refugees went."

"So your family crossed over to Baghdad?" Tony continued to probe.

"Yes. My grandpa took a job as a financial manager in a local bank branch. They barely had enough to get by even with a small one-bedroom apartment, but my dad put himself through engineering school."

"Did they ever consider going back to Tehran?" James asked.

61

"I'm sure that they did, more than once, especially after the shah fled in 1979." She looked down at her hands clasped together on the table. "Of course, then Khomeini came back to Iran and installed his own Islamic government. There was bloodshed in the streets and then the hostage crisis broke out."

"I don't want to overstep, but I have to ask: How do most Iranians view that whole time period? It's such a polarizing subject that I've never tried to have a discussion about it." Tony tilted his head to the side as he gazed at her intently.

Petra blinked rapidly before looking back at him. "I don't think there's anything that my grandparents have ever been more ashamed of. They don't talk about it much since it's so emotional for them. It was such a terrible situation. I've never understood how people could think something like that was justified. Threatening so many people caused so much harm, but it wasn't just the American embassy. Thousands of people died in the protests, in the clashes, in the executions." She shuddered.

The room was silent for several moments before Petra continued.

"Things were much better for my family in Baghdad, though. When my dad finished engineering school, he got a job at a foreign telecom company and they moved into a bigger apartment. They were one of the few Shia families in their community, but it didn't seem to be an issue."

"Shias are a particular sect of Islam right?" James appeared to be a bit embarrassed as his mother spoke.

"Yes. Most Muslims are Sunni, but in Iran most people are Shia."

"What happened after that?" Elizabeth asked. Everyone at the dinner table was looking at Petra with bright, focused eyes.

"Relations between Iran and Iraq worsened. Iraqi troops invaded Iran in 1980 and my family was scared of being singled out as Iranians living in Baghdad. So they crossed the border into Kuwait. My dad started working for another telecom company and my aunt started teaching art at the British Council. My grandma started a small catering business and one of her first clients was a British family. My aunt actually married their son, Franklin, but she didn't meet him until a year later at work. A year after they moved, my dad needed to see a dermatologist, and Uncle Franklin recommended that he see Dr. Danielle Thomas, my mom. My dad was her patient and once she discharged him, he got the guts to ask her out."

"That's a great story. Did they get married in Kuwait?" Lea asked as she returned to her seat after putting away leftovers in the kitchen.

"No, in San Diego, my mom's hometown. They were working in Kuwait until the spring of 1990, but when things between Iraq and Kuwait began to get tense, they decided not to take any chances. They did immigration paperwork for my grandparents and moved to San Francisco. A few years after the Gulf War, they moved back to Kuwait."

"So you were born there? After the Gulf War?" Tony asked.

"Yes."

"You don't have an accent at all. Do you speak English at home?" he inquired further.

"My dad and I speak Farsi most of the time. Mom and I speak English, and also when it's all three of us."

"How did your dad learn English?" James piped up.

"When he first moved to Kuwait with my grandparents, his company sent him on exchange to Ireland to learn English." Petra grinned. "It's actually pretty funny—he speaks with a mixed Irish and Iranian accent now."

"That is pretty funny. How many languages do you speak?" Tony asked.

"Um, about five," Petra said, hesitating slightly.

"Wow. What's the list?" Tony exclaimed.

"English, Farsi, Arabic, Hindi, and French."

"Well, that's just amazing," Elizabeth said, echoing the sentiments of the others at the table.

"Really, it's just a function of how I grew up. My dad is Iranian; my mom is American. I grew up in Kuwait. Our housekeeper was from North India, so that's how I picked up Hindi. We had to take a foreign language in school, so I took French."

"Well, if I ever need an interpreter, I'm going to call you," Tony said, laughing.

The conversation drifted a bit and Tony began recounting some of his own stories as part of the air force. He told them of his different postings in Europe and Asia, and how he flew from one place to another.

"Well, you were jetting around like that until you met me and I calmed you down," Elizabeth butted into one of his stories.

"Now, now, dear. You know that I am incredibly grateful for that," he said smiling.

"Sometimes I just need to make sure. When you get all caught up in your glory days—"

"Don't you ever underestimate how important you are to me." Tony walked around the table and gave his wife a kiss.

Sitting on the other side of the table, Petra smiled at how sweet James's parents were.

The rest of the evening passed in a flurry of lighthearted jokes and storytelling. Tony and Elizabeth told the story of how they met and then the discussion shifted to summer vacation plans until Petra excused herself to catch a late evening train back to Philadelphia.

An hour later, Tony and Elizabeth drove back to their home in another suburb. Before going to bed, Tony went into his home office and called a former colleague with a particular intelligence service.

"I have someone for your next class of recruits," he said in a voicemail message. "You would be crazy not to recruit her."

## New York City, United States – Two months later, July, 2015

"I know I'm supposed to be available for a new assignment," Carlos Santiago said to Alex Mittal. "But until you need to deploy me, I was hoping to spend some time with my sister and my new nephew. My mom is in town too, and it would mean the world to me."

Alex responded with a smile. "Sure, Carlos, take a bit of time with your family. We all risk our necks enough. I only need one thing from you."

Carlos's eyes narrowed. "Come on! Can't I just relax for a bit before the next urgent deployment?"

"Don't worry, buddy. It won't require too much of your time."

He raised his eyebrows. "Fine, what do you need?"

"Really, I promise it won't," Alex continued, taking in Carlos's expression. "One of our satellite reserves called in a potential new recruit a few months ago. We did some screens and have done most of our initial due diligence. We are really interested in this kid. I want you to check her out and then give her the pitch. Let's hope that she's interested and we can pursue it from there."

"She?" Carlos's tone did not mask his skepticism. "How many promising women do we really get in field ops? Especially those referred to us by idle college professors with experience from before the Cold War?"

"I know women usually aren't referred by our satellite contacts, at least not many good candidates. But most of those women wouldn't pass our initial screens, and this one did. Plus, she was referred by a friend of Sir Robert's. She's already made the cut, so we need to pitch to her and see what happens."

Carlos finally shrugged and nodded in agreement.

\*\*\*\*

Four days later, Carlos Santiago quietly sat at a table near Bryant Park while pretending to read the newspaper in his hand. For the past forty-five minutes, he had been observing and listening to the conversation at the next table.

During the summer months, Bryant Park was a place where New Yorkers flocked to sit around and enjoy lunch, a midafternoon coffee break, or drinks at the bar after work. The park is located just behind the New York Public Library. In the building's shade, several bars offered both indoor and outdoor seating. Just beyond the bars' tables, there were tables open to the public for anyone to sit without spending any money.

Carlos had situated himself next to some of the tables belonging to the Bryant Park Grill's bar. He could clearly hear the conversation among the group of girls sitting just within the bar area and did not have to worry about being interrupted by a nosy waiter looking for a better tip.

For the past four days, he had observed Petra Shirazi's movements—from the start of the day at her current home in Midtown West, to the office near Bryant Park, to dinner and drinks with friends, and finally, when she returned home. Her movements did not suggest anything out of the ordinary for a young woman her age. He was far from sold on her potential as an agent, but he had decided to make the pitch tonight so that he could skip town and spend some time with his family. So far, he had been unable to catch Petra alone.

In the meantime, he observed the group of girls. All of them were generally attractive, but one in particular, Cristina, was wearing a low-cut blouse that highlighted a voluptuous torso and a short skirt that crept up steadily as she sat.

Carlos wasn't the suave, sexy James Bond-type of agent who could sweep almost any woman off her feet and out of her dress in less than an hour. Unfortunately, Carlos fell decidedly into a different category of spy. Although not bad looking, he was on the shorter side and was a major tech geek, and neither quality got him much action. That being said, he was well qualified and had a good reputation professionally. Still, while deployed on secret operations, most male agents engaged in a fair amount of meaningless sex whenever the pace of the mission permitted such indulgence. Carlos had not gotten laid in six months, so as he listened to the conversation, he ogled at Cristina's legs and bust and envisioned her lying in his hotel room on Madison Avenue.

He tried unsuccessfully to force his eyes away from the plunging neckline. It was only because of his training that was he able to follow the conversation in spite of the distraction.

"I have to go to my judo class now," Carlos heard Petra say as she stood up.

He waited a minute and then followed her from a safe distance. As he walked, he recalled how his own recruiting process had differed. He followed Petra to the judo studio and watched her go inside for her class. Before heading inside, he made a quick phone call.

"Hi, Stella," he said as his sister picked up the phone.

"Carlos! Hello! When are you coming to see us? You told me you would be in town two days ago."

"I know, I know. I'm sorry, I should have called earlier. I'm in town for a conference, remember? I thought I would be able to skip out, but that wasn't possible."

"Damn you for being such a hotshot. I know you love it at GE, but I wish they would give you more personal time."

"Personal time? Come on, sis. You know I didn't take this job for its work–life balance, but I do wish I could be home more to hang out with you."

"As if. You were so excited to get away. And you left me with all of Mom's attention to myself."

"Thank heaven for that," he mocked gently.

"Joking aside, when do you think you can come by?"

"Well, I'm hoping to make it to Hoboken tonight."

"Tonight? You need to give me more warning! Mom is going to want to cook up a storm. I have to call her right away."

"Now, now, don't go crazy, sis. I'm just coming over to see my new nephew. And it's still not for sure."

"Okay, okay. I'll try to keep her under control."

"You do that. See you tonight, Stella."

"See you tonight."

He walked into the studio and signed up as a walk-in for the next class. The intermediate class that he had registered for took place at the same time as the advanced one and in the same large gym. He was hoping he could get the teacher to bump him up so that he would have a better chance of speaking to Petra.

The class started as expected with a series of warm-up exercises and muscle strengthening. Later, it proceeded into the rounds of sparring. He watched intently as Petra held her own with the mostly male class. The first signs of respect crept into his eyes.

As he'd hoped, the instructor sent him over to the advanced ring for the last fifteen minutes of class. He sparred with a couple of people there, allowed himself to be beaten, and then began doing some exercises at the bench. In between sparring rounds, he observed Petra doing the same. When she came to continue her exercise sets, he struck up a conversation.

"How long have you been doing judo?" he asked.

"For about seven years. How about you?"

"About ten years or so. My name is Anton, by the way. Anton Garcia," Carlos said, using one of his favorite cover identities.

"Hi, Anton. I'm Petra," she replied and shook his outstretched hand.

Their small talk continued and Carlos attempted to turn on the charm. "This might be kind of random, but do you want to get coffee or a drink after class? I'm thinking about signing up for more classes and would love to hear what you think of this place."

Petra hesitated for a second and then shrugged. "Sure. Let's grab a coffee."

He nodded, grinning to himself. They met outside the studio after class and walked to a nearby café. Once they sat down, he cut straight to the point. "So, Petra, here's the thing. I work for a government agency that wants to recruit you. We think you're a good fit, and we'd love to talk to you about some opportunities."

Petra raised her eyebrows at him. "Right. Is that your idea of a pickup line?"

Carlos squirmed. "I'm not trying to pick you up. I really am here to recruit you."

"No shit. Did the police academy send you?" she said, grinning.

Carlos shrugged and pulled out an FBI badge. "Are you happy now?"

"Oh…sorry," Petra said, taken aback.

They sat in silence for the better part of a minute. "You said you're trying to recruit me? Into the FBI?"

"Not into the FBI, but another agency."

Petra looked at him surprised. "Wow."

"Here's my card, and a flash drive that will give you a bit of detail on the work we do. Unfortunately, I can't stay, but watch the video on the flash drive and see what you think. I'll be in touch."

A few minutes later, he was standing on the platform at the nearest subway station with access to the Path trains to New Jersey, excited to go see his nephew. On his way to the station, he sent a message through the Agency's server to Alex. *Pitch made. TBC.*

\*\*\*\*

# Chapter 6
# Heading to Paris

*Kuwait City, Kuwait – September, 2015*

Kasem could barely contain his excitement as he walked out of Selim Kharafi's offices in Kuwait City.

"Kamran, we got the investment pledge from Kharafi!" he shouted into his superior's voicemail.

For the past few months, he had been back and forth from Tehran to Kuwait City every few weeks hoping to engage Kharafi as a key investor in the Basra and Flower of Eden projects. Kharafi was well regarded in both the business and development worlds, so his stamp on the projects would give them more credence to ask other investors and development finance institutions for funding. Normally, development finance institutions such as the World Bank would be their initial target. Because of Iran's reputation, Kasem had strategized that approaching such organizations after they had secured some initial funding would be the better way to go. "After all," he had explained to his boss, "the development implications of these projects are pretty clear; they will be contributing a large amount to the local economies and creating jobs. If we also get one monetary investor on board, we build credibility with the overall project returns as well. That should help us to get both development finance people and other investors on board."

He walked across the parking lot toward the Sheraton Kuwait Hotel and got into a taxicab parked in front of the entrance. "The airport please," he told the driver.

On the drive to the airport, Kasem's phone rang. He looked at it and saw Kamran's name on the caller ID.

"Hi, Kamran," Kasem said as he answered.

"Great news, Kasem. I was glad to get your voicemail. Are you on your way back?"

"Heading to the airport now."

"Do you have enough time to talk about the next step?"

"Yes, actually, I was hoping to talk about that. I need more time to get other investors on board with these projects. Once we get another one or two on board, we can initiate talks with contractors for the detailed design and implementation plans."

"Sounds like a good plan."

"I'd like these two projects to become my exclusive focus now—at least for the next couple of months. I spend most of my time on them anyway." Kasem fidgeted as he waited for his boss's response.

"Hmm…We would have to reorganize to cover your smaller projects."

"Yes, but I think Taleb or Abdullah can handle them."

"If you arrange it with them and make sure that they are willing and able, then I don't have any issues with it."

"Thanks, Kamran."

"See you tomorrow, Kasem. Have a safe flight."

They reached the airport a few minutes later and he proceeded straight through check-in to the Pearl Lounge to refresh before boarding the flight. As soon as he took his seat on the flight, he slipped into a deep sleep, dreaming of how he and Jamal would celebrate later that night.

### Philadelphia, United States – October, 2015

Carlos Santiago glanced at his watch as he waited for his new recruit to arrive at the small café just off Locust Walk on the Penn campus in Philadelphia. He was growing impatient and tried to pass the time by taking in the surroundings.

Philadelphia in October hardly boasted pleasant weather, but the real cold spell was still to come. In spite of the weather, though, the setting was beautiful. The trees that lined the path glittered in reddish gold as the fading sun caught them with its last rays. In stark contrast to the general beauty, giant signs were scattered across the brick walk detailing whereabouts for haunted houses, candy drives, and of course, the numerous Halloween frat parties that would feature copious amounts of alcohol and women dancing around in sexy, figure-hugging costumes. He had already seen a few people walking around in costume, but the provocative part of the weekend had yet to begin.

He smiled when he saw Petra approaching from the distance. *Wow,* he thought, taking in her knee-length red dress with black boots that highlighted every curve in her perfectly proportioned hourglass figure. *Way better than the judo uniform!*

She walked over to the table and took a seat across from him. "Hi, Petra. Thanks for meeting with me today."

"Hi, Anton. Nice to see you again, I guess."

"I wanted to follow up with you since I was passing through Philly."

Petra nodded. "I went through the information you gave me, but I'm not sure what to make of it."

"Well, for starters, if you take a posting with us, for each year that you serve, we will pay back your entire student debt for that year on top of your salary."

She smiled. "I did pick up on that detail and it's a great draw, but I still don't understand. What do you actually do?"

"Basically, we are looking for people to gather information in the field."

"What kind of information? The flash drive didn't even explain who you are."

"We're an intelligence agency."

"Yeah, I got that much. So you work for the CIA? I thought you showed me a badge from the FBI."

"I did, but that was just to get you to talk to me. And no, I'm not with the CIA either."

"But something along the same lines?"

Carlos nodded.

"Can you tell me what you do? You specifically," Petra probed further.

"I travel and gather information that pertains to security here and in other countries. Usually, I work with sources on the ground."

He watched for visual cues as she nodded in understanding. *Bet she's thinking about that giant college debt,* he conjectured as he observed the tightness in her features. *Probably more than two hundred thousand dollars? That was enough to make it a no-brainer for me.*

"So what do you think? Would you be interested in coming to training after you graduate this December?"

"Going to training isn't a full commitment is it?"

"Not officially, but it's a strong signal." He paused. "Why don't you tell me about your concerns?"

She averted her eyes. "I don't know if I'd be cut out for it."

He met her gaze and then pressed further. "Cut out for what?"

"You know, being a spy."

Carlos nodded. "I didn't think I would be either, but I needed the money." He shrugged his shoulders. "I didn't qualify for any normal grants or other funding, and I didn't want my mom to pay for school. As for being a spy, we wouldn't have picked you if we weren't sure that you could handle it. The training prepares you well for everything that you have to do on the job."

"How were you recruited? Did they identify you?"

"I was working on my PhD in cryptology and I was interested in working with the government, so I went to a few different employment presentations. I ended up talking to one of the recruiters for a while. He asked me about my work in cryptology, my goals, stuff like that. A few weeks later, someone else approached me and asked if I'd be interested in going to training. We talked about the potential pros and cons of the opportunity. It sounded intriguing, but I was pretty uncertain and skeptical about the whole thing. But, like I said, the money tipped the balance for me. I needed it to help repay my debts."

"Is the person who recruited you still there?"

"Yeah, I work with him regularly."

She looked pleasantly surprised. "Is that typical?"

"We're a small organization, so in general, yes, it is typical. That's something that sets us apart from the CIA."

"What was the training like?"

"Training was the hardest six months I've ever spent doing anything. It was great, don't get me wrong, but I've never been pushed so hard. Not like that."

"What do you mean?"

He took a deep breath, considering how best to describe it. "The program pushed me intellectually, emotionally, physically. Since it pushes you on all of your personal dimensions, it's incredibly strenuous. I also found it to be tremendously rewarding."

"Do people ever leave after training?"

"Most people who complete training do stay. Many actually leave during training, though."

He watched her blink rapidly as she responded, "What happened when you finished, Anton?"

"I started being posted on assignments. Most of mine were in Latin America. I worked on seeking out sources, monitoring targets, acquiring and dealing with evidence."

"Have you ever recruited anyone before me?"

Carlos hesitated. *Should I tell her the truth?* "No, actually, you would be my first recruit."

Petra tilted her head to the side and looked at him intently. "How many people have you killed?"

He looked at her, surprised by how quickly she had come to that point. "Three, two in self-defense. The third one was about to get away, so I shot him. It wasn't supposed to be a kill shot." He sighed heavily. "It never gets easier. Sometimes it seems necessary, but you always wonder if it really was."

She looked down at the table for a moment to take that in. "So if I come to training and then decide to leave, what happens?"

"We would pay off six months of your tuition and living loans, which I think in your case is about thirty thousand, correct?" He paused and Petra nodded. "While you're in training, we'll cover all your costs—food, housing, everything. You don't get paid, but you won't be out any money."

"Can I have some time to think about it?"

"Sure. Give me a call at the number on my card. If I don't pick up, just leave a message with your name and either a yes or no."

"Okay." She paused as she picked up her purse. "I think that's everything I wanted to ask you, so I'll get going then."

"Enjoy Halloween weekend."

As she walked away, Carlos watched her dress sway with each step. Across the Agency's server, he sent an update to Alex: *"Decision imminent."*

****

Petra left the classroom after her last final exam and sighed with relief. The stress of turning in final papers and studying for exams had prevented her from really enjoying her last few months on campus. *I'm going to miss it here.*

She walked home with her boots crunching on the salt scattered across the icy snow. When she reached her dorm room, she collapsed on the bed for a few minutes, staring at the ceiling. The room was barely larger than the furniture it contained—a single bed, a desk, and a decent-sized closet. The view that looked straight across Philadelphia to the southeast made up for a ton, though. She took in the view and stretched out on the bed. After reaching for her phone, she called her mother in New York. "Hi, Mom."

"Hello, my dear. All done with your tests?"

"Yup. All done. No more papers, tests, or anything like that."

"Amazing. How do you feel?"

"I can't believe it. How about you and Dad? How was the move?"

"Well, as usual, Homeland Security hassled your father. You know how immigration control is. If they see anything about Iran, they freak out. It doesn't matter how many years he's been a citizen, or that he hasn't even been back there since his family escaped in the seventies."

Petra could hear her mom fuming on the other side of the line. "I'm sorry you have to keep going through this, Mom."

Danielle sighed. "Don't worry, we're both fine. It just gets so frustrating."

"I'm so excited you're close by now. It will only take me a couple of hours to drive to the house!"

"Well, we can't wait to see you. The house is such a mess, so don't expect anything else. We've only been here for a week. And everything is so different. It's hard doing things around the house without all the help we had in Kuwait."

"You know I don't care about that, Mom. Just a few weeks of home cooking and relaxing sound great to me."

Danielle beamed. "I'm glad to hear it. I wish you could stay longer. I can't believe your company said that you have to start training on January fifteenth."

"Yeah, I wish it wasn't so soon."

"We understand. We'll just miss you! Anyway, dear, I'm going to go help your father with some more unpacking. See you this weekend? Do you need us to get anything for you?"

"Just be at the house when I get there."

"We will."

Petra said goodbye and pulled out her copy of the contract she had signed and given to Anton Garcia already. For the millionth time, she skimmed through it. The contract outlined her commitment to attend and complete training with the "Agency." *Doesn't it have a real name?*

Upon successful completion of training, as Anton had said, she would be able to sign a second long-term contract. If she elected not to do so, she would still receive six months' worth of student loan repayment.

She sighed, second-guessing her decision once again when a knock on the door drew her back to the moment.

"One second," she called out, hastily putting the contract away. "Come in!"

"Hi, Petra! How was your last final?" asked her friend Alice, as Petra opened the door.

"Alice! I'm so glad you came by."

"Are you kidding? As if I wouldn't come by." Alice gave her a big hug. "I'm going to miss you. I can't believe you're missing the second semester of our senior year."

"I know it sucks, but school's too expensive to stick around," Petra sighed.

"I know, but I wish you were going to be closer."

"New York isn't that far!"

"Yeah, but you're not even joining the company full time anymore. I thought you liked consulting. We get to travel and work with different companies. We had such a great time last summer that I thought for sure you would take the offer to come back."

"It just wasn't right for me," Petra explained.

"You never told me, though—why aren't you signing with them?"

"It was a lot of fun. I did have a great summer. The people are great and the travel is fun, but I didn't really care for the work. I don't think finance is the right place for me."

"What are you going to do instead?"

"I'm doing this three-month training program at another consulting firm. It's more government related. If I like it, I'll stay. If not, I'll figure something out then."

Alice perked up. "You could come back and work with us."

"Maybe. We'll see."

Later that night, Petra finished packing and threw her suitcases into her car to drive to her parent's new house. "Time to move out and move on," she whispered, repeating the phrase her father had said that had helped him through the many moves during his childhood and adult life.

## *Tehran, Iran – February, 2016*

When his phone rang at 4:15 p.m., Kasem was about to doze off at his desk. "Kasem Ismaili, Iranian National Securities Exchange," he said, picking up the handset.

"Hello, Kasem. It's Victor Black."

Kasem sat up quickly. "Victor, great to hear from you. How are you doing?"

"Fine, fine. I won't take too much of your time, but I wanted to let you know that, unfortunately, Selim and I will be traveling out of Kuwait for our next meeting at the end of March."

"Oh, that's fine. Should I speak to your assistant to reschedule our meeting then?"

"Actually, we have a very tight schedule for the next six weeks or so." Victor's voice sounded stiff and unyielding.

"I see…" Kasem said, unsure of how to respond. *They're pulling out of the deal?* His heart sank into his stomach. "When would work best for you then?"

"Actually, could you meet with us during our trip?"

Kasem perked up immediately. "Sure, no problem."

"Okay then. Most likely, we'll have to push the date forward a bit for the meeting, and move the timing around. Selim and I will be in Paris the first half of April, so we hoped you could just join us there. We can have the meeting at the Georges Cinq Hotel where we'll be staying."

"Of course. That sounds great." Kasem felt elation creeping through his body.

"Perfect. I'll have my assistant call your office to figure out the details. Speak to you later then?"

"Okay, thanks. I look forward to her call."

"Great. Bye."

"Bye." Kasem barely had the word out before the line went dead. A wide grin spread across his face. *Paris, here I come!*

Two hours later, he drove home and went straight to Jamal's apartment. "Jamal! We are celebrating tonight. In a few weeks, I'm going to Paris."

## *New York City, United States – March, 2016*

"As most of you know, the results of this evaluation will determine who is able to remain with the Agency. For all of you, we commend your abilities and efforts and wish you the best in your future endeavors, whether you're with us or another organization."

Petra was lined up with her class of fellow recruits in front of Chris McLaughry. Each of them was at the point of extreme exhaustion. The latest evaluation had consisted of the most strenuous five days she had ever experienced, both mentally and physically. She could feel her eyes glazing over and forced herself to focus.

Chris nodded at Alex Mittal before continuing. "Alex is handing each of you an envelope with the results. Feel free to open this at your leisure."

Petra felt her stomach tighten as Alex handed her an envelope. She ripped it open and stared at the paper with confusion. All it contained was a note.

*"Petra, please speak to me once you read this note. – CM"*

Taking a deep breath, she extracted herself quickly from the silent, seated group. *Does this mean that I failed?* Chris had just walked out of the room into the hallway and she fully intended to catch him.

At the exit, she bumped straight into him. "Chris! Why did I get a note to speak to you instead of receiving my evaluation?" She held the note up.

"Yes, I wanted to speak with you. Let's go to my office."

He led her down the corridor to the left toward his training office. They walked in and he closed the door behind them, gesturing for her to take a seat as he sat down behind his desk.

Petra sat down in silence, unsure of how to begin. She placed the letter face up on the desk to start the conversation. "What did you want to speak to me about?"

"Before we get to that, let's talk a little bit. Tell me, how did you feel about this evaluation?"

*Shit.* Her stomach was tying itself in knots as alarm bells went off in her head.

"Honestly, I thought it was incredibly challenging—exhausting in every way. Still, I felt that I performed reasonably well." She met his eyes and tried to mask her apprehension. *Let's get this over with.*

"Good. Here are your results." He handed her a report card that gave her a score for each part of the evaluation: weapons training, marksmanship, fitness, psychological integration, combat tactics, etc.

She frowned as she read the numbers.

"As you can see, your results are very good, actually great. You scored the highest in our class of recruits."

A hesitant smile appeared on her face.

"We have an operation that we'd like to staff you on."

Petra recoiled slightly with shock. "Wow, I thought I still had another couple months of training to complete."

"We think you're ready. The mission is quite short, so you can still finish training and attend the final ceremony with your fellow recruits."

"Well, okay then." Petra kept her uncertain emotions to herself. *Don't I have another two months left to decide if I want to do this?*

"For the mission, you are going to work with a government bureau. The details are here," he said, handing her a small USB stick. "You'll report to your controller tomorrow morning. All the details are on that flash drive. Memorize them tonight. The encryption on the drive is programmed for a memory wipe at midnight."

Petra took the USB stick and her evaluation report, and then stood to leave the office. As she closed the door behind her, she heard him call out, "Good luck, Petra."

**\*\*\*\***

# Book III
## 2021

# Chapter 7
## An Off-Book Mission

*New York City, United States – May, 2021*

On the morning of the internal department head meeting, Petra arrived at the conference room next to her office at 8:00 a.m. sharp, where she had asked one of her research team members to meet her. He had been working for the past two hours already.

"Morning, Russell. Thanks for coming in on your Saturday, and this early in the morning too."

"No problem," he responded, still engulfed in the reams of paper spread out across the table in front of him.

"So before we go any further, let's talk about where we are," Petra said, taking charge. "We have information connecting Fayed to Khaled Majed's family. Have you learned anything else about them that will give us a better idea of what they are planning?"

At this point, Russell looked up and shook his head.

Petra frowned and studied the papers on the table until a thought occurred to her. *Focusing on General Majed's nephew is not rational—it's emotional.*

"Let's explore a different angle. If we forget Khaled Majed for now and focus on Fayed, where might he get that kind of money?"

"Well, campaign contributions are pretty small in Kuwait, certainly a lot smaller than here," he said, pulling out some of the research they had done on the National Assembly.

Petra gave him a brief nod.

"Most of Kuwait's big businesses are owned by different families, like the Al-Ghanims control electronics, and the Al-Shayas control retail. Some of the parliamentarians come from one of the big families, so they get their money from there," Russell added.

"But Fayed isn't a member of any of those families, is he?"

"No, but he did remarry recently into a well-known family," he continued.

"Yeah, they're big in the industrial space. Wasn't that before his campaign though? What about his sources of funding for previous campaigns?"

"I checked into it, but didn't find anything unusual."

"Maybe that's a dead end then." Petra leaned back in her chair and pursed her lips. "What about people in his inner circle? Let's go through who's in it."

"There's Fayed, his wife, his three senior aides, including Khaled Majed, his brother, and the rest of the Islamist section of Parliament."

Petra ran her fingers through her hair. "You did some research on the other Islamists, right? What did you find?" She searched through the papers she had projected on the screen and picked up the list of parliamentarians Alex had sent over in his first set of documents.

Russell pointed at the first few names on the list. "So those are the people who are affiliated with other segments. The ones that I would say are Islamists are at about the halfway point."

"You would say?" she asked, looking confused.

"You know what I mean," he shrugged. "None of them are affiliated officially with any particular party, since none of the parties actually exist anyway."

"True."

"It's such a strange system."

"You mean a democratically elected Parliament versus a monarch who represents progress? Yeah, it makes you wonder about democracy, but we can talk more about that later."

Russell nodded and Petra looked back at the list.

After contemplating the list for another minute, she pointed at one of the names. "What about that one? Hamsa Zayeedi. I think I've seen it somewhere."

"Hamsa Zayeedi? Yeah, Khaled Majed actually visited him three times in the past two weeks. It didn't seem like anything unusual though."

"Still, let's follow that one through. Our intel says that Fayed went with him one of those times. What did they do?"

"They met at a dewaniya, ordered some sheesha, and then were left alone."

"And they were there for three hours? So it was a social event."

"Yeah, must have been," he agreed.

Petra's brow furrowed. "Did you do any research on Zayeedi? I know he wasn't the focus, but let's see what we've got."

Russell opened up a couple of files on his computer. "Zayeedi is very well connected, and is extremely wealthy. Do you think he's the source of Fayed's funding?"

"Maybe. What else do we know?"

"They've been working together on more Islamist legislation for a while, along with mobilizing the movement in Kuwait."

"But they haven't done anything related to foreign policy." She took a seat at the table and concentrated on the screen. "Let's figure out every point of contact between the two of them over the past few months."

"Well, there have been a number of public meetings, a few TV sessions, and then some social things." Russell hit a few keys on his keyboard and a joint calendar appeared that displayed where and when Fayed and Zayeedi had met in the past six months.

"Wait a second. Go back to their individual calendars," Petra said.

He tapped out a few shortcuts and the two calendars appeared on the screen side by side with matching dates without the filter for meetings. Russell scrolled through them both together, wondering what his boss was looking for in the calendars.

"Stop," she said suddenly. "A month ago, they were both in Abu Dhabi at the same time."

"It looks like leisure travel."

"Isn't that when the conference was, though?"

"The one on Sharia law in international politics?" A concerned look crossed his face as he pulled up the dates. "You're right. They did go there on those dates."

Petra leaned back in her chair, thinking. "So they went to the conference together."

"Why doesn't the government put a stop to the conference?"

She let out a huge yawn. "Everyone just monitors it closely and lets it continue. The conference is nonviolent, so we judged that there wouldn't be much harm done by people discussing how to integrate Sharia law and Islam into modern society."

"Still, I'm going to check the list of attendees." He turned back to the screen and hit some keys rapidly.

"Sure. Let's look at it together."

The two of them reviewed the list on Russell's screen for a full five minutes before one of the names struck them.

"Shit," Russell said, pointing at the screen. "Is that?"

"Fuck! That's Mohammed Jamal Ibn Qasem. How could we miss something like this?"

"I don't know," he said, looking dumbfounded. "The last report we had on Ibn Qasem said he was in Afghanistan. Wouldn't it have shown up on our radar that he was in Abu Dhabi?"

"Shit, shit, shit." She reached for the phone on the table and hit Chris's cell number.

"Petra?" they heard Chris answer from the phone's speaker. "I'm on my way in for the meeting."

"There's no discussion needed. I have the recommendation."

"That doesn't sound good."

"It isn't. Chris, is it too late to cancel the meeting?"

"You're not seriously asking me that."

"No, I guess not. I'll just see you there then." She sighed and hung up, and then looked back at Russell. "Thanks for your help today."

"I need to get going before the meeting, right?"

"Yeah. Sorry, you know how clearance works. It's above your pay grade. For now, anyway," she said with a smile.

"No worries." He tapped his finger against the table a few times. "Petra, I have to ask. Do you really believe it?"

"What?"

"That Fayed is a terrorist."

She shook her head. "Honestly, my gut says no. Maybe I'm wrong. Maybe this was a big disguise and he's been involved with Al-Qaeda for years. Regardless, we can't ignore what we just found."

"I don't think so either. I've researched him a lot, and I almost feel as if I kind of get him. He's a bit of an oaf, arrogant, pompous, but I don't think he's capable of doing something that would kill a lot of innocent people."

"We'll just have to investigate further."

He nodded. "Okay, I'll see you on Monday then," he said as he grabbed his things and headed out of the conference room.

She gathered the papers together and headed back to her office where she dumped them on her desk. After taking a seat, she leaned back in her chair to try to get a few minutes of naptime, along with some perspective. Her eyes fluttered open when she heard her six-foot Californian boyfriend stop in the doorway.

"Hi, Petra," Grant said. "How are you doing?"

She beamed, happy that he had come by to check on her. "Hanging in there."

He walked around her desk and kissed her softly. He smelled like fresh citrus because of the Davidoff cologne he always wore. Pulling away, she smiled and linked her hands behind his neck, mussing his chin-length brown hair. "I'm glad you're here," she said, peering into his blue-green eyes.

"Well, I always try to check on you when I come in. What time did you get here?" He nodded at the piles of papers spread across her desk in complete disarray. "You've been busy."

"Yeah. I came in early to prepare for the staff meeting. But what are you doing here on a Saturday?"

"We had a bit of an IT issue yesterday, so I called the team in to make sure the server is operating properly. It was a close call." He glanced around her office. "I'll never know how you manage to organize things with all of these printed files. Did you find what you were looking for?"

"I hate reading on the computer screen, you know that."

"Yes, I do." He smiled as he remembered the first time he had gotten the courage to talk to the young woman who only had been appointed a little less than three years ago. She had been fumbling with the printer as she tried to find page thirty-seven and forty-eight of a sixty-page document that she had insisted on printing rather than reading on screen.

"Do you really need it? You know you will probably only read the executive summary anyway," he had told her. That first conversation had been one of many over the next several months before he summoned the courage to ask her out. At first, she had refused, saying that she was hung up on an ex-boyfriend. When she finally agreed to go out with him more than a year later, he was both surprised and excited. Their relationship had progressed slowly, but the past couple of months had been exhilarating.

She smiled back at him and stood on her tiptoes to give him another kiss. "I'm going to get back to this now," she said as she pulled away.

"Okay. Good luck in there." He squeezed her hand and headed back toward his office a few floors away.

Turning back to her desk, she began running through her notes and typing them to make sure she was clear on everything for the meeting. She felt the caffeine wear off while she stared at her computer screen. Before realizing it, she had dozed off to sleep with her head resting on the desk next to her computer.

Twenty minutes later, a knock on the desk woke her with a start. "Oh!" she said.

"Morning, Petra," Chris said as he stood in front of her desk.

"Shit. It's already eleven. I'll be right there for the meeting." As she stood, her chair rolled backward and crashed loudly into the cabinet behind her desk.

Chris looked at her, clearly amused. "Petra it's only ten forty-five, you have a few minutes. You didn't sleep here last night did you?"

"Phew! No, of course not. I just stayed late and got in early this morning."

"Ready for the meeting?"

"Yeah, it's not going to be pretty though."

"You're not going to recommend the Agency Watch List, are you?"

With a sigh, she nodded. "We'll have to send an agent in as soon as possible, and we don't have the luxury of time and effort to deal with internal protocols. Whoever we choose will have to go in alone."

Sensing her discomfort, Chris countered, "At least the assignment will be in Kuwait. There are worse places we could send an agent. I know Kuwait isn't exactly like it was when you grew up there, but it still has good relations with the West."

"I guess...." She thought back to her own experiences. "The agent won't be able to access any support network and could be blind to any intelligence we collect after deployment."

"We'll be able to set up some sort of communication. Try not to worry."

Petra nodded again reluctantly, still unconvinced. *It is necessary,* she kept repeating to herself.

The two of them walked to the meeting, both wishing they had a different recommendation.

****

After a draining two-hour meeting, Petra and Chris walked out of the meeting room on the twentieth floor of the Agency's building. Similar to most office buildings, each floor housed a different regional or service department. Most floors had their own conference rooms, but extremely important or supremely classified meetings took place in the situation room on the twentieth floor. Security swept it on an hourly basis for bugs and listening devices, and every night the room was tested for any potential issues with its soundproof wall insulation system. The system ensured that no one would ever be able to listen in on conversations from outside the room and the building.

Before entering, all personnel went through a full-body scanner that used a combination of electromagnetic radiation and x-ray technology to create an image of a person's body. Images of all items that agents carried or wore were stored in an "impenetrable" Agency database housed separately in both the Technology and Counterintelligence Departments. Agents were scanned again when exiting the room, just in case a comparison was necessary.

Petra and Chris walked through the scanner separately followed by several others. Petra smiled as she saw Veronica walk out with Matt, another senior department staffer. Although their relationship was not public, she (and almost everyone else in their division) knew that the two were dating.

More than a year earlier, in February, Veronica had left a company party quite early, citing exhaustion as the reason. One of her close friends, Sharon, had gone with her. Within ten minutes, Sharon returned and pulled Matt toward the exit, saying that she needed to speak with him. Petra had enjoyed the rest of the evening with the other department heads, all of whom had become quite close friends, but decided to leave fifteen minutes later. Four of them—Petra, Jesse, Brian, and Chris—were all hungry and chose to trek to one of the many diners open within a ten-minute walk from the bar. Before they left, Sharon returned and rejoined them, saying that she would come to the diner as well.

The five gradually made their way to the bar's exit, stopping to pick up their coats from the extremely slow and crowded coat check. Then Brian spotted the scene. About thirty feet away, just on the other side of the exit, Matt and Veronica were kissing passionately. The five of them watched, with everyone but Sharon surprised, and tried to restrain their laughter. Shortly after, they all crowded into a cab and left.

"Are they official yet...?" Chris asked inquisitively as they walked toward the staircase.

"You're kidding? You mean those two are a *couple*?" Petra said, grinning cheekily.

He rolled his eyes. "It's been more than a year since that time we saw them, right?"

"Outside the party, when they both left because they were 'tired'? Yeah. And no, they're not official yet, although they are still together."

"So everyone knows except for HR?"

"Everyone who knows them knows, but once HR finds out, they'll broadcast it over the intercom. So they're keeping it quiet for now."

Chris winked at her in amusement. "Did Brian tell you the story from a few weeks ago?"

"When you guys went out in Brooklyn?"

"Yeah."

Petra raised her eyebrows. "No, I don't think so."

"Finally, I know some gossip before you do. We were out in Brooklyn—me, Brian, Matt, and a couple of other people. At the end of the night, we were about to get a cab when Matt says, 'Actually, guys, I don't feel like paying for a cab tonight. I'm going to take the F train home.' And then he turns down the exact street where Veronica lives."

Petra smirked mischievously. "The F train? So that's what they're calling it these days, huh? Guess we all need *that* from time to time."

"Exactly." Chris giggled as they walked down the next flight of stairs and they fell into a comfortable silence. As they rounded a corner, he spoke up again. "How do you feel about this whole thing?"

"The mission?"

He nodded.

"Not great." She shrugged, thinking back to the meeting.

"Are you thinking about what that analyst said?"

"About how the agent going in would be completely exposed? Yeah."

Chris waved his hand in front of him in a dismissive gesture. "Don't worry about what he said. He's a total rookie. He never should have been in the room in the first place."

"That may be so, but that doesn't mean what he said isn't true." She paused on a landing and turned her gaze toward the floor as her shoulders slumped slightly.

"Petra, you wouldn't have come to this decision if we could do anything else right now."

"I guess you're right."

Chris sighed and they continued to walk in silence. He was glad they had taken the stairs because it gave them a semblance of privacy that a packed elevator didn't provide.

"Maybe it's time we move past the decision and start planning this thing."

Petra took a deep breath and then nodded.

"What kind of agent do you think we need for this?"

She paused for a moment before responding. "For starters, we need someone who speaks Arabic."

"And Farsi, so the agent will be able to follow Majed too."

"Yeah, that's right." Petra crossed her arms as she thought. "We'll need an agent with some previous experience in the Middle East, preferably even experience in Kuwait."

"Preferably male?"

"I don't know. It would be easier for a guy to become Fayed's friend, but—"

"That would take a lot longer. So maybe someone who can pose as a new assistant?"

"Something like that. We could set up a cover through a family friend looking for work for his daughter. I still have to think it through."

He stopped midstep and gawked at her with his mouth open. "Hold up for a second. So we need a female agent who speaks Arabic and Farsi with a decent amount of experience in Kuwait. Sound like anyone we know?"

Petra glared at him. "We need an *active* agent who fits that profile. Agents who retired from the field do *not* qualify."

"Sorry, I just couldn't help myself." Chris cocked his head to the side with a goofy smile on his face. His features turned serious again as he continued. "Going back to what you were saying, do we have enough assets in the region to set up that kind of cover story?"

She pursed her lips. "It should be doable. I'll work with Alex on the details."

"So now the fun begins."

Petra grimaced. "It does indeed."

## *Salmiya, Kuwait – May, 2021*

The Ahriman was waiting in the hotel lobby when John Matheson walked in to pick him up. "Hey, John. Thanks for picking me up."

"Well, look at you. You look like a natural in that nightgown," John exclaimed as he looked his friend up and down.

"As do you."

They headed out to the car together. On the way, John stumbled as he tripped over the skirt tail of the dishdasha.

"Damned dish…dishdata!" he grumbled in his Texan drawl.

The Ahriman snickered, not bothering to correct his friend.

Dewaniyas were a central part of social life for Kuwaiti men. Reception areas were set aside for men to sit and mingle with friends, colleagues, and guests while smoking sheesha and sipping tea, coffee, or other drinks. Since women traditionally kept separate social circles, dewaniyas typically were still all male.

The sun was setting in the distance and it lit the sky in a blaze of pinks and oranges. All of it framed the brilliant blue Salmiya seafront as if it were a postcard.

"Gorgeous sunset," the Ahriman said, gazing out the passenger side window.

"We get those sometimes here. I know it's not New York or London, but you should give this place a chance."

"We'll see. I have to give it to you on the food. It's great."

"Wait till you try the kebabs they bring out at these dewaniyas. And sheesha—well, you already know sheesha, and kebabs too, I guess."

"Yeah, but not in the past few months."

The two rode in silence until John took the highway exit for Surra. "You know what I think is strange, Mustafa?"

The Ahriman looked at him quizzically. "What?"

"That now we are in a whole other city." John gestured toward the yards of villas stretching out around him. "Kuwait is a small, funny place. People think everything is so far away when it is just a twenty-minute drive," he said as he parked the car and turned off the engine.

They walked slowly toward the dewaniya tent. Even from this distance, he could catch a hint of the apple- and grape-flavored sheesha pipes that people had already started. "I can smell it from here," the Ahriman said with his eyes lighting up in anticipation of some real company.

"Best scent around. We're over there in the VIP tent," John commented as he pointed ahead.

When they first entered the tent, it was rather empty. They called for the waiter and ordered two apple sheeshas and some of the traditional lemon mint drink that Kuwaitis consumed in mass quantities to combat the summer heat. The Ahriman took a seat and fidgeted as he tried to get comfortable.

"I wouldn't even bother trying," John remarked, amused by his friend's attempts to find comfort. "Dewaniya couches are not made to be comfortable. I just sit halfway on the seat and lean forward."

The Ahriman tried it and scowled, shaking his head in discomfort.

"You'll get used to it. Or you'll get so stoned that you won't care."

"Let's bring it on then!" The Ahriman tried to lean back on the couch as he sipped his lemonade. "This drink is amazing," he exclaimed.

"Refreshing, isn't it? I've tried to copy it at home, but I can't get the proportions right. I never know how much mint to add."

They each took a drag and the tent began to fill up with smoke and a few other people.

John introduced him to several of the men entering the gathering. He pointed out one of the men in particular, wearing a dark-colored vest over his white dishdasha. "That's Othman Al-Sabah."

"Al-Sabah?" the Ahriman asked, trying to play dumb. "You mean one of *the* Al-Sabahs?"

"Yeah, he's one of the local business partners for *Total*. I think he's the king's cousin's son or something."

"You mean the Emir?"

"Yeah, same difference."

The Ahriman curiously observed the crowd as it grew larger. Over the evening, he struck up conversation with a few people.

"What are you doing in Kuwait?" one of the men asked.

"I'm here working on a project with *Total*. John over here is my boss." he said and pointed to the man on his right.

"Are you living here now? Or here temporarily?"

"Looks like I'll be here for a few months or so."

"Well, you should come around again."

The Ahriman beamed. "Absolutely."

The six of them smoked their pipes calmly and then Othman Al-Sabah took out a tiny metal flask. "It is whiskey—a twenty-one-year-old Balvenie Portwood single malt. A friend of mine brought it in for me." He poured a tiny amount into his empty water glass, and then peered around the group. "Care to try it?" he asked as he savored the first sip.

The Ahriman watched in amusement as the men passed the flask around the circle. *No need to be subtle.* He took a long swig. The strength of the taste shocked him—it had been years since he had indulged in his old favorite. He handed off the flask and forced a big smile.

He clenched his teeth together and pulled at the sheesha pipe as a distraction from the strength and memories that came with the taste of the whiskey. He took a deep breath and exhaled the apple-flavored smoke in a series of rings in front of him.

"You must smoke sheesha pretty often if you can blow smoke like that," someone said.

The Ahriman let out a dramatic sigh and shook his head. "Not as often as I'd like. I need to get one of these to keep at my hotel."

"Where are you staying?"

He gestured toward the seafront. "Over in Salmiya."

"How do you like Kuwait, Mustafa? Where are you from?" someone else asked.

"My family is from Jordan, but I grew up outside of New York. I've been living in London for the past few years."

"Your Arabic is excellent."

The Ahriman could not help but glow with pride at the compliment. "Thank you."

"Did you live in Manhattan? I went to college there." They spent the next thirty minutes exchanging stories about the merits of the New York City bar scene.

"Where in Jordan is your family from?"

"Close to the Dead Sea."

"The Dead Sea? It's great, isn't it?"

"It's nice to be able to walk through the water, that's for sure," the Ahriman responded.

"Oh, don't hold back on us. It's nice because everywhere you look you get to see all those girls in bikinis."

The Ahriman joined in as the room erupted in laughter. When the room quieted a bit, he added, "The best girls are on the Mediterranean. In the south of France."

"No! I'll tell you where the best-looking women are. They're in Turkey."

The room dissolved into a series of jokes and commentary about where the best-looking women in the world lived. The next couple of hours passed slowly.

"Now, Mustafa, can you do this?" Othman asked. He inhaled a large amount of sheesha smoke and then blew it out in the shape of a crescent moon.

The Ahriman threw his hands out to the side. "Are you crazy? How did you even do that?"

"It's easy! Just try it."

"Easy for you to say," the Ahriman responded, still laughing. He made a feeble attempt. John followed his lead and blew out a strange cylindrical stream of smoke.

The men around him broke out in laughter.

"*Mabrouk,* Mustafa! And *mabrouk,* John!" one of the attendees congratulated them. "The two of you have managed to blow shapes that look like the map of Kuwait and some sort of sausage."

Each of them then proceeded to attempt the same stunt on their own. Of the group of six, Othman was the only one who seemed to be able to do it effectively. Laughing, one of the other men proclaimed him the obvious winner.

"This youngblood will do it for you! Seems like you still need to work on it, Mustafa. Now I must return home to my wife, or she will cut off my balls for being too late. When do we meet here next?"

"Next week! Mustafa, will you join us?"

"In sha'allah," the Ahriman said, smiling.

"He'll be here," John said with a nod. "I'll make sure of it."

A half hour later, John dropped him off at his hotel. "Holy shit," the Ahriman said. "I used to be able to easily drink half a bottle of whiskey."

"You meant it when you said you didn't drink a lot, huh? Well, don't worry, you'll build your tolerance right back up with this crowd," John scoffed.

"Thanks for taking me. I'll see you in the office."

"No problem, man. Let me know which days you're coming in."

John drove away and the Ahriman trudged through the lobby and upstairs to his hotel room. When he got inside, he collapsed into bed, barely managing to take off his shoes. *Guess I'm already in my nightgown,* he thought as he passed out.

**\*\*\*\***

# Chapter 8
## To Accept or Not?

*Surra, Kuwait – May, 2021*

Marzouk Fayed felt rather satisfied as he stretched out in bed with a beautiful dark-haired woman by his side. She was lying on her stomach and the light from the window caught the curve of her back exactly. *This is the life.*

"I have to get back to work," she said as she rose leisurely from the bed.

"If you must," he acceded. "I'll come by your desk later then," he declared and then sat up and placed his hands behind his head against the headboard, beaming as he watched her.

"Yes, Marzouk," she said hastily, searching through her clothing. "We should be careful."

"Why are you worried? I'm the boss." She gave him a tentative smile to acknowledge the statement. While he watched her dress, he congratulated himself. He had managed to bag her shortly after she began working for him four months earlier. He and his wife spent little intimate time together and his workplace rendezvous helped to contain his urges. Like many politicians, he owned apartment space above his offices that he used specifically for this purpose.

"Did anything happen this week? Are you worried about someone suspecting?" he asked with a puckered brow.

"No, not really. I did some paperwork to start your campaign for reelection. Khaled also had me research which foreign VIPs are expected to visit in the run up to the elections. Oh, and he had me provide some information on Kuwaiti dewaniyas to a friend of his who works at *Total*."

Fayed straightened up in surprise. "He had you give some information to a friend at *Total*?"

"Yes. Apparently this guy just moved here—I think he's supposed to be in Kuwait for a few months."

"Do you remember his name?"

She frowned as she zipped up the back of her ankle-length black skirt. "I'm not sure. I think it was Mustafa something or other."

"Do you remember what information he asked for?"

"I didn't really talk to him much. He came by, said hello, picked up the papers I had ready, and left." She buttoned the front of her blouse as she continued. "Khaled asked me to give him some information on VIP dewaniyas and Kuwaiti customs. I just used one of the papers the National Assembly gives to foreign guests. I figured it was only a personal favor."

Fayed nodded in understanding. *Khaled has been talking to him without me?*

She looked back at him with concern as she began putting on and adjusting her *hijab*, or headscarf. "Did I do something wrong? It only took a couple of minutes. I didn't think it was a big deal. Do you not want me to do any more personal favors like that?" she asked timidly.

"No, no, it's completely fine. I was just curious," Fayed responded, trying to placate her worries. *What else does she know?*

He waited impatiently while she finished getting dressed. His mind was too perturbed to enjoy the remainder of the process. When she left for her desk downstairs, he grumbled while he got dressed quickly. *I have to go in to the office on a weekend now.*

Fifteen minutes later, he walked into his office and buzzed Khaled Majed through the intercom system with an urgent signal.

\*\*\*\*

Moments later, Khaled rushed into Fayed's office. "I'm sorry, sir. I didn't realize you were coming in to the office today." He knew that Fayed often spent a large part of the weekend napping in the room upstairs to avoid his wife. In spite of Khaled's best efforts, a snicker escaped from him. *You've descended to the ground floor—how wonderful.* He cringed, expecting a backlash.

"Khaled, do you see me here in front of you? What is so funny? Why are you laughing?"

"N-nothing, sir. I am glad to see you, sir."

"Well, I am *not* glad to be down here. The weekends here in Kuwait are different from your hometown in Iran. *You* work six days a week the way you did there, but *I* don't."

"Yes, sir," he responded while looking straight into Fayed's eyes as he tried to contain his annoyance.

"My weekends are supposed to be from Thursday to Saturday. I shouldn't be wasting that time down here. I pay you to work every day except Friday. Is that clear?"

Khaled nodded in response.

"Have I made myself clear?"

"Yes, sir!" Khaled drew his shoulders back and pulled his neck up as if he were about to salute Fayed.

"Very well then. Now, I want an update on the Ahriman."

"Okay, sir. Th—" Khaled halted when Fayed threw up a hand to interrupt him.

"Before you start, I want to make something else quite clear. I am down here on a weekend because I heard from one of your secretaries that she met with him a few days ago. She said she gave him information on going to one of the VIP dewaniyas. Now, when were you planning on telling me about this?"

Khaled exhaled loudly. "I do apologize, sir. I thought you wanted me to run things and only bother you when absolutely necessary."

"Yes, but to an extent! You cannot go around arranging for key parts of the operation without informing or involving me."

"Yes, sir."

The two men stared at each other for a good thirty seconds before Fayed decided that the point had sunk in enough to continue. "Very well then. Proceed with your update."

Khaled gave his boss a slow nod before he began to speak. "All right, sir. The Ahriman has begun putting things in place. He has made initial contacts with the inner political circle through the dewaniya and will be using that to move closer to our target."

"That's it? That's your update?"

"Y-yes, sir." Khaled's posture stiffened. His immediate instinct was to stand at attention when challenged by a superior, even one whom he did not respect.

"It has been a few weeks since he arrived here. Hasn't he done anything else?"

"Positioning himself properly requires a great deal of planning, effort, and time. Since we did not provide him with the target before he arrived, I believe he is taking the necessary steps to prepare. He cannot move into political circles without establishing himself first."

Fayed scrutinized Khaled. "Perhaps you are more competent than I realized. I thought your uncle just wanted to make sure you were employed when he asked me to take you on, but it seems you are quite valuable, particularly on this project."

*Is that a compliment?* "Thank you, sir. I do appreciate your compliment." He wagged his head vigorously, as if to seek further approval.

Fayed looked at his aide bemused. "When will you provide him with the weapon components that he asked for?"

"In the next two to three weeks, I believe."

"Great. We are making progress then?"

"Yes, sir."

"Good. I'll head back to my chambers now. Please provide these updates on a weekly basis from now on." Fayed shook his finger dramatically.

"Yes, sir."

"Okay. Dismissed."

Khaled bowed his head slightly and then straightened, turned, and quickly exited the room. On the way to his office, he passed the secretary whom he had asked to provide information to the Ahriman. He stopped in front of his office door and glanced back at her. *How did he...? Oh.* He shook his head in amusement as the realization struck him. *Lucky oaf!*

Several hours later, he called to update his handler.

"Be careful," his handler said. "That was a close call. We can't let him figure out the real target."

"I know. He found out through one of my assistants. I think he's screwing her."

"See if you can take advantage of that, Khaled. You can use her to pass on some selective pieces of information."

"It will be done."

### Kuwait City, Kuwait – May, 2021

Omar walked slowly toward the Emir's family dewaniya while balancing a large tray of Irish coffees. After making them, he had kept enough whiskey and Baileys to make one for himself when he returned to the kitchen later. To an outsider, the cups appeared as if they only contained average coffee. It was another story as soon as you got close enough to smell them, though.

He reached the door and listened quietly. The group inside was discussing the financial reform package the Emir planned to push through before the next parliamentary elections. He waited a while, hoping for something interesting. After glancing at his watch several times, he yawned in boredom. *Nothing new.* The Emir had put forward the plan publically and then to Parliament before disbanding it. The monarch had made no secret about his push for a financial stimulus to help resuscitate the ailing economy.

Omar pushed the door open and served the mugs of Irish coffee to the men seated around the dewaniya.

"Thank you, Omar."

"You're welcome, sir. Is there anything else you'd like?"

"Not for the moment, thank you. We'll call you if we need anything."

Omar nodded and left. He waited near the door, trying to focus on the boring discussion once again. The conversation grabbed his attention when he heard them shift the discussion to who might receive the contract for the newly discovered oil field. There was some disagreement over whether to give it to some American company or another much smaller one.

He listened for a resolution to the conversation, and when there was none, headed back to the kitchen where he took out his phone. He quietly texted, *"No news to report on elections. Some disagreement on oil contract, no decisions made."*

The recipient replied, *"Continue to monitor and update."*

Omar received the message and proceeded to make an Irish coffee for himself.

## New York City, United States – May, 2021

Petra skimmed through the potential agent profile that Alex had sent her the previous evening. As she got to the end, she slammed the folder shut.

"Computer, dial Alex Mittal on a secure line with hologram projection." The phone clicked as it connected, and a projection of Alex materialized in front of her.

"Hi, Petra," he said.

"Hey, Alex."

"How's the cover story? Any thoughts on the file that I sent you?"

"I'm surprised by you. So far you've sent me two different agent profiles over the past few days, yet you know full well that these agents don't meet the criteria I sent over to you." Petra frowned as she waited for his response.

"Well…" Alex crossed his arms and Petra could tell that he was stalling.

"You of all people should know that time is of the essence here? And you know that we can't just have anyone on this mission. This agent will be going in alone and has to be really good."

"Yes, I know. Petra, the two I sent you are the best I can do right now. If we use anyone else, we'll have to pull them off a mission that is already in progress."

"You can do that if required. This is top priority." *It's not as if you haven't done it a million times before now.* Petra stood and slapped her hands palm-down onto her desk.

"Okay, look, I did find a couple of agent profiles from missions currently in progress," Alex said and reached for a file. "Let me pull them back out and see if one of them is a good match for your criteria. But I am only pulling someone off of a mission if the agent is *perfect* for this one."

Petra assented with antipathy, "All right."

"I'll send you what I have in the next hour."

She spent the next forty minutes working on the cover story that one of her researchers had produced. In general, the story was fine, but they needed to match it to an agent. She remembered one of the most important things Alex had told her before he sent her on her first mission. "As a field agent, you can never just accept the cover story that you've been given. Work on it and try to make the part about your past as close to reality as possible. The best cover stories are the ones that are easy to remember, meaning they are actually true, or at least as close to the truth as we can make them."

*Damned protocol.* Petra leaned back in her chair, thinking back to her days in the field.

Fifteen minutes later, the phone on her desk rang sharply. The loud *bling-bling* noise dragged her away her from her work as she pushed a button to accept the call and transmit her own hologram.

"Petra Shirazi," she said as the projected image in front of her desk went from hazy and unidentifiable to an image of Alex.

"Hi, Petra. Is now a good time to go over the options?"

"As good as any. What have you got for me?"

"Other than the two options I sent you already, there are only two that might work. Actually, one really fits the bill."

"Okay, so we use the new agent, the one who you think fits."

Alex responded reluctantly, and she scowled as she detected discomfort in his voice. "Look, Petra, it's not my call."

"What do you mean?"

"I sent the agent files to Chris. You'll have to talk to him about it."

"Talk to him about what?"

"You know how protocol works," Alex said. "The criteria you sent over were difficult to fill. I have two options, and the whole thing requires him to sign-off before we can move forward, whichever direction he decides to go."

Petra attempted to swallow her irritation. "What aren't you telling me? Chris doesn't normally get involved in prepping agents. And if there is a decision to make between two potentials, you and I should make it together since we are in charge of putting this mission into play."

"You really need to talk to Chris. He can explain."

"But why did you go over my head? You need to tell me what's going on."

Alex shook his head. "I haven't made any decisions, Petra. I just sent over the two possibilities. None of the profiles I reviewed fit your criteria properly. There are issues with both options and you know as well as I do that he does get involved if there are trade-offs to make between operations. I'm surprised he hasn't talked to you yet, but you do have to go through him."

"Alex, the whole point of an off-book mission is that we can move the pieces quickly enough to react to a pending threat. If it takes almost a week just to pick an agent, we are running way behind schedule. I do not want to compromise this mission to follow random protocols that we should be able to bypass."

"I know you don't, Petra, and believe me, neither do I," he griped. "I only involved Chris because it was necessary. We can't do anything else until he makes a decision. I'm sure he's working on it, so as long as everything else is ready to go, the mission can still be deployed within the next couple of days." After a brief pause, he continued, "Just talk to Chris."

"Okay, fine," she said, reluctantly acceding to his point. "Sorry I got so riled up. Can you give me anything else to go on? I'm worried. Is Chris getting involved because we need to pull someone off another high-priority mission?"

Alex shrugged. "It makes sense that you would be worried. An off-book mission with someone from General Majed's family in the vicinity? Anyone in your position would be concerned."

"I guess. It just seems like there's something else..." Petra could not shake the nagging doubt in the back of her mind.

"I'm sorry, but I really have to go. Let me know what you and Chris decide." Alex sighed and then his image dissipated as he ended their connection.

Petra sat back in her chair with a puzzled look on her face.

## *Istanbul, Turkey – May, 2021*

At the other end of the line, Alex leaned back and closed his tired eyes. *She is not going to like this.* He took a long sip from his large mug of green tea, wishing that it would magically change the situation. *Damn it, Chris, you should have decided by now.* Whatever Chris did decide, they would have to find a way to move forward. Petra was right; that process needed to begin as soon as possible.

Looking around, he surveyed his field office of five members. They were hunched over files while working on the twelve active missions the Agency currently had running out of their hub in Istanbul. *Need to focus on something else.*

He glanced down at the thin file in front of him containing the list of requirements Petra had sent over and the profiles of the two potential agents he had identified for the mission. *I'm not going to be the one to tell her.*

## *New York City, United States – May, 2021*

Chris had been avoiding the file on his tablet for the past two and a half hours because he was unsure of what to do since he had spoken to Alex, the director of mission deployment for the Agency's Middle Eastern field operations. They had gone over the two options—together and separately. Either they had to pull one of their currently deployed agents, Rajul McStevens, off a current high-priority mission, which would jeopardize both her life and the mission, or they would have to send in an operative who hadn't been in the field for years.

"There's no easy solution to this," Alex had said during their conversation.

"No, definitely not," Chris had responded. "I'm going to mull over it. Hopefully, a solution will present itself."

Alex had shrugged skeptically and said, "I wouldn't hold my breath."

Chris groaned at the file on his tablet once more. He reviewed the status of Rajul McStevens's current mission. It was ranked in the second Agency risk category, indicating a "moderate to high" level of risk. The mission they were trying to staff would rank higher at category one. Even so, Chris knew very well that no mission could have an agent pulled out suddenly without considerably increasing its risk level. That left the answer right in front of him; he would have to ask a retired field agent to deploy on this mission.

Taking a deep breath, he stood and picked up the tablet from his desk. *This won't get any easier.*

As he turned to leave his office, he saw Petra standing in the doorway.

****

Petra stepped inside Chris's office, her eyes fixed steadily on his face.

"Petra, hi," he said, falling back into his desk chair. He placed the tablet back on his desk and his right hand moved immediately to the button on his blazer, which he unbuttoned and then rebuttoned. Her eyes narrowed as she took in his obvious nervousness.

"You are a hard person to track down these days," she said, tight-lipped, as she walked into the office and took a seat on the other side of his desk. "I tried calling your office several times. Clearly, you had a ton of meetings, since you weren't available."

Chris let out a long exhale. "I was just on my way to talk to you."

"I hope you mean about the off-book mission that we authorized. Alex said I should talk to you because there is some big holdup. Let's figure this out now so that we can get moving. I don't want any more delays." She silenced the doubts in the back of her mind.

"Oh, right," Chris said. "So Alex told you that I had to make a decision?"

Petra watched his microexpressions as he paused and made a feeble attempt to school his features and look at her blankly.

"I have been trying to track you down all afternoon. We need this decision to move forward. You know this is important, so why are you stalling?"

He looked at her, still unsure of how to proceed. "Yes, well..."

"Jeez, Chris! What is going on? I've worked with you for over three years and never seen you like this." She waited for his answer, watching him in complete exasperation. Still hearing no response, she continued, "Okay, I'm no idiot. I know that Alex wouldn't have involved you unless you had to make a difficult call. So just tell me what the fuck is going on and then we can figure out how to deal with it. We can't afford to jeopardize this mission."

Chris let out a dramatic sigh. "Alex didn't tell you why he involved me?"

Petra's face scrunched into a frown. "No, you know he wouldn't do that. Alex does everything by the book. It's your turn to tell me what's going on. If you don't want to tell me because of this need-to-know bullshit, then I get it. Just tell me your decision so we can move forward." She paused and watched him fidget. "I need the agent's profile to put this mission together. If the candidate isn't ideal, I can work around that, but only if I have the time to do so."

She watched him hesitate yet again. "What is it, Chris?" she said, raising her hands in disbelief.

"Okay, fine, I'll tell you, if you'll let me," he said, interrupting her.

"Oh, okay." Petra's posture relaxed as she sat back in her chair. "Go ahead then."

"This is the file that Alex sent over with the profiles of two potential agents for this mission," he said while pushing the tablet across his desk toward her.

Petra swallowed slowly as her annoyance began to subside and hints of concern made their appearance. Without opening the file, she picked the tablet up in her hands. "If this whole thing was so secretive that Alex went over my head, and the situation so precarious that you are hesitant to tell me about it, why are you just handing this over to me?" She raised her eyebrows, looking for answers on his face.

He shook his head. "Just open it."

Hesitating, Petra looked down at the screen, her stomach tightening into knots. *This can't be good.*

Gingerly, she tapped the screen to open the file. On top was the agent profile for Rajul McStevens, currently deployed on a category-two mission in India. Sliding her finger across the screen to turn the page, she skimmed through the mission details. "So you're involved because our only option is someone who is currently deployed? And even then her qualifications are far from ideal?" she asked, looking up at him confused. "It's unfortunate that she is still learning Farsi, but why was that so hard to tell me?"

Chris shook his head again. "Keep going."

She bit her lip and turned through the first few pages that provided more detail on Rajul McStevens. When she got to the next profile, she stopped and straightened up in shock. The photo of the agent was someone who had been out of the field for years.

Petra stared at her own picture taken the day she had finished training. "Wow. I, uh, wow," she said, unsure of what to say.

When she finally looked up at him, she felt as if a haze of pain and memories clouded her vision. "You want me to go back?" She felt as if someone had stabbed her in the chest, and she could barely force the words out.

Chris nodded slowly.

"I don't understand how you could ask me to do that." Petra's heart rate was rising as her memories of the field rushed back to her. "You made me go through months of therapy for PTSD. Sometimes I'm not even sure that I'm better. And you want to send me *back*?"

"Petra, believe me, if the situation were different, I would never ask you to do this. But you were one of our best, and right now, we need you out there."

She turned away, trying to control the mix of emotions washing over her. "I can't go back," she said aloud. "I haven't been in real training for years. I don't even know if I could still handle it—being out there on a mission, so cut off from everything." She crossed her arms over her stomach and fought to keep her breathing steady. "This is crazy, Chris. This mission is extremely high risk. Why would you send in an agent who has been out of the field for almost three years?"

"We don't have a choice. If I pull Rajul from her mission, it puts both her and the mission in jeopardy. And you said it yourself—she isn't nearly as qualified for this posting as you are. Her Farsi isn't good enough for this operation."

Petra gaped at him. "So you and Alex really are saying that I'm the only agent we have who speaks Farsi and Arabic? That can't be possible."

"We have some people with varying proficiencies in each, even a couple with both languages, but you already saw their profiles. No one can speak both as a native." Chris watched her and took a deep breath. "Does that really surprise you? You had to have known that the qualifications you and your team put together for this mission would be hard to meet, and that they almost seemed written just for you."

She sighed and her fingers started to tremble. She clasped her hands together to try to steady them. "I did notice, but I guess I chose not to think about it. I should have known this was coming after I talked to Alex today."

Chris cleared his throat. "I doubt there's much I could say to make this situation easier. This is a tough thing for the Agency to ask of you."

She looked up at him, her eyes clearly displaying the wide mix of emotions she felt. "I don't know what to say or do. I can't imagine going back. The very idea paralyzes me."

"I want you to understand that this is entirely your decision. I do think it is in the Agency's best interest if you go back, but I also know how difficult that would be for you."

"Chris, you have to be straight with me. This isn't just my decision. If it were entirely up to me, Alex would have been able to ask me himself. He wouldn't need your approval. We both know that my career here hinges on whether or not I take this mission."

"Well, that isn't *entirely* true."

"Come on. This is a turning point for me. Will I put myself before the Agency? Above that of our sponsoring countries whom we are trying to protect? Or will I rise to the occasion and put everything else first. If I want to have a career here, then I have to serve as if I don't give a fuck about anything else."

Chris averted his eyes. It was enough of a signal that she knew he was acknowledging that she was right. After what seemed like an eternity of silence, he finally said, "Honestly, I don't know what I would do in your place. If you don't take this mission, your career here will stall, but you'd still have a future outside of the Agency. You're well qualified, so I'm sure there would be plenty of opportunities for you. But if you do, you will be serving millions of people around the world, not just the Agency."

She began to blink away tears. He pulled a tissue from the box on his desk and handed it to her before he continued speaking.

"We both know that terrorism is not just any individual attack. It inflicts people with fear and anger, who then react by lashing out at others, whether or not they helped create that fear. It's the brainwashing and the indoctrination that lead one person to believe that people of a different background or religion are more violent or destructive than others in our society. We try to treat terrorism as something we can actively fight with troops and security forces, random bag searches and infringing on people's rights by monitoring phone calls or e-mail. Really, the only thing we can do is try to bolster the barriers to keep that sort of fear out of our population."

Chris stood and walked around to the front of his desk, stopping to the left of Petra. He crossed his arms and leaned against the edge of the desk.

"Petra, no one knows Kuwait better than you do. How many times have you had to explain the political system there in the past few weeks? Hardly anyone knows about the situation, yet you have had to explain repeatedly how democracy can be so at odds with progress. Most people here would advocate for democracy without a second thought, but democracy and progress in Kuwait are almost mutually exclusive. Who else at the Agency would know how to navigate that system?" Chris took a breath and exhaled loudly.

She looked up at him and decided to lighten the palpable tension in the room. "Quite a speech you've got there, huh, boss?" She forced a smile, but could not stop her voice from quivering.

He managed to chuckle and smiled back at her. "Why don't you take the rest of the day off and think about it."

She nodded, put the tablet back on his desk, and walked out of his office. She stopped by her office long enough to get her bag and then headed straight for the elevators. On her way down to the lobby, she sent Grant a text message.

*"I need to tell you something. Please come by my place when you get off work. Bisous, Petra."*

Within thirty minutes, she was back at her apartment, indulging in the world of potential scenarios. *To accept or not?* The thought echoed in her mind.

She reached for her phone and searched her contacts for the number Carlos had given her when he left the Agency. Petra recalled what he told her on his last day. "I know I could only give you an emergency contact number when we were both out on missions, but now you can call me even if you just want to say hello. Don't be a stranger."

The thought of leaving the Agency seemed unfathomable. She had started working there right after finishing college, and in spite of everything she had been through, she felt a deep bond with the organization and the people working for it. If she declined this mission, though, her career there would be essentially over. While they would not force her out, a reassignment to some pure paper-pushing division would be the equivalent. She would have no choice but to find work elsewhere.

She hit the call button and waited for Carlos to pick up. After a couple of rings, she heard a voice answer, "Hello."

"Carlos?" she responded.

"Yes. Who is this?"

"Hi, it's Petra. Petra Shirazi. I'm sorry it's been so long since we last spoke."

There was a long pause on the other end of the line. "Petra? Wow, I'm surprised to hear from you. It really has been a while."

"A couple of years. Like I said, I'm sorry."

Petra waited through another awkward pause and then asked, "How are you, Carlos?"

"I'm doing great. I got married a couple of years ago. I sent you a wedding invitation, but we never heard anything from you. I thought something must have happened to you. We've been worried."

"Carlos, I'm so sorry. I was in a bad place the last time I talked to you. Things went pretty bad on my last mission."

"Your last mission? But we spoke almost three years ago."

Petra sighed. "Yeah, that's when I came back from my last mission."

"What happened? Did they do something to you? After what they did to me, I wouldn't put anything past those scumbags."

Petra struggled to come up with the right words. The situation that had caused Carlos to leave was very similar to the dilemma that she currently faced.

He broke the silence in a halting voice. "Sorry, I shouldn't have said that, it just slipped out. Anyway, what have you been doing since?"

"I head the Middle East research team now."

"Research?" His tone turned to concern. "Things must have been pretty bad, huh? I'm sorry to hear that."

"Thanks," Petra said. "It's no excuse. I should have called you ages ago."

"I wish I'd known. Maybe I could have helped you out."

"Thanks, Carlos. I'm sure you would have been very supportive."

"So, not to put a damper on this party, but to what do I owe the pleasure of this call today?"

"I'm in the middle of something, kind of an Agency dilemma." Petra paused, unsure of how much she could say.

"Not much you can say, huh?" She could tell he was smiling on the other end of the line. "Don't worry, I know the drill."

"Yeah." Petra forced a smile as well.

"Just tell me whatever you feel like you can."

"Okay," she said, nodding to herself. "Well, they are asking me to do something. It's important, but also could jeopardize my own personal health and future, something I'm not even sure that I can actually do."

"So then you shouldn't do it, right?" Carlos interrupted.

"Well, if I don't do it then—"

"Then your career there is over. You would have to leave the Agency."

"Yeah. That's basically all I can tell you."

"They want you to go back don't they?"

She gawked at the phone. *What can I say?*

Before she could respond, he eliminated the question. "Don't worry about answering that. I shouldn't have asked."

Petra let out a nervous laugh.

"So what's stopping you from making a decision either way?"

"It's hard to decide what's more important, you know? I know that it won't be good for me, but I don't think I can say no, knowing what I do."

"Does leaving the Agency scare you?"

"Yeah, of course. It's a big part of my life. It's the only place I've ever really worked." She paused. "Did it scare you at all? To leave? To walk away from a career you spent so long building?"

"Are you kidding? Of course it did."

"How do you feel about it now?"

"I left because of Diane and everything that happened. I haven't looked back for a second. We couldn't have a real life together if I still worked in the field. I just needed to walk away."

"Do you think you would have felt the same way if Diane worked for the Agency? Or if you were with the Agency, but not in field ops?"

"Petra, I can't answer this question for you. If you're wondering what your life might be like without the Agency, I can promise that you would be just fine. You are a smart, amazing young woman. This wasn't even the only job opportunity you had when you left college, so clearly it isn't the only option you would have now."

"How could I get a job without actually being able to talk to anyone about this one?"

"Oh, come on, kid. Who do you work for now? Chris McLaughry? Is he still the head of Research?"

"That he is, so yes and yes."

"Since I know how awful it is to work with you, I'm sure he wouldn't mind giving you a recommendation. Heck, I could even give you a recommendation. I was the agent who recruited you."

She let out a long exhale. "Yeah, I guess you're right."

"So? What are you going to do?"

"I don't know. I just need some more time to think."

"Petra, come on! That's exactly what you don't need to do. You can figure this out pretty quickly. You're not the kind of person who needs to dwell on things and mull them over. I'm pretty sure you already know what you're going to do."

Petra's heart sank as she realized that he was right.

"Don't worry, I'm not waiting for you to answer me. I know that you can't tell me anyway. But I do know you pretty well and you'll figure out the right decision."

She ran her fingers through her hair. "You're right. I guess you always were when it came to me."

"All right, kid, I have to run now. I want you to be in touch more regularly from now on, though. It's sad if a mentor never hears from one of his star students."

"Always such a charmer." She looked away from the phone and glanced at herself in the mirror. "Thanks so much for letting me talk through this. Even if I couldn't tell you much, I needed to talk to someone who I knew would understand."

"Happy to be of service." He stopped abruptly. "Look, judging from your tone, I have an idea of what you're going to do. So just be careful out there, okay? And you can always count on me. You know that, right?"

"Thanks, Carlos," she smiled. "I'll call you soon. I promise."

"I hope you do. Take care, kiddo."

She hung up and then caught her own reflection in the mirror above her dresser. With just that glance, she felt more confident in her decision. *I know what I have to do. I'll never be able to look at myself again if something happens and I could've stopped it.* She glanced at the clock. It was close to six o'clock, when Grant normally left the office. *How am I going to explain this?*

She was in the kitchen making a cup of tea when Grant came into the apartment. He walked over to the kitchen and gave her a kiss. "Hi, babe. What did you want to talk to me about?"

Petra looked into his eyes and said, "I think you should sit down for this." She leaned back against the counter of her open kitchen that faced the living room couch.

Grant noticed her expression and then his eyes danced around the room before returning to her. "I take it from your expression that it isn't good news." He stopped speaking and sat down on the couch. "If you're pregnant or something, it's okay. Whatever it is, we can handle it together."

She gave him a woeful smile. "If only, babe."

He frowned. "Hmm, okay, but you know you can tell me anything, right?"

She nodded and opened her mouth once and closed it immediately, searching for the right words. "I'm not even sure how to begin."

Grant fidgeted in front of her. He was obviously trying not to let his confusion and apprehension show on his face, but she noticed it anyway because she recognized his microexpressions.

"Are you, are you breaking up with me?" he stuttered.

*Maybe you'll break up with me after I leave.* She ignored his question and pushed forward. "I never told you what happened before I joined the Research Division."

"No, you didn't. You never really wanted to talk about it."

"There's not much I can say about what I was doing before I joined Research, but you should know that I was a field agent."

Grant smiled, clearly trying to feign surprise. "Oh, yeah."

Petra tilted her head to the side, bemused. "You already knew?"

"There were a bunch of rumors when you joined Research." He paused for a second and then continued. "It was hard to miss, to say the least. The rumors combined with how competent and stunning you are."

"Do you ever turn off the charm?" she said, still laughing.

"Absolutely not." After a moment of silence, he said, "Okay, I'm sorry. I was just trying to lighten the mood. I do that when I'm nervous."

"I know."

"I'm sorry. Keep going. Just tell me whatever it is."

"Well, like I said, I was a field agent for a couple of years." She took a deep breath, struggling with the memories of the different missions. "Until one particular mission."

Grant got up off the couch, walked over to Petra, and put his arm around her. He pulled her toward the couch and the two of them sat down together.

"On that mission, things, well, things got really bad. I was working with an asset and he got compromised."

"And then they came after you?"

"Yes. I was lucky. He took the fall completely. Once I got out, we were trying to put together an extraction plan, but before we could get him out, they executed him for treason." She hadn't talked about what happened since she stopped attending therapy for her post-traumatic stress disorder a year earlier. It made her feel as if she were back in one of her sessions.

He reached out and grabbed her hand. "Do you feel like it was your fault?"

Petra glanced down at her feet for a moment before giving him the tiniest nod. "Sometimes. Rationally, I know it wasn't. We went over the details a thousand times. There's no way I could have seen it coming." *Because of everything else.* "But sometimes I still don't believe it."

He took a deep breath. "I can't imagine how hard that was." He rubbed her shoulder and back with his right hand.

"It was…difficult, to say the least."

They sat in silence and she leaned her head on his shoulder, enjoying the comfort he brought.

Finally, Grant broke the silence. "Maybe I'm wrong, but there was something about your tone that made it seem as if there's a lot more to this conversation. I don't want to push you to tell me anything you aren't ready to say, but I'm scared of what you might say next." He took a deep breath. "Is there some particular reason you are telling me about this now?" The apprehension in his voice was tangible.

She sighed against his chest and then pulled away to look at his face. "A few days ago we discovered a huge potential terrorist threat. I can't tell you much about it, but…" She blinked rapidly, wishing that would make things easier in that moment. "But we can't find an active agent who is qualified enough to go in and gather the kind of information that we need."

Grant's breathing turned shallow. She could tell that he knew what was coming, even if he could not bring himself to say so.

"So they asked to me to go back."

"They want to deploy you? Shit." He looked up at the ceiling and exhaled. "What are you going to do?"

Petra stood up, walked over to the large windows of the living room, and looked out across the cityscape. "I thought about it a lot today. I even spoke to Carlos, one of the agents who recruited me. He's not with the Agency anymore. It just seemed so crazy that they would try to send me back when I told them that I could never even contemplate the idea again."

She turned back to face him. "But given how important this mission is, I don't feel as if I can place my own personal well-being over everything else—"

"No! They can't make you do this. Haven't you already done enough?" Grant lashed out. She met his eyes as they passed over her face and then the rest of her.

"There's no way I could stop you. I can't even ask you to stay," he whispered. "You have such a big heart. It's one reason I fell in love with you in the first place. And now it's the reason you're going back." He shut his eyes for a moment and smiled grimly. "You know this is going to drive me crazy, right? I already think about you all the time, and I can see you every day, so I know you're fine. Now you're going to be halfway around the world and in danger…" His voice trailed off and she walked over to the couch to cup his face with her left hand.

They looked at each other for several moments. He started to speak and stopped a few times before he could muster the words, "How long will you be gone?" She could tell that he was trying not to think about the worst-case scenario.

She returned to the window and leaned against it, still facing him. "I don't know, babe. There's not a lot of clarity about this mission."

She watched him struggle with his thoughts until the words seemed to burst from him. "How, er, how risky is this mission going to be?"

She met his gaze and shook her head. "Grant, I don't want you to go there. We don't know anything. It could be risky, but it might not be." Her voice cracked slightly as she forced out the last few words and she turned away from him to gaze at the city beyond her apartment.

He got up off the couch and walked toward her again. When he reached the window, he stood behind her and wrapped his arms around her waist to hold her tightly. They stood there in silence, studying the view.

She turned around and looked up at him, trying to ask the question that she knew repeated in both of their minds. Finally, she asked, "What does this mean for us, Grant? I don't, I can't expect you to wait. I don't know how long I'll be gone. I don't even know if I'll make it back."

As he looked into her eyes, Grant shook his head. "Stop," he said forcefully. He put his hands on both sides of her face and kissed her softly. "Petra, I love you and I will wait for you. Do you know how long I waited before I finally had the courage to ask you out?"

Her eyes twinkled. "I know it was a while."

"You don't know the half of it," he smirked. "Besides, if anything dangerous is happening, I am going to swoop in and rescue you. No buts about it."

"Oh, yeah? You'll be the Agency's newest Batman, called for whenever we need help?"

"Batman? Come on, babe. Why do you think I do all that freehand rock climbing that you hate so much? It's not dangerous for me because I'm actually Spiderman, ready to rescue you at a moment's notice."

She threw her hands out to the side. "I really wish you wouldn't do all that ridiculous climbing. Is it really that hard to put on a harness?"

"I know, I know. I will next time. I promise." They smiled at each other and he pulled her into a strong hug. "I mean it, though. If anything goes wrong, I am going to show up and get you out of there," he said, putting a brave face on his obvious worries. "Wherever *there* is."

She gave him a soft kiss and considered what Grant had said earlier. She looked back up at him and spoke up slowly, "Grant, I...I'm not sure if—"

"If you're ready to say those words back to me? I understand. I love you and I know I'm ready to say that. We haven't been together very long, though, and I don't want you to say them before you're ready."

She looked up at him, her eyes filled with a soft inner glow. He kissed her on the forehead and said, "We'll have plenty of time when you come back for that."

She forced herself to smile. "Can I take you with me? Will you fit in my suitcase?" she teased.

"I wish," he said. "When do you have to leave?"

"As soon as possible once we have everything set up. Maybe a few days or a week?"

"Well, let's not waste any time."

She stood on her tiptoes and kissed him deeply. He picked her up and carried her into the bedroom. The moment overtook them and the night passed as they got lost in passion and embrace.

****

# Book IV
# Five Years Earlier
# 2016 – 2017

# Chapter 9
## Lila Tabbas
## Five Years Earlier

*Paris, France – April, 2016*

Kasem Ismaili walked out of his hotel in Paris and headed toward the Jardin du Luxembourg, one of the city's many beautiful gardens. He took in the morning air, breathing deeply. The weather was perfect—the sun shined brightly from a beautiful periwinkle blue sky. The trees that were scattered around the sidewalks sparkled in the morning light. It was chilly, but fresh, or *frais* as the French called it. He had arrived in Paris less than twelve hours earlier and had spent much of that time enjoying a typical French night of decadence at a wine bar, chatting with a couple of beautiful women.

This morning, though, he fully intended to prep for his meeting with Selim Kharafi and Victor Black the next day. He stopped on the way to enjoy a few macarons from Jean-Paul Hevin, an artisanal *patisserie* on the south side of the gardens. Then he settled down at a small café past the garden gates with the overstuffed bag he had lugged with him containing his laptop and a few manila file folders.

For the next hour, he sipped slowly on a small espresso and flipped through the documents in the files. A couple of hours later, the smell of fresh-baked bread lured him into one of the sandwich places just outside of the garden. Without realizing it, he had walked into a specialty Italian bakery. A mass of people were standing in front of the deli display and calling out to the chef in a combination of Italian and French. To Kasem, it all sounded like complete gibberish.

"*Vous voulez commander?*" the guy behind the counter shouted at him.

*What the hell did he say?* He stood there looking befuddled as the guy behind the counter kept shouting the same thing.

"Excuse me, do you need some help?" a woman said in heavily accented English as he felt a tap on his shoulder.

Kasem looked back to see a pretty girl standing in line behind him. "You speak English?" he asked, waiting for her nod before he continued. "Yes, I do need some help. Normally, I can understand basic French, but I'm completely lost at the moment."

She smiled and her whole face lit up. "Do you eat everything?"

"Yeah, pretty much."

"Not a vegetarian or allergic to anything?"

"Nope and nope," Kasem said with a grin.

She stepped in front of him and shouted out an order. A few minutes later, he was handed a bag with two overstuffed sandwiches on warm Italian focaccia wrapped in wax paper. Kasem paid for them and looked at the girl intrigued.

"Thank you," she said. "You didn't need to buy me lunch."

"It's the least I could do." He gave her a mischievous wink and pointed at her with the hand that held the bag of sandwiches. "You saved me there. Besides, I have an ulterior motive. Will you join me for lunch?"

"I guess I can't refuse since you still have my sandwich," she said with a smile. They walked to a park bench and sat down. For the next few minutes, they exchanged meaningless stories about Italian sandwich shops and food.

"Oh, I'm sorry. We've been talking for the past few minutes and I didn't even introduce myself. My name is Kasem." He held out his hand.

"I'm Lila," she said, shaking his hand.

"What do you do?"

"I work for the French Ministry of Foreign Affairs here in Paris. What about you, Kasem?"

"That sounds interesting. I work with the Tehran Stock Exchange in Tehran."

She raised her eyebrows. "Did you grow up in Tehran?"

"No, my family is from there, but I grew up in the US. What about you, Lila?"

"My mother's family is Moroccan and my father's is Iranian, but I grew up here in Paris."

"Where did you learn English?"

"Isn't it obvious from my accent?" she asked, again with a bright smile. "Of course I learned it here in France. I went to an international school and spent a couple of summers in London when I was a teenager, but I could never get rid of my accent."

"Actually, I think your accent is quite nice," Kasem said, looking at her keenly.

Their conversation continued for the next hour until Lila suddenly glanced at her watch. "I'm sorry, I have to go. I've taken a full lunch break!"

"That's too bad. Maybe I could see you again during my trip?"

"I'm sorry, but I don't think that will be possible."

"Ouch! You know how to hit a guy hard."

"Oh I'm sorry. Your life is so hard, isn't it?" She paused to consider for a moment. "Give me your card. I'll call you if I do end up with any free time."

"I guess I'll take what I can get," Kasem said, handing over his card. "Lila, you're killing me."

She took his card and stuffed it into her purse.

"Will you at least give me your number? Or your card?"

"I'm sorry, but I cannot," she said and then her eyes twinkled as she held back a grin. "If I have time over the next few days, I'll call you. You return to Tehran at the end of the week?"

"Yes, on Sunday, the seventeenth."

"Okay. Thank you for lunch. Goodbye, Kasem."

"Thank you for saving me earlier. Bye, Lila."

*Will I ever see her again?* Kasem watched her as she walked away.

****

After the meeting with Selim Kharafi and Victor Black, Kasem decided to make the most of his last few days in Paris. He was heading from the Georges Cinq Hotel toward the La Durée bakery on the Champs Elysees to sample the *pain au chocolat pistache*—a pastry with chocolates and pistachios recommended by a friend—when his cell phone rang.

"Hello, Kasem Ismaili speaking."

"Hi, Kasem," he heard a woman with a French accent say from the other end of the line. "This is Lila from the Italian place yesterday. You gave me your card at lunch, remember?"

"Hi, Lila. Of course I remember and I'm so glad you called. I wasn't sure if I'd hear from you."

"I wasn't sure that I would call." She sounded amused, as if she were holding back a laugh.

Kasem grinned. "I guess it's my lucky day. So when can I see you?"

"In a bit of a rush aren't you?"

"I try not to let good things get away."

"That's very sweet of you. How about this evening?"

"Sure that sounds great. Where should I meet you?"

"Have you seen much of Paris, Kasem?"

"Not really. Just the area around the Jardin du Luxembourg and the Champs Elysees."

"Meet me at the Place Contrescarpe at seven this evening."

"Yeah, okay, sure, b—" Before he could finish his question, he heard the line go dead. *Where is the Place Contre—what?*

He spent the next couple of hours wandering around the area near Trocadero and the Eiffel Tower and then returned to his hotel to get ready to meet Lila. He studied a map for ten minutes before finding the Place Contrescarpe. When he finally found it, he realized it was quite close to his hotel, so he walked there. After he saw Lila waiting for him, the rest of the evening passed in a blur.

Toward the end of the night, he found himself looking at her intently once again. *I feel as if I could tell her anything.*

They enjoyed each other's company until around midnight when she excused herself. "It is getting late and I need to catch the metro home."

"When can I see you again, Lila?"

She looked at him, clearly considering her response. "I don't know. You leave so soon."

"Can I see you tomorrow? During the day?"

"I have to work tomorrow!"

"It's Friday. Take the day off." *If only...*

She gave him a half smile. "I cannot take the day off, but I will be attending a conference outside the office that ends at three. I can meet you then."

"Tomorrow at three then." He stood up and pulled her into a deep, long kiss.

After a few moments, she pulled away and he released his hold on her. "I will see you tomorrow," she whispered.

The next two days in Paris flew by for Kasem. He and Lila spent almost the entire time together, walking around the Seine, exploring museums, drinking wine, and eating macarons. Try as he might, though, Kasem could not get her to come back to his hotel.

On Saturday evening, he was forced to say goodbye. "I got you something last night after you left." He handed her a small box.

"Thank you." She opened the box to find a circular locket made of shimmery white gold. "It's beautiful. Help me put it on."

"Of course," he said as he took the ends of the necklace from her and fixed the clasp.

"Thank you again. I really like it."

"I wish I could see you again," he said, gazing into her eyes. "You don't have any trips planned to Iran, do you?"

Her mouth curled upward as she spoke. "No, not really, but maybe some time."

A tentative smile spread across Kasem's face. "Really?"

"Don't look so shocked. I told you my father is Iranian."

His smile spread across his face. "I really do hope so. Please call me if you ever think about coming to Tehran."

She nodded, stood on her tiptoes, and kissed him. "Goodbye, Kasem."

"Goodbye, Lila."

He watched her walk away again, realizing it could be the last time he would see her. *I really know how to pick them.*

Kasem thought back to his ex-girlfriend, his only serious relationship. The two of them were together for most of his college years. The entire experience had left a scar that was still sore and painful. He could remember some of their happiest moments— doing things together in college and in groups. He also clearly recalled the evening when she told him that she had been sleeping with another guy for more than two months.

His mind wandered back to Lila and he smiled at the contrast. *I hope I can see her again.*

That thought continued to occupy his mind on his flight back to Tehran the next morning. He was considering taking a nap when the in-flight magazine caught his eye. He flipped through the magazine until he landed on the article entitled, "Kish Island: One of the Middle East's Hidden Spots of Ecstasy."

*Kish Island is getting media attention?*

The article focused on Kish Island being the place in Iran where locals and foreigners could escape the local realities. People could dance, drink, and party there. One particular paragraph stood out to him.

*Kish Island is one of the few places in the Middle East where people can enjoy the best of the East and West. Foreigners and residents have access to numerous bars and clubs to enjoy a hopping nightlife after spending the day at the island's beautiful beaches. The sun shines incessantly and the buildings are decorated in traditional Persian facades. Hotels, bars, and restaurants even serve beer and giant piña coladas on the beach.*

He read on, amused. *Can't wait to go there!*

The article continued, "Not many people outside of the Middle East have heard of Kish Island, but it is one of the few tourist resorts in the region, and probably the world, that allows visitors to enjoy both the culture of the area and all of the typical resort pleasures: beach, beer, and nightlife."

Kasem leaned back and pictured himself dancing with Lila at a beachfront bar on Kish Island. He smiled and continued to daydream about it as the flight passed over the European continent. *Jamal and I need to make a trip.*

## *Tehran, Iran – May, 2016*

"The design phases of the Basra project will be laid out as follows…"

Kasem tried to listen to the principal architects outline their updated design plans for the Basra project. He doodled in the margins of the report in front of him to appear as if he were taking notes. *Damn thing could be made of feathers for all I'd know.*

He had been back from Paris for several weeks, but it felt as if an eternity had passed. His thoughts bounced between the Jardin du Luxembourg, the time he had spent with Lila, and the in-flight magazine he had read on the flight back to Iran.

He shifted in his seat and sat up to try to force himself to pay attention.

"This development planning will allow for both infrastructure development for tourism and local economic development along the border…"

When the team of architects sat down, Kasem's boss chimed in. "Could we have an update on the finances for both projects before we move on to the design of the Flower of Eden?"

Kasem nodded, trying to push past his post-lunch coma. "Based on our estimates, the required investment for this development, the Basra project, is approximately eight billion US dollars. The initial investment is closer to nine billion rials, which is about six hundred million US dollars. We have thus far secured slightly more than two hundred million dollars through a combination of funding from Kharafi and other regional investors."

"And the Flower of Eden project?"

"Again, it has a similar status. The total project cost is estimated at seven billion US dollars, with an initial investment of six billion rials, or about four hundred million US dollars. We have raised slightly less than two hundred million dollars."

"Where do we see the remainder coming from?" his boss asked.

"Most of it is likely to come from international finance and development institutions. I've just set up a meeting with the International Finance Corporation in London for three weeks from now. We still need to determine the team to attend and try to set up some other meetings for the same week."

"Great. Okay, now let's hear about the design plans for the Flower of Eden."

The design team stood up once again. "Essentially, the Flower of Eden project is a hotel and tourism development for Kish Island. Because of Kish Island's status as a tourist destination for locals, this project is aiming to bring it to the attention of international tourists."

The team droned on about design while Kasem waited for the end of the day and thought about the upcoming meeting in London. *Maybe I can see Lila?*

## New York City, United States – June, 2016

"And, finally, the last member of our entering class, someone who I am proud to say that I recruited personally—Agent Lockjaw, Ms. Petra Shirazi!"

Petra chuckled as she stepped onto the small stage the Agency had set up on the training grounds to commemorate the new "graduating" class of recruits. She looked down the line at the other ten recruits, most of whom she did not recognize from the initial training session just a few months earlier. *Where did the rest of them go?*

Kevin Smith, a member of the graduating class, nudged her out of the daze. "Wake up, Petra!"

She looked at him with a goofy expression. "Who cares? There are no more tests left!"

Since returning from her first operation several weeks earlier, Petra had thrown herself back into the final stage of the training program. She was paying the price for it now as exhaustion seeped into every pore of her body. The debriefing process for her last mission had completely wiped out all of her remaining energy reserves.

Petra could recall every detail of the exhausting debriefing. "Since this is your first operation debriefing, I'll help you out by giving you a bit of theory behind it. What I'm going to do is ask you difficult and challenging questions about the mission you were on and why things ended up as they did," Carmen de Nicola, the Italian agent who conducted her questioning, had said.

Later that evening, she went up to Kevin, told him, "I never knew that I could have so many different emotional states over a two-week period," and then collapsed into his arms. Thankfully, he had enough presence of mind to put her in bed where she remained until the next day.

Petra thought back on the experience now with a shudder. She was most concerned with the intensity of the debriefing, even for a simple information gathering operation. Because of that intensity, she was not sure how she would get through the same process for a more complex or high-priority mission.

Chris was speaking from the small podium in front of them. "Now, without further ado, I am honored to introduce one of our esteemed founders, Sir Robert Irvine."

An elderly man who appeared to be in peak physical condition for his age took the podium. "Good afternoon. It is my great pleasure to speak to you today. I have spent much of my life in this line of work, and I am excited to see the current generation moving forward in this area. Most of you probably know about the work that we do, but I'd like to provide a little history about this organization and how it came to be." He paused to survey the graduates before continuing.

"A number of years ago, a few individuals, many of whom were powerful at different points in time, decided to take action due to increasing issues with intelligence agencies around the world. Some of you may have heard stories or perhaps legends of a league of deadly and traitorous British spies known as the Cambridge Five, as well as the Aldrich Ames fiasco on this side of the Atlantic. These were, and are, far from the only cases when intelligence agencies of different NATO and allied governments have been severely compromised. Under a secret pact—and with a large degree of difficulty, may I add—we created a special organization to cater to intelligence needs around the world without being bogged down in needless and annoying political maneuvering. The Agency, as we decided to simply call it, is a swift, action-oriented organization, rather than one of the slow-winded intelligence organizations from which it was born. And that is the beauty of it—we are able to fly completely under the radar and attend to issues where government intelligence agencies' hands are tied, issues they are unable to attend to because of political, competency, or security issues." Sir Robert cleared his throat and then reached for a glass on the table next to the podium for a sip of water.

"The cases we deal with are still of monumental importance and are often sourced from these government agencies. Still, we house our own field and research teams, both of which operate in close proximity and are crucial to each other's success. I will not spend too much time discussing the detailed workings of our organization at this moment, but I wanted to give all of you here an understanding of the significance of this organization. We are not the CIA or MI6, but we do play a significant role in what happens around the world today. As a founder of this organization, I must express my gratitude that you are all joining our efforts and I bid each of you a wholehearted welcome. Completing our training program is a supreme achievement that should not be taken lightly. So, welcome to the Agency and congratulations!"

Sir Robert smiled as the recruits applauded him and he stepped away from the podium. Then Chris and another recruiter began handing out champagne glasses to the small group of recruits. Just after everyone had received a flute of champagne, Petra noticed someone else walking across the park. "Carlos!" she cried out excitedly.

He waved at her from across the field. "Nice work getting Carlos here, Lockjaw," someone said to Petra's left. "Looks like we have all of our recruiting officers present after all."

Petra glanced at Sergei, the only Russian member of their class, and smiled. "Thank you, Agent Pegleg. I knew that I could make it happen."

Carlos walked up to the stage and Petra stepped down from the platform to give him a hug. "Good to see you, Petra. And I'm glad you've finally stopped calling me Anton," he ribbed.

She rolled her eyes before saying, "I'm glad that you made it. Thank you for coming. It means a lot to me."

"I wouldn't miss it. You are my first recruit." He winked at her cheekily and said, "Now get back up there. I want my glass of champagne and you are holding up the toast."

"Here you go, buddy," Chris said as he handed Carlos a champagne flute.

Chris looked around at the small group standing around him and raised his glass. "It is my pleasure to welcome our new batch of recruits into the Agency. You are the first class of recruits I supervised and I hope to work with many of you in the future. I don't say that lightly. As one of the junior heads of staffing, I would not hesitate to shuffle you onto someone else if I didn't believe it. Congratulations on completing your training. Now let's raise our glasses to welcome the newest members of the Agency."

The group of eleven recruits touched their glasses together and hugs went all around. After a couple of sips from her glass, Petra stepped away from the laughing bunch to get a bottle of water.

"Hey, Lockjaw, would you mind grabbing one for me too?" Kevin called out as she reached the table.

Petra gave him a searing look. *Damned call signs.* "Sure, *Kevin.* I can get you some water," she yelled while shaking her head.

"Those call signs are going to stick around no matter what you do."

Petra looked up and winked at Carlos. "You should know, Agent Puppy."

His eyes widened in obvious indignation. "I'm not even going to ask who told you about that."

"I wouldn't tell you. What on earth did you do to get that name in the first place? And how did you get rid of it?"

Carlos shook his head, laughing. "Everyone loses their training nickname after their first mission. No one would actually put Agent Lockjaw or Pegleg or whatever on a mission file."

"But how did you get that name?"

"That's for me to know."

"Oh, come on! It's my graduation day."

He tilted his head and smirked. "I'll tell you the story of how I got my nickname if you tell me about yours."

Petra looked at him amused. "Okay, you've got a deal."

"Fine," he said, his face turning red.

She handed him a bottle of water from the table. "Here you go."

"Oh, thanks."

"You're welcome," Petra said smiling. "I got my nickname because they pulled one of the captor simulations on us during a training drill. We didn't know it was a drill at that time."

Carlos felt his jaw begin to set in annoyance. "You totally played me. I thought I would at least get a good story out of you?"

"As part of the simulation, they tested each of us separately to see how long it would take to get us to break under isolation and light torture. I lasted the longest, managed to make up some stuff to throw them off, but didn't tell them anything. So I got the nickname Lockjaw."

Petra leaned over and gave Carlos a kiss on the cheek. "I'll be back to hear about Agent Puppy." She turned and walked toward the stage, grabbing another couple of water bottles on the way.

"I'm not sure if I'm more amused or annoyed," he called after her.

"Looks like we found quite the recruit, Carlos," Chris said from behind him.

"That we did."

"Who's going to tell her about her next mission?"

Carlos gestured widely with his arms. "Oh, you can't push that off on me. You know that's all on you now."

"Fine. I'll tell her. You just need to make sure that she is ready for this."

"She's the best person for it. It fits perfectly with her background."

"On paper, absolutely, but what about emotionally? Do you think she can handle it?" Chris probed.

"It'll be tough, but she's still the best person for it. And, yeah, I can make sure she's ready."

"Just remember, Carlos. We aren't supposed to get too close to any of them. Especially right before we send them out."

****

# Chapter 10
## Just a Source

*New York City, United States – June, 2016*

Petra sat back in surprise and gaped at Alex. "I just finished training, and you want to send me on another secondment?"

"Yes, that's what I just explained."

"You know all about the actual mission, but you can't tell me anything about it yet because it's up to the Brits? They'll just explain it to me whenever they think it, oh, might be kind of important to tell me where I am going?"

"I'm sorry, Petra. They asked for one of our top recruits. You're available, so we're sending you over."

She sighed. "It's just frustrating not knowing anything about a mission when it's about to start. It was the same last time with the French. And last week, Chris told me about another operation, the long-term assignment that all of you think should be my priority. How am I supposed to focus on that if you are seconding me off to the Brits? How many operations do you want me to cover at once?"

"Try to take it as a compliment. Being seconded to other agencies is a good sign for your career. Besides, there's nothing immediate that you need to do for that long-term operation. You'll get to it when the time is right."

Petra rolled her eyes. "Okay, whatever. Just give me the mission file, which, I know, won't say anything about the actual mission." *Will I ever see a real Agency mission?*

Alex handed over a USB key that she tucked into her purse. "Same drill as usual. Look through it, memorize it, and then it will erase itself."

Petra nodded rather than giving him a verbal response because she was afraid she might sound too sarcastic.

"There's also something else—an asset we want you to cultivate before you start with the Brits. It's 'need to know' classified, so make sure you don't talk about it once you get to the UK."

"Are those details on here too?"

"Yes."

"Okay."

"Look, Petra," Alex said, hesitating before continuing. "The operation is pretty important for the Brits based on the information they gave me. You'll do a couple weeks of training with them and then they'll let you know what's next. I'm sorry I can't tell you more."

"Fine, fair enough. I should probably get used to this 'need to know' business."

## *London, United Kingdom – June, 2016*

Kasem walked out of his meeting with the International Finance Corporation with mixed feelings.

"That could have gone better," his boss Kamran said quietly, echoing his own thoughts.

"They do want to keep the dialogue open, so hopefully that's a positive sign."

"We'll see what happens. Each of these donors is a giant bureaucratic machine."

"Yes, indeed," Kasem concurred. "Are you off to the airport now?"

"Yes, catching the first flight this evening. How many days are you staying?"

"I'll be back in the office next week."

"Okay, see you then. Have a nice weekend, Kasem."

Kamran hailed a cab and headed to the airport. Without waiting any longer, Kasem took the bus from the IFC's Westminster location to King's Cross station where he would meet Lila when her Eurostar train arrived. *She'll be here in less than an hour! I can't believe she agreed.*

Once he reached the station, he stood in front of the arrivals zone to wait. Thirty minutes later, he wrapped his arms around her and kissed her deeply.

"Kasem, we are in public!" she exclaimed in her halting French accent, shying away.

"You love it," he teased. He kissed her again and then grabbed her bag. "Let's go get you set up in the room."

"How far away is the hotel?"

"It's right next door."

Her eyes widened as he led her through the terminal to the lobby of the St. Pancras Renaissance Hotel. She gawked at the Victorian red brick façade accented with arch work in beige and blue. "It's beautiful," she said, taking it all in. "Is this where we are staying?"

"Just follow me." They took the elevator to the fourth floor and he led her to a south-facing room that looked out over the London cityscape.

"I'm happy to see that you're wearing the locket," he whispered into her ear.

She took in the view. "Kasem, you shouldn't have done all of this."

He stood behind her and wrapped his arms around her in silence. They kissed softly and he slid his hand down her back. "Stop," she said, pulling away and looking at him uncomfortably.

"I, I'm sorry! I didn't mean to make you uncomfortable."

"This is wonderful—staying here and seeing you. You didn't have to do all this, but that doesn't mean I'm ready to rush into anything."

"I know. I'm sorry. I didn't mean to make you uncomfortable. Lila, I promise you can take as much time as you need."

She looked up at him. "I don't know whether to believe you or not. I wasn't sure if I should come here because I didn't want to send you any mixed signals."

He put his hands on her shoulders and gazed into her eyes. "I'm so glad you're here. I just want to enjoy your company. Don't feel pressured into anything that you don't want to do. You don't even have to hold my hand if you don't want to."

He hugged her and when he let go, she smiled and grabbed his hand. "Well, I actually do want to do that."

He pulled her close to him. The next three days passed by quickly until they once again had to say goodbye.

### Secret MI6 Facility, southeastern coast of England, United Kingdom – June, 2016

"Great job, Petra. You dropped your time by ten seconds on that run."

Petra saluted her trainer. "It's all because of you, Sean!"

"Oh, don't flatter me! Now, go get cleaned up and I'll see you for the tactical planning session."

"Will do." She walked off the cross-country track toward her cabin. *When can I get back to London?*

Two hours later, she sat in a tactical "planning" session that entailed, once again, more training. Petra could barely resist the temptation to take a nap. *Heard all of this before.*

The instructors droned on until suddenly something grabbed her attention. "Tonight, each of you will receive a psychological evaluation and then your first operation details."

At the end of the session, she headed over to her evaluation room in the main house. She walked in, set down her messenger bag, and took a seat at the table, waiting for her instructor to enter.

"Hello, Petra," said a man who she had not yet met. He dropped his own shoulder bag on the floor by his feet, set down a file and a legal pad on the desk, and sat in the chair across from Petra. "My name is Mike Abbot."

"Hi," she said as she shook his hand. "I thought Sean would be doing my evaluation."

"No. We think it's best for people who haven't spent time in your circles to do the final psychological evaluation."

She gave him a quick nod and he continued.

"Petra, how have you enjoyed your stay in England?"

"Well, it's beautiful and the people I've been working with are great."

"But...?"

"To be honest, I'm tired of training drills. I already went through training in New York. Why do I need to sit through the same stuff again here?"

Mike pursed his lips and nodded. "Understandable. Anything else?"

Petra shrugged. "I'd really like to find out what I'm doing here. I'm going through training for the second time and no one has told me anything about the operation that I'm going to be involved in here."

"Fair enough. You will hear about that tonight, provided that you get a favorable evaluation."

*More psychological evaluations?* Petra kept her thoughts to herself and waited for him to continue.

"Now, could you tell me about the trip that you made before you came out to the countryside?" he said.

"I was told that I could fly over a few days ahead of time, so I did. I spent a couple of days in London and then took the train out here where a car picked me up at the station and brought me to this location."

Mike made a few notes on the pad before asking his next question. "Tell me about your trip to London. What did you do?"

"I wandered around, saw some of the sights. Nothing crazy."

"And I see in your file that you were already sent on one mission? Another secondment?"

"Yes."

"What was your role?"

"I'm sorry, that's classified. I can't tell you about a previous operation." Petra kept her posture straight and steady so as not to give anything away.

Mike nodded again and wrote something on his notepad.

*I thought this was only a formality? Is he just being a hard-ass?* She waited impatiently for him to finish.

He flipped through her file quickly to see her latest performance evaluation. "Your test results have been very good. Do you think there's any reason I should hold you back?"

Petra looked at him, taken aback. "No, I don't believe so."

"Very well. I don't see any reason to either." He reached into the bag next to the desk and removed a slim file. "Your next mission will take place in Ireland. You'll be reactivating an asset of ours who is now living just outside of Galway in a town called Kinvara."

Petra took the file and opened it. "Reactivating this asset? Wouldn't someone who actually worked with him be better for this?"

"Ideally, yes, but all of his previous handlers are either retired or recognizable in Ireland."

She tilted her head to the side. "So you want someone who won't be recognized to go in?"

Mike grinned. "That is correct."

"But it says here that all I'm required to do is give this guy some money."

"We don't expect that anything else will be required."

She threw her hands up in front of her. "So you flew me across the Atlantic to run an errand? Am I missing something?" *What the fuck?*

"Your immediate task is to attend this meeting."

"And after the meeting? Should I just head back home? Or is there a reason I had to go through training for a second time?" She gritted her teeth to stop herself from saying more given his position of authority.

"Fly back to London and head to our active duty station. The address is in the file. Once you get there, you'll receive details on how to proceed."

*Seriously?* Petra sighed. *Great, more jumping through hoops.* "Okay, then. Thank you," she responded.

She shut the file, slid it into her bag, and shook his hand.

She was almost out the door when she heard Mike call out from behind her. "Just remember to burn the file once you've memorized everything."

## *London, United Kingdom – June, 2016*

"Good afternoon, Petra."

"Good afternoon," Petra said, looking across the table at the young man who had just entered her debriefing room.

"I'm Brendan Collins. I'm with the Agency on permanent assignment here in the UK. I'm going to be your temporary handler until you leave for your next operation," he said in a thick Irish accent.

She gave him a tight smile. "Nice to meet you, Brendan."

"I trust everything went well on your assignment in Galway?"

"It did. I already debriefed with someone this morning. I told her everything that happened, although there wasn't much to say. It was pretty simple. I handed over the money and instructions, and that was it."

Brendan nodded with his eyes twinkling. "Yes, I've looked through the details of your debriefing already."

"If I'm done here, I'd really like to find a hotel room and get some sleep. Unless you're finally going to give me some information on the mission I was brought over here for."

"You'll be able to do that in a few minutes." He slid a USB key across the table.

Petra raised her eyebrows as she slid the key into her messenger bag. *Didn't think they would ever give me the info,* she almost grumbled aloud.

"That key contains the details of your mission. Most of your questions should be answered on there, especially those that relate to the last two trips you've made for us."

"I'm sorry, but how do you know all of this? The information about my trips is supposed to be restricted. Unless…?" Her voice trailed off.

"Unless they have something to do with your current operation. And yes, they do."

"I see."

"You'll leave in one week, if that's all right with you. Unfortunately, because of your cover story, going out earlier will be difficult. You'll be installed as an employee at the embassy and then can operate as many sources as you believe possible. Under all circumstances, you are an employee of their government and have nothing to do with the Agency or any official organization—British, American, French, or otherwise."

"I understand." She paused for a moment. "Why did I need to go through all of this extra training if you were going to send me on the mission I was slated for already?"

Brendan let out a hearty guffaw. "One of your recruiters suggested it. He wanted to make sure that you were ready, so he decided to send you over to us first. It's a big mission, after all. We didn't want to send you out on something that risky unless you were ready."

"And the assignment in Kinvara?"

He shrugged noncommittally. "It was just an errand we needed to be handled by a foreigner. You were in the right place at the right time."

Petra bit her bottom lip in irritation. *I'm going to kill Alex. Being seconded is good for my career, huh? What bullshit.*

"You're free to go, Petra. Good luck."

"Thank you."

### Tehran, Iran – June, 2016

Kasem had spent the past hour looking at a set of pictures from London instead of working. The memories were wonderful and heartrending. He pictured Lila smiling in front of him and a sheepish grin crept across his face. *Why hasn't she answered my calls? It's been almost a month.*

"Kasem, did you see the e-mail from IFC?" said someone behind him, abruptly pulling him from his daydreams.

He sat up suddenly. "E-mail from IFC? No, no I haven't seen it." Hurriedly he refreshed his Outlook inbox and opened up the e-mail message. The grin on his face grew even wider as he read it.

"They are moving forward. They will fund both Basra and the new Flower of Eden. I can't believe it," Kamran exclaimed as he approached Kasem's cubicle.

Kasem skipped to the bottom of the e-mail, which outlined the funding amounts. "Just a token for Flower, but still, we have their stamp!"

A group from the office went out to a long lunch to celebrate. Kasem left his phone on his desk and did not see the e-mail that arrived while he was at lunch for several hours. Lila had sent him a message to let him know that she was going to arrive in Tehran within two weeks. She had been assigned a posting at the French embassy.

**** 

Kasem could barely contain his excitement as he drove toward the embassy-issued apartment where Lila was staying. *She's actually here!* He was grinning from ear to ear.

He stopped at the compound gates and handed his ID card to the guard. "I'm here to see Lila Tabbas. She's expecting me," he said.

"Okay, just hold on one second."

Another guard walked out of the post and used an under-vehicle search mirror on a telescoping handle to inspect underneath the car. After returning Kasem's ID, the guard asked Kasem if he could search a gift bag sitting on the passenger seat that contained a box of earrings for Lila. Both guards then looked around inside his trunk and under the hood before finally signaling him through the gates.

*Thought the French would be more lax.* Kasem remembered how immigration had just waved him through passport control in Paris a few months earlier.

He parked the car and then walked through the compound to the address that Lila had given him. The compound boasted beautifully kept gardens and buildings sporting the architecture of the French countryside.

134

Once he found Lila's apartment, he rang the bell and stood fidgeting in a mix of excitement and apprehension. She opened the door smiling. "Hello, Kasem!" she said, immediately wrapping him in a hug. He moved to kiss her, but she pulled away. "Come in, silly."

He walked inside and she shut the door behind him. Then Lila went to the living room windows and pulled the blinds shut. "Now, Kasem, where were we?" she said with a smile.

He walked over to her and pulled her into a deep kiss. "I am so happy that you're here," he said as he gazed into her eyes.

"It does feel quite surreal," she said.

"You've been here for three days, but didn't let me come see you until today."

"I know, I know. I'm sorry, but we had a whole slew of mandatory training and I didn't want things to be too obvious."

"Do you need to keep us a secret?"

She smiled again. "Not entirely, but I'd rather keep it out of the gossip circles. It's fine for you to come over, but you shouldn't spend the night. The security logs will show when you enter and leave, and I don't want people to get too many ideas."

"Oh, so you're worried about what everyone will say about you and the dashing, handsome young man who is always coming to visit?" Kasem said as he tried to look serious, but his lips twitched into a smirk anyway.

"You know what I mean." She pulled him to the sofa with her. "I work and live here, so I have to be careful. I want to make good impression, and I hate gossip. I don't really care what the guards think, but we should be subtle about this. That's all I meant. And I can come see you from time to time."

He nodded, feeling somewhat placated.

"Oh, come on. We'll be able to see each other so much more than we have over the past few months."

"Lila, can I ask you something?"

"Of course."

"What does this mean to you?"

Her eyebrows scrunched. "You mean our relationship?"

"Yes. We've never discussed it." He took a seat on the couch as he waited for her response.

"Well, I care about you and I assume that you care about me. What else do you want to discuss?"

Kasem answered tentatively, "You aren't seeing anyone else, are you?"

"It's always about that with men isn't it?" She rolled her eyes and turned away. "No, I am not seeing anyone else. I sort of thought that we had something here."

Instead of responding in words, Kasem kissed her again and they lost themselves in the moment.

Over the next two hours, they made a simple dinner while laughing and flirting constantly. He kept trying to distract her from cooking by pulling her into kisses. "Be careful!" she told him repeatedly. "The oven is hot."

While they ate, they talked about a multitude of different things. He told her about his work and his projects. She talked about the post she'd received at the embassy and how she was unsure of how much she would actually like it.

After dinner, he kissed her and prepared to say goodbye. "I can't tell you how much I actually want to stay," he said. "But I know that it's better for us if I leave."

"Thank you for understanding, Kasem."

"When can I see you again?"

"Call me and we'll see."

Lila watched him walk away toward his car and settled back into the apartment. She booted up her computer, logged on to the secure server, and began going through an inbox full of messages from the past couple of hours.

## Tehran, Iran – Nine months later, March 2017

Lila watched silently as Kasem slept beside her. He rarely slept over at her place, but tonight was one of those rare nights. She crawled out of bed quietly and logged on to her computer. She typed a message to her handler. *"No news from any of my sources. Just the normal 'I'm okay' signs."*

Her handler's reply arrived a couple of minutes later. *"Glad to hear it."*

She turned back to look at the bed. *I guess this one is fine too,* she thought, as she fiddled with the locket that Kasem had given her. She blinked tears away from her eyes and tried to think clearly. *I need to tell him. It's been almost a year.* She took a deep breath. *How did this happen? He was supposed to be just a source. But now...*

136

Her mind flitted across memories of the past few months. From the beginning, she had cultivated him as an asset, but she always had known the real reason that she wanted to spend time with him. He had given her very little information, but every moment with him had felt too short. So she had pretended he was still a key value asset in her reports, but she had fallen head over heels for him, against every bit of advice and training that she had ever received.

Before she could lose her nerve, she whispered loudly, "Kasem, there's something I have to tell you."

He stirred quietly without opening his eyes.

Shaking him, she said again, "Kasem, I really need to tell you something."

He opened his eyes sleepily. "What is it Lila?" He took one look at her face and sat up. "What is it? What's the matter? Tell me."

"I haven't been honest with you."

He frowned and blinked rapidly, scrunching his eyes to push the sleepiness away. "What do you mean?"

It took all of her nerve to get the words out. "I am not just an attaché to the French embassy here."

"Oh," he said, confusion written across his scrunched brow. "Okay, that's not really a big deal, is it? It's a bit strange that you didn't tell me, b—"

"Kasem, I work for the French government."

The first hints of concern appeared on his face. "Of course you do...You work at the embassy."

"It's more than that. I've been giving them information about Iran. Information they need."

"What do you mean?"

"I'm a source. I provide them with intelligence."

The color started to drain from his face. "Intelligence? Like a spy? For the French?"

"Yes."

"Holy shit." Kasem put his right hand on his forehead and stared steadfast at the floor. "I feel like I'm in a bad dream." He bit down on his lip. "Is that why you came here?" His breathing was rapid and shallow as he started to feel the weight of what she said.

"When we met, I lied to you. I was working under a cover ID with the Ministry of Foreign Affairs. It was a preparatory exercise to come to Tehran."

His face crumpled as if she had just driven a knife into his back. "So when we met, you knew the whole time you would be coming to Iran?"

"Yes," Lila admitted. "I'm sorry. It was all part of my cover, and they thought you could be a source for me. I was kidding myself. I tried to convince myself that I didn't care about you, that I didn't love you."

He buried his head in his hands. "I need this nightmare to end," he muttered. "This has to just be a bad dream." He paused, and then his voice sounded cold. "Wait, have I actually been a source for you?"

Lila shook her head. "Not really. You haven't given me anything that we couldn't have gotten from other sources. I kept you as a source so that I could keep seeing you without anyone asking any questions."

She saw tears well up in his eyes, which he blinked away. "I don't know what to say, Lila. How do you expect me to process this?"

She put her arms around him and squeezed his shoulders. "I really do love you, Kasem. More than you know. I couldn't tell you this otherwise. I would have told you sooner, but I was scared." She sighed. "There's something else."

He gave her a bitter glance. "What could you possibly add to being a spy?"

"I'm so sorry I lied to you, but you need to know what to do if I ever get compromised, or if there's any danger."

He turned toward her and grabbed her shoulders. "Lila, stop. Just stop. I can't handle this right now."

"I'm sorry." Lila ignored his plea and met his eyes. "I'm sorry, I know you need time to process, but this is important. You have to hear this." She paused to figure out how to tell him without causing him more anxiety. "I'll take you to see a friend of mine tomorrow. She's one of my other sources. If I ever need to get in touch with you because I've been compromised or whatever, I'll give her my locket and make sure you get a message from me through her. Her name is Nurah Bahar and I trust her completely."

****

# Book V
# 2021

# Chapter 11
## The First Set of Components

*Salmiya, Kuwait – June, 2021*

The Ahriman drove back to his hotel from the third dewaniya he had been to since arriving in Kuwait almost one month earlier. *Damned white nightgowns.* He glanced down at his dishdasha, which desperately needed to be cleaned.

In an effort to stay alert, he turned up the radio and rolled down the window. He blinked quickly as the summer dust stung his eyes and tried to focus on the reddish sand-stained roads through his slightly drunken haze.

When he pulled into the hotel parking lot fifteen minutes later, he breathed a sigh of relief. *Next time, cab!*

He entered the lobby and headed toward the elevator when a woman at the concierge desk called out to him. "Mr. Mubarak? We've received a package for you."

He turned back surprised. *Already?*

"Oh, that's great," he responded. "I'll take it with me now."

"Certainly." She walked into the storage room and emerged with a large cardboard box marked 'fragile.' "Looks like it arrived from your company in Paris," she said, noting the address on the box.

"Yes, I was expecting some marketing materials." He took the box and gave her a polite smile. "Do I need to sign anything?"

"Yes, if you could just sign here." She handed him a delivery receipt and a pen.

He signed the paper and returned the pen. "Thank you, Miss Hamada," he said as he tried to look at her badge subtly.

"Oh, you're welcome, sir. Please let me know if there is anything else that you need." Her tone lingered on the end of the phrase and she held his gaze steadily.

He took in her glance with surprise. *Is she flirting?* "Er, thank you. I'll be sure to let you know."

Grabbing the box, he turned toward the elevators.

"Actually, would you mind leaving me a message in my room each time a new package arrives? I'm expecting several sets of marketing materials from *Total* headquarters."

"Certainly, sir. There isn't anything else you need tonight, is there?" she said while actually batting her eyelashes.

"No, that's fine, thank you." He went straight to his room. *Women,* he thought, shaking his head.

He put the box down on the table in his room and pondered opening it, but decided against it. *Might as well wait for the rest.* With that, he stuffed the box into the closet, and called down to the front desk for some room service.

When Miss Hamada delivered the food thirty minutes later, he sent her away in a hurry. Entranced by his computer screen, he didn't notice that she'd left her phone number on the bill.

## New York City, United States – June, 2021

"Talal Al-Kazemi is a wealthy businessman in Abu Dhabi who became an asset after one of our agents saved his father's life five years ago," Petra told Chris. "He's agreed to give us access to some of the people he's done business with in Kuwait."

"Okay, but who are you going to be? He can't exactly provide you with a cover identity," Chris said while looking at the information Petra was showing him on a holographic screen projected vertically over the conference table in front of them.

"I'm going to pose as his daughter, Mariam Al-Kazemi, a young woman in her late twenties studying international policy and journalism."

"And where is the real Mariam going to be?"

"She's in Washington, DC, taking a course for the summer."

"I see," Chris paused, considering it. "How do you know she isn't going to travel home or anything?"

"If she does, her father will notify us and we can come up with an alternative. The course runs until the end of August, though, so barring an emergency, we don't expect her to leave the country."

"What about after the end of August?"

"We'll have to figure it out on the fly."

"I know it's not ideal to have Petra posing as a real person, but it's the best we can do so quickly. We need a name that will give her access to multiple politicians," Alex added via the videoconference link they had initiated with the Istanbul field office.

"But won't people be able to access her picture online? Are you sure we shouldn't just create an identity for you?"

Petra grinned. "Talal Al-Kazemi has five daughters and there aren't very many pictures of them in wide circulation. And look at her picture." She tapped the projection twice to open and display the photo.

Chris scrutinized it, frowning. "Your features are similar enough, but no one would mistake you for one another in person."

"No one who's actually met Mariam, but she's never been to Kuwait, so this should be a safe bet. And anytime I interact with Talal's contacts, I'll make sure to wear a *hijab*, which will make it harder to recognize me."

Chris stared at the photo of Mariam and tried to imagine whether Petra could pass for her while wearing a traditional headscarf. "Fair enough. If both of you think this is the best course, then go with it," he finally agreed.

"Now that we're all set on the Petra's cover, let's talk about how you are going to get information," Alex said, redirecting the conversation to Petra.

"Sure," she replied.

"As the daughter of Talal Al-Kazemi, you shouldn't have any issues getting an interview with Fayed's office. Still, it might be harder to get more than one point of access."

"Yeah, I'll have to think on my feet. It should be enough to plant a couple of bugs, though. Maybe I can request follow-up interviews based on current events or something. I'll figure it out."

"To lend credence to the whole thing, you also should interview some other politicians. It'll get around within the circles and should help you gain better access," Alex continued.

"It will be kind of a pain to do research on multiple politicians, but whatever. I'm supposed to be a green master's student, so it's fine if I don't have everything perfectly laid out."

"Yup. Just make sure you are dressed right."

"Yes. Think sexy but conservative," Chris added.

She gave him an amused look. "I grew up there, remember? I definitely won't cross that line."

"But remember to get as close to it as possible."

She rolled her eyes and then nodded her agreement.

"Okay. Petra, I'll take care of things on the Kuwaiti end if you take care of things on yours," Alex said.

She looked at his image and forced a half smile. "I guess I should start packing."

## *Kuwait City, Kuwait – June, 2021*

Petra could feel the heat wave seeping into the airplane when she arrived at Kuwait International Airport. *Perfect.*

Before exiting the plane, she glanced through her documents and ran through her cover story. Alex had quizzed her on it multiple times over videoconference, and even though she had managed to memorize everything, she still felt uneasy about being back on assignment. After grabbing her bags, she went straight through immigration controls by way of the GCC countries' citizens' line.

A contact they had set up through her cover's father, Talal Al-Kazemi, met her at the airport.

"My name is Orestis Andrianis. Your father and I used to work together in Europe. I work with one of his suppliers here," he said as he greeted her.

"Hi, Mr. Andrianis. I'm Mariam. Nice to meet you."

He took her straight to a small apartment in the Surra area where he had arranged for her to stay.

"Please make yourself at home here. Feel free to stay here for as long as you like. From what your father said, you are expecting to be here about six weeks?"

"Something like that."

"Just let me know once you figure things out. You are in Kuwait for an internship, yes?"

"Not exactly. I am studying international policy and journalism, so I wanted to interview and work with some of the prominent politicians and their senior aides who aim to enter and return to the Kuwaiti National Assembly with next month's elections."

Orestis raised his eyebrows. "That sounds interesting. Look, I have to go in to the office. I'll let your father know that you've arrived safely." He tapped his foot against the floor and looked at her with narrowed eyes.

"Thank you, but there's no need. I'll call him later today."

"Okay. My card is on the table. Please call me if you need anything. Also, there are some taxi service numbers by the phone that you can use."

"Thanks, Mr. Andrianis. I'll probably get a rental car later this week, but that will be very helpful in the meantime."

"Well then, bye, Mariam."

He walked out of the apartment still grumbling and she chuckled as he walked away. *Probably thinking that rich kids are ridiculous!*

After he left, Petra proceeded to set up her computer before unpacking anything else. The Agency had issued her a new computer just prior to the mission under the guise that her old one had broken down. In reality, this computer was specially equipped with a double encryption platform that would transmit automatically to the Agency's satellite as a check-in point.

She booted it up, entered a password, and then waited as the retinal scan device confirmed her identity. After logging on, the computer connected automatically to the local broadband with a signal that masked its location. Upon connection, it also automatically transmitted a short blip indicating her safe arrival.

Three days earlier, she had been briefed on how the computer worked. "You can even rig this computer to self-destruct if the retinal scan doesn't confirm that it is you. You won't really need that because you'll only be using the computer on Agency premises here in New York, but we've included that functionality as part of our update to the field computers."

"That's exciting," Petra had said to the tech, noting that she would have to remember to implement that security mechanism if she ever felt that her cover had been compromised.

For now, she set the security settings to "Automatic memory wipe" if anyone else attempted to access her system. *Hope that doesn't backfire.*

Petra spent the next hour unpacking her things and then made several calls to set up meetings with members of the National Assembly for the next three days. It was easy for a wealthy business executive's daughter to be added to their calendars.

She felt a yawn coming from her waist up. Looking at her watch, she saw that it was about three in the morning in New York, so she had been up all night essentially. Taking a deep breath, she called a rental car company and asked for delivery later that afternoon. As soon as they confirmed the details, Petra hung up and curled up on the bed for a long, well-deserved nap.

## New York City, United States – June, 2021

Grant Antrobus knocked sharply on Chris McLaughry's office door when he arrived at the Agency's office on the Monday morning a week after Petra had left for her mission.

"Come in."

"Hi, Chris," he said, opening the door.

"Grant, hi, how are you doing?"

"Not so great."

Chris tried to sideline the conversation he knew was about to start. "Will I see you at the Canadian Consulate Ball?"

"Well, my date had to go out of town, so I'm not really up for it now," Grant said with a glare. "Have you heard from our mutual friend?" His tone was curt and tense.

Chris sighed. "We both know that I can't tell you that."

"Come on. She's been gone a whole week already. I just want to know if she made it to wherever you sent her in one piece."

"You've been here long enough, so you know how field ops work. I can't divulge any of that information."

"Seriously? I just want to make sure that she's okay." Grant's breathing grew heavy.

"Look, I'm really sorry, buddy. I can't tell you anything."

"You guys are making me crazy. First, you send her back in after three years without training. You ripped apart our lives without a second thought and now you can't even tell me that she's okay?"

"Okay, Grant, try to stay calm about this."

"I'm not asking you to tell me where the fuck she is. I just want to know if she got there alive and well. Just give me a yes or no. Is that really asking too much?"

"You can't keep coming in here to ask me that every few days."

"So I can't simply ask if my girlfriend made it in one piece to wherever you sent her? What the hell is wrong with you? I thought you were her friend, not just her boss, but I guess the Agency always comes first, right?" Grant slammed his fist into the desk.

"Okay, okay. Look, I need you to calm down before the entire hallway hears you yelling at me."

"Stop telling me to calm down, Chris! Just tell me if she made it there."

"All right, all right. Her computer's checked in a couple of times a day since she got there. She's fine."

Still searing with emotion, Grant held his gaze for a moment. "Thank you. Now, was that so hard?" he finally said before turning around and exiting.

Later on that day, Grant scowled at his computer monitor feeling utterly helpless.

"Hey, boss," he heard someone say, wresting him from his thoughts.

"Oh, hey, Nikhil," he said with a glance to his office doorway.

"Sorry if I interrupted what you were doing. I finished up with the diagnostics I was running. There aren't any tech emergencies at the moment, so I was wondering if I could take a longer lunch break."

Grant smiled sheepishly, glad that Nikhil could not read his mind. *He's done and I'm only on my first diagnostic!*

"Sure, that's fine. Everyone else has already gone to lunch, so just enjoy the temporary reprieve. I'm sure there will be a whole series of tech emergencies this afternoon."

Nikhil grinned. "Well, at least I can get just a little bit of sun before diving back into ridiculous complaints about slow download speeds for iTunes."

Grant rolled his eyes. "Get out of here before you distract me even more."

After Nikhil left, Grant spent ten more minutes staring blankly at his computer. His mind was spinning and unable to focus on anything but Petra. *I just need to know where she is.* His mind went through every potentially dangerous place where the Agency might have sent her. *DR Congo...Afghanistan...Libya...Iraq.*

He slammed his fist down on the desk in frustration and then glanced around in concern. No one had seen his display of emotion. The department was quiet in the tech bays outside his office door since Nikhil was the last to go to lunch. An inkling of an idea appeared and persisted in the back of his mind. *I'm the only one here.*

He exited from the diagnostic program he was running and turned off the internal monitoring system on his computer system. He hesitated for a moment. *How can I get away with this?*

From the general database, he tried to open the mission files directly. The screen began overflowing with a list of files, all of which were protected documents. He pressed a few keys rapidly to override the protection system as a general supervisor. *All too easy,* he thought as he saw the small padlock icons next to the file names disappear.

He opened the first file and saw that it belonged to the South American Protection Department. Sitting back for a second, he opened the DOS command on screen and entered "Middle East." A loud *beep* came from the computer with a large red error screen. He tried again, entering "Mid East" with the same result. *Maybe the Arab World?* The same loud *beep* greeted him after typing that.

Exasperated, he typed in "MENA" and an hourglass appeared on screen. When the hourglass disappeared a couple of seconds later, only five files remained on the screen. *Thank goodness we're such a small operation.* He opened the first one. The mission was titled "Operation Ramses," with lead agent Tyberius. The mission included several other agents' names. The second file was similar— "Operation Sheikh."

*No fucking clue.* He paused while trying to decide what to do. On a spur of the moment, he grabbed an encrypted USB stick and copied the five files. *Now I just have to walk out the front door.*

Grant looked at the USB stick. *Way too noticeable.* He searched through his drawers and found a large, metal case with a lighter inside it. He shook the case open, dumped the lighter into the drawer, and slipped the USB stick into it. *Perfect.* He sat back and admired his handiwork. He stuffed the lighter case into his jacket pocket and then returned to his computer screen. Within a few moments, all evidence of Grant looking into the mission files had disappeared, the monitoring system was reactivated, and his computer was back to running diagnostics.

A couple of hours later, Grant feigned sickness and checked out of the Agency building to go home. *This had better work.* The metal detector at the front entrance noted that he was carrying a metal lighter case in his jacket pocket, but nothing else.

### Salmiya, Kuwait – June, 2021

"It's Imran from the front desk, Mr. Mubarak. I'm sorry to disturb you. Another package has arrived for you. Should we send it up to your room?"

"Could you send it up in about fifteen minutes, please? I'm about to jump in the shower."

"Certainly, sir."

The Ahriman was still in his towel when he heard a knock at the door.

"I'll be right there." He hurriedly pulled on some clothes and answered the door.

"Good evening, sir. Here's the package that just came for you," Miss Hamada said and gestured toward the bellhop trolley with a large box on it. She leaned against the doorframe toward him, trying to catch his eye.

"Thank you. I'm sorry you had to carry such a heavy package upstairs. I should have come down to get it."

He lifted the box from the trolley and placed it just behind the door. "Here's something for your trouble," he said as he handed her a one-dinar note, the equivalent of about four dollars.

Miss Hamada frowned as she accepted the bill and hastily rebuttoned the top two buttons of her blouse while walking to the elevator. He watched her leave and then slowly proceeded with his work now that the final package had arrived.

He opened the closet and removed the other five boxes he had received over the past couple of weeks. Two of them were large and heavy, while the other three were not much larger than a small briefcase. He grabbed a knife and tore the first large one open to find a sheaf of marketing materials. *"Total est un des leaders mondiaux dans l'industrie du pétrole et du gaz naturel,"* he read aloud from the top page. *Marketing materials in French? For people in Kuwait?*

As he pulled out shrink-wrapped stacks of generic marketing letters and company information sheets, he noticed that some were in English and some even in Arabic. *Slightly more credible.* Finally, at the bottom he found the component he needed. For the next hour, he proceeded to open the other boxes, dig through the different brochures, branded pens, notepads, folders, and USB keys to remove the other four components he required.

He cleaned each piece slowly and then put the six components together, making sure each one fit exactly. Three hours later, he sat back and admired his handiwork. *Only one thing left.*

He waited a few moments and then proceeded to deconstruct the newly built device. When each piece was separated once again, he hid them throughout the room. He stuffed a bunch of flyers and notepads back into the different boxes and then shoved them into the closet.

He glanced at his watch, which read 2:00 a.m. Stretching out on the bed, he mentally ran through his plan. *I'll head to the supermarket later this week,* he decided before letting a wave of sleep wash over him.

## *Kuwait City, Kuwait – June, 2021*

"Uncle, I think we need to postpone the elections," Omar heard the Crown Prince say forcefully to the Emir.

The voices began to escalate.

"No! We cannot give the Islamists fuel to hate us any more than they already do."

"But you took a big risk appointing me as your prime minister. Shouldn't you let the public get used to it?"

"No, the more time that passes, the more the politicians can manipulate the public. The number of people that listen to those who say I have turned my back on democracy and Islam will just keep growing."

"If you rush into the next election, we may not even be able to put the stimulus package in motion before Parliament tries to put a stop to it!" the Crown Prince declared emphatically.

Omar listened keenly as the Emir maintained his stance. "We have to take that risk. The more time we give them, the more they can convince the public that they represent progress."

"Who would believe that, Uncle? They have been trying to repeal coed education for the past fifteen years. What kind of progress is that? Doesn't your track record speak for itself?"

Omar was standing in the kitchen adjoining the room where the Emir and Crown Prince were conversing, making a pot of Turkish coffee at a slow pace. He listened for a few more seconds as the argument continued, snickering to himself. *I could be on the other side of the palace and still hear them argue. I wonder what they'll decide.*

He carried the tray of Turkish coffees to the office chambers, still listening intently. The discussion had grown quiet and he could no longer catch much from outside the office. He frowned and leaned against the door to try to hear any part of the conversation. When he heard nothing, he knocked on the door and entered to deliver the coffee, taking note of the tension in the room.

After delivering the coffee, Omar returned to the kitchen and sent a text message through his phone.

*"Delay of elections being discussed. Decision TBD."*

A moment later, he received a reply. *"And the oil contract?"*

Omar answered, *"No decision yet. Textron VP arriving in two days to discuss."*

A moment later, he read another response. *"High priority: monitor and update anything regarding elections or the contract."*

Omar pocketed his phone and glanced down the hallway to make sure that no one would see him. He snuck over to the office door and attempted to listen further, still carrying the tray so he would appear to be collecting empty cups.

## *Surra, Kuwait – June, 2021*

Petra walked into Marzouk Fayed's offices in Surra fifteen minutes before her scheduled interview time of three o'clock. She checked in with one of the secretaries. "Hello, my name is Mariam Al-Kazemi. I'm here for an interview with His Excellency Marzouk Fayed."

"Okay, no problem. He will be ready to meet you momentarily."

"Thank you." She paused for a moment. "Would it be all right if I used the restroom?"

"Go ahead. Take the corridor to the end and then turn right. It's the door right before the staircase."

"Thank you," Petra said as she started to walk down the corridor. She smiled to herself as she began to explore. *Maybe I do miss the field sometimes.*

Fayed's office was housed in an old apartment building with a newly refurbished interior and exterior. He shared it with three other politicians, with each of them owning two floors that had separate entrances. The politicians also owned apartment space above the six office floors, although it was unclear whether they actually used the space.

The hallway was paneled with dark oak wood plastered with gold-toned design work. Petra shuddered at the gaudy design. At the end of the hallway, she turned right and saw the bathroom doorway just ahead of the stairwell. Judging from the décor, she guessed that Fayed's office would be upstairs.

She ventured further down the corridor, walking past several small offices looking for Khaled Majed's office. None of the doors had his name posted on the outside. *I hope he's nothing like his uncle.*

Going back to the stairwell, she made her way up slowly, trying to act obviously lost so that she could claim ignorance if anyone saw her. From the top of the stairwell, she could see two large conference rooms and then two offices at either end of a small hallway. The smaller hallway was decorated in the same fashion as the downstairs hallway. The larger of the two offices sported a bright red carpet at the entry. She choked back a nervous laugh. *That has to be Fayed's.*

When she reached the far end of the upstairs hallway, she was satisfied to see the door marked with "Khaled Majed – Senior Aide." Quickly, she moved back toward the stairwell; the emptiness of the hallway made her nervous.

She glanced around looking for cameras and made her way back downstairs. Before returning to the reception desk, she stopped at the restrooms and pulled her long hair into a loose bun. She left a few tendrils out to frame her face—a technique that she had found to be quite successful in capturing the male eye. Since she would not encounter anyone who knew the real Mariam Al-Kazemi, Petra had elected not to wear a hijab to this meeting, especially since she would need to employ every possible distraction to plant the bugs. On her way out, she flushed the toilet so that no one could question her reason for wandering the halls.

When she walked back to the entrance, the secretary spotted her and asked, "Did you find it all right?"

"Yes. I passed it by it at first by mistake, but I found it."

"One of Mr. Fayed's aides will be out to meet you in a second."

"Great. Thank you so much." Petra paused and then continued. "I was wondering—would it be possible for me to also speak with Mr. Fayed's senior aide?"

"You'd like to speak with Khaled Majed?"

"Yes. You see, I'm thinking of taking on a similar position in the UAE when I finish my master's next year and I'd like to have some context about what it's like to work with politicians."

The receptionist frowned and then shrugged. "They are both at the same meeting. If Khaled is free, I'm sure he'd be happy to speak to you. Otherwise, maybe we can schedule something in the next few days."

"That would be great. Thank you." Petra took a seat in the lobby to wait. Finally, thirty minutes later, both men emerged from the elevator bay. Fayed headed straight down the hallway toward the stairwell.

"Reema, sorry we're late," Khaled said to the receptionist. "What's the next meeting scheduled?"

"Mr. Fayed is scheduled to speak to this young lady, Mariam Al-Kazemi from Abu Dhabi. If possible, I believe she'd also like to speak with you."

Khaled raised his eyebrows. "Mariam Al-Kazemi? As in…?"

The receptionist nodded before he could finish his thought.

"Oh. Well, then yes, of course. Just have her come to my office after her meeting."

"Great."

Petra pretended to be deeply engrossed in a magazine during this conversation, but actually took in every word. *Got to love being an Al-Kazemi.*

Over the next hour, Petra interviewed both Marzouk Fayed and then Khaled Majed. She asked them detailed questions about the upcoming elections, their plans, strategies, and general feelings about the direction of the government. The interviews were well rehearsed due to her preparation with other politicians over the past couple of days and she was able to ask a few provocative questions. During both sessions, she dropped her pen on the floor and had to lean over to pick it up from under the desk. The men were too engrossed by the cleavage from her V-neck blouse to notice when she planted bugs directly underneath their computer stations.

\*\*\*\*

# Chapter 12
# Family Emergency

## *New York City, United States – June, 2021*

Grant cried out, throwing his pen against the wall. *Fuck me.* After the third night in a row spent going through the files he had stolen from the Agency's database, he was at a loss. He had let himself into Petra's apartment to see if any of her stuff would help him. In the past couple of days, he had gone through the files on the missions in the Middle East, trying to compare them with papers that Petra had left in her apartment, but so far, he'd been unable to connect any links.

He stretched out on the couch to clear his mind and figure out what to do. *I need help with this.* He tried to think of any of Petra's friends who might be willing or able to help him. From what he remembered, all of them were still with the Agency, except for her recruiter.

Grant sat up, trying to recollect what he knew about Petra's recruitment. She had told him there were a few people involved. She had mentioned Chris and some guy named Alex, but only one person outside of the Agency. *Who is he?*

He went into the bedroom to search through some of Petra's things, wishing he could look at the contact list in her phone, but it had been put in an Agency vault. He wracked his brain. *What was his name? She mentioned him the other day.* Grant closed his eyes to concentrate and it came to him. *Carlos? It was Carlos.*

He rummaged through one of Petra's drawers where she kept old cards and postcards. He found a bunch of stuff from her parents. He found a postcard from Tehran toward the bottom of the pile with a message written in what appeared to be Arabic or Farsi. He considered it for a moment, but then dismissed it. *Probably from her family.* He continued going through them and found what looked like a wedding invitation, a white envelope with "Miss Petra

Shirazi" in calligraphy across the front. *Maybe this has something useful.*

He pulled the invitation out of the envelope. While looking for contact information, he saw that the RSVP card was still stuffed inside. *Guess she forgot?* He scanned the invitation that read, "Your presence is requested by Carlos Santiago to witness when the beautiful Diane Starshinina agrees to officially become his better half for life. Please join us for the wedding on June 17, 2019 at 6:30 p.m. with a dinner reception to follow." *Yes, finally got something!* At the bottom of the invitation, he found RSVP contact information for Diane Starshinina. *Good enough.* He reached for his phone and dialed the number.

"Hello."

"Hi, is this Diane Starshinina?"

"Yes, speaking."

"I was hoping to speak to your husband, Carlos. I'm sorry to call so late."

"Oh, that's fine. Carlos is in the den. I'll get him. Who's calling?"

"My name is Grant. I'm Petra Shirazi's boyfriend. I think they used to work toge—"

"Oh, okay. One second." He detected surprise in Diane's tone.

A couple of minutes later, a male voice answered the phone. "Hello?"

"Is this Carlos?"

"Yes. You're Petra's boyfriend? Is everything all right? Has something happened to her?"

Grant cringed. "I hope everything is all right. I need to ask you for some help."

"Of course. What do you need?"

"Actually, Carlos, would you mind meeting in person?"

Carlos was silent for a moment. "Sure. How does Sunday night sound?"

"That works. Where should we meet?"

"Let's meet at your apartment. Something tells me that this conversation may not be entirely kosher, so someplace private might be best."

"Since this is about Petra, let's meet at her place," Grant suggested.

"Okay, sure. She still has the apartment on Sixty-Ninth Street?" Carlos asked.

"Yes."

"I'll be there at ten on Sunday."

"Carlos, thank you so much."

The phone clicked as Carlos hung up. Grant looked around Petra's apartment where he had spent the past few nights. *I really need to get out of here.*

## Salmiya, Kuwait – June, 2021

After being outside in the summer heat for almost two hours, the Ahriman stretched out in his hotel room sipping a cold 7UP. He looked down at the 7UP bottle in his hand. *Wish I had a beer.* Recent events had led him to many alcohol-related memories, one of which was a cold beer on a hot summer day.

He relaxed for about thirty minutes and then walked over to the kitchen area where he had deposited his shopping bags earlier. Going through each bag, he placed some produce and perishables in the fridge and then put a couple of cans in the cabinets above the sink. Once he had cleared up the kitchen, he stood back and admired his handiwork. *No one would suspect a thing.*

He headed back to the bedroom area and pulled out one of his notebooks. The recipe he needed was written in a sort of personal code. *My personal cookbook.* He flipped the pages until he found the right page, and then he read the recipe. He sat back and calculated mentally how much time he would need. Preparation would require about forty-eight hours, so he elected to start on June 30 to have enough time.

He leaned back against the headboard. *Just have to wait now.* He began to smile, but stopped when he looked out the window. He shook his head to rid himself of the image of yet another billboard with the photograph from his file. *How will I...?*

## Surra, Kuwait – June, 2021

Khaled walked into Fayed's office on a Saturday afternoon. Once again, he was surprised that Fayed had come in during the Kuwaiti weekend, which was Friday and Saturday, especially since Fayed did not even normally come in on Thursday.

"Khaled, please take a seat," Fayed said and gestured toward the chair in front of his desk.

"Is something wrong, sayeedi?"

"I called you in because I am concerned about the upcoming elections. Do we have any updates from Bayan Palace? I heard a rumor in the dewaniya today about a possible delay in the election date. I don't need to tell you how much that would inconvenience us."

"The latest update from my source is that the Emir has been quite adamant that he will not postpone the elections next month."

"Good," Fayed said. "Since I have you here, can you update me on our plan?"

Khaled nodded. "We received an update from him yesterday. He said things are moving along and he will be ready ahead of schedule."

"So everything is ready?"

"Yes, I believe so."

A wide smile spread across Fayed's face. "Has he figured out his strategy for planting it? Security around the palace will not be light."

"Sir, I'm quite sure that he has a strategy. It's better if we don't know. That will make it easier for us to claim denial."

"Very well."

"I'll let you return to your work, Khaled. Thank you for coming in on such short notice."

The two of them walked out of the office together. Several miles away, Petra studied the conversation on her computer screen that was transcribed automatically by the bug she had planted. *Time to dissect every word.*

****

An hour later, Khaled walked out to his car and made two quick phone calls during his drive home.

"Omar, have you heard anything else about the oil contract?" he asked his contact at Bayan Palace.

"The Emir wants to give it to that American company, but he is still worried about the backlash from Parliament."

"What has he decided to do?"

"The Crown Prince has advised him to wait until after the elections," Omar responded.

"I see. Have they said anything more about when the elections will be?" Khaled held his breath as he waited for the answer.

"The Emir is holding firm for July fifth."

"Okay. Let me know if you hear anything more. You'll get your next check tomorrow."

"Thank you."

The line went dead. A few minutes later, Khaled dialed a number in Tehran while sitting in traffic. Since the windows were up, he had the air conditioning on full blast.

"I have news."

"Tell me," replied the raspy voice of his handler.

"The Crown Prince advised the Emir to wait to award the contract until after the elections."

"Did he agree?"

"Yes," Khaled answered. "He's worried about potential backlash from Parliament if he does too much while they are out of session."

"Did you talk to our contact at Textron?"

"Yes. He made sure to emphasize the importance of awarding the contract prior to the elections."

"Good."

"Are you sure that they will ask Reynolds to intervene?" Khaled asked.

"There's too much money at stake for them to do anything else. He will be there right on schedule."

Khaled felt reassured by the confidence in his handler's voice. "I trust your judgment."

"Just make sure that no one figures out that he is the real target."

**\*\*\*\***

Petra listened to the conversation for what felt like the hundredth time.

*"Good. Since I have you here, can you update me on our plan?"*

*"We received an update from him yesterday. He said things are moving along and he will be ready ahead of schedule."*

*"So everything is ready?"*

*"Yes, I believe so."*

*"Has he figured out his strategy for planting it? Security around the palace will not be light."*

*"Sir, I'm quite sure that he has a strategy. It's better if we don't know. That will make it easier for us to claim denial."*

*"Very well."*

Frowning, Petra switched off the recording from Fayed's office. *What the hell?* She had spent the past twelve hours going through files, notes, and transcribed conversations trying to figure out what the latest discussion between Marzouk Fayed and Khaled Majed described.

*Fayed, Majed, and a "him"? Planting something in a palace?* She frowned, recalling the original conversation that had precipitated the whole operation. *Thirty million euros.*

She tapped the screen, pulled up the transcript of the original conversation in Arabic, and stared at it. *Nothing.* She tapped her screen again and switched to the bug's time log to look through the full records of Fayed's conversations and computer activity. *Tell me something, anything.*

Fayed's log showed a series of conversations with secretaries and other Parliament members, the conversation with Khaled, and numerous e-mails sent through the computer. Thankfully, the bugs were sophisticated enough to give her a full picture of his day-to-day activities.

She scrolled through the subjects listed for the e-mails that he had sent. Most of the e-mails were categorized as social or about the upcoming elections. *Maybe Khaled Majed's log?* As the log loaded, she noticed that it was quite different from what she would have expected for a senior political aide. There were several messages between Khaled Majed and an "OZ":

*June 24, 2021 – Khaled Majed received from OZ: "E priority election date. Decision TBD."*
*Khaled Majed sent to OZ: "Continue high-priority monitoring."*
*June 25, 2021 – Khaled Majed received from OZ: "E remains adamant. Decision made."*
*Khaled Majed sent to OZ: "Good. Continue to update."*
*June 26, 2021 – Khaled Majed received from OZ: "Status quo unchanged."*
*Khaled Majed sent to OZ: "Continue to update as needed."*

Petra frowned. *Who is OZ? Are those someone's initials, O. Z., or a codename? Someone who reports to Majed? And what about E?*

She studied the log for a minute before she remembered something from the beginning of the conversation between Fayed and Khaled. She quickly reopened the transcript of it in Fayed's log. The first thing Fayed had asked about was, of course, the election date.

She leaned back in her chair as the realization struck her. "Majed, you crooked twit. You have a spy in the Emir's office. E is for Emir," she said, chuckling. "But what are they planting? And who is doing it?" She sighed, wishing she had more insight.

She logged onto her Agency server and pressed a few buttons to dial Chris through the computer.

"Hello," she heard a moment later.

"Hey, it's Petra."

"Hey. Can you speak freely?"

"Should be fine."

"Good. How are you doing?" A projected image of Chris from the shoulders up appeared from the sidelight of her computer as her own screen began transmitting like a videoconference.

"I'm fine. Just trying to figure out all of this shit."

"Your boyfriend came by asking about you."

"Seriously?"

"Yeah. He got a little worked up the other day in my office just wanting to know if you're okay. He calmed down once I finally told him that you had checked in."

Petra looked aghast. "You did? He must have been really upset. Thanks for telling him that."

Chris chuckled as he recounted the incident. "You know, he somehow seems to get even taller when he's angry, like a character from a comic. I felt bad for the guy because he's never worked in the field and he's just worried about you. It's sweet."

Petra sighed. "Yeah, it is. So he's okay now?"

"He'll live. Anyway, update me."

"There are still a lot of gaps, but I did figure out one thing that's interesting."

Chris rubbed the stubble on his chin. "Which is?"

"Fayed has a spy in the Emir's office. Someone with the initials O. Z., or at least that's the codename they're using."

"I'll get you a list of the Emir's employees."

"Sounds good."

"Anything else?"

"I sent you a transcript. Fayed and Majed had a conversation about someone planting something at a 'palace.' I'm still trying to figure out what they mean." She ran her fingers through her hair, considering the details of the conversation.

"Let's talk it through. I'm not as good at research as Russell, but hopefully we can still figure it out."

"Yeah, I guess you're stuck helping me since he doesn't have clearance," Petra said with a laugh. "The big question is what exactly do they mean by the 'palace'? I need to try running some database searches."

"Okay, share your screen so we can talk through it."

"Got it." She opened up the Agency database on buildings considered to be credible targets for terrorist agencies. Accessing the search function, she typed in "palace OR castle" as keywords.

"Should we use both of them?" Chris asked.

She hesitated for a moment, thinking about the Arabic words Khaled Majed and Fayed had used. "The word they used definitely implied palace. I think that should give us enough information."

"You're the expert." Taking the gamble, she retyped only "palace" as the keyword.

"There are palace hotels all over the place," Chris said, skimming down the list of more than one hundred results. "For thirty million euros, maybe we should strike hotels with fewer than one hundred rooms, except for those that usually house VIPs."

"Sounds like a plan." Petra keyed the criteria into the search engine.

On his end, Chris watched the search screen. "Damn. There are still more than fifty places. Should we add Kuwait to the parameters?"

She shook her head. "No, I don't think so. It must be a global target. There's no way Fayed would target something within his own country."

"Yeah, I agree."

Staring at her screen, she increased the search sensitivity by relevance. "Let's try 'known as anti-Islamic,'" she said as she typed it into the search bar. Her face crinkled as the results appeared on her monitor.

"All that did was give us a location function. The further away from the Middle East, the more likely to be known as anti-Islamic," Chris scowled at the search engine.

She closed her eyes for a moment and pondered how to fix it. After a few moments, an idea struck her.

"Let's try this: 'known as pro-Western AND anti-Islamic AND Middle East relevance.'" She reopened the sensitivity search and typed in the new keywords, along with shifting the function to use agent reviews rather than location as the basis. A list of ten places appeared that she and Chris began scanning quickly.

Before she could dive into the list, she glanced at her watch. "It's 3:34. Shit. I have to be at an interview at 4:15. Oops!"

Chris winked at her, bemused. "Glad you're keeping your cover intact by interviewing some other people. We can pick this back up later."

## *New York City, United States – June, 2021*

When Carlos rang the doorbell at Petra's old apartment, it felt like pure déjà vu.

Grant answered the door. "Hi, Carlos. I'm Grant. Nice to meet you finally. Thanks for coming over. Come in."

"No worries. Anything I can do to help Petra."

"I really appreciate it."

"I can't believe she's kept this apartment since she joined the Agency five years ago," Carlos said as he walked into the foyer. "We had some good times here." A wistful expression crossed his face as he thought of the occasional parties Petra had thrown when she returned from missions for short stints. "She's like my little sister. I hope she's okay."

Grant returned his melancholy smile. "I hope so too. Would you like anything to drink?"

"Sure. Some tea would be great."

"You sure you just want tea? I've got some high quality gin here." He gestured toward his own glass of gin and tonic on the counter.

"Nah, just tea would be great."

Carlos sat down on the couch in silence, watching while Grant proceeded to make tea in the open kitchen. He tapped his fingers against the couch as he waited.

"Grant, just tell me what's going on. I spoke to Petra a week ago and she seemed pretty torn about something."

"Yes. She's gone back into the field."

Carlos nodded. "I figured as much after our conversation. So what's the matter? She's only been gone for a few days so far, right?"

Grant clenched his right fist against the counter. "The whole thing is just so frustrating. She can't have any contact with anyone here—at least nothing personal—and I don't even know where she's gone."

"Didn't you know it could be like this? That's standard Agency protocol."

"Sure, Carlos, because I've been involved with so many field agents before Petra."

"Okay, okay, fair enough. It's difficult. Trust me, I know. Just tell me what's going on."

Grant sighed. "I looked into the Agency's database trying to find out where she is."

"You did what? Why the hell would you tell me something like that? Do you know how much trouble you could get in for doing that? How much trouble I could get in for knowing about it?" Carlos gaped at him. "Oh, jeez. I thought something might have actually happened to her. I didn't realize I was just dealing with a worried boyfriend." He stood up to leave. "There's nothing I can do. Right now, I should be calling the authorities to report your ass. Heck, I should call the Agency even though I'd rather stab myself with a hot poker. I'm just going to leave and pretend that I don't know a damn thing about this."

"Well, it's not as if you're so perfect. You left the Agency because you couldn't take it anymore."

"That's true. I wouldn't do what they asked me to do and I couldn't take what they did to me when I declined. But when I was there, I didn't act like a lunatic. Why do you need me? You can probably figure out her mission and its status from the files on your own. I don't want to be involved with this."

Grant stepped in front of him with pleading eyes. "I'm sorry. I shouldn't have said that. And you're right, I probably shouldn't have hacked into the database, but I can't shake the feeling that something bad is about to happen. It's driving me crazy. I just need to know where she is. I can't decipher the mission files on my own. So please, will you help me figure it out?"

Carlos rolled his eyes. "I can't be a part of this."

"Come on, man, please? They sent her back in the field after three years with barely even a week to prepare. She could die out there." Uttering those words made his chest tighten and his stomach churn, and then he started to shake. Grant immediately swallowed the rest of his drink in one gulp to calm his nerves. "I just need to know something. No one will tell me anything."

Grant held Carlos's gaze steadily until he conceded. "Fine, I'll help you out, but just the basics, nothing deeper. Tell me about the files."

"One second. Let me pull them up on my computer."

"You transported stolen files out of the Agency?" Carlos's mouth fell open and he stood up to leave again. "What the fuck is the matter with you?"

Grant ignored the comment as he started up his laptop on the coffee table in front of them and opened up the computer files.

"This is too much. I can't be an accomplice to something like this. What do you even want me to do, Grant?"

"Please. What would you want Petra to do for Diane?"

Carlos glared at him. "Diane would never do anything like this."

"I bet she would if she thought it could help keep you safe."

Carlos was fuming as he fell back onto the couch. "Fine, let's get this over with." He glanced at the first file. "Operation Ramses. Well, that's been going on forever, so it's unlikely they would need Petra for it." Grant clicked to display the next file. "Operation Sheikh? I guess that's a possibility. Let's see the rest and then we'll figure it out."

The two of them looked through the remaining three files.

"So based on what I know, I would say it has to be either *Sheikh* or *Rehla*, the one from the last file. Both of them were initiated recently with small teams—actually *Rehla* is just one agent—and both have the sort of mission profile that fits Petra's expertise." Carlos leaned back on the couch with his arms crossed.

"How do we figure out which one it is?"

"Do you have any files from Petra's office? Something she was working on?"

"I couldn't get the files from her office, but I have the papers from her desk here."

Grant retrieved a stack of papers that Petra had left scattered on her desk and they began flipping through them. Toward the bottom, Carlos found a sheet that made him take notice.

"What's that?" Grant asked and glanced over at the piece of paper.

"Some kind of a diagram. She has someone, or something called 'MF' pointing to 'KM' with a question mark toward 'GM.' Then she has a bunch of squares at the bottom with 'KC,' 'Thrn,' and 'AD' in them."

Grant scratched his head. "T-H-R-N? Tehran? Do you think either of those missions is taking place in Tehran?"

Carlos squinted at the two files on screen again. "I don't speak Arabic or Farsi, but let me try something." He opened up a translation engine and used the automatic translate for both words. "*Sheikh* is a commonly used word in the Middle East. The subheading underneath it is *shafafiyah* though. *Shafafiyah* in Arabic means 'transparency,' but the Farsi word is *shafafiyat*. So it seems as if that mission would be in an Arabic-speaking country. Let me try the other one."

He typed "*rehla*" into the same translation engine. "*Rehla* doesn't come up with any results in Farsi, but in Arabic it means 'journey or trip.'"

"So it's safe to say that neither is in Tehran?" Grant's expression brightened slightly.

"Seems like it. But if Tehran is in a box, then the other two boxes are probably for places as well. 'KC' and 'AD' must be somewhere in the Arab world."

"Kuwait City, maybe?"

Carlos nodded. "And Abu Dhabi?"

"Seems right," Grant agreed.

They peered at the two files again. Carlos pulled them up alongside one another and compared them. "Shit. That's it. Operation Rehla!" he exclaimed.

"What? What do you see?" Grant asked excitedly.

"Operation Rehla is an off-book mission."

"How do you know that? And does that make a difference?" Grant took a swig from his drink and forced himself to swallow slowly. "How do we know that's Petra's mission?"

"Petra was one of our best recruits. If they were going to pull her out of retirement, it would have to be for a critical mission, and an off-book mission is as critical as it gets."

"But how do you know that Operation Rehla is an off-book mission?"

"Do you know what an off-book mission is?"

"Not exactly. I've heard rumors about missions that we don't record accurately in the books. It's something along those lines, right?"

"It is, but an off-book mission also bypasses Agency protocols. The mission doesn't need to meet any basic requirements. *Sheikh* has three team members. *Rehla* has one. *Sheikh* was initiated six weeks ago, based on the file creation date, and *Rehla* only two weeks ago. *Sheikh* has a location code number, agent ID numbers, and linked files. *Rehla* has no location code, no ID numbers, no linked files, no access to any other information. It has to be an off-book mission."

"Off-book missions can do that because…?"

"Because they are considered to be highest priority. And because it would take too long to put together a team that fits normal protocols. Off-book missions are created when taking the time to do that would jeopardize the mission."

Grant leaned forward onto the coffee table. "So because it's an off-book mission, we know for sure that she's on that one?"

"This is intelligence, kid," Carlos mocked. "We never know anything for sure, but I'd be willing to bet that they would only send her on a mission with that level of priority."

"Is there anything else indicating that it's *Rehla*, so we can be more certain?"

Carlos returned to the files, scanning them for anything else that stood out to him. Grant had been fidgeting for several moments when Carlos finally turned toward him chuckling. "She put the signal right there in front of us. The agent in charge of *Rehla* is listed as Agent Anahita."

Grant looked at Carlos quizzically. "Anahita?"

"Anahita is a Farsi name. It means 'the goddess of love and fertility,' or some such nonsense."

Grant raised his eyebrows. "What does that have to do with Petra?"

"It's the name of one of Petra's roommates in college. I remember it from the recruitment file that I put together. We investigated her and did a check on all of her known close associates. Petra always said an alias is easier to remember if it means something to her."

Grant's face lit up. "It's like she wanted us to figure it out."

"I seriously doubt that."

"You're probably right. Okay then, how do we figure out more about the mission?"

"Already ahead of you," Carlos said, starting to go through Petra's papers again. "Wait a second." He looked back at the paper with KC and AD. "Look at that. In the corner. She's written something. Can you read that?"

After squinting at the piece of scratch paper, Grant finally said, "I think it's an abbreviation for national assembly. But I'm not sure."

"National Assembly? Well, then she's in Kuwait."

"Of course. Abu Dhabi is in the Emirates and they don't have a national assembly," Grant said with a smile of relief.

"That also makes sense given Petra's background, living there for so many years and all."

The two of them sat back quietly. "So based on all of that, can you tell me anything about how much danger she may be in?" Grant asked.

"I don't know for sure. Off-book missions can be risky, but Kuwait isn't a high-risk destination. It depends on the mission, of course, but the location is important as well. This file doesn't give me much to go on."

"Since it's an off-book mission, they've kept all the details out of the file."

"Exactly." Carlos looked at Grant, tilting his head. "So, if you don't mind my asking, why are you so worried?"

"I just have this feeling that something bad is going to happen to her. I can't shake it."

"It's not as if you can do anything from here anyway."

Grant's expression brightened. "Do you think I could do something about it if I went over there?"

"Whoa, Kuwait isn't a tiny village. Do you think you could just walk down the street and run into her? We may have figured out where she is, but we don't know a damned thing about her cover identity, her target, or anything else. There's no way any of us could find her without that."

"Yeah, of course, you're right. I just wish I knew—"

"Grant, you can't do anything more. Look, Petra is the most skilled agent I've ever met. She can take care of herself. So just sit tight and wait." Carlos stood to leave. "Anyway, I have to run. It's been over two hours and I need to get home."

"Sure, Carlos. Thanks for coming." Grant stood and shook Carlos's outstretched hand.

"I hope that helped a bit. Wish I could do more."

Fifteen minutes after Carlos left, Grant made his decision. He logged on to his travel account and booked a flight to Kuwait for later that week. Once the booking was confirmed, he logged on to his Agency e-mail server and sent a message about his upcoming trip. He cited a "family emergency" as the justification for his urgent last-minute leave of absence.

\*\*\*\*

# Book VI
# Three Years Earlier
# 2018

# Chapter 13
## Everything Went Black
## Three Years Earlier

*Tehran, Iran – May 28, 2018*

"Is this Kasem Ismaili?"

"Yes," he said as he groggily rubbed his eyes. "Who is this?"

"It's Nurah Bahar. Do you remember me?"

Kasem sat up abruptly and frowned. "Yes, of course. You're that friend of Lila's. Is everything all right?"

"I have a message from her."

Kasem's heart started to race. "What is it?"

"We can't talk about this over the phone. Can you meet me in an hour?"

He reached over to his bedside table to grab his digital alarm clock. He blinked twice in astonishment at the bright red numerals that read 2:04. "In an hour? You mean meet you at three in the morning? Are you crazy?"

"You're both in danger. Do you want to hear the message or not?"

"Yes, of course! But I have to get to work in a few hours."

"I'm already breaking the rules by trying to get this message to you. It will all be irrelevant in twenty-four hours."

"Oh, come on! You have to give me more than that to go on. How do I even know that you've spoken to Lila?"

"I have the locket that Lila wore. Will it be proof enough?"

"The locket?" he said, taking a deep breath. *Lila said that would be the signal.* His thoughts began to run toward dark places. "I guess another sleepless night wouldn't do me any harm," he finally conceded. "Where should I meet you?"

"The place where we first met. I'll see you in an hour. Don't be late."

The line went dead. *Where we first met? It'll take almost an entire hour to drive there!* Kasem groaned as he fumbled around the room to get dressed.

He was en route to his car when he remembered his friend Jamal was huddled on the couch after locking himself out of his apartment down the hall. *He just had to forget his keys tonight.* He pulled out his cell phone and typed a hurried text message while stopped at a traffic light.

"*Running urgent errand for L on other side of town. See you in few hours.*"

Forty minutes later, Kasem pulled up in front of the empty lot where he and Lila had parked the last time they visited this flat on the other side of the city. Choosing the safety of the garage next door instead, he parked his car and walked over to the building.

It was eerily quiet at close to three in the morning. Cars passing by on the nearby highway were few and far between. Kasem shuddered. *This had better be an emergency.* His thoughts drifted back to Lila and he could feel his stomach tying in knots. He tried to push his mind away from the worst-case scenario to no avail and shuddered once again.

Kasem entered the lobby quietly and walked toward the elevator, which still had a large worn-out sign written in Farsi that read, "Elevator out of order." He pushed open the door to the stairwell and rushed up to the third floor.

He knocked softly when he reached the apartment door. A few moments later, Nurah opened the door a crack.

"Did you come alone?"

"Are you fucking kidding me? Who would I bring with me? It's three in the morning!"

"I had to be sure. Come in," she said while opening the door to let him inside the dimly lit apartment.

He stepped past her into the living room and felt something sharp jab him in the neck. "What the h—?" he cried out.

Kasem's eyes widened as he fought to maintain his vision. In his peripheral vision, he could see two burly men appear from the shadows of the dark room and grab his arms. He tried to lash out, but his muscles refused to respond. His legs started to sway and the room grew even hazier. "Nurah, what are you doing? Who are these men?" He tried to shout, but could barely hear the whisper that escaped from his throat.

His legs buckled and he fell, first to his knees and then over onto his right side, landing hard on the side of the small couch near the entryway. Without realizing it, his phone slipped out of his pocket.

"I'm so sorry, Kasem. They already knew everything. I have to protect my family."

In the back of his mind, he could hear the echo of Nurah's voice.

The room faded as they thrust a dark sack over his head. "Where are you taking me? What do you want with me?" he tried once again to shout.

Then everything went black.

## *Tehran, Iran – Two days later, May, 2018*

"Kasem? Answer the door! Are you there?" Jamal Soroush yelled, knocking repeatedly on Kasem's door. He then took out his phone and dialed Kasem's number. "Dude, it's Jamal. Where are you? Why aren't you picking up your phone? Did the battery die? Because it goes straight to voicemail every time I call," he said, leaving yet another voicemail for Kasem.

Jamal opened the last text message from Kasem on his phone.

*"Running urgent errand for L on other side of town. See you in few hours."*

He banged his fist on the door again. *What the hell, Kasem? It's been two days!*

Jamal pulled out the key Kasem had given him a few months ago—the first time he had crashed on the couch. He entered the apartment and the living room looked exactly as it had two days earlier. *Has he even been home?* He walked through the living room and into the bedroom to confirm. The sheets were rumpled and the comforter was thrown to the side.

*Why hasn't he been home?* He checked the time on the message again, and that concerned him more than anything else did. *An errand at 2:17 a.m.?*

Jamal took a deep breath. It was possible that Kasem had stayed over at Lila's, although generally he came home. He scrolled down to the entry 'Lila – Cell' and hit the call button.

Two rings later, she picked up. "Jamal? Hey, how are you?"

"Hi, Lila. Not bad. How are you?"

"I'm okay."

There was a long pause while Jamal mustered the courage to ask Lila about Kasem's whereabouts. "Look, this might be kind of awkward, but are you with Kasem by any chance? I haven't heard from him in a while, and he's not at home."

"No, I've been traveling for a few days. I thought you were having a boys' night or something."

"Yeah, but I don't know where he is. I crashed at his place a couple of nights ago and I haven't heard from him since he sent a text message about some errand for you."

"An errand? What errand?"

"I...I don't know. His message just said he had to run an errand for you on the other side of town. It was kind of weird. He sent it at close to three in the morning."

"He said he had to run an errand for me at three in the morning?" Jamal could hear the surprise in her voice. "Where exactly did he say he was going?" she asked.

"The message just said the other side of town."

"Listen, Jamal, I'm sure it's nothing. He's probably running late because of work tonight."

"Er, sure, okay, I guess."

"I'll try to find him, and I'll have him call you when I do."

**** 

Lila's eyes widened and she felt her blood pressure rise several notches. Her throat tightened and she felt a pressure on her chest as she hung up the phone. She had just returned earlier that day from a three-day visit to one of Iran's smaller cities and had wondered why she had not heard from Kasem while on her trip.

She grabbed her bag and keys, bolted the apartment door, and ran full tilt for the parking lot. Once she got to her car, she drove directly toward a small flat on the outskirts of the city.

**** 

Lila circled the main road near Nurah Bahar's building before pulling over into an empty parking lot across the street. Instead of heading straight to the building, she walked over to a small convenience store on the other side of the lot.

She headed into the store and purchased a pack of cigarettes. "Do you have a light?" she asked, taking a cigarette out of the pack.

"Sure." The shopkeeper held out a lighter and she lit the cigarette.

*Ugh, I hate the taste of cigarette smoke.* She pretended to take a puff as she left and then walked around the store to a small alley in the back. She stood in the alley, looking up at the third-floor window of Nurah's building. Finally, after making sure that no one was around, she dropped the cigarette and put it out.

She took out her phone and quickly removed the SIM card. She then pulled out the locket that Kasem had given her from the pocket inside her purse. While away on her mission, she had hidden her necklace instead of wearing it. From inside the locket, she retrieved a half-size SIM card, a new smaller size issued by the Agency, and inserted it into the phone. The locket was just large enough to hold the half-size SIM. She keyed in her emergency number and waited for someone to pick up.

"What happened? Why are you using this number?" her handler asked, sounding frantic.

"We've got a serious problem. I think Nurah Bahar has been made."

"How do you know?"

"She left the painting of red flowers in her east window. She must have thought she was being watched." Lila could hear the blood pounding in her ears as she spoke.

"Fuck. How much does she know?"

"I'm not sure how much they could have gotten from her yet, but she's been in touch with another one of my other assets."

"She knew about another asset?"

"It's a long story." Lila had no idea how to explain the situation to her handler.

"You have to come in immediately. It's not safe for you."

"There's something I have to find out first." She closed her eyes in an attempt to keep her tone sounding calm and collected.

"You're the one who called the emergency number. An emergency means you come in."

"I'll be in by tonight. You need to warn my other assets. If Nurah has been compromised, I have no idea how deep it goes."

"Who else could she know about?"

"She knows about Kasem, but that's it. But if they already know about me, then the game's over."

"Okay. Come in as soon as you can." He sighed. "And—?"

"Yeah?"

"Don't get dead."

"I'll be fine," she said and hung up.

Lila walked back across the lot and headed toward Nurah's building. She looked behind her many times to make sure that no one was following her. She felt inside her purse and found the hilt of her Colt pistol. *Hope I don't need it.* She blinked rapidly and tried to push away the other thoughts that persisted in the back of her mind.

*This is my fault. I never should have introduced them to each other. I'm so sorry, Kasem.* She took a deep breath, trying to think clearly. *Why would Nurah call him?*

She crept into the building's stairwell and moved slowly up to the third floor with one hand on her gun. Her footsteps echoed in the empty stairwell.

Nurah's building had two apartments per floor, each with a bathroom window looking into the stairwell. The windows were frosted and had shutters, which locked from the inside and were usually kept shut.

Lila reached Nurah's bathroom window and crouched beneath it, listening quietly. *Nothing.* The room was silent. After waiting for about five minutes, she made her way up the last half flight of stairs that led to the front door of the apartment, holding her breath. She made quick work of the lock with a lock pick kit that she had in her purse.

The living room looked mostly as she remembered it. Everything seemed in order. She walked through to Nurah's bedroom, looking for signs of a struggle. She looked over Nurah's desk and noted the large space in the middle without a speck of dust. *No computer.* She checked the bathroom and the kitchen. The apartment was in such an orderly condition that it gave her the creeps.

Frustrated, she made her way to the bar area in the living room after grabbing a small bottle of water from the kitchen. She was about to take a sip when she noticed scuff marks on the grey tile of the entryway. She examined them closely, kneeling down and feeling around the individual tiles. There were several dusty footprints close to the door, as if a number of people had stood there recently. A few feet away from the door there were two low couches, one full-sized and one smaller loveseat, in the living room.

Next to one of them, there was a darker spot on the greenish-grey carpet. *That could be anything.*

She sank down into the loveseat while still staring at the scuffmarks and the larger stain on the carpet. She fidgeted a bit, trying to collect her thoughts. As she leaned against the back of the sofa, something pushed the cushion up so that it jabbed her in the butt.

She moved to the side and pulled up the cushion. *What the hell?* Her heart stopped when she saw what had been poking her. *Kasem's phone.* She picked it up and tried to turn on the phone, but the battery was dead. She bit her lip and thought back to what her handler had said. *You need to come in. It's not safe.* It certainly wasn't safe for her. *But what about Kasem?* She stuffed the phone into her purse and moved quickly to get out of the apartment, first making sure she had left the place as she had found it.

When she reached the car, she dumped the contents of her purse onto the passenger seat to find the car charger for her phone. Half of its contents spilled over the edge of the seat and she grabbed at them haphazardly while searching for her charger. When she found it under a notebook on the seat, she hastily plugged Kasem's phone into the charger and started the car. A minute later, it blinked on and she looked at the call log.

*Lila, Lila, Jamal,* she read. *Definitely his phone.*

She revved the engine and drove straight toward the center of the city, calling the emergency number again. "Kasem and Nurah have been taken."

"Are you sure?" her handler questioned.

"Yes. I found his phone in her abandoned apartment."

"Jesus, he knew where she lived?"

"I don't have time to explain. We have to figure out what's happened to them." She forced herself to focus on the road as she drove downtown at breakneck pace.

"Okay. Just come in. Once you're safe, we can work on them."

She reached for Kasem's phone and dialed Jamal's number.

"Kasem? Finally!" he said as he picked up.

"Jamal? It's Lila."

"Oh, okay. He's with you now, though? So everything is fine."

"No. I'm going to pick you up."

"What? Lila, what's going on?"

"I'll be downstairs in ten minutes. Just be there."

"Okay, of course, whatever you say." She could hear the combination of worry and confusion in his voice as he hung up.

Ten minutes later when he got into her car, she pulled away from the building without a word and drove like a stuntwoman straight toward the French embassy.

"Lila, what's going on? Where are we going?"

"Will you just shut up? I can't drive when you're talking like that," she yelled. The car was moving along even faster than her drive downtown. A moment later, she spoke in a calmer voice. "I'm sorry. Look, you just have to trust me."

Jamal nodded, clearly taken aback by her reaction.

She pulled up at the back gate of the embassy and rolled down her window. She pushed her thumb against the gate fingerprint scanner and opened her eyes wide for the retinal scanner.

*"Veuillez fournir le code d'urgence."* Please provide the emergency access code.

A keypad appeared on the screen and she tapped in a series of letters and numbers.

*"Accès accordé."* Access granted.

She breathed a sigh of relief and drove to the back of the embassy compound. She let Jamal into her apartment and turned to leave.

"Lila, where are you going? And why did you bring me here?" He stepped in front of the doorway to block her path.

"You'll be safe here. The embassy staff will take care of you."

"What are you talking about? I don't understand."

"Jamal," she said and bit her lip, struggling to find the words. "Kasem's been arrested. I brought you here to make sure that you're safe."

"Kasem's been arrested? For what?"

"I don't know the details, yet. Just stay here okay? I'll send someone to fill you in and I should be back in about an hour, but I really have to go."

He gave her a hesitant nod and stepped out of the way. "Okay. You'll explain everything later then?"

"I will."

Lila walked out of the apartment and headed to one of the decorative buildings within the embassy compound. She used her thumbprint to get through several access doors until she reached a secure conference room. Her hands were trembling as she dialed the number.

"Hello?"

"It's me. I'm safe now."

She could hear her handler sigh in relief. "Don't ever pull this kind of shit again."

"I won't. I understand."

"Now, let's get you in to debrief. I want to know what the fuck happened out there."

## *Tehran, Iran – Two weeks later, June, 2018*

Kasem had been imprisoned in a windowless gray cell with a solid metal door. Without daylight, he had lost all perception of time.

His captors had tied his hands to a ring hanging from the ceiling. The rope had started to cut into his wrists, leaving deep, red, open sores, and every part of his body screamed in pain. He could see that the skin on his chest and abdomen had turned black from bruising. The deep gashes on his back seared with even the slightest muscle twitch.

*She will get me out.*

Kasem had faced continual torture since he'd been captured. Somehow, he had managed to keep his resolve. Occasionally, he dozed off in spite of the pain and numbness in different parts of his body. When he slept, his dreams were always of the future he still yearned for with a home, a family, a career, and Lila by his side. He ached to hear his mother's voice, even when she was scolding him over the phone, and he yearned for the sound of one of her petty arguments with his father. His parents always squabbled, but each disagreement only lasted a moment and it was usually quite endearing to watch. He still hoped that he and Lila could build such a future together.

The door to his cell opened and his face recoiled as the light blinded him. General Majed stood before him yet again, but this time without the torture kit that he usually brought. Kasem attempted to raise his head a couple of inches, but he could barely make eye contact.

"Since you refuse to discuss your dealings with the West, despite our attempts at persuasion, I have come up with a better idea."

Kasem tried to focus his eyes on the general, attempting to hide how deep his fear ran.

"We have managed to locate your girlfriend."

Kasem snickered. "Yes, you've found out that she's no longer in the country."

"Actually, we've arrested her."

"You're lying! That's not possible!" Kasem yelled, trying to reassure himself.

"Perhaps this will prove that I am telling the truth."

The general held up a locket dangling on a silver chain—the one Lila always wore, the one he'd given her the first time they had said goodbye in Paris.

Kasem choked as tears clouded his vision.

"I will leave you now. I trust that you will be more forthcoming now that she is in our grasp as well."

The general turned and exited, slamming the door behind him. As the door shut, all of Kasem's remaining hope vanished with the departing beams of light. Sobs began to wrack his chest. *No! Could it all really be for nothing?*

****

# Chapter 14
## The Forgery

*Tehran, Iran – June, 2018*

Lieutenant Afshar was disturbed when he hung up the phone. His superior would not be pleased once he informed him of what he had just heard. General Majed demanded immediate updates on the search and attempt to capture Lila Tabbas. Kasem Ismaili had been shackled to the ceiling in a cell for sixteen days. He had hardly swallowed a morsel since they had informed him of her capture, so Afshar had now given the guards standing orders to force-feed him if he did not comply. They had yet to present Kasem with their offer, hoping that by the time they did, the news they had fabricated might actually be true.

He turned and walked down the hallway toward the general's chambers.

"General Majed, I've just received word," he said as he knocked on the door.

When there was no response, he knocked again. He pressed his ear against the door and heard movement in the room. "Sir, are you all right?" he asked as he pushed the door open.

He gasped in embarrassment as he surveyed the scene. The general was fully engaged with one of his mistresses. She screamed when she saw him and Afshar shouted, "Apologies! I did knock, sir!" He kept his eyes cast downward as he hastily retreated and slammed the door behind him.

A few minutes later, a disheveled General Majed arrived in the situation room. Once a chamber for an Iranian prince, the room was poorly designed for any kind of surveillance gathering or analysis, but the lieutenant had been taught never to complain. Still, it did add a certain grandiose air to the atmosphere.

"Good afternoon, General, sir."

"Yes, Lieutenant," the general grunted. "What do you have to report?"

"Unfortunately, the girl was able to flee the country before our men got to her. We won't be able to extract any information from her."

"No! You people are incompetent!"

The lieutenant kept quiet and listened to the general's rant, trying to keep any visible responses to a minimum. He had heard that the general was a bit unhinged and did not want to provoke him any more than necessary.

"She's a secretary, for goodness' sake! How could you lose her? How could they extract her so easily?"

"He must have communicated with his contacts that they needed to get her out immediately. Once he realized we had tracked his contact through a foreign agent at the French embassy, he had to work quickly." Lieutenant Afshar squirmed as he waited for the response.

"Have we found any valuable information he could have had access to?"

The lieutenant shook his head. "It doesn't appear that he could have communicated anything of value to either the Americans or the French."

"In that case, perhaps we can use her betrayal to our advantage."

"What do you mean, sir?"

"The news of her death could have a powerful influence on our young prisoner."

"Her death?"

"Her death, or at least her impending death." A conniving smirk appeared on the general's face.

"So you mean—?"

"Lieutenant, we can manipulate the situation to our advantage. We may even be able to turn him into our ally. It's clear that Western agents have extracted her. He still thinks that we're holding her because of that locket you found in the rental car she abandoned at the airport." The general paused and considered his next step. "If he does know nothing of value, then he must hope that the West will pay a ransom to save them both. We will make him believe that they are refusing to pay the ransom and allowing the two of them to remain in our custody. That should be enough for him to listen to our proposition."

****

As the door to his cell creaked open, Kasem's eyes recoiled from the bright lights of the hallway. Two days earlier, a guard had released the shackles that secured his wrists to the ceiling. The guard took pity on him when he saw the deep, raw cuts on his wrists and allowed him to remain in a heap on the floor.

His stomach had felt as if it were in knots ever since they informed him of Lila's capture. As far as he could tell, they were accusing him of selling state secrets as a spy and they hoped to derive some information about his activities from her. He knew that revealing the truth was out of the question. At least Nurah had only provided them with his name without mentioning that Lila was actually her handler. So far, they had been unable to break him with torture; he was too scared of jeopardizing Lila's well-being to say anything, but he shuddered at the thought of further waterboarding. Now that Lila was a bargaining chip, though, he was at their mercy. The general had left him to ponder these thoughts until now.

"Do you remember our last conversation?"

Kasem felt that the question scarcely deserved a response, so he remained quiet and motionless.

"We have someone of value to you."

Kasem began to quiver, but gave a slight nod.

"Now we have more information."

Then fear gripped him so hard that Kasem felt as if a rod had just been jabbed into his stomach. He gathered the strength to look up at the general, barely able to keep his eyes steady.

"We have verified the story you provided. We no longer believe that you sold anything of value to the French."

His stomach tightened further. If they believed that he had no more useful information, there was no reason to keep him or Lila alive.

"Since you can no longer give us anything of value, we have contacted your girlfriend's family for ransom."

"But she's from a poor family," Kasem said with a scratchy voice and all the energy he could muster. "She hasn't done anything wrong! There must be something else, right? The government will never allow—"

"Both the American and the French governments have refused her ransom."

The weight of that news caused Kasem's chest to tighten so much that he could barely gasp for air. *Refused? How could they? She's...?*

"But that's impossible!" he cried out, wishing he could convince himself as well.

"They have left you both to die. We can accuse her of being your accomplice, and we have more than enough to justify execution for both of you."

"No! There has to be something I can do. I'll do anything!"

"We might be able to come to an arrangement, but you would have to be willing to work for us."

"Work for you?" Kasem's disbelief was clear.

"If you refuse, then you leave her to die as well."

The general had cornered him and they both knew it. Even if he and Lila never could have a life together, even though she never would have allowed him to compromise himself for her, he had no choice. He would do whatever it took so that she could go free.

"She is unharmed?"

"For now, yes. I can make no guarantees if you do not comply."

"Will you free her?" Kasem asked shakily.

"We will release her into American custody."

Tears began building in his eyes. "Before I agree, I want proof that you have released her, that she is alive and free."

"You will have it."

General Majed turned and walked out of the stinking, dank cell. As he shut the door behind him, his face broke out into a conniving grin.

**** 

Lieutenant Afshar cursed with frustration as he looked at the most recent newspaper forgery attempt. "This is supposed to be a simple forgery of an American newspaper. How difficult is it for you to print something that looks real?"

"B-b-but, sir, we were supposed to receive a new printing press three months ago. The old one is not up to the task," said the manager of the commercial printshop.

"Do you want General Majed to come here to tell you himself how important this is?"

"N-no, but sir what can we do without the right equipment?"

"You make it work. Do you think that when we're out in battle we have the most effective artillery? The most effective camouflage? The most effective radar?"

The middle-aged printshop manager stared back at him, clearly unsure of how to respond.

"Well, we most certainly do not. We make it work. And that is exactly what you are going to do. If not, I will pull all of your government financing. Do you understand me?"

"Er, yes, sir." The printshop manager squirmed uncomfortably.

"Good. And make sure that one of your web designers puts the article in the *Washington Post*'s archives. I don't care how you get it there. Hack into their server and just get it in there."

"But, sir, what if they find it?"

"Bury it deep in the archives where no one who isn't looking for it would find it."

The manager averted his eyes and let out a long sigh. "Very well, sir."

"We put you on this assignment because you supposedly have the best printing facility in the city. I imagine that you wouldn't want us to discredit your sterling reputation?"

"Of course not, sir."

"And I am certain that you wouldn't want to face the consequences if you fail."

Without waiting for a response, the lieutenant walked out of the shop. General Majed would not be pleased that the newspaper forgery would be delayed another few days. Of course, he still did not understand why the general wanted such a document. *Who cares if the prisoner works for us? He's just some American traitor.*

Twenty minutes later, he walked into headquarters to report to the general. As he entered the situation room, the general turned and glared at him. Without any greeting, he shouted, "Do you have any news, Lieutenant?"

"Unfortunately, the printing will be delayed another few days, General."

"You useless scum, I gave you the slightest bit of responsibility and you cannot deliver. Be careful or I will make sure that you are never promoted."

Lieutenant Afshar fought to contain the laughter bubbling inside him. As a general, Majed had complete control over whom he promoted within his direct line of command. So, no matter what happened, the general controlled the lieutenant's promotion possibilities. Such threats were highly improbable because the general wouldn't send out a directive about something that he already controlled.

However, the manner in which the general made such threats was quite comical. His face turned red and his cheeks puffed out, much like a cartoon character the lieutenant remembered from his childhood. Even though the general was considered to be one of the most brilliant tactical minds in the country, his constant need to intimidate those around him made him seem as if he were a bumbling idiot, in addition to other actions. Really, who in his right mind did not lock the door when enjoying certain pleasures with a mistress?

Stifling his laughter, the lieutenant responded. "I-I-I'm sorry, sir. I will make sure that the, uh, that the printing is not delayed again."

"Why are you stammering? You are a military man. Get control of yourself."

As the general continued to glare and seethe, the lieutenant's laughter became even harder to control. In haste, the lieutenant excused himself. "I, uh, do apologize, sir. If you'll just, uh, just excuse me for one second."

Afshar heard the general growl at him as he rushed out of the situation room. When he was safely down the hall, giggles overtook him as he thought of how funny the general looked when he was trying to be intimidating. For most people, intimidation tactics were extremely effective. After all, few people could glare as powerfully as General Majed could. However, after spending so much time with him, Afshar could tell the general's glares apart—the severe glares from the momentary ones. He had seen other men in the military react similarly, and all of them would rally behind the general in a second if the need arose. Within military circles, men often joked about how the Iran-Iraq War would have gone very differently if General Majed—then only in his midtwenties—had been in charge of the Iranian troops. In battle, there was no one better to command them, but there was also no one more entertaining in his efforts to be intimidating on a day-to-day basis. The lieutenant settled his laughter and then walked back to the situation room, hoping he could control himself this time.

When the lieutenant entered, the general glared at him once more.

"You simply don't understand how much we will gain from this situation, Lieutenant. That boy is going to be one of our biggest assets." The general gave him a cunning smile. "He already hates the West for refusing to free his beloved Lila. He will succumb to whatever we ask and do whatever we require to pay his debt for letting her go."

"Yes, sir."

"I will never understand how something like love can cloud a man's judgment. I, myself, simply enjoy the pleasures a woman has to offer. I have my wife and she has borne me four sons, and I have my mistresses, but I would never let a woman have power over me!"

"Yes, sir." The lieutenant nodded, thinking of Farah, his mistress.

"Well, then. Shouldn't you be on your way? To encourage the wonderful men at the printshop to complete this assignment? You should stress its importance once more."

"Yes, sir."

"And please make sure that they understand the consequences if they are unable to deliver what we need from them."

"I will, sir. If there is nothing else, I will be on my way then."

"Dismissed. And Lieutenant—"

"Yes?"

"I cannot stress enough the consequences for you if you do not deliver, either. Your little dalliances will have to end."

"Sir?"

"Do not underestimate how much I know about your activities."

"Yes, sir." Lieutenant Afshar turned and exited the room fuming in anger. *Who the hell do you think you are? Farah is my business.*

Afshar sighed. No matter how angry the general made him, he had no recourse. He had no power in the military without the general's approval. Still, he and Farah would have to be more discreet about their relationship. As long as none of the men realized that he saw only one woman, they could not threaten her to get to him.

He did have control over his own actions, though. The lieutenant did not intend to return to the printshop today because there was little more he could do to impress upon them the importance of a good forgery. Besides, the printshop manager was hardly enough of an idiot to refuse a military request.

He walked down the hallway toward the empty chambers. Farah was his favorite mistress, and actually his only mistress. He tried to visit her at least once a day. Affairs in his home were in disarray. His mother and father had been pushing him to find a bride, but he saw little need for such commitment when he would rather spend time with Farah. They could spend hours lying in each other's arms, talking about how they had each grown up. He had shared stories about his childhood, about an accident that had left his brother permanently injured. He had even told her of how his father had forced him to join the military. In turn, she had spoken of how she was forced into the harem to settle her family's debts. She never told him about the other men she had seen that day because his emotions were too fragile. He already grappled with a tremendous amount of anger and jealousy at the thought of her life in the harem and his inability to provide for her and couldn't bear to actually hear about another man touching her.

Since she was a woman in the military harem, marriage was not in their future. It would destroy his career and both of them would be shamed publicly for the nature of their initial relationship. In all likelihood, the military would discharge him without pay and she would be unable to set foot in many of the more religious neighborhoods. They would be penniless and he would have no way to support her.

The time he spent with her, though, was the best part of his day. If supervising the execution of the newspaper forgery ensured that he spent more time in the Tehran command center, he would happily do it to stay close to her. They both fervently hoped that he would remain in Tehran as long as possible.

He entered the chamber and sat down on the large king-size bed. He reached over to the phone and pressed the number eight on the intercom. A few minutes later, she entered the room. "You summoned?" she asked in a deliberately husky voice.

"I would come immediately if you summoned as well."

Her eyes sparkled and she closed the door behind her. As the lock clicked, he stood behind her and wrapped his arms around her tiny waist. Turning around, she gave him a quick peck on the lips and attempted to escape from his hold. Giggling, they fell over each other onto the bed.

### *Tehran, Iran – Fourth of July, 2018*

Lieutenant Afshar walked out of the printshop smiling. After almost two weeks of consistent effort, he finally had managed to procure a credible forgery of the *Washington Post*. The shop had also managed to hack into the newspaper's servers and insert the article deep into its archives.

When General Majed first put him in charge of this assignment, the lieutenant had scoffed. During training, his superiors had deemed him a commander to watch, and he'd been optimistic when he received his first posting under such a renowned military leader. However, the general had no intention to teach his subordinates and ruled the ranks with an iron fist. Still, on occasion, even someone as frustrated as Lieutenant Afshar had to admire the general's foresight. Afshar had expected that procuring a credible forgery of a well-known American newspaper would be a simple and easy task. The government, and thus the military, unofficially owned the Islamic Republic News Agency. He thought that a request made to the manager of a government-funded commercial printshop would suffice for such a forgery. However, the process of creating an adequate forgery also had required Afshar to recruit one of the Islamic Republic News Agency's most talented print editors.

In addition, the antiquated printing press required six separate recalibrations to produce the copy that Afshar needed. According to Afshar's new best friend, the forgery would have required only one recalibration with the new, modern equipment they had been promised for more than a year. Since each recalibration took about sixteen hours on the archaic machines, they had to wait almost two weeks for the finished forgery.

As he walked back to headquarters, Afshar skimmed through the newspaper. "*Washington Post*, July 4, 2018," he read aloud. Details about various Independence Day celebrations occurring around the country littered the front page. Toward the bottom of the third page was the most important article, with the headline: "President Invites Tabbas to White House for Fourth Celebration." His eyes breezed through the first couple of sentences. As the general had ordered, the article mentioned that Lila had been released after a rescue attempt mounted by the US military.

*On June 29, Lila Tabbas, a French and American citizen, was rescued from Iranian custody by a SEAL team after being wrongfully imprisoned for stealing state secrets. She was held in an Iranian prison as a suspected spy for Western governments.*

General Majed had scoffed when he first read the fabricated article to be printed. "That is exactly how the Americans would portray a prisoner's release, even if they had negotiated or bargained anything of value. They are too patriotic to allow for weakness in the public eye. So much for their so-called freedom of press. They just allow this democratic republic bullshit to make it seem as if their people are free to say anything they wish. That government is completely in charge of its people, as any government should be to operate effectively."

Lieutenant Afshar did not agree with the Iranian government placing such tight controls on the press. He was a devout Muslim and believed in the Islamic Republic News Agency, but also felt their message would be stronger without the government forcing people to read only one point of view. Still, he could see the passion in the general's eyes when he spoke of it. In General Majed's twisted reality, the only hope for the Iranian people did indeed lie in government-exercised controls. The general genuinely believed that Iran would fall into chaos and ruin without such control.

Afshar stopped suddenly when he realized he had reached the headquarters building. He headed inside to speak to the general, newsprint in hand. *This had better convince him.*

\*\*\*\*

For the past two weeks, Kasem had been left alone to dwell on his fears for Lila's safety while he believed that she remained in General Majed's clutches. He tried to remember every moment that they had spent together, including their happiest times and a number of terrible fights. It seemed as if they could conquer the world together. Sometimes, he would fall asleep with those thoughts and dream of those moments.

He dreamed of touching her smooth café-au-lait skin and stroking her long black wavy hair. Sometimes he could almost see her big hazel eyes that seemed to pierce into his soul. She was always able to see the best in people, the best in him. He remembered some of their most romantic dates, such as the trip to Kish Island where they stole away from the glitz and glitter of the parties to walk along the beach alone. He recalled an elegant candlelit dinner at an expensive French restaurant, as well as a relaxed night at home when she made tacos for him because he missed the Mexican food he had grown up eating in New York.

The simplest things always stood out the most—how she fell asleep when they curled up on the sofa to watch movies or how her eyes sparkled with laughter when she teased him. His favorite memory was waking up next to Lila in his bed and wrapping his arms around her. He liked to cuddle her when they could sleep in on Friday mornings, the only day when neither of them had to be at the office early. If he really focused, he could conjure the faint smell of her coconut shampoo with traces of vanilla from her perfume.

Occasionally, he even had a sex dream and relived some of their most passionate moments. When he woke up to the emptiness of his dark cell, sometimes he was able to smile, but more often the loneliness was overpowering.

Even though his dreams were his biggest torment, he could not help but hold on to them. They were the only place where he could spend time with her, where he felt he could almost touch her. Most of the time, the details from his dreams escaped him though, and he clung to his memories, not wanting to forget any detail of her face or her mannerisms.

In his moments of greater clarity, he pondered the agreement he had made. He knew that she never would have let him do this. No matter what, though, he could not let her die.

At points of greatest weakness, he contemplated what he would do if General Majed did remain true to his word and freed her—maybe it would be better to die than fulfill his debt. However, somewhere deep within his subconscious, he still hoped that they might someday be together, and that, of course, would be impossible if they were both dead.

As the days passed, he grew angrier, allowing his rage to overpower his fear and grief. One night he yelled out into his empty cell, "Why do I have to face this choice? Damn you Americans! Damn you French! You left her to die!" His body shook with anger and grief.

That night he dreamed of her alone in a cell, chained to the ceiling just as he had been. Gaping sores covered her back. Powerless to help her, Kasem watched as a guard entered, released her shackled wrists, and pulled her to the ground. She screamed as the officer mounted her and she clawed at his face. Finally, with her face covered in a mixture of tears and grime, she gave up and let him have his way with her.

Kasem awoke weeping. *I can't let that happen to her.* He glowered into the emptiness. *They did this! How could they refuse ransom? How could they leave her behind?* After staring blankly at the darkness before him for some time, he finally dozed off again and succumbed to his dreams.

*Kasem once again was a spectator in Lila's cell. She was lying in a heap on the floor when the guard entered. He smacked her awake and she pleaded with him.*

*"Please, please, sir,"* she whimpered.

*The guard paid her no mind as he climbed on top of her. She was so weak that she did not even attempt to fight him.*

"No!" Kasem jolted awake. Pain radiated through his body. *She couldn't even fight back?* When his pulse began to slow, he felt a few tears roll down his face. His eyes fixated on the cell door with new resolve. *I have no other choice.*

The nightmares began to occur several times a day. Anytime sleep granted him respite from his solitude, his nightmares forced him to watch the future that awaited Lila if he did not comply with the general's wishes. Even in his daydreams, he visualized her being whipped and tortured.

The guards nearby made no attempt to help him. They delivered one or two meals each day and snickered at him from the hall. A day earlier, one of them had said, "Well, it is the Fourth of July for his lovely Lila. I wonder what she is doing to celebrate?" Bouts of laughter then overcame both men. In Kasem's mind, he envisioned breaking down the cell door and beating them with a baseball bat, again, and again, and again.

\*\*\*\*

As Lieutenant Afshar and General Majed approached Kasem's cell on July 5, they were surprised to find the corridor remarkably quiet instead of hearing the normal yelling that characterized the insanity eating away at Kasem's psyche.

"Prisoners who remain in that state for too long lose track of reality," General Majed explained to the lieutenant after the first outburst. On occasion, he would surprise the lieutenant by his genuine desire to teach. Of course, this desire only appeared for about five minutes every few weeks.

As they approached the door, Lieutenant Afshar forced himself to focus on the upcoming encounter with the prisoner.

"Lieutenant, before we go in, do you have any thoughts on this?"

190

The lieutenant looked at him surprised. "I hope this article is enough to convince him."

"That's why the forgery was so important."

Lieutenant Afshar nodded as the general continued, "When we get inside, I'll take charge."

"Yes, General."

"You will remain at my side and only respond if I direct you to do so."

"Yes, sir."

"Very well. It seems that he is quite calm today. This love business makes men as weak as kittens. They'll do anything to make sure they can keep chasing after their milk!"

The lieutenant nodded and tried to push thoughts of Farah out of his mind. For the second time since he had procured the newspaper forgery, he felt doubt creep into his mind. He knew how much the broken man in front of him must love this Lila to have sacrificed so much for her. It also concerned him that they had not been able to identify the crime that the prisoner had committed. *What would I do for Farah?* He blinked, trying to erase the sympathy building up in his eyes.

The general opened the door, allowing the hallway light to flood into Kasem's cell. Kasem looked up at them from the floor. He was half sitting, half lying down, as if he had just awoken from a dream. The lieutenant peered into his eyes, seeing the pain rooted deep within them. *Resignation,* the lieutenant thought, understanding the emotions smoldering within the man in front of him.

The general spoke first. "Get up, you filthy oaf! You stink."

Kasem rose slowly, putting weight onto his legs gingerly. When he finally reached his full height, he stood taller than both the general and the lieutenant. At the time of his capture, he was a well-built, intimidating figure. The lieutenant recoiled, appalled by Kasem's shaky limbs and emaciated form. After six weeks in a Tehran prison, the man in front of him looked like a shadow of his former self.

The lieutenant silenced his own thoughts and looked expectantly at the general.

"Yesterday, the American government had quite a Fourth of July celebration."

Kasem glanced toward the ground and then raised his eyes slowly to once again meet the general's gaze.

"You asked for proof that your Lila is alive and we have it." General Majed turned to the lieutenant who removed the newspaper forgery from his briefcase and handed it to Kasem with the third page on top.

"This is a copy of the *Washington Post* we managed to acquire from the American embassy. I believe the third page should be adequate proof for you, yes?"

Kasem's eyes scanned over the page. The lieutenant watched him squint as he struggled to focus after days in the cell with dim light.

"Can I have some time to read it?" he asked, his voice beginning to break.

"If you insist."

Kasem nodded.

The general's eyes softened, much to Lieutenant Afshar's surprise.

"You will be ready to begin your work tomorrow, boy?"

"Yes."

"In that case, I leave you to read the paper."

The two military men turned and walked out of the cell, leaving the guards to shut the door behind them. As they walked back to the situation room, both remained silent. The lieutenant wondered if he could have imagined the show of empathy from the general.

"General, sir?" said the lieutenant before he could restrain his curiosity.

"Yes, Lieutenant?"

"Permission to speak freely?"

"Granted," the general responded with a grunt.

"Why did you leave the newspaper with him? What if he suspects it is a forgery?" the lieutenant asked and then sighed. He had lost his nerve to ask the general anything personal about what he had seen while they were in the prison cell.

"The forgery is quite good, Lieutenant," General Majed responded. "I doubt he would be able to detect that it is fake after being stuck in that dark cell."

"Oh yes, of course."

"Somehow I doubt that was what you intended to ask me."

"I, I'm sorry, sir. I was just surprised you gave him the day to spend with the article."

"His training will wait a day. He is no good to us if his psyche is completely wrecked. If he remains quiet all day today—no more yelling, no more rages—then we have him. He will be ready for assignment as soon as we put him through training."

"Isn't that what training is for, sir?"

"Training should include more of the mental components. Our military training is for those who have joined for very different reasons. Can you think of anyone from your training class who joined because he was trying to repay a debt?"

"Only a financial one."

"But nothing of this kind."

"No, sir."

"We are hardly going to use him as a foot soldier. It would be too risky to include him in tactical support. He needs a rather *different* preparation."

"I see, sir."

"Lieutenant, you will understand in due course."

## *Paris, France – July, 2018*

"You have to help me get him out of there!" Lila exclaimed into the phone.

"I don't know how to tell you this."

"What is it?" Her voice grew shakier.

She heard her handler exhale loudly. "We just got word from another asset in the Iranian government."

"And?"

"There's been no word about your asset since you left Tehran."

She could feel her chest constrict as she forced out the words. "What are you saying?"

"Well, for starters, there's no way we can send in anyone to rescue him."

"But he could still be alive! We've been waiting on intel for weeks. Why don't we just send someone and find out ourselves?"

"You know we can't do that. If your asset is alive, there's no indication a new agent would be able to get him out of there."

"Fine. Then I'll go." Lila braced herself, waiting for her handler to refuse.

"We both know that there is no way you could get back into the country without notice. And if you did, you certainly wouldn't get out alive."

"I don't care, Alex. He's my asset, my responsibility."

"He knew the risks when you recruited him."

*He didn't, though.* "I don't care."

Alex was silent for a moment. "Fine, I'll send someone over to help you."

"Thank you."

**** 

Lila's handler, Alex Mittal, hung up the phone and then dialed another number.

"I need to place one of my agents in emergency asylum care due to severe PTSD." He spoke without a trace of hesitation. There was no doubt in his mind that this must be done. His agent needed help and he had to make sure that she received it as soon as possible. "I want you to bring her back to the States as soon as possible, but until then, she is not allowed to leave Paris under any circumstances."

****

# Chapter 15
## Training the Prisoner

*Tehran, Iran – July, 2018*

"You two will be in charge of the boy's training," General Majed instructed Lieutenant Afshar and Khaled Majed. "I expect you to take him to a point where he is as strong, swift, and clever as one of our best-trained spies."

Khaled noted Lieutenant Afshar's gesture of agreement as the general pulled him aside.

"Uncle, you pulled me away from my assignment to train this prisoner?" Khaled asked as he launched into a tirade at the general. "This traitor, whom you call 'the boy'? I cannot even disclose this assignment because it would detract from my career record! The only reason I'm still standing here is because we're family."

"And you honor me and our family by doing so," the general responded. "I ask you to trust me, not just as your uncle, but also as your commander and a military tactician. This boy is the key to my plans. You should not underestimate how manipulating someone's heart can yield a powerful ally or enemy."

With a sigh, Khaled nodded reluctantly. *Do I have a choice?*

"In this case, we are lucky enough to have gained a potential ally, but we need to set things up to make the most of him."

"I see. How would you like me to proceed?"

"You and Lieutenant Afshar can divide the training as you see fit. Use a minimal amount of delegation. I do not want this to become public."

"Because you think other commanders in the military would object?" Khaled scoffed at this idea.

The general glared at his nephew. The two men were the same height with widely built shoulders and stocky frames. Their features were remarkably similar, although the general had become considerably heavier over the past few years. Both boasted beady black eyes that could bore into another man's mind. Lieutenant Afshar shuddered as he observed the two from a distance.

"No," General Majed finally retorted. "I have a plan that must remain secret. There are few people that can be trusted with what I hope will happen."

Khaled's eyes widened with surprise. "You trust Lieutenant Afshar to that extent? Why? I must say that I'm surprised."

"He serves honorably, although we do not always agree, and he is clever. There is much you could learn from each other."

"Just because I did not follow in your footsteps does not mean that I am any less of a man," Khaled bellowed before he could stop himself.

"Calm yourself," General Majed snapped to interrupt his nephew. "You are foolish if you think that I would involve you in something of this magnitude only because you are family. Indeed, you are my brother's son, but my sources tell me that you are one of our best intelligence agents. So stop jumping to conclusions that make you look like an idiot."

Khaled gawped at his uncle, taken aback. "But I thought you disapproved of my choice to join intelligence instead of the military? I thought you believed that I was weak and unworthy because of it."

The general sighed. "I know that I must have made you feel as if I didn't approve of your choice not to follow our family's legacy. You were not without cause for thinking that. I did make you feel unworthy because of it, but the intelligence community can keep only so much secret from someone like me. I have heard much of your success in the past two years and there is no one, family or otherwise, whom I would trust with this task more than you."

Khaled felt as if a weight had been lifted from his shoulders. He had chased his family's approval for more than a decade. General Majed was the incredibly accomplished and decorated military man in their family, and neither Khaled nor his father, Yasser, had ever stood out in their schooling. Khaled had always felt like a failure compared to one of his cousins who seemed to follow General Majed's footsteps exactly.

Khaled's cousin Navid graduated from school at the top of his class and then attended one of Iran's best engineering schools. Navid entered the military and breezed through training. Khaled, who was eight years younger, always felt as if he lived in Navid's shadow. He watched at Eid as his father and General Majed praised and commended Navid. When Khaled finally started at university in a mediocre computer science program, his cousin received his first official military commendation for his efforts to protect a battalion from an attack by the Kurdish minority. In college, Khaled finally began to show real promise for a career track; he excelled at manipulating and decoding messages.

A family friend noticed this prowess and recommended that he consider an opportunity with intelligence. "You will have a more difficult life than you would as a programmer, but it will be far more exciting," he pitched to Khaled six years earlier. He went through basic military school followed by a full suite of intelligence training, and had risen through the ranks swiftly.

"The intelligence community is seducing you," the general once warned. "Be careful what you sign up for."

Khaled had disregarded the warning even though it was the only constructive comment he had ever received from anyone in the family, until now. *Does he actually believe in me now?* A wave of both calm and shock washed over him. He remained silent, absorbing everything his uncle had just said.

"Thank you, Uncle," he said, finally able to muster a response.

"You're welcome, nephew," the general replied, allowing a note of pride to drift into his voice.

Khaled felt a smile creep onto his face as he recognized the small but noticeable trace of pride. He took a deep breath and accepted the assignment. "What would you like me to do?"

"I will give you more details as the plan materializes further."

Khaled nodded, waiting for his uncle to continue. The pause lasted for what felt like ages.

"The boy must be trained in everything of value for an intelligence officer. He must be able to enter a room and blend in with the people there. He must be able to figure out how to infiltrate the tightest of social circles. He must be able to handle a weapon while acting as if he knows nothing about one. Whatever you know, whatever you have learned in your training, you must teach him. I trust your judgment. You know that world much better than I do."

"It will be difficult with his background, although it should be possible. Uncle, why do you want to recruit him? What's so special about him?"

"Nothing really. He's intelligent, athletic, has the right kind of build for what I'm looking for," the general smirked. "Really, he was just at the right place at the right time. We captured him and have the means to turn him, and we can capitalize on that."

"I see. What types of situations do you want him to be able to handle?"

"Anything and everything. He must learn Arabic. He already speaks English as an American and Farsi as an Iranian, but he must learn Arabic."

"You want him to speak as a native?"

"Yes."

Khaled frowned, uncertain of how to proceed. "It can be quite difficult for people to learn languages that well at such a late age."

The general's eyes widened. "He must speak well enough to natives that they believe he is from a different Arab country. So, to Kuwaitis, he could sound like a Jordanian, or to an Egyptian, he might sound like a native of Syria."

Khaled let out a long sigh. *No easy task.* "As you wish. I will start him on daily sessions of a minimum of two to three hours. He will be fully immersed in the language during those sessions."

"Is that how you were taught?"

"I was much younger, but yes, Uncle. I will teach him the same way that I learned Arabic."

The general crossed his arms, waiting for further details.

"I will also begin a training program that includes artillery, basic confidence training, self-defense, and situational adjustment. Will you permit me to involve one of my trainers?" Khaled continued.

"No. This must be kept as secretive as we can make it."

"I will have to report what assignment I am currently pursuing to my intelligence superiors."

"I should be able to handle that. You are taking part in a special family ritual to honor your cousin Navid's untimely death. The two of us will go through it together since both of my brothers cannot be with us today."

Khaled looked up sharply. "Navid is dead?" he asked, shocked. In spite of all the resentment he bore because of the attention Navid had received, Khaled had always admired his cousin.

General Majed looked decidedly surprised. "You had not heard? No one told you?"

The realization dawned slowly on Khaled. "I have been on assignment for the past six months," he said, his voice unsteady. "When? How? What happened, Uncle?"

General Majed took a deep breath. "Navid was posted on another security mission in the Kurdish area. Three months ago, on the way back to the base from an operational raid of a rebel building, their car drove over a stationary landmine." After another deep breath, the general continued. "They were too far away from a hospital to get help in time. You know how it is over there without any real infrastructure. Only one member of his unit survived, a Commander Tehrani. He said that Navid died shortly after the blast."

Khaled felt his chest heaving as he fought to keep his emotions in check. "And this Commander Tehrani, did he say anything else?"

"He was transported to a military hospital here in Tehran with several third-degree burns and shrapnel wounds, but they were able to save him. The doctors expect him to make a full recovery, physically, at least."

"Have you spoken with him directly?"

"Briefly, yes. He spoke well of your cousin. Commander Tehrani resigned his commission shortly after recovery, so I have not seen or spoken to him since."

"At least Navid died with honor." The pressure on Khaled's chest began to ease.

"You may be in intelligence, nephew, but you have a military heart," the general said.

Khaled gave his uncle a bittersweet smile. "Will we actually do anything to honor his death?"

"Yes. I will take leave to help you and Lieutenant Afshar in the beginning stages of the project. During that time, we will also conduct a family ritual to honor Navid and his memory. Most of the time will be focused on training the boy, but we shall still be able to do that."

"How long do you intend to take leave?"

"My leave period will be for about four to five weeks. After that, you and Lieutenant Afshar will be on your own. At that point, we'll come up with some sort of assignment for you to report to your superiors."

"All right, Uncle. I will send a notice to the base that I am going to take an emergency family leave to honor my cousin."

The general nodded. "I wish I didn't have to mar our first meeting after so long with such news."

"I know, but I am still glad that it was you who told me."

The two men looked at each other solemnly. "This is the first time we will work together," Khaled said.

"I look forward to it." General Majed turned to look out at the city of Tehran that stretched out below the rooftop where they stood. "Together, nephew, we are going to write a new chapter of our country's history."

## *Tehran, Iran – Three months later, October, 2018*

"As you can see from his most recent test results, he has made major progress over the past three months in overall fitness, weapons training, and marksmanship," Lieutenant Afshar concluded, waiting for the general's response with apprehension.

General Majed listened in silence to the progress report on Kasem's training. "What about his results on war tactics, situational integration, and the more psychological aspects of the training?"

"I have schooled the boy in some basics of war tactics, but so far, that has been more Khaled's area. He is conducting his own assessment on those aspects and he will be here presently, I'm sure," the lieutenant responded.

General Majed snickered. "I see you have also started to refer to him as 'the boy'?" he said with raised eyebrows.

Lieutenant Afshar stood in silence, unsure of how to respond. Deciding to ignore the jab, he continued, "If we were preparing to send Kasem Ismaili into a war zone, he would be reasonably prepared. To send him in as a spy, as someone who has to blend into the surroundings, that will require more time and work."

"Lieutenant, what are the next steps?"

"Khaled and I will have to discuss how best to increase the intensity of his training going forward."

"How is he behaving emotionally? Psychologically? Are you convinced that he has converted to our cause?"

Lieutenant Afshar paused, considering his answer. "Honestly, sir, I do not believe he is a true convert to our cause. Bu—"

"So you would recommend his cancellation?"

"No, sir. I was about to say that while he may not align with us on all convictions, I am quite certain of his commitment to us. He considers himself indebted for releasing his beloved Lila, and his

200

anger at the West for denying her ransom is real. It is a powerful force in our favor."

"Do you think he is ready for a first mission?"

"Pending Khaled's evaluation, yes, I believe he is ready for a simple mission."

Khaled interrupted their conversation when he rushed into the meeting room carrying a stack of papers. He saluted his uncle before taking a seat next to Lieutenant Afshar, still trying to catch his breath. "My apologies for being late, sir. The psychological session with the boy took longer than expected."

"So you both have taken to calling him 'the boy.'" The room was silent for a few moments before the general continued. "Lieutenant Afshar has provided me with an update on the aspects of the boy's training that he is overseeing. Please update me on your side, Khaled."

"I have been working with him on his Arabic, use of force tactics, situational integration, and any other psychological aspects of training."

The general gestured with his right hand to indicate that Khaled should continue.

"His Arabic has made quite a bit of progress, but I do not believe he could pass as a native speaker. He also has made progress with military tactics, and depending on the mission, may already be able to integrate into a number of psychological situations."

"So your prognosis is generally positive?"

"Yes, but I believe we will need several more months to work on his Arabic. He has a talent for languages, but it has never been cultivated, so it will take some time to bring it out properly."

"I see."

"The other caution I have, sir, is that he has been able to hold something back from me. I'm not sure what it is yet, but he is definitely hiding something."

"And what do you think that is?"

Khaled shook his head. "Honestly, I haven't a clue. Something about his past, but I haven't been able to access it."

"But you believe in his commitment to us?" General Majed said as he rubbed his chin.

"I believe he will honor his debt to you. Love was a powerful force to use against him."

"The lieutenant believes the boy is ready for his first mission. Would you agree?"

"Yes, as long as it is simple and doesn't require native Arabic."

General Majed's face crinkled with obvious satisfaction at his nephew's response. "No, the first mission I have in mind does not require native Arabic. I want him to tail a British diplomat, Sir Nigel Shaw. I believe Sir Nigel is a spy who controls an asset within our government. We need to find out who it is and then use that to our advantage."

"Do you have a file on this Sir Nigel?" Lieutenant Afshar asked.

The general pushed a folder across the table. "I'm sure there will be further information required, but this is what I had in my own personal records. It should give you enough to start preparing for the mission. Oh, and I want him to take care of this mission alone."

Afshar and Khaled glanced through the file together. "We should be able to work with this," Khaled agreed.

"Okay then. This meeting is adjourned. Keep up with the boy's training and let's see how he does on this operation."

The general rose to leave the room. "Sir, before you go, can I ask one question?" Khaled squirmed in his seat.

General Majed raised his eyebrows.

"Why is it that you want Kasem to take this mission rather than someone in counterintelligence?"

"This mission is purely for training purposes to ensure that he will do as we order. If we have to cancel him, I would rather figure it out on something that is relatively low priority. We can always put counterintelligence on it later. Give it some time and you will see why I want to use the boy over one of our own operatives." Without waiting for a response, the general turned and walked out of the conference room. Before he stepped out, he turned back toward the table and issued another directive, "Oh, and teach him some basic Kurdish. It might be useful."

## New York City, United States – October, 2018

"We have word on what happened to your asset in Tehran."

Lila stared at Alex, waiting for him to say what she already knew but had refused to acknowledge openly, even to herself.

"He was executed two days ago. I'm sorry."

She focused her gaze on the wall behind him. "Who gave the order?"

"The order was issued by General Majed, but it was executed by one of his lieutenants."

"Which one?" It took all of her willpower to keep her voice steady.

"A Lieutenant Afshar. He's a rising star in the military, but we don't know much about him. Do you want us to investigate further?"

She bit her lip to stave off tears. "No, that won't be necessary."

"Is there anything else?"

"No. Thanks for looking into this. I know you had to go out on a limb to send someone."

"You're welcome. I just wish I had better news. Are you going to be okay?"

"Don't worry about me. I'll be fine." She blinked rapidly, waiting for him to leave.

"I'm here if you need to talk to someone outside of your sessions."

"Thanks."

She watched the door shut behind him and finally allowed a stream of tears to fall slowly down her cheeks.

## *Tehran, Iran – October, 2018*

Kasem waited in silence for Sir Nigel Shaw to emerge from the British embassy on Ferdowsi Avenue in Tehran. He ran his hand through his hair. Under Khaled's instructions, he had let it grow longer, along with his facial hair, which he grew into a beard to disguise his face naturally. He was parked across the street from the embassy gates watching everything around him in supreme boredom. *Is this what a stakeout feels like?* He groaned. After waiting for more than an hour, he was trying not to lose focus. The afternoon heat had begun to dissipate with the first tendrils of dusk. The autumn air felt crisp, but it was marred by the heavy cloud of pollution that sat stagnant over the cityscape.

Leaning on the passenger seat, he grabbed the file he had put together on Sir Nigel. According to the file, Sir Nigel had entered Tehran under the name of Richard Stevens, a British engineer who was doing some kind of work at the embassy. Their reports thus far had showed that he moved around the city with minimal entourage.

For the past couple of hours, he had watched cars pour in to the embassy compound. Some fancy function was scheduled for networking among the diplomatic staff. Because of the timing, Kasem knew it would be next to impossible to watch everyone once the party ended in the next few hours.

He leaned back in his seat in an attempt to clear his head and shake off his fatigue. *Just want to sleep.* The doubts in his mind lingered and refused to be quiet, though. She was free now, so he knew that he should try to escape. He let out a long sigh, knowing he would never be able to elude them, especially with the tracking anklet he'd been forced to wear at all times. His only chance would be to stick around long enough to get a mission outside of Iran.

Several cars exiting the embassy compound caught his attention. He watched intently, hoping one was marked with the license plate number 896EM9 or 907YIN. *No luck,* he thought as they drove past him.

His mind shifted to Lila. *Wish I could see her.* The thought that he would never see her again made him feel as if lead weights restrained his entire body. Kasem shook himself and tried to envision being free of General Majed and the military forever. He smiled wistfully. *Maybe someday.*

From the corner of his eye, Kasem noticed two figures in ill-fitting suits about to pass through the embassy gates in a black Lincoln with plates 896EM9. He squinted to get a better look at the passenger. *Looks like him.*

Kasem clicked a couple of photos of the driver as the car waited for the embassy gates to open. A couple of minutes later, he started his car to follow the diplomats as subtly as possible. Two blocks away from the embassy, the sedan stopped and the two men exited the car. Sir Nigel Shaw and the man accompanying him slowly walked down Ferdowsi Avenue and then veered to the right onto a narrow side street. Kasem stopped his car a block behind them and exited quietly once they disappeared around the bend. He moved quickly to the corner ahead of the alley and peered around.

*Where is he?*

Cautiously, he made his way around the corner and walked down the alley. It was a dead end and Kasem could see Sir Nigel and the other man standing behind a giant dumpster. He sniffed the air in surprise. *Hash? Here?*

He watched them smoke their cigarettes, trying to get a good look at the other guy. From what he had been able to see, the man did not look like the picture of Sir Nigel's senior aide in the file.

To keep out of sight, Kasem crept up to the other side of the dumpster. There was a gap about a foot wide between the container's edge and the wall behind it. He watched through the gap and waited until he saw the diplomat put out the cigarette and then toss it to the ground. Sir Nigel then turned around and began walking back down the alley, followed closely by the other man.

*Shit.* Kasem squeezed into the crevice between the wall and the dumpster while trying to keep himself from throwing up at the smell; his nose was pressed against the side of the dumpster.

When he peered over the edge, he saw Sir Nigel walk back to the end of the alley toward the car, which was still waiting for him on the main avenue. Kasem squirmed out of the crevice and limped over to the end of the alley. They started the car and drove away before he could follow. From where he stood, he could see the car reenter the embassy's gates without any other stopovers. *Damn,* he thought, heading back to his car.

Later that evening, Kasem tailed Sir Nigel back to his home in a locked compound. He watched the lights in the apartment go dark. *No leads.* He sighed and turned to drive back to the military base where Khaled Majed had provided him with a small barracks-style studio. Something about the scene in the alley irked him, though. It was unusual for a visitor to walk around Tehran alone, even with a car nearby, especially in the evening. Smoking hash was by far the strangest factor since Sir Nigel hardly seemed like the type.

Before heading home, he drove back to the area near the embassy and walked down the alley with a flashlight. It was dark and dank, as expected. The air smelled like putrid garbage and sewage. He walked to the end where he had seen Sir Nigel smoke the cigarette. He shone the flashlight on the alley's walls to look for any sign that the diplomat might have left. He saw no chalk marks or visible signs on the walls that could be used to communicate with a source. *Nothing.*

He was exiting the alley when a realization struck him and he ran back past the dumpster to where the men had smoked the hash earlier that day. Instead of shining the flashlight at the walls, he shone it on the ground where Sir Nigel had stood. It had been cleared. *No cigarette butts. Got you.*

In his room that night, Kasem spent several hours trying to figure out who was with Sir Nigel in the alley. He compared the photos he'd taken of the driver with a number of other shots from the embassy's manifest. Sir Nigel smoking hashish with either a bodyguard or a driver seemed strange enough, but with someone not in the records at all?

For the next several days, Kasem kept watch on the alley. He saw many different people go there to smoke, usually in groups. He even saw a couple sneak back there. Kasem looked on engrossed as the man lifted the woman up against the wall, pulled down his paints, and they had passionate sex. When she started to scream, he covered her mouth to keep her quiet until they were finished. After watching the scene in front of him, Kasem felt even more deprived.

One week later, he finally had a stroke of luck. Kasem watched as Sir Nigel Shaw's senior aide, Edward MacIntyre, ventured down the alley. This time he smoked an ordinary tobacco cigarette rather than one with hashish. *Maybe it's a different signal?* Kasem thought as he observed.

Later that night, Kasem watched another man enter the alley for what seemed to be a quick smoke. Before leaving, the man gathered all the cigarette butts left in that part of the alley into a plastic bag. Kasem took a number of pictures of the encounter and then followed the man, wondering if he was the driver from the previous day.

He tailed the man on foot for a few blocks, trying his best to stay out of sight. After turning the corner, he saw the man jump into a parked car and veer away. Before the car was out of eyeshot, he did manage to catch the license plate number. "0-9-7-L-K-8," he said repeatedly to himself as he walked back to his car.

When he reached the military compound, he logged on to his database of government employees. As part of the operation, Khaled had provided him with a government-issued computer, albeit one that was stripped of much of its functionality. Still, he was able to do a search on the license plate number, which he found belonged to a local car rental agency. He noted the phone number and address of the rental company.

Early the next morning he drove to the rental agency's nearest office. He walked up to the reception desk and pulled out a police officer's ID and badge. "I'm with the police. I'm afraid we've found one of your rental cars abandoned on the outskirts of the city. We've already contacted your corporate office about someone picking it up at our impound lot, but I'd like to track down who rented it to see why it wasn't reported stolen."

"I'd be happy to help you, sir. Do you have the license plate number?"

"Yes, it's Tehran, 0-9-7-L-K-8."

The receptionist typed the numbers into the computer and they waited. "Here it is, sir. The car was issued to a Naveen Arzani. It was leased by someone on his behalf, though—Abdullah Ghazi. Would you like the phone number and address provided as well?"

"Yes, please." Kasem wrote down the information she relayed in a small spiral notebook. "Thank you," he said before he walked out.

Later, a quick search in the computer database yielded details on Naveen Arzani, who worked for the Ministry of Defense. The next morning he reported the information to Khaled Majed.

"Very good, Kasem. I think this is enough to confirm that Naveen Arzani is indeed providing information to this British diplomat."

"It could be either Arzani or Ghazi. They are both with the Ministry of Defense. That's why the guy didn't show up in the database when I searched with just the picture. I don't have clearance to view full profiles of internal staff."

Khaled nodded. "We can use this to our advantage. I'll continue to have Arzani and Ghazi tailed. You can focus on your training. When we need you back on this operation, I will let you know."

Over the next month, General Majed proceeded to feed false information to Naveen Arzani through the Ministry of Defense while Kasem continued his training. He had almost forgotten about the mission when Khaled summoned him one evening.

"We need you to finish the operation related to Naveen Arzani and Sir Nigel Shaw."

Kasem's heartbeat quickened. "What do you want me to do?"

"We need you to set up a car bomb."

"A car bomb? For Arzani?" Kasem blinked several times, trying to remain calm.

"Yes. Please take care of this within two days and make it look like one of the ethnic minority separatists groups is to blame."

"I didn't agree to this. I never agreed to kill someone." Kasem could barely get the words out.

Khaled looked at him solemnly. "I believe you did when we released your girlfriend. Just in case, I thought we might need a bit of leverage. Here," he said as he handed Kasem a picture of Lila sitting in the backseat of a car.

Kasem swallowed slowly. "What are you saying?"

"There's a date on the picture. It was taken in Paris a couple of days ago. We still have access to her if we need it." Khaled reached across the table and snatched the picture from Kasem's hand. "Do you understand?"

Kasem's voice caught in his throat and he walked out of the room shaking.

Two days later, Kasem watched with tears in his eyes as a car bomb exploded in the middle of Imam Khomeini Square. That night he listened to the news report about the event.

*"A car bomb exploded at 18:30 this evening in Imam Khomeini Square. The death toll currently stands at twelve people with another eight seriously injured. The incident is being blamed on a Kurdish rebel group, although no group has yet claimed responsibility for it."*

Kasem lay in bed and tried to blink away his tears. *How could I?* The question repeated in his mind until the sandman granted him temporary reprieve as he fell into a restless sleep.

\*\*\*\*

# Book VII
# 2021

# Chapter 16
# The Final Component

*Al-Rai, Kuwait – June, 2021*

The Ahriman growled as he circled the underground parking lot at The Avenues, a mall in the Al-Rai district just off Fifth Ring Road. Located outside the more frequented parts of the city, The Avenues was the largest mall in Kuwait. As usual, the mall was packed over the weekend and it was impossible to park close to the cinema.

He squeezed his compact Toyota Yaris rental car into a parking spot partially occupied by a giant Mitsubishi Pajero sitting well over the dividing line. Gingerly, he managed to open the door and exit the vehicle while cursing the other driver under his breath. He headed straight to the entrance of Carrefour where he inhaled the chilly air-conditioned air from inside the mall. Bypassing the hypermarket, he walked straight toward the cinema on the other side of the mall.

A short line at the ticketing counter meant he only had to wait for a couple of minutes. "Two VIP tickets for the new *Star Wars* movie," he said when he reached the ticketing agent.

"Certainly, sir. That'll be ten KD, please."

"Thank you," he said as he handed over the money and pointed at the seating chart. "Could you please give me those two seats in the back?"

"Certainly, sir."

After grabbing the tickets, he headed to the snack counter and bought a large bag of popcorn. *Perfect way to design a drop,* he thought, grinning as he helped himself to a handful and walked toward theater number six. He got in line at the entrance and studied a large advertising cutout next to the women's bathroom.

When the queue outside the theater started to dissipate, a young woman exited the bathroom and walked up to him.

"Did you remember to get the caramel popcorn for me?" she asked.

"I did," he said, looking back at her. Instead of noticing her curvy figure, he checked for the three items she was supposed to have on her person. *Red Fiorelli purse, navy blue Pierre Balmain watch, and a pair of red-tinted sunglasses on top of her head. Check, check, and check.*

"Would you like to try some now? Or should we wait until we're inside."

"Let's head inside," she said, grabbing a handful of popcorn from the bag in his hand anyway. With her other hand, she took his arm and they walked into the theater.

"Next time, ask for the sweet and salty popcorn to be mixed," she instructed.

"Sarah, Sarah, Sarah, you do like to be difficult," he teased, shaking his head.

Once they found their seats, he handed her the popcorn. "I know you'll eat more of it than me."

The Ahriman sat back and enjoyed the movie. Halfway through, she handed the bag back to him. "I left you a little bit," she whispered into his ear.

He nodded and they watched the rest of the movie in silence.

When the credits rolled, they walked out of the theater and she gave him a hug. "Let me know if you need me to take care of any more errands," she whispered seductively into his ear. "I'm always game if I get a free movie out of it, or anything else."

With that, she turned and walked away. The Ahriman headed back toward Carrefour where he purchased some fruit to eat back at his hotel. He stuffed the almost empty bag of popcorn into his shopping bag. When he got to his car, he checked the inside of the bag for the three items that he had requested. He found a small airtight container and the remaining two components. *I'll assemble the parts tomorrow.* He started the car and headed back to his hotel in Salmiya.

## Surra, Kuwait – June, 2021

"Petra, I just pulled up the list of places you sent over to me." Alex's image appeared on her computer screen via the teleconference encryption software installed on her laptop. He rubbed his eyes as he scanned through the list of ten places.

"Great. Any thoughts?" Petra asked.

"I'm concerned. Are you certain that you used the right screening criteria? We'd get more hits with just the word 'palace.'"

She frowned visibly. "I went with my gut."

Alex gave her a skeptical nod. "Can you quickly run me through your process?"

"I started with the big picture and then went through the logs from Majed's and Fayed's offices. Both of them are focused on the elections, and my guess is that Majed has a source inside the Emir's offices. Someone called 'OZ.' I couldn't get anywhere with that lead, so I went with the word 'palace' and ran it through the Agency's database. To limit the search size, I put in a few criteria: anti-Islamic, pro-Western, and Middle East relevant. That gave me the list you have in front of you."

"Okay, so assuming that this list is correct, what should we do with it?"

"We should heighten our intelligence presence around those places for starters."

"Okay, that's fine." Alex scrolled down toward the bottom of the list and frowned.

"What is it?" she asked, noticing the expression on his face.

"Did you see number ten on the list?"

Petra looked back at the list. "Bayan Palace? Yeah, I saw that. Somehow, I don't think they would have a target within their own country. It must be a global target. I'll keep monitoring the bugs to see if anything would suggest that."

"Why would the Emir's home show up under a search with 'anti-Islamic' as the criteria?"

"You know how the search works, Alex. If the Agency has intelligence that cited something that way, it'll show up in the search."

"Meaning that some of the newspapers or other sources we use have labeled the Emir as anti-Islamic? Isn't that a bit excessive?"

Petra shrugged. "It is, but for extreme Islamists, that might be the case. It's not that farfetched. For one thing, Fayed has implicated the Emir as someone without a commitment to Islam on several different occasions. Still, like I said, I doubt they would target something within Kuwait."

"Okay. I'll keep you posted on anything we turn up in any of these places."

"Great. I'll talk to you later then."

"Sure." Alex paused, about to hang up the call. "Wait, just give me a second." He opened up the internal Agency database on the different places on Petra's list and keyed in agent alerts for the top nine potential targets she had unearthed. "Petra, I've got a bad feeling about this. If there is a threat in Kuwait, will you be able to do much on your own? We should ask Chris to send a team in to help you. You might need backup."

"Aw, Alex that's sweet of you. You're a good mentor, you know? Even if you did recommend that I do something that I swore I would never do again. And now you want to be protective to make yourself feel better." She gave him a tight smile. "Don't worry, I'll be fine. If I need backup, I'll call it in."

"All right, fine. So when are you going to stop holding that against me?" he retorted. She hung up without bothering to give him a response.

When her irritation with him subsided, Alex's words echoed in the back of Petra's mind. *I've got a bad feeling about this.*

## *Salmiya, Kuwait – June, 2021*

The Ahriman let himself sleep in and relax the next morning before he headed into the kitchen at around eleven to begin his recipe. He pulled out a large pot and began mixing small amounts of different ingredients.

He ground up some sugar, charcoal, sulfur, and saltpeter separately. Before mixing them together, he added a small amount of water to the saltpeter. He then mixed it together slowly, poured the mixture through a sieve, and left it to dry on a large tray next to the window.

Separately he mixed some saltpeter and sugar in a skillet on low heat. He slowly stirred the mix together until it liquefied. Laying out a piece of foil, he poured the liquid onto it, folded the foil around it, and placed it into one of the components he had received in the mail. The component was shaped like an elongated cylinder with a translucent white lid attached to the bottom. It was made from a special sort of durable plastic used as a substitute for metals in assembling machinery that needed protection from rust.

On top of it, he attached another white lid that had arrived separately and then placed a second plastic cylinder on top of it. Each lid was equipped with a notch system that allowed the two cylinders to fit together exactly.

He checked on the powder he had left to dry. It wasn't ready yet, but that did not concern him since he would not need it until later.

Going back into the kitchen, he removed the last component he'd received in the mail. It was a small jar without a lid made from a similar high-density plastic featuring the same notch system of the other components. He grabbed the Carrefour shopping bag with the empty bag of popcorn. From inside the popcorn bag he removed two of the pieces that Sarah had given him. After placing one of them inside the jar, he attached the whole thing to the bottom of the cylinder containing the liquefied sugar and saltpeter mixture and attached the detonator.

It was a perfect fit.

### *Kuwait City, Kuwait – July 1, 2021*

Grant had been sweating constantly since he had arrived at Kuwait International Airport. He stood in his boxers just below the air conditioning vent in his hotel room as he tried to cool off and figure out what to do next. He turned to the mirror and glared at his reflection. After trying to imagine a solution, he finally gave up and dialed a US number from his hotel room's landline.

"Hello," he heard from the other end.

"Carlos, is that you?"

"Yes. Who's this?"

"Can you hear me?" Grant shouted over a wave of static. "It's Grant Antrobus. Petra's boyfriend."

"Grant?" Carlos said, sounding surprised. "How are you? Are you on the subway or something? I can barely hear you."

"Not exactly. It's an international line."

"International?" Carlos paused, inhaling sharply. "No, you didn't. Please tell me you didn't. Did you go t–?"

Grant swallowed loudly. "Yeah. I'm in Kuwait."

"What the fuck? Are you insane? What are you going to just walk up to her and say hi? How the hell do you think you're even going to find her? We don't have a clue what kind of cover she's using or a—"

"I don't know, Carlos. I didn't really plan this out."

"No shit! You asked for my help so that you could stop worrying and now you could jeopardize her entire operation. Do you realize you could blow her cover?"

"Er, I hope not."

"You have got to be kidding me. Do you understand what could happen to her if you blow her cover?"

"Well—"

"You could compromise her safety and you might even get her killed! You're lucky she's not in Tehran or somewhere else, buddy. At least Kuwait's an ally of the fucking Agency countries."

Grant waited in silence as Carlos cursed him steadily. The line was fuzzy enough that he could not catch every word, but the gist was clear.

*He's right. What the fuck am I going to do?*

Several moments later, Carlos stopped lecturing momentarily. "Are you still there? Did this damn line get cut off?"

"I'm here," Grant said meekly.

"So, what the fuck are you planning to do?" Carlos's tone still reeked with frustration and disapproval.

"I don't know. I just know that I need to find her." He took a deep breath. "And for that, I need your help."

"You want my help again? I can't believe I listened to you before. I thought I was helping you to get some peace of mind. I know Diane could have used some back when I was still going on missions. I didn't realize that you are a total dumbass!"

"Carlos, I'm going to find her with or without your help. My best chance at not blowing her cover by accident is having someone help me, someone who knows the game."

The line was silent for what felt like an eternity. Grant bit his thumbnail as he looked at the handset. *I'll never find her without his help!*

"Fucking shit. Okay, I'll help you because I'm done with those assholes at the Agency making everyone choose the job over everything else. I can give you a way to get a message to her."

Grant's heart leaped into his throat. "Really? Okay, thank you."

"But if you don't hear from her today, and I mean *today*, then you get your ass back on a plane to New York. Is that clear?"

"Yes. Absolutely." *Hell no.*

"Okay. I'll give you an emergency frequency code."

"What's that?" *How have I never heard of this?*

"Every agent in the field carries an emergency com device. It's standard field tech that's usually issued to a field agent right when they're recruited. If they are using the same one for Petra that she used to have, you can get an emergency message to her with it. It'll be encrypted so that if anyone else finds it, the message will look like gibberish or spam."

"Oh..." Grant stopped, considering. "What if they've changed her code?"

"Nothing I can do then, buddy. There's no way I could get her new code. If you're completely desperate, you could try sending her an e-mail. She might be checking, but she might not."

"Okay..."

"You have to try not to worry so much. They asked Petra to go back because she was actually really damn good. She knows what she's doing."

"But that doesn't mean nothing can go wrong."

"Something can always go wrong. Anywhere, anytime. You just have to wait and see."

Grant sighed. "Okay, let's try the code."

"One second. I have to go find it."

Carlos left the phone on hold. Grant's hands continued to grow clammy as he held on to the phone. *What the fuck am I doing?*

"Okay, I found it," Carlos finally said through the static.

"Go ahead," Grant said, grabbing a pen and a piece of paper.

"W-X-N-8-9-5-6-8-J-K-X-L-E-X-4-8-9. Did you get the whole thing? It's seventeen characters."

When Grant finished writing, he read it back to Carlos to confirm that he had correctly transcribed the code.

"Okay, so how do I do this?"

"Send a message to her usual e-mail address and put that in the subject line. The encryption will happen automatically," Carlos explained.

"You mean she's checking her usual e-mail address?"

"Probably not very often, but yeah, she might check it. This is an emergency frequency message. She'll get it whether or not she's checking her e-mail."

"What do you mean? How could she ge—"

"The message will forward to her special com device because of the code. All agents are required to check their coms at least once a day," Carlos interrupted.

"I see. Which e-mail should I use? Agency or personal?"

"Agency."

Grant nodded slowly. "Okay, then I guess that's it."

"That's all I've got, so good luck. And hey, Grant, memorize the code and destroy that piece of paper. It would be bad if that got into the wrong hands."

"Okay. I will."

"Bye then."

"Carlos?"

"Yeah?"

"Thank you. This means so much." Grant wished he could reach through the phone line and shake Carlos's hand.

"You're welcome. I just hope you don't fuck things up too badly."

"I hope so too."

The dial tone *beeped* back loudly as Carlos hung up the other end.

Grant looked at the phone and then at his face in the mirror. Resisting the urge to punch the mirror, he walked over to his computer and spent a moment looking through the files he had gathered.

He stared at his screen, thinking it over. *Here goes nothing.*

He clicked through the Agency's messaging system and wrote her a short e-mail message with the emergency encryption code in the subject line.

*Arrived in KWT. Staying at JW Marriott, room 507. Would like to see you. – G*

He hesitated before finally pressing send. *Hope this doesn't ruin everything.*

## Surra, Kuwait – July 1, 2021

"I just received word from our contact at Textron," Khaled whispered into his phone.

"And?"

"They have requested that Reynolds intervene with the Emir. They want to award the contract before the elections."

"Did he accept? When will Reynolds arrive?" Khaled could hear the excitement in his handler's voice.

"He'll be here in three days. You were right about the timing."

"Just make sure that he delivers."

"I will, Uncle."

**\*\*\*\***

# Chapter 17
## The Uninvited Guest

*Surra, Kuwait – July 2, 2021*

Petra groaned as the early morning sun streamed through her window. *My alarm still hasn't gone off. It's not even seven in the morning!* She stretched her arms and pulled herself out of bed.

After freshening up quickly in the bathroom, she sat down at her computer and skimmed through the most recent logs generated by the bugs in Fayed's and Khaled Majed's offices. As she started reading, she typed in the passwords for the Agency's server login process, which took several moments.

She was in the middle of reading a conversation between Khaled Majed and his source in the Emir's office when the server buzzed, indicating a video chat request for her. It was from Alex, also working early in Istanbul. She accepted and his image appeared on screen.

"Hey, Chris told me you needed a list of the Emir's employees."

"Yeah, I asked for it a few days ago."

"Sorry about the delay. Must have slipped through the cracks. Here it is."

Petra opened the message's attachment and started skimming through the list.

"Do you need any help right now?" Alex interrupted.

"Actually, yeah. I'm trying to figure out who Khaled Majed's source is in the Emir's office. The logs show someone tagged as 'OZ.' Hopefully, it's just initials, but it could be something else." She sent Alex a copy of the relevant log and then continued looking through the list of several hundred names.

"Is there a way to segment this list?" Petra asked, feeling a bit daunted by its size.

"We can try."

"The mole would need to be someone in the Emir's house or office. I don't think it could be a driver or delivery person. Also, the person must be someone with regular access, so no decorators or contractors."

"Okay." Alex looked at the list he had received from one of his researchers. "Damned rookies put this together," he muttered. "Complete mishmash of a list." He scowled. "I think the last two pages list people with regular contact with the Emir's home."

"Thanks."

"Wouldn't the source just need to be there once? He could plant a bug the way you did in Fayed's office."

Petra drummed her pen against the desk, thinking. "The Emir's office is checked often. It would be pretty risky."

"Fair enough. These are the names that have some relationship with the letters 'OZ.'" He keyed in four names from the last two pages. "Unfortunately, we don't have enough access to give you more information than that."

Petra leaned forward onto her elbow and sighed. "Yeah, that's why you needed me to go in there in the first place. I'll see what I can do from here. Try to find out anything else, if you can. If we can turn the source, it might get us some information on what Fayed and Majed are doing."

"Will do. Based on what you've read, what do you think?" he asked.

"Of the source?"

"Yeah."

"He's a snake."

"For gathering information on the Emir? Petra, isn't that the pot calling the kettle black?"

She grinned, thinking of how many sources she had used during her previous missions in Europe and the Middle East. "Very funny. I may look good in black, but that kettle is extra slimy. Any alerts on the locations we discussed?"

"Nothing special. I'll send you anything that comes up."

"Thanks, Alex. Hey, do you have a few minutes to look at these logs with me? I'm not making much headway."

"Sure."

She sent over the most recent logs and gave him some time to skim through them. "There doesn't seem to be anything new or definitive. I'm not sure what to think."

"This is the full record of the conversations, on and offline, that your bugs have picked up?" Alex asked.

"Yeah. Did you notice something?"

"Maybe with the log times. Both Khaled Majed and Marzouk Fayed disappear from their office computers for the entire afternoon on several days."

"Really?" Petra glanced back through the log times. "You're right. If they aren't spending the whole day in their offices, then where are they spending that time?"

"That's the question you have to answer."

"Between June twenty-third and today, they have been out of the office for at least half the day on six separate occasions. Maybe I should have planted a tracker on them," she grumbled. Looking back at the computer screen, she rubbed her chin, trying to figure out what to do.

"You might be able to track them depending on how often they go. It must be some other office. It's not possible for them to be at that many four-hour meetings when Parliament is out of session, especially with both of them gone at the same time."

"Yeah, it can't be a coincidence. I could try tailing them. Can you track them on satellite just in case?"

"Sure, no problem," Alex agreed.

"Great, thanks."

He scrutinized the schedule further. "It looks like they usually clock in for the mornings and then disappear in the afternoon."

"Yeah. I'll start at their offices. Maybe they'll go somewhere together."

"We could try to track them separately via satellite if required, but it would be difficult." Alex pursed his lips.

"Yeah, we'll see if they stick together first."

"Send me a message on the emergency com system a few minutes before you want me to start tracking. I'll use the GPS from your device for the satellite lock."

"Thanks, Alex. Will do. Talk to you later then."

"Yup."

Petra disconnected and proceeded to get dressed. She then pondered strategy for the next thirty minutes. She was on her way out the door when she remembered what Alex had said. *Shit, my emergency com.*

She began rummaging through her purse for her emergency com device. *Hate big purses.* Petra had forgotten about checking the device the previous day and she knew how important it could be. When her hand finally closed around the palm-size device that looked like a soft pink lipstick container, she pulled it out and clicked the slider on the end to transmit her "I'm safe" message code. Only then did she notice that the outside rim had turned from its normal shade of gray to bright red. *A message? Alex didn't mention anything.*

She slid the cap in the coded configuration she had learned years ago to release the interior screen. Without the code, the container would open up to reveal an old, dirty-looking lipstick that most people would never attempt to test. A moment later, the screen lit up and a message from Grant appeared. She read it and her blood started to boil. *What the fuck? He came here?*

Quickly, she checked the bug logs to see if Khaled Majed was already in the office. She hoped fervently that he would stay there for a few hours. In the meantime, she would find Grant and kill him for being so foolish. She grabbed her car keys and then picked up her computer as well. Since Grant had unilaterally decided to show up in Kuwait, he might as well make himself useful.

Fuming the entire way, Petra drove into the main part of Kuwait City. She parked across the street from the Marriott Hotel and called the front desk.

"Marriott Hotel, good morning."

"Hi, I'm calling to speak to one of your guests, Mr. Grant Antrobus," she said.

"I'll put you through. Hold, please."

After three rings, Grant picked up. "Hello?"

"Hi."

He recognized her voice immediately. "Hey P—"

"Shut up and listen to me. I'm heading upstairs to your room."

"Um, okay. Great."

"I'll be there in five minutes," Petra said before hanging up on him.

She walked into the hotel lobby and went straight to the elevator lobby in the back. When another couple arrived, she ducked into the elevator after them and waited until they unlocked the keypad with their room key. *I hope it doesn't require floor-by-floor access,* Petra thought as she watched them press the button for the eighth floor.

"Could you get five for me please?"

"Sure."

The button for the fifth floor lit up and Petra smiled politely. "Thank you."

When the elevator reached the fifth floor, she walked straight down the hallway and knocked on the door to room 507. She took a deep breath. *I'm going to kill him.*

Grant opened the door and went to put his arms around Petra, but stopped abruptly when he saw her glare.

"C-come in."

"Thank you for being available for this interview, Mr. Antrobus."

"No problem at all."

He shut the door and she pulled out a small device from the bottom of her phone. She scanned it around the room quickly and nodded.

"Sorry, I had to check. It detects most kinds of bugs."

Instead of saying anything, he walked over and tried to kiss her. She pulled away and glowered at him. "Why did you come here, Grant?"

"No other greeting for your boyfriend?"

Petra gave him a short kiss and crossed her arms. "I don't understand why you came here. You could put everything at risk. What the fuck do you think you are doing?"

Grant tried to make a puppy dog face at her. "I'm sorry, Petra. I was going crazy. I didn't know where you were, if you were okay, when to expect you back. You said you couldn't tell me anything."

"For good reason! To prevent something like this. You could blow my entire mission! If I was in deep cover, our lives would be in serious jeopardy."

"I know, I know. I'm sorry."

"You're so infuriating. You just decided to show up here without thinking about the consequences." Petra scowled at him and sank down onto the couch. "This isn't like when we were skiing and you came to fucking rescue me from a double black-diamond slope. And I didn't even need to be rescued then. I was doing just fine on my own."

He looked as if she had stabbed him in the gut. "You weren't doing fine. You always say that as if you don't need anyone, but sometimes you do. And, as I recall, you tumbled fifty feet down that slope and lost both your skis. I'm just glad that you fell feet first because you could have gotten a concussion. If I hadn't come back to check on you, you never would have made it down that hill on your own. You even tried to convince me to keep going instead of helping you." He sat down next her and grabbed her hand. "That's why I'm so scared. I'm afraid that you wouldn't ask for help if you needed it."

"It isn't your place to decide that here. I was trained for this job, and I'm good at it. I don't need you to swoop in and rescue me."

His jaw set stubbornly as he spoke. "I was trained for some version of this too, but it was years ago, so forgive me for wanting to be here for you."

"Damn it, Grant! I didn't ask for this kind of support."

"Well, I'm sorry, but that's what you're going to get from me. When you're in danger, I can't focus on anything. When I'm with you—when I know that I can help you—then everything is clearer. I couldn't shake the feeling that I had to be here for you."

She watched him with a furrowed brow and then relaxed and sighed, letting her emotions subside before she spoke. "You really messed up, but I don't have the time to stay mad at you for it. Now tell me, how did you find me? That's something serious that the Agency needs to correct."

She noticed the grimace that passed across his face and raised her eyebrows. "What did you do?"

"I hacked into the Agency database," he admitted, with his gaze fixed on the floor.

"Holy shit. Do you know what they could do to you if they find out?"

"I covered my tracks pretty well."

Petra rolled her eyes. "Great. So it'll take them a little bit longer than usual to figure it out." She paused for a moment. "Wait a second. This is an off-book mission. How did you even figure out which file it was? Or where I was deployed?"

"I had some help," Grant said sheepishly.

"From who?"

"Your friend...Carlos."

"You involved Carlos? Grant, you made him your accomplice. How could you do that?" She paused and ran her fingers through her hair. "What did you expect to do here anyway? Be my sidekick? As you can see, I'm perfectly fine, and right now, you are keeping me from the operation. You need to go back to New York."

"No. I'm going to help make sure that you come home."

Petra closed her eyes as she tried to contain her frustration. "This is crazy and stupid," she said before taking a deep breath. "If you really aren't going to leave, then you better make yourself useful."

"What can I do?" His expression brightened.

"You can help me hack into two computers. I planted bugs on both of them, so I have the present-day logs. Each bug isn't a full hack, though, so I can't access online activity and e-mails prior to them being planted."

"Okay, sure. That I can do. Are they standard Agency-issued bugs?

She ran her hands through her hair again. "I think it's the most recent model. It records conversations in the vicinity and provides a full record from the computer's base after it's attached."

"So it's one that attaches to a computer or keyboard from underneath the table."

"Yes. That's it."

"All right, that shouldn't be too difficult."

Petra logged on to her computer and opened up the log files. "Here you go," she said, handing it over to Grant.

He spent fifteen minutes using simple hacking software that modified the bug protocols to access the full memory associated with Marzouk Fayed's and Khaled Majed's computer IP addresses. "Done. You should be able to access everything you need now."

She took the computer from him and started going through the files. "Wow, this is amazing. Thank you."

"You didn't think I could do it?" He gave her an indignant expression.

"I didn't say that! But why isn't the bug programmed to do this automatically?"

He leaned over and kissed her. "It's not exactly a simple protocol, and it's decidedly illegal."

"This is the Agency we're talking about. Does that really matter?"

He shrugged.

"Okay, okay, whatever," she said. "Can you help me some more? We have to figure out who Fayed hired, what they are up to, etc."

"Sure. Let's transfer one of the logs to my computer and I'll go through it and you can do the other one. Give me the simpler one since I don't know anything about this case."

Petra nodded and they transferred Khaled Majed's office log to Grant's computer. They spent more than two hours piecing through the e-mails, documents, and files used by the two different computers.

At some point, Grant stopped her in exhaustion. "We need to debrief. What have you found? I'm not sure I get what's going on with this whole thing."

"Well, let's start with the big picture. What we had before was Marzouk Fayed and Khaled Majed talking about someone in charge of planting some device. They spent thirty million euros on something, so they must have hired this person for that sum. And the device, whatever it is, is going to be planted in a palace." She bit down on her lip, thinking it through.

"I don't really know anything about that, but Khaled Majed has had two streams of odd, secretive messages."

"Two streams? I only know about one. Show me."

Grant pulled up a series of messages exchanged between Khaled Majed and the mysterious 'OZ.'

"Okay, I've seen these," she said. "He must have a mole inside the Emir's office. What about the other one?"

Grant opened a second series of messages. "The messages start in May of last year."

*May 15, 2020 – Khaled Majed sent to G: "Just installed myself."*

*September 22, 2020 – Khaled Majed sent to G: "Beginning to convince MF."*

*September 23, 2020 – Khaled Majed received from G: "Good. Continue to update."*

*January 15, 2021 – Khaled Majed sent to G: "Please prepare Ahriman."*

*January 16, 2021 – Khaled Majed received from G: "In progress."*

*May 10, 2021 – Khaled Majed received from G: "Ahriman to arrive KWT on May 15."*

*May 15, 2021 – Khaled Majed sent to G: "Ahriman has arrived. Preparations have begun."*

*June 15, 2021 – Khaled Majed received from G: "Components being delivered."*

Petra stared at the stream of messages. "Oh my God." She sat back in her chair thunderstruck.

"What is it? What does that mean?"

Her tone was flat and she shivered. "Ahriman is a Farsi word. It was a name used in Persian mythology."

"And?"

"In Middle Persia, the Ahriman was the spirit of destruction."

"So the spirit of destruction has arrived in Kuwait?" he fumbled.

Petra could barely form the words. "After the June attacks, Agency chatter indicated that a figure called the Ahriman was responsible for what happened at the Suez Canal. We never got anywhere with the intel, so we finally abandoned the project."

Grant's eyes widened. "So the spirit has arrived. Does that mean...?"

"There's going to be an attack here. They are planting a device on the royal family." She shook her head. "I can't believe I was so stupid. Bayan Palace is such an obvious target. It's the symbol of the monarchy! I didn't think Fayed would attack his own country, but he considers the Emir to be someone who has betrayed Kuwait."

Grant looked at her with a frown. "Forgive my ignorance, but I don't understand."

"You don't understand what?"

"Why would Fayed want to assassinate the Emir? What good would that serve? The Emir would just be replaced by another monarch."

She tilted her head and frowned back at him. "It's because of how politics works here. The Emir is a symbol of everything progressive about this state. He stands for how women achieved the right to vote, for greater civil liberties among the population, for education that focuses more on teaching algebra than teaching religion. If the Emir dies, so does that symbol."

"But isn't he a dictator?"

She shook her head. "No. He's a monarch, not a dictator. There's a difference. He derives his power from the constitution."

"But what about Parliament? Shouldn't they have power as well?" His brow furrowed.

"They do. Parliament is responsible for all legislation when it is in session."

"You said that the Emir can fire Parliament whenever he wants. What kind of legislative power is that?"

"You'd be surprised, Grant. Parliament has managed to hold back or at least delay some of the most beneficial and progressive reforms for this state."

"I'm sorry, but it still doesn't make sense to me. If he can fire Parliament whenever he wants, how does democracy have any power?"

"The Emir can only disband the National Assembly when there is just cause. It's a power check similar to the presidential veto on legislation back home."

"Come on, Petra. The president can't just fire the House or the Senate."

"No, of course not. The way it works here is that the Emir can disband Parliament if they are moving in a direction that is detrimental to the country. While they are out of session, he can often correct the issue before they're back in power, but it's only a temporary bandage. The same people who caused the stalemate or problem in the first place are reelected."

"If the Emir stands for progress, what does the Assembly stand for?"

"There's a progressive faction within the Assembly too, but they are outnumbered by the ultraconservative Islamists."

Grant scratched his head. "I see. So this is a failing of democracy."

"Exactly."

"By supporting the Emir, do we undermine the democracy?"

She looked at him concerned. "I don't know. Maybe. All I know is that I would choose progress over democracy any day."

"I don't know what I would choose. I've never had to consider something like that," he whispered.

"We can't worry about that right now. Whether or not we agree with the existence of the Emir, we have to try and stop his assassination."

"You're right. What can we do?"

Petra started pacing the length of the room. "I don't know. We still don't know enough. When is it going to be? How the fuck can I figure that out?"

"You have to stop and relax."

She ignored him and continued pacing.

"Could you stop pacing, please?"

"No, this is how I think." She continued to pace as her thoughts sprinted along. "What does Fayed talk about? Nothing that would indicate a target. The only thing he ever fucking mentions is the elections." After closing her eyes for a moment, it struck her. "That's it! The elections. He's planning to hit the royal family after the election results are released."

"Okay. You're the expert, so I'll take your word for it. What can we do?"

"We have to send all of this to Chris. Maybe he can use some diplomatic channels to get the Emir to delay the elections, or to at least cordon off his family."

"Okay. It's the middle of the night there so he won't see this stuff for a few hours." Grant pressed a few buttons that transmitted their annotated files to Chris.

"It won't be enough. Today is July second! The elections are in three days. We have to do more."

"And we will, but you have to sit down."

She held his gaze and took a deep breath, then nodded and took a seat on the couch.

"Now, babe, just tell me what you need."

"We need to find this Ahriman. We need a name, a location, something."

"How can we do that?" Concern was etched across his face.

"Go through the logs again. Put together a list of all the names they mention in e-mails that aren't included in Fayed's staff list. Maybe that will give us a clue."

"Petra, what are you going to do?"

"I'm going to go through Khaled Majed's file again to see if I can figure out who 'G' is. If we find out who Majed is messaging, that might give us a clue about the Ahriman."

The rest of the day passed as they lost themselves in the research. *What am I missing?* Petra thought frantically as she scoured the records.

### Surra, Kuwait – July 3, 2021

Khaled smiled when he looked through the messages left on his desk by his secretary.

*From: Mustafa.*
*Message: Prepped and ready.*

He immediately logged on to his computer and sent an update message. He leaned back in his chair and savored the moment.

Several minutes later, he walked over to Fayed's office and knocked on the door.

"Sayeedi?"

"Yes, Khaled, come in. I'm going through the election prep materials that you gave me. Did you want to add anything?"

"Actually, I've just received word from our friend Mustafa Mubarak."

Fayed perked up. "And?"

"Everything is set and ready to go. He will be at the dewaniya tomorrow."

Fayed's face broke out into a smile. "And we shall toast the day of his arrival."

*For so many reasons,* Khaled thought, giving Fayed a conniving smile.

The bug underneath Fayed's desk recorded and transmitted the conversation to a computer in the JW Marriott Hotel.

\*\*\*\*

# Chapter 18
# Fourth of July

*Kuwait City, Kuwait – July 4, 2021*

"Here are the people mentioned in e-mails who aren't on Fayed's staff list. One of them was mentioned again in yesterday's logs."

Petra groaned as she stepped away from her computer. Every muscle in her body ached from sleeping in front of the computer screen the last two nights, trying to figure out the target. She looked over Grant's shoulder, surveying the list. "Do you mean Mustafa Mubarak? He came up in the logs from yesterday?"

"Yes, he's the one."

"Can you pull it up?"

Grant tapped the screen and the log appeared. They read it together.

"Our friend Mustafa Mubarak, huh?" Petra mumbled. "Hmm. And he's going to be at the dewaniya today."

"Isn't a dewaniya just a social gathering? They could be having a get-together or something to celebrate Fayed's reelection."

"That's true, but toasting the day of his arrival?" She stretched her arms over her head, considering the conversation. "Holy shit."

"What is it?"

"It's the dewaniya. That's how they're going to do this. They're going to plant a bomb in one of the royal family's dewaniyas. Mustafa Mubarak must be planting it."

"Couldn't it be anyone attending?" he asked.

"But why would they specifically toast his arrival? That's too much of a coincidence."

"So Mustafa Mubarak is the Ahriman?"

"Yes, I believe so. Let's call Chris and see if we can get access to the flight manifests for the past couple of months."

"It'll take us forever to go through all of that! Besides, that still won't tell us where he is."

230

Petra sighed. "You're right. I'm not sure how to do this."

"What about hotel records?"

"He wouldn't stay at a big hotel, so we can't just hack into records for any of the big chains."

"We could just monitor the dewaniya, couldn't we? The Emir can't have very many of them."

"You might have a point there," she said frowning. "We could monitor the dewaniya and catch him in action. If we just knew which bloody dewaniya. There are hundreds in Kuwait. It probably isn't even at Bayan Palace! It just has to be one that the royal family goes to regularly, and the royal family is freaking huge."

"Hundreds of them?"

"Shit." She stood and began pacing again. "Which of them would be the Ahriman's target?" She stopped suddenly. "Okay, we need a list of all the dewaniyas that members of the royal family go to on a regular basis."

Grant nodded and started to type a search into his computer.

"Not just anyone in the royal family," she directed. "Concentrate on the Crown Prince and the Emir. Find out where they go."

"Isn't that a bit risky?"

"We don't have time to check everyone else. We'll just have to take the gamble. They would be the most high-profile targets for Fayed to hit. It has to be the Emir or the Crown Prince."

"But, Petra, what if you're wrong?"

"Let's pray that I'm not."

Grant stared at her for a couple of seconds and then nodded again, still somewhat convinced. "Even if we find the dewaniya, what are we going to do? How can we stop him? We have no idea what kind of device it is."

"Khaled Majed said Mustafa Mubarak will be at the dewaniya tonight. He must be planting the bomb tonight, if he hopes to get out alive. That way he can detonate it remotely sometime tomorrow. If we can figure out which dewaniya it is, then we can catch him in the act."

He looked back at his search screen. "It looks like the Emir and the Crown Prince go to the dewaniya at Bayan Palace regularly, but frequent several others on occasion." He turned the screen toward Petra so that she could see. "What do you think?"

She peered at the screen and took a deep breath. "Security around the palace will not be light," she whispered, remembering the conversation between Fayed and Khaled that had perturbed her. "They probably wouldn't go anywhere else around the time of an election."

She reached for her bag to check for her gun. "Come on. We have to get you a dishdasha and find a way into the Emir's dewaniya."

His eyes were wide. "So the Ahriman will be at the dewaniya at Bayan Palace."

"Yes, and so will we."

\*\*\*\*

"Before I get to what you asked for, you need to tell me what the fuck is going on." Chris's on-screen image looked grim. "Your boyfriend comes to see me here in the office and then he fucking shows up in Kuwait? How the hell did he know to go there? Petra, if you told him, you know what I have to do, right?"

She heaved a long sigh. "I didn't tell him anything. He figured it out somehow. Found it in the Agency's files."

"The Agency's files? How the fuck did he do that? Does he realize that he could be looking at jail time? I have to report this shit."

"I know, and I think that he knows too. I don't know what got into him. He just went crazy worrying or something. And I guess being a senior manager in IT probably gave him a slight advantage when it came to figuring out the files."

"I will have to get our people to address this security breach. At least he didn't show it to anyone outside."

Petra gulped. *Don't mention Carlos.* "Yeah."

"Fine, let's move on. You can tell him to come back in. I'll deal with him later."

"Okay, give me a second." Petra placed the call on mute and moved away from the video feed toward the bedroom area of the Grant's hotel suite. She opened the door and saw Grant sitting on the bed, stooped over and biting his nails. "You can come in now."

"What's he going to do?"

"I don't know. He didn't say. We'll deal with it later. Let's just try and stop this bomb."

Grant followed her back into the room and they both stepped in front of the video feed. Chris would be able to see them both now.

"Hello, Grant," Chris said curtly. "Normally, I would pull the plug on this right away, but I can't distract Petra by asking her to ship your ass back here, so we're going to postpone all discussion about what the fuck you thought you were doing by accessing our secure files and then showing up in Kuwait. Is that clear?"

"Yes," Grant conceded.

"Okay. Petra, I called in a couple of favors about what you sent. There is no way to cancel the Emir's dewaniya tonight without making a lot of people suspicious, but both of you will have access to it. I also requested that the blueprints of Bayan Palace be sent over to you. You should have them in the next half hour."

"Great. Thanks, Chris. I know today's your day off."

"Security around the holidays is indeed problematic," he grumbled. "But Petra, we've got a much bigger problem."

She tilted her head. "What do you mean?"

"Do you remember that oil deal we talked about?"

"The one here with Textron? Yeah, of course. Have they made it official?"

"No, that's the problem. They haven't made a decision about giving it to Textron yet. And good old President Reynolds has decided to make sure that they do, and that it happens before the election."

She gaped at the image of her boss. "What are you saying Chris? You don't mean…?"

"Unfortunately, yes, I do. The president arrived in Kuwait on an unscheduled visit this morning. I believe he's meeting with the Emir now."

"What the hell are we supposed to do now? How did we not know about this? We're an intelligence agency! I know the Secret Service is not always forthcoming, but didn't they think this piece of information might be relevant?"

"I don't know what to tell you, Petra. I only heard about this today."

"What the fuck? He's such a weasel that he'll personally negotiate what's supposed to be a free-market contract for his best friend who is perfectly capable of negotiating on his own?"

"I know. We can't do anything about it, though. You've got to make sure nothing bad happens at that dewaniya today."

"The dewaniya? Are you kidding me? As if the stakes weren't high enough without this added on!" She glared at Chris's image on her monitor. "Wait a second. Why would the president go to the dewaniya if he's here on an unscheduled visit?"

"Didn't you see the message Alex forwarded to you? The Emir is closing his dewaniya to everyone but the Crown Prince and the president tomorrow, so today is our only shot at this. None of them will be there today, but tomorrow is a different story."

"So the Emir is going to the dewaniya tomorrow with the Crown Prince and the fucking president of the United States? How many targets could they possibly put in one place? Fucking shit. Have you informed the Secret Service about the bomb threat?" She clenched her fists tightly.

"That'll be my next call. I wanted to update you first."

"What the hell am I supposed to do, Chris? This is fucking insane!"

Grant looked over at his girlfriend who had once again begun pacing around the room. "Okay, Chris. We've got it. We'll do our best."

"I know you will, but, both of you, be careful. Don't do anything crazy."

"We'll be careful," Grant said.

Petra paced around the room for the next fifteen minutes before Grant was finally able to calm her down. She was still reeling from the new information when they headed to the bedroom to get dressed in traditional Kuwaiti clothing.

"Women's clothing here is so unflattering," she said as she looked down at the black *burka* she wore. "It's convenient cover though and at least the dress I am wearing underneath is pretty nice."

"I hope I get to see you wear that dress again," Grant grinned. "Will they really let you through just like that?"

"Not tomorrow, since POTUS will be there, but tonight I should be okay. I only need to get past the initial gate. After that, I'll shed the burka and do some investigating while you are in the dewaniya."

"I'm going to sound ridiculous. I don't even speak Arabic!" He threw out his arms in exasperation.

"Your cover is that you are a friend of the Crown Prince's eldest son Hamad. Trust me, you'll be fine."

"What if the Crown Prince's son is actually there? It's not as if he'll know who I am."

Petra gave him an exasperated look. "Of course he won't be there. We specifically picked someone who is out of town. Don't worry so much."

"Fine," Grant said with a roll of his eyes. "Let's test out the earpieces before we go."

"Sure." She pressed one of them into her ear and Grant did the same.

"Do you copy?" he asked.

"Yup. And you?"

"It's working."

"Perfect. Let's go," she said.

They headed down to Petra's rental car. Grant drove as Petra directed him toward the Bayan Palace dewaniya.

## *Salmiya, Kuwait – July 4, 2021*

The Ahriman poured exactly 250 grams of the black powder into the top portion of the device he had assembled several days earlier.

*It's ready,* he thought as the powder settled into the bottom of the device. To secure it, he wrapped a few pieces of duct tape around the device and then taped the entire thing to his thigh. When he pulled his dishdasha on afterward, he was satisfied with the concealment. No one at the security gate would notice the device he was carrying. The dewaniya had only one entrance and the guards did not dare search any of the Emir's guests.

Before leaving, he slipped the canister Sarah had given him into his left pocket. *Just in case.* He surveyed the area to make sure the kitchen was clear of the substances he had made and walked out toward his car. *Time for my last dewaniya.*

## *Kuwait City, Kuwait – July 4, 2021*

Petra and Grant arrived at the gates to Bayan Palace and each held their breath until one of the guards waved their car through toward the dewaniya.

"Where is the women's event?" he asked.

"It's on the other side of the palace. I should have a good excuse to get lost."

"Just be careful, babe. Okay?"

She smiled. "Don't worry, anyone who sees me wandering around will take one look at me and direct me over to the women's event."

"Not if it's this Ahriman guy," Grant mumbled under his breath. Petra glanced at him and decided to ignore the comment.

They got out of the car and she readjusted her dress and burka.

"How are you going to approach the men's section?" he asked.

She pulled up the blueprints on her phone, which she had received en route. "The women's event is held over here on the north side of the palace compound. The main dewaniya is here, on the other side. An attic crawl space goes over the main dewaniya with old vented access points here, here, and here. They probably use it for storage. The vents will be covered up inside now because of the air conditioning system, but I'll be able to use my pinhole camera to view the dewaniya. Based on these plans, I can probably enter the attic through one of the access points in the main palace. It looks like there is one in this store room." She pointed at the map to show the entry point to the attic.

"But how are you going to enter the main palace?"

"I'll figure something out."

"I don't like this," Grant said, shaking his head. "When can I get us both back home?"

"Soon, babe. Soon." She reached out and squeezed his hand.

"There's a reason I never had any interest in the field. I was always much happier sitting behind my computer, or even better, reading about every aspect of the history of any random place." His expression brightened momentarily as he pictured himself at a country house pouring over artifacts from an archaeological dig. "Instead, I'm here pretending to be a nonexistent friend of the Crown Prince's son, about to sneak into a dewaniya with my girlfriend to capture an assassin so dangerous that he's named after the Persian spirit of destruction." He banged his head on the headrest a couple of times. "This is exactly what I pictured for our Fourth of July weekend.

She leaned over and gave him a kiss on the cheek. "It's going to be okay."

"I just wish I had more control over this whole damned situation."

"Try not to worry. I'll be fine."

He glared at her for trivializing the situation.

"Grant, I know. I promise I'll be careful."

He studied her for a moment and she looked at him quizzically. "What is it?" she asked.

"Nothing really. I can see why they wanted to send you back into the field. You freaked out for a bit, but now you're so calm."

"I wouldn't have taken this operation if I'd really had the choice." She forced a small smile and tried to focus on the moment instead of letting her mind wander back several years.

"Grant, look at me." She grabbed his other hand and met his eyes. "All you need to do is go straight into the dewaniya. Everyone there will speak English, so don't worry about not being able to speak Arabic. Just take a seat and look around for our future friend Mustafa Mubarak. If there's anything particularly visible about him, try to let me know if you can."

He exhaled sharply. "Okay, I can do that."

"And try not to attract too much attention to yourself. If you think he's suspicious of you, excuse yourself and get out of here. Just let me know as much about him as you can on your way out."

"But then what will you do?"

"I'll improvise." Her eyes softened. "Try not to freak out about what Chris told us either."

He shuddered and looked away.

"What did I tell you? Don't worry! We'll be fine." After glancing around to make sure that no one was watching, she leaned over and gave him a deep kiss. When she pulled away, she tried to give him a reassuring look in spite of her fears.

The combination of her training in how to read people and the time they'd spent together made it easy for her to decipher his expressions. She could tell there were so many questions he wanted to ask her. They were the same ones that she had often asked herself when she started fieldwork. *How is it possible to focus without being distracted by emotions? How is it possible to remove emotions all together?* The moment passed before either of them could speak their minds.

She fastened her Colt pistol into her calf holster underneath her burka. "Let's get this over with."

\*\*\*\*

# Book VIII
# Three Years Earlier
# 2018 – 2019

# Chapter 19
## The Conversion
## Three Years Earlier

*Tehran, Iran – December, 2018*

Since executing the Khomeini Square mission more than a month earlier, Kasem had thrown himself back into his training. His nightmares raged, wracking him with memories of Lila, the car bomb, and the hopelessness of his situation. Every morning he woke up and tried to distance himself from those memories. After trying countless mornings in a row, he came to a decision. He would continue to serve General Majed until he could get a mission outside of the country, when he hoped he would be able to cut the anklet and break free.

He kept news clippings about the car bomb inside a book in a drawer next to his desk. It served as a reminder of all the pain he had caused by following the general's orders. The pictures from the clippings fueled a quiet need for vengeance the moment he found a way to escape.

His Arabic lessons were going well and he pushed himself hard to ensure that he would eventually get a mission outside of Iran. He knew that if he could figure out how to disable the tracking system in his anklet, then he might have a chance. Any tampering with the device would set off an alarm. The skin beneath it had become chafed and raw, but he had found ways to protect the area with special layered socks and lotions.

On the morning of December 22, he rose and logged on to his computer. It would be the first Christmas he had spent alone in a long time. Last year, he had spent it with his parents. They sipped wine around the tree and told jokes and stories. He had planned to introduce them to Lila this Christmas. His chest ached as he imagined the four of them sitting around the tree at his parents' home in Brooklyn. They would have been informed of his death by now. *Wish I could just call and hear their voices.* He remembered his last camping trip with his dad in the Catskills. When they returned, his mother had signed Kasem up for a cooking lesson because she thought he was too thin. No matter how many times she had tried to teach him, he couldn't master even the most basic Persian recipes.

He forced himself to continue with his morning routine rather than dwell upon his loneliness. Kasem opened his message server to check for summons from Khaled Majed or Lieutenant Afshar over the past twenty-four hours. The two of them generally had left him to his own devices since the Khomeini Square operation. He was about to head to an Arabic lesson when a message arrived that was marked "urgent."

The message simply read, *"Report to base operations at noon."* Kasem looked at his watch and saw that it was only ten, so he went to his class, although he had difficulty focusing on anything but the upcoming meeting. Khaled Majed had finally allowed him to start taking group lessons at the military barracks in addition to their personal sessions, although he attended under a strict cover ID.

After class, he headed to the operations room where he now had most of his sessions with Khaled Majed, Lieutenant Afshar, or both. When he arrived, both of them were seated already and Lieutenant Afshar was sweating and holding a small USB key.

Kasem took a seat, wondering why the lieutenant seemed so nervous. He had never seen the lieutenant look so anxious.

"Kasem, thank you for coming on such short notice," Khaled began.

"Not a problem," he replied. *Did I really have any choice?*

"We have another mission we'd like you to take. Actually, another two missions."

Kasem nodded. "What are the details?"

"You'll find most of the information on this USB stick. One of them will involve you participating in a military initiative," Lieutenant Afshar said while handing it over to Kasem.

"Okay. Is there anything else I need to know?" Kasem turned his eyes toward the lieutenant, wondering if his obvious nervousness was related to the mission.

"No, the USB key will give you everything that you need."

"Okay. In that case, I will return to my room to review and plan."

Lieutenant Afshar gestured toward the door. "Go ahead."

As Kasem turned to head back to his room, he felt confused. It was strange that the two of them had summoned him to a meeting in person when anyone could have delivered the USB key. That, along with the lieutenant's anxiety, made the entire encounter perplexing. Of course, something personal may have put the lieutenant on edge. The encounter made Kasem unpleasantly aware of how little he knew about the personal lives of both Khaled Majed and Lieutenant Afshar. He would have to remedy that if he wanted to find something he could use to his advantage. Such knowledge might be critical to force their cooperation and disable his anklet's monitoring system.

One thing was certain, though: the lieutenant and Khaled Majed had not both been there simply to say hello to him. General Majed had to be the one behind it. Kasem contemplated what the general might be up to now. He let his thoughts continue to run on until he reached his room fourteen minutes later, ready to view the contents of the USB key.

## *Tehran, Iran – New Year's Eve, 2018*

A team of men dressed in black crept slowly into the gardens outside the boundary wall of a moderate-sized villa on the outskirts of Tehran. The family inside was celebrating the upcoming New Year with loud music playing and laughter drifting out of the open windows.

"All men in position. Wait for my signal," Kasem heard through his earpiece as he crouched silently next to the wall.

"Do we really have to raid them tonight? If Commander Derderian is plotting against General Majed, surely nothing will happen tonight? We could take him some other time, like when the commander is alone," Kasem whispered to the man crouched next to him. The man glared at him and then turned back toward the house.

Kasem looked at his watch as he heard the laughter and yelling from the house growing louder. "Ten, nine, eight, seven..."

"It's time. Throw in the grenades," a voice bellowed on the com.

The man next to him reached for his grenade, removed the pin, and threw it over the boundary wall. Kasem crouched with his hand on the other grenade, paralyzed at the thought of throwing it toward the house. "Throw it in, you fucker! Damn it, give it to me."

Before Kasem could react consciously, he released his grip on the grenade. The other man grabbed it, removed the pin, and threw it over the boundary wall in one swift motion. Seconds later, a slew of explosions coincided with the stroke of midnight. The sound made Kasem's jaw clench as he pulled a gas mask over his head. The grenades were a new breed designed for small explosions that would trigger the release of a high concentration halothane vapor.

He saw one of the men further along the wall gesture for them to climb over it. Kasem stood up slowly and hauled himself over the wall using the stone irregularities for traction. The halothane vapor had already begun working as an anesthetic within the home.

Kasem followed two of the men as they broke through the main door at the front of the house. The explosion from the grenades had knocked out several of the windows and the main door was hanging on its hinges already.

When they reached the dining room where the family had been celebrating, Kasem surveyed the room and let out a sharp breath of relief. The grenades had knocked out the windows, but the house walls had acted like a trench, fortifying the family from the explosion. The gas was another story—it had been seeping through the windows for the past few minutes.

"Members of the family are out cold, sir," Kasem heard the man ahead of him radio in to their mission commander. "Should we proceed as planned?"

He couldn't hear the response, but the question was clarified when his own earpiece crackled a moment later. "Proceed as planned. Take in all family members."

They pulled out the nine members of Commander Derderian's family, placed large sacks over their heads, and bound their hands with cable ties. "Put the family in the second van. The commander goes in the first one, alone," the man in charge ordered over the com.

Kasem complied with the orders and helped pile the women and children into the second van. *Why do we need the family? Isn't this a bit much?*

They drove the family to a locked horse stable facility further outside the city. Inside there was a barred off room that once had functioned as a breeding house. They placed the family inside while locking up the commander in an adjoining stable with three guards posted outside of it. Kasem and another guard were assigned to monitor the family overnight. He took the second watch to allow the other guard to sleep.

Early into his shift, Kasem saw that they were beginning to wake up. One of the children was crying while holding her stomach and shivering. He recognized that they were experiencing some of the common side effects of halothane gas.

Kasem picked up the blanket he'd been sleeping on earlier and held it between the bars. "Take it," he said in Farsi to one of the women. "It will help her." He gestured toward the little girl shivering on the floor.

The woman took it, glaring at him. "What have you done to us? Where is my husband?" She wrapped the blanket around her daughter and spoke to her softly. "Take this, it'll keep you warm. Everything will be all right, you'll see. We're going to get out of here."

With a sigh, Kasem stepped away from the bars. He had just dozed off again when he heard the warehouse door open. He kicked at the other guard and they both stood hastily at attention, waiting to salute whoever was coming inside the stable.

Two men entered, dragging along a gagged and beaten Commander Derderian. Behind them, Kasem saw General Majed walk in followed by Lieutenant Afshar and another man he didn't recognize. Both the lieutenant and the other man were carrying guns, Kasem observed in surprise. *Seems a bit excessive for a kidnapped family.*

The procession stopped directly in front of the barred room so that the family could see Commander Derderian.

"Daddy!" one of the children called out.

"Why are you doing this, General?" the commander demanded, turning toward him. "I have done nothing wrong. You don't have a shred of evidence against me, and yet you kidnap my entire family? I'll make sure you hang for this."

General Majed smirked at his prisoner. "Really? You are going to make sure that I hang for this? I have all the proof that I need. I don't take kindly to people in my line of command plotting to kill me." The general gestured toward Lieutenant Afshar. "Lieutenant, hand me your weapon, please."

"Sir, is that really necessary?" Lieutenant Afshar asked shakily while drawing his gun from its holster.

"Are you contradicting me, Lieutenant?"

Lieutenant Afshar handed the gun over in silence.

The general disengaged the safety and held it to Commander Derderian's head. "You will now reveal every detail of your plan to me."

"There was no plan! I haven't done anything wrong."

"You will tell me what I ask, or your family will die," the general snickered and motioned toward Kasem and the other guard. "Bring me those two children."

Kasem gritted his teeth as they each grabbed one of the children and pulled them out of the barred stable. The door latched shut behind them.

"Would you want to be shot in front of your children? Do you want your blood splattered across their faces?" the general challenged, still holding the gun at Commander Derderian's head.

"I haven't done anything!"

"You Armenian scum. If you don't tell me your plan, I will shoot every single member of your family and let you watch them die."

Derderian seemed to shrink as his resolve fell away. "I'll tell you everything. Please don't hurt my family. They were never a part of this."

"Take him outside and set a few bombs inside here. Let's make sure that the commander has every reason to cooperate."

Kasem watched as the man who had entered with the general set the charges. When he was done, he gestured toward the rest of the men guarding the family and they followed him outside. There they waited for the general and the rest of the men to return. Derderian's wife and his sister were bawling and trying to attend to the children while Derderian's brother sat with his mother.

The first hour crept by slowly while Kasem waited outside the barred horse cell. When the general and the other men finally reentered, it felt as if an eternity had passed.

"Lock him in there with his family," the general said.

Two of the other guards pushed past Kasem and threw Commander Derderian into the cell.

"Get the children out and take them to the car."

Kasem pulled the shivering little girl from her sobbing mother's arms and followed the men shepherding the other two children out of the warehouse. They ushered the three children into the back of a navy blue van waiting outside and locked the door.

"Officer Ismaili, set off your charges," General Majed said as soon as the children were locked in the truck.

244

"S-sir?"

"Is that really necessary, sir?" Kasem heard Lieutenant Afshar say, echoing his own thoughts.

"Do you want the children to be inside when this place blows up? If not, then set the bombs off now." The general glared at him. "Did I not make myself clear? Set the bombs off. Now."

Kasem stared at the general as the man retrieved the trigger from his shirt pocket. He handed it over to Kasem.

"Set the bombs off. Now."

"W-what?"

"You heard me. Set the bombs off. Now!"

Kasem felt paralyzed and continued to stare at the general.

"We're waiting on you boy," General Majed said, glaring at him. "You know what the consequences are if you do not comply."

Kasem squeezed his eyes shut and remembered the photo of Lila that they had shown him. His fingers were shaking as he gripped the detonator and tried not to push the button. Finally, he opened his eyes.

"May God forgive me," he whispered as he pressed the button.

\*\*\*\*

"Set the bombs off. Now."

*"Set the bombs off. Now."*

*"Set the bombs off. Now!"*

*The warehouse lit up in a ball of red, orange, and yellow flames.*

Kasem woke up in a cold sweat in the front seat of his car. He glanced around to get his bearings and then closed his eyes again, wishing he could shake off the newest recurring nightmare. He tried to calm his racing heartbeat with thoughts of the children who were still alive, but he knew that the conditions of a Tehran orphanage left much to be desired, and they would never recover from the explosion. With considerable effort, he put his mind on the mission at hand, even though it was pointless to try to forget what he had done. He could never erase that memory.

For the past three weeks, Kasem had been researching and tailing Nicholas Diaz. The USB stick Khaled Majed and Lieutenant Afshar had given him identified Diaz as a potential source of intelligence for the Iranian military, although he did not see what value Diaz could possibly provide. Diaz was pro-Iranian with potential anti-Western sympathies, but he had limited access to any embassy or ministry. In Kasem's mind, Diaz was a glorified Spanish shopkeeper—a civilian who was hardly worth his time. The one attraction of this operation was that Diaz used a freight service through the Suez Canal. Kasem secretly hoped he could turn this local operation into one where he monitored Diaz's dealings outside of the country. If he could make that happen, he had a chance to cut his anklet and make a break for it without being caught.

Kasem lifted his pant leg and looked down at the monitoring device latched around his ankle. *Damned technology.*

Over the course of the morning, Kasem had watched Diaz go to several meetings. From the listening device Kasem had planted in the car, he learned that Diaz would be alone in his store on the outskirts of Tehran that afternoon. He waited until then to make his approach.

Kasem walked into the store and made small talk with Diaz, asking about how he operated the chain of antique stores.

"Not too many customers are interested in the actual business. What do you do?"

"I work as a contract designer here in Tehran," Kasem replied.

"Oh great. What kind of design?"

"Mostly small commercial buildings—small shops, office space, the occasional house."

Diaz cocked his head to the side. "That's quite a coincidence. I'm actually looking for a redesign of one of my storefronts."

"Really? This is my lucky day. I came in to pick up a present for my sister, but I might leave with a project."

"Now, don't get ahead of yourself," Diaz chuckled.

Kasem went on to purchase a small sculpture for his nonexistent sister and handed over his business card.

"Jamal Simrani, contract designer," Diaz read aloud. "Jamal, I'm Nicholas Diaz." Diaz handed over his card as well. "Do you live around here?" he asked as Kasem took the card.

"No, I live downtown. I wanted to take a few days away from all the smog."

"But the city is beautiful."

Kasem grinned. "It is, and don't get me wrong, I absolutely love it. I don't know if I'll ever be able to move away from there, but sometimes I need a break from the intensity."

"Your sister lives around here then?"

"Yes. It's an easy trip."

"Ah, I see. That makes more sense. Well, Jamal, how about you join me for a coffee later this week?"

"That sounds great."

Back in his car, Kasem glanced down at his anklet once again. *I wasn't lying about not being able to leave.* He jerked the gearshift as he drove to a hotel nearby on the outskirts of the city.

\*\*\*\*

"All right. Next on the agenda is an update on the boy's progress. Please tell me he is doing well." General Majed sat in a conference room across from his nephew and Lieutenant Afshar.

"On the overall operation or on his training?" Lieutenant Afshar took a deep breath, trying to calm his racing pulse. Since the general had first told them of his plan, he had been breaking out into cold sweats and palpitations. He wished more than anything that he could run away from General Majed's insane plot.

"On both please. Start with his training."

"Kasem has continued to make progress on his marksmanship, fitness, and war tactics," the lieutenant started.

"And his Arabic?"

"His Arabic has improved considerably since our last update," Khaled added.

"Considerably? Which means what, exactly?" the general probed.

"Well, he can speak comfortably in both social and intellectual sit—"

"Stop. Both of you. I don't care how comfortable he is or how much he's improved. I care about how someone listening to him will react. If they think he sounds like a foreigner, then the whole thing is a damned waste. Can he pass for a native?"

Khaled shook his head. "He has retained some sliver of his American and Farsi accents."

"You need to work harder! The boy must lose all traces of those accents. I don't care if a Kuwaiti thinks he is Syrian or an Egyptian thinks he is from Saudi. We can work that into his cover stories, but he must sound like he grew up in an Arab country! This is your responsibility."

"General, sir," Afshar said to interrupt the tirade. "Most foreigners are unable to pick up native accents. Maybe we could work that into his cover stories somehow?"

"You are both incompetent." General Majed stood and stormed out of the room.

Lieutenant Afshar and Khaled looked at each other in surprise and disbelief.

"Do you think he'll come back?"

"He's your uncle. What do you think?"

Before Khaled could answer, the general reentered the room in a huff.

"If you believe he is incapable of materializing a real Arab accent, what do you propose to do about it?"

Afshar gestured at Khaled, indicating for him to continue.

"We could create his cover as an Arab who was raised outside of the Middle East but has been back for several years. There are many immigrant families in the West who have been ineffective at teaching their children proper Arabic."

General Majed crossed his arms and scowled at his nephew. "And what about the remnants of his Farsi accent?"

"I believe that only a native Farsi speaker would be able to discern them. Most individuals would accept that his accent is a bit odd because he grew up in the West while speaking Arabic at home."

The general scratched the back of his head. After a moment of silence, he responded, "Very well. If that is our only way around this, then we can use those cover stories. I want you to double your efforts to make his accent as untraceable as possible."

Khaled nodded and the lieutenant gave him a sympathetic glance. They both knew that teaching a language was hardly an exact science.

"What about his psychological evaluations?" The general continued to probe his nephew.

"The results are similar to our previous meetings. He will act in our benefit even if he does not believe in our cause."

"And Khaled, have you managed to figure out what he is holding back?"

"I am chipping away at it slowly."

General Majed frowned, looking rather unsatisfied. "Now, please update me on the overall mission."

"Kasem has been providing new design plans to Nicolas Diaz for the past six weeks. Diaz appears happy with them and we are moving along with development plans on schedule." Lieutenant

Afshar paused. "Diaz's shipping contacts have also been researched further and we believe we can use them to our advantage."

"When do you think we will be ready to move forward?"

"Sometime during the summer, Uncle."

General Majed stared across the table at his nephew and the lieutenant. Afshar squirmed under his gaze and tried to force himself to sit still.

"Very well. Just remember to keep to appropriate timing as we discussed. I do not need to remind you of what is at stake," General Majed snickered at the lieutenant.

Afshar swallowed as he thought back to the conversation when he had challenged the general's plan because of the casualties that would result. He had threatened to take it up the command chain to get the general court-martialed. The general had responded with a sly smile and had threatened to hurt Farah and her family if the lieutenant did not comply. Afshar stared back, trying to hold his gaze steady.

"Oh, and both of you, let's keep the boy occupied," the general ordered. "There are several other lower-priority missions he can attend to while plans for this one develop."

## Urmia, Iran (West Azerbaijan province near the Turkish border) – February, 2019

"The mission will be to flush out the exact headquarters of the Kurdish rebellion movement. They are assembling in Urmia. You have to find their headquarters and give us a diagnostic on the amount of weaponry they've gathered and when they are planning to strike."

Kasem exhaled loudly as he thought about the mission assignment. He now understood why Khaled Majed had required him to learn basic Kurdish. Based on what had happened with Commander Derderian's family, Kasem could see that the general did not take kindly to many of the minority ethnic groups in Iran—the Armenians and Kurds to name a few. According to some of the rumors Kasem had heard, one of the general's pet projects was to flush out and destroy a number of the Kurdish rebellion groups. This was, of course, the first Kurdish operation he had participated in, though.

He had been sitting in his car watching a seemingly deserted warehouse on the western boundaries of the city. After spending a couple of weeks wandering around the city while posing as a travel journalist exploring Kurdish culture, he had tracked a suspicious cargo shipment to this warehouse. He tapped his com system to begin transmitting. "Sir, this is Officer Ismaili calling in," he said to Khaled Majed.

"Do you have an update?"

"I'm concerned that my hunch about this warehouse might be wrong. I've been surveying for the past two days and I'm not sure that anything is happening here."

"What do you suggest?"

"I await your orders, Commander. I can head back to base and try to find some other leads, or I can continue surveillance on this warehouse." *Or I could drive west across the Turkish border.*

"Hold your post for now."

Since arriving in the West Azerbaijan province more than four weeks earlier, Kasem had been monitoring a group of militant Kurdish rebels. According to the briefing file, they were responsible for several bomb blasts in Tehran. The file had some huge gaps, though. It contained minimal information about who might have provided the group with financial funding and weapons. Clearly, they had some high-powered connections, but finding information about them was next to impossible. The reports in the file also stated that their main base was likely to be outside of Urmia, but so far, the trail had gone cold.

Two days later, Kasem finally noticed something abnormal happening at the warehouse. "Commander, it looks like I may have something," he radioed in to Khaled Majed.

He photographed four different people entering the warehouse, all at different times. "Must be some kind of meeting. There are at least four of them in there now, although they all went in at different times. I'm heading inside to see if I can find out more."

"Take pictures of the attendants. The controller will want to see them."

"Yes, sir."

Kasem got out of his car and walked slowly toward the building, taking a long detour. As he got closer, he made sure to be as quiet as possible. He was about to dart inside when he noticed a reflective panel on the upper right corner of the door. *Cameras.*

Taking his time to avoid the cameras, he reached one of the windows and knelt below it. The window opened toward the outside. He frowned, realizing he was still too far away to hear the discussion.

He stood up slowly and peered through the open window. There were several large crates in front of it. Placing his hands on the windowsill, he raised himself over it slowly and dropped down behind the crates. The giant upright fans humming around the meeting room muffled the *thump* of his drop so that it was lost in the ambient noise.

The crates were arranged in several rows. He moved quietly through them until he was within earshot of the conversation. *Time to test my Kurdish.*

He hit the record button on his cell phone and listened quietly. His face was knotted in concentration as he tried to catch every word with his basic knowledge of the language. Even with his best efforts, he was unable to follow the conversation completely, although he did pick up bits. They were discussing a facility or prison of some kind in Tehran and swearing a lot. He grinned as he heard the words *dayk heez* and *goo zil* said repeatedly, respectively meaning "son of a bitch" and "big shit."

Without pausing the recording, he pressed a few buttons on his phone and sent a message to Khaled Majed. *"Located meeting. Discussion regarding some kind of prison. Please advise."*

Khaled Majed replied: *"Forward photos of attendants immediately."*

Kasem hit a few more buttons and sent the pictures he had taken from the car documenting who was attending the meeting. He waited in silence as he tried to catch more of the dialogue.

The conversation continued, still focusing on a prison and an inmate, and some kind of bomb, when suddenly it hit Kasem even with his rudimentary understanding. The former head of the group had been arrested and was being held in a prison facility in Tehran. The meeting was to figure out some kind of plan to rescue him.

He pulled up a copy of the file on his phone. *Akam Yazdani, formerly Akam Yazade,* he read on the top line, noticing that the man had been required to change his Kurdish name. *"Dayk heez…"* he whispered, repeating the Kurdish phrase for son of a bitch.

He skimmed through the rest of the file and frowned when he saw that Yazdani had spent three years in prison for having alcohol in his Tehran apartment. *We used to do that all the time,* he thought, remembering his days with Jamal. Simply because they had raided Yazdani's apartment, Kasem knew that there had to be a cover-up involved. Yazdani must have been planning something that someone higher up in the police force or the government had found threatening.

He sent another message to Khaled Majed. *"Discussion regarding Akam Yazdani. Request permission to investigate further."*

Shortly thereafter, a reply arrived. *"Permission denied. Terminate all individuals in warehouse."*

Kasem eyed his phone in shock. *Terminate them?* He pulled out his gun and attached the silencer to the end.

He shook off his inhibitions and then turned around to climb onto one of the large crates. *Not my problem,* he thought. Glancing down at his anklet, he clenched his teeth. *Whatever it takes.*

From his elevated vantage point, all of the targets were in his sights. He crouched down on top of the crates and lined up his first shot. Less than a minute later, the warehouse was spattered with blood and Kasem could only hear the echo of his own footsteps as he walked away.

****

# Chapter 20
# The Ahriman

*Tehran, Iran – April, 2019*

Kasem glared at his computer monitor. According to the message on his screen, the final objective of his operation with Nicholas Diaz would be to plant recording devices on several of Diaz's freighters. *This whole thing was utterly pointless.* He had spent months cultivating Diaz's trust while he was under the impression that Khaled Majed, or rather General Majed, wanted to turn Diaz into a source. Now, after all of that time and work, they pulled a switch on him. He could have placed recording devices without spending nearly as much time to butter up the target.

On the brighter side, he would not have to break Diaz's trust by asking him to become a spy. The assignment was simple enough that it would not require huge amounts of time going forward. The result would ruin the business, but Diaz would never know who was responsible.

After staring at his computer for the next few minutes, Kasem opened up the shipping schedules Nicolas had sent him. The first schedule was for the raw materials they would use in the redesign of his storefront as part of Kasem's cover. The schedule would be useful in planning where and when to plant the recording devices.

He reviewed the information that Khaled had sent him as further background information. Khaled had held back most of the information initially, but now he disclosed the real motivation for the operation. The general believed that Diaz was running a smuggling operation through his shipping business. If Kasem had known the real motivation, he would have used a much less friendly approach with Diaz. Now that he had cultivated their relationship, Kasem realized that he genuinely liked Diaz. He was the closest thing Kasem had to a friend since Jamal, which made the rest of the operation far more disconcerting. *I have to ruin him.*

He was still reviewing the schedules along with the freighters' routes to calculate a possible approach when he heard a knock on the door. A moment later, he opened the door to see Lieutenant Afshar.

"Lieutenant?" he exclaimed.

"May I come in?"

"Of course." Kasem took a step back to allow the lieutenant to enter his small studio in the military barracks. "I'm sorry, I wasn't expecting you, sir," he said, gesturing at the messy desk.

"At ease," the lieutenant said, taking a seat at Kasem's desk. "I wanted to speak to you about your next assignment. Have you figured out an approach yet?"

"I'm still reviewing the schedules and the route, but I have a couple of ideas."

"Let's run through them together."

"Okay, great," Kasem said, surprised. He pulled up a stool from the kitchen area to take a seat next to the lieutenant. "Here are the schedules and the map. I've marked some of the different routing and refueling points."

The lieutenant leaned over to look at the map. "So the freighters typically come in from Europe by passing through the Suez Canal. After that, they head south through the Red Sea and turn east into the Gulf of Aden. Then they come around the Arabian Peninsula through the Gulf of Oman to finally dock at Bander Abbas." Afshar traced the route slowly with his finger.

"Exactly. There are a few points where we could plant the bugs. We could plant them at Bander Abbas when the freighters leave Iran, or somewhere else along the route."

"Bander Abbas would be the easiest spot since you wouldn't have to leave Iranian territory," Afshar said as he retraced the shipping route on the map.

"Yes, but if the aim is to catch Diaz in the act of smuggling, we might as well try to figure out who works for him at customs."

"And if we plant the bug while in Iran, then we will never know."

Kasem gave a brief nod, trying to pretend to be as emotionally detached from the location as possible. *Please send me out.*

"You know, Kasem, if we send you out of the country, you should be aware of a few things."

"What do you mean, sir?" Kasem focused on keeping his breathing steady.

"It's possible that your anklet might, well, you know, malfunction. It's possible that we would have some difficulties in locating you if needed, especially right after you complete the operation."

He regarded the lieutenant blankly. *Is he really hinting at...?* "I, I'm not too worried about that, sir."

"Good. I just wanted to make sure that would not be a concern for you."

He nodded again, still trying to understand the implications of what the lieutenant had just said.

The lieutenant looked back at the map and pointed to a spot. "One of their biggest delivery sites on the way back to Europe is in Aqaba, at the southern tip of Jordan. It's a beautiful port, not too large, and it should be manageable in terms of security."

"It would be the ideal place to plant the bugs," Kasem agreed.

"Then we are in agreement. Now you need to figure out how to convince Khaled to give you clearance to carry out the operation there. You should also come up with a plan to explain to your new friend why you need to be in Aqaba so that you won't blow your cover."

"It's easy enough to explain to Khaled. As I said, this is the best way to catch the customs officials that are in Diaz's pocket. I'll have to think about how to broach the topic with Diaz, though."

"Good. Once you have Khaled's approval, we can set you up with a few fake passports so you can travel to Aqaba without an issue."

*A few?* Kasem gulped and nodded, watching the lieutenant, unsure if this was too good to be true. "I will be ready to present a full plan to both of you as soon as possible."

"Remember one thing, Kasem. We never spoke about this operation today. If anyone asks, I came by to speak to you about something regarding your weapons training. When you run it by us for our official clearance, it will be the first time that I hear about it. Is that clear?"

"Yes, sir."

Kasem watched as the lieutenant let himself out, and then he collapsed backward into his chair, reeling in disbelief. He glanced down at the monitoring device on his ankle. *I could disappear.* He shut his eyes as he contemplated the possibility. Even if he had to ruin a friend's business to do it, he knew that he could not turn back from the opportunity the lieutenant had given him. Kasem looked back at his computer and furiously typed out an e-mail that made the full case for why the operation should take place in Aqaba. He focused on the need to bypass Iranian security forces, which tended to be far stricter than those in Jordan were, at least by reputation. He concluded with the point that if he loaded the bug system onto the freighter during its journey back to Europe, they would be able to use the data it collected to implicate a number of corrupt customs officials operating in Bander Abbas.

Two days later, Kasem presented the strategy to Khaled Majed and Lieutenant Afshar, who feigned complete ignorance on the subject.

**\*\*\*\***

Lieutenant Afshar was at his wit's end, staring at General Majed and Khaled. "But, sir, are you sure that you'd like to alienate some of the black market operators to this extent? If Diaz is really smuggling the amounts that we suspect, then the operators will not be happy with us for ending his operations. Drug money is a huge part of their revenue and we cannot operate without their support."

General Majed had just finished affirming his commitment to the mission he had laid out months earlier.

"Lieutenant, I have heard your concerns and I do not agree with you. The mission will proceed as planned. If you have any problems with that, it would do you well to remember our agreement."

The lieutenant shivered, recalling the general's threats to Farah and her family. "Yes, sir."

The general turned toward Khaled. "Now, tell me about your end of this, please."

"Kasem has developed a friendship and business relationship with Nicholas Diaz. Since he is working as Diaz's store designer, he has access to the schedule of Diaz's shipping program. We've laid out plans to set up a bug system on several freighters that should record all shipments that Diaz transports and discharges."

"So the bug system will be laid in Bander Abbas?" the general said as he traced the shipping route with his finger.

"No. We've elected to do it at Aqaba, just before the freighters enter the Suez Canal."

General Majed raised his eyebrows.

"If the trap is set on our own soil, we will not be able to catch the corrupt customs officials involved in Diaz's scam. We need to catch the big guys and planting the trap in Jordan is our best bet."

"Very well. I trust your judgment, Khaled, as long as the boy is ready for it."

"We both believe that he is, sir," Lieutenant Afshar interjected.

"In that case, proceed as planned. With the other initiatives we have planned, we are going to destroy every last one of the drug smuggling operations these scum have been running through our country. And at the same time, we'll drive a stake into the Western scum who finances the whole damned thing."

"We will, sir," Khaled said.

General Majed stood and then turned to Lieutenant Afshar. "Lieutenant, please attend to an urgent query at the central command center. I will join you there shortly."

"Yes, sir." The lieutenant stood quickly and exited the room. It was clear that whatever else the general wanted to discuss, Afshar's presence was not welcome.

"Was there anything else, Uncle?" Khaled asked when the lieutenant was out of earshot.

"Make sure that the self-destruct mechanism on the bug system is operating properly. There cannot be any mistakes."

"Yes, sir."

## *Aqaba, Jordan – June, 2019*

Kasem smiled as he walked back to his hotel room in Aqaba. The sun was setting across the Red Sea and he could see the Israeli-Egyptian border clearly marked by the two white Taba monuments on either side of it. The operation to set the bug system had gone as planned and he knew that his chance to escape was dangling in front of him. He had arranged with Lieutenant Afshar for the security system on his anklet to go blank for a few minutes the next morning. He would use that time to stage a car accident to fake his death and get away.

The possibility of escape was both enticing and scary. He knew that his life would never be what he had hoped for years earlier. He would never be able to build a life with Lila, nor would he ever be able to settle down without having to look over his shoulder. Regardless, he would no longer be subjected to the whims of a rogue Iranian general and his minions.

Before falling asleep for the last remaining hours of the night, he reviewed his plan. Early in the morning, he would leave the hotel in the rental car. There was a deserted old parking lot further down the street. Under the cover of dawn, he would douse it in gasoline and light it from a few feet away. He would time it so that he could cut his anklet exactly when the monitoring light blinked off and then throw it into the fire before stealing away. The scene would never stand up to a full investigation, but he was banking on the general's need to cover up Kasem's death rather than investigate it. Khaled would have some difficulty maintaining his cover if he launched a full police investigation into the crash, so he was more likely to arrange for a cleaner and then forget about the whole thing.

After reviewing his plan, he surveyed his empty hotel room to make sure he was not forgetting anything important. He checked his pockets to make sure that he still had three of his passports. His plan was to throw the Jordanian passport into the fire and use the other two for exit. He sincerely hoped the guy who Afshar had arranged to make the other two passports was worth the exorbitant price they'd paid.

Taking another deep breath, he thought through the rest of his plan. As soon as he made it out of Jordan, he would ditch both of the passports and get another one that would be untraceable if the general figured out Afshar's role in his escape.

Thinking about the rest of his plan made him sigh. He had no idea what he would do with his life now that so much had changed. He hardly thought he could return to life as an investment banker. In vain, he tried to silence his doubts to focus on the next few hours. They remained, though, nagging at the back of his mind.

He only slept for a few hours and awoke just after four in the morning. He gathered his passports, some money, a bottle of rubbing alcohol, and a Leatherman multi-tool with a knife to cut through the ankle monitor. The previous day, he had filled a gas can full of fuel and left it sitting on the passenger side floorboard. *I hope this works.* He pushed away thoughts of what he would do if it did not, and what he would do if it did.

Before driving to the abandoned parking lot, Kasem took a short trip around the city. He switched on the radio to listen to the news, and reveled in the fact that these would be his last few minutes as a slave.

His posture stiffened at a report about a bombing.

*"A number of explosions in the Suez Canal have caused an oil tanker to go up in flames. Authorities believe that the explosions were caused by several bombs placed..."*

He had just entered the abandoned parking lot and continued to drive to the space he had chosen to carry out his plan. Kasem's thoughts began to blur. *Bombs? In the Suez Canal?* Diaz's freighters had left the Aqaba dock the night before to head for the Suez Canal, shortly after he had planted the bugs. *Oh my God. Did I...? How? Those were just bugs!*

He frantically thought back to how he had set the system of bugs; images of the different rooms flashed through his mind. He had set the devices all over the group of freighters. To get complete coverage of each ship, he had placed the bugs in the supply rooms, the captain's lodge, on the bridge, and even in the engine rooms.

He slammed his right fist into the steering wheel. "No!" he screamed. In that moment, he knew the whole thing was a ruse. Khaled had told him the bugs were in large, fully enclosed capsules for a reason; they were supposed to be more difficult to destroy and would transmit and erase data if someone without the proper code tampered with them. It was so elaborate that Kasem had bought the story completely.

*Bomb charges. How could I let this happen?* He slammed his foot down on the brake pedal, causing the car to careen to a stop and hit the wall at the parking lot's edge. The air bag failed to release and he crashed into the steering wheel.

Kasem lifted his hand and felt a small amount of blood dripping from a wound on his head. Part of him wished the crash had just killed him. He clenched his fists, enraged about how much of a monster General Majed really was. His body was shaking as he tried to get control of his thoughts. *How did this happen?* He recalled their meetings when they had planned whole mission. *How could I not have seen it?*

A moment later, the realization struck him. From the beginning, he had been willing to do anything for the general if it meant a mission outside of Iran. Kasem wanted to cling to the idea that he had been duped, but he had always known something about this mission was not right. He never could have predicted the extent of the plan, but he had decided to ignore all the signs that there was something larger at play than simply bringing down a ring of drug smugglers.

*Does that make me any better than General Majed?* Just asking such a question made him wince. *I allowed this to happen. And all those people....* The possibility of escape had made him willing to do anything for the general, no matter what the cost.

Still shaking, he pulled himself out of the car and surveyed the giant dent in the front of the hood. The news was still blaring from the radio as the Al-Jazeera correspondent continued with details about the attack.

*"It appears that at least seven or eight freighters were consumed by fire. Authorities are trying to determine the extent of the damage, but the real danger is to the oil tankers, which are so close to the fires. So far, the death toll is in the hundreds as rescue crews try to search the burning freighters for survivors. There are still no reports about who is behind this terrible attack. No organization has claimed responsibility yet ..."*

One of the details gave him a slight ray of hope. *Seven or eight freighters?* His mission had been to set bugs on only the four freighters belonging to Diaz's shipping business. Although he knew it was next to impossible, he allowed himself to hope that Diaz's ships were not the ones that had exploded.

He stared at the Leatherman still sitting on the passenger seat despite the abrupt stop of his crash. *Were the explosions my fault?* If he cut the anklet now, he could get out and be free of all of it, but he would never know the answer for sure. He walked around the car, reached through the open passenger window for the folded multi-tool. He flipped the knife blade out and pulled up his pant leg to cut the anklet. His hand shook as he reached down with his left hand to hold the anklet still. His palms were sweaty and he had trouble holding the knife steady in his right hand.

He was about to cut through the band when he realized he was deceiving himself once again. *There is no way that I wasn't part of this.* His eyes squeezed shut and pictured the conference room where Lieutenant Afshar, Khaled, and the general had first given him the assignment to investigate Diaz's shipping company. He imagined walking into that room and shooting them all. *What good would that serve?* Breathless and infuriated, he opened his eyes. *I am the one who allowed this to happen. What right do I have to freedom? What place do I have but to continue being his lapdog?*

In that moment, he felt there was no other choice. He had left behind every part of his former self. All he had left was what he had done and what he would do in the service of the general. *I have to go back.*

Instead of cutting the anklet, he tossed the multi-tool aside, opened the passenger door, and grabbed the can of gasoline he had brought with him. He slammed the car door shut, pulled the extra passports from his pocket, and tossed them next to the wall a few feet away from the car. He doused them with gasoline and lit a match.

The blaze incinerated the papers and destroyed his last chance of escape. He wiped his face with the back of his hand, smearing dust and sweat across his face with salty tears.

Denying himself another moment of self-pity, he climbed back into his dented car, somehow successfully started it, and drove back to the hotel, his face and clothes streaked with smoke and grime. He would follow orders and head straight back to Tehran.

## *Tehran, Iran – June, 2019*

Kasem waited outside of the conference room where he'd been summoned. He had returned to Tehran a few days earlier and still had difficulty collecting his thoughts.

He looked down at his anklet with regret. If he had decided to run, he would have been gallivanting in Europe by now. He had tried calling Diaz several times since his return to find out what had happened to the freighters and the shipping company. The upcoming meeting ought to shed some light on the events, but he knew not to trust information from Khaled and the general.

The news about the extent of the damage to the Suez Canal was worse than even his most terrible fears. A number of neighboring oil tankers had caught fire, including two docked tankers. The damage to the docks would take years to repair, not to mention the massive casualties and mangled bodies that poured into Egyptian morgues and hospitals.

Deep down, he knew that this meeting would not yield any new answers. It was too much of a coincidence that he had planted a whole fleet of bugs the night before the explosions. He had made a conscious decision to ignore all of the signs of the bombing that were right in front of him. Escape was the only thing that he could see, no matter what the cost. He had lost the ability to think for himself, to weigh his own life with everyone he had killed. By seeking escape, he had inadvertently strengthened the chains that bound him to this life.

*This is my life now.* He rested his head in his hands and took a deep breath. He wanted to shout at the top of his lungs. *It's not my fault!*

With another deep breath, he tried to lower his heart rate as he'd been taught during training. He was still shaking when Lieutenant Afshar came out of the conference room to summon him.

"Hello, Kasem. I wasn't sure I would see you again."

*Did you know?* He wanted to yell at the lieutenant. Instead, Kasem spoke curtly, glowering at him. "Yes."

"Well, you can come in now."

Without saying a word, Kasem stood and followed Afshar into the conference room. He was shivering, but he clenched his teeth to try to control it.

"Sit down, boy," General Majed said as he entered. Kasem took a seat next to the lieutenant.

"There is an operation we need you to attend to immediately."

Kasem blinked twice in astonishment. *What about what just happened?*

"You must capture this man," the general said, sliding a photo across the table along with a USB key. "The rest of the information you'll need is in the file. Once you have him, burn down the house. If he tries to escape, kill him."

Kasem picked up the photo in silence. The general stood, nodded at his nephew and Lieutenant Afshar, and walked out of the conference room.

"I need to get going as well," Khaled said, following his uncle.

After they'd both gone, Lieutenant Afshar turned toward Kasem. "Let's, um, debrief your last mission."

Kasem raised his eyebrows. "What is there to debrief? I planted the bug systems as instructed. And then I left."

"I assume you've heard the news."

"Yes." Kasem gazed intently at the table for a moment, and then asked, "Did you know?"

Afshar sighed and for a moment, Kasem saw some of his own pain mirrored in the lieutenant's face before he looked away. "I knew the bugs had a self-destruct mechanism, but I thought Majed only wanted to bring down some of the drug smuggling business. I never imagined…the Suez Canal…all of those people."

"So it was my fault." What little hope had remained buried in his consciousness slipped away.

"There were other people involved, Kasem, but I don't know who or how many."

"And this man that General Majed wants me to capture, who is he?"

"They haven't kept me in the loop for a while. I don't know anything about it."

Kasem's eyes narrowed. "I know why I got stuck doing this, but what about you? Why the hell do you work with them, for him?"

Afshar glared at him. "Don't accuse me of anything. I have my reasons just like you have yours. It's not my fault you didn't get out when you had the chance." The lieutenant glanced around the room and whispered, "Look, there might still be a way for me to get you out."

"What?"

"I need a couple of days. We both have to act as if everything is normal."

"Okay, but this mission is supposed to be executed immediately."

"I can't figure things out any sooner."

Kasem gave him a bitter look. "Why on earth should I trust you? Why are you helping me?"

"Because I need to get out too."

They sat in silence. Finally, Kasem responded with a shrug. "Okay. I'll wait a couple of days. It's not like I have any other choice."

\*\*\*\*

Kasem took a seat at a table facing the large model ship displayed in the window of Café Lorca in the Armenian quarter of Tehran. He gazed wistfully at the edge of Daneshjoo Park with the sunset as a backdrop. He and Lila had gone to the park together several times. He remembered sitting with her in the Shahr Theatre and telling her his parents' stories of when they went there on dates.

Adam Saroyan had been seated at the table closest to the model ship for more than an hour. He had ordered two coffees and a large piece of cake, and showed no signs of moving. He seemed completely caught up in the book he was reading.

Kasem took a deep breath and forced himself to focus on the book he was pretending to read while sipping on one of the few good cups of coffee he'd found in Tehran. The target was taking a very long time to finish his coffee and alarm bells rang in Kasem's head. He knew that Saroyan was experienced in intelligence, so it was possible that Kasem had been made. The longer they sat there, the more obvious it would be that Kasem was only hanging out to keep watch.

Kasem shut his book and walked over to the counter.

"Would you like to settle your bill, sir?" the barista enquired.

"Actually, I wanted to order one of your pastries."

"Certainly. Which one would you like, sir?"

"I'll have that one in the corner, with the chocolate and pistachios," he said, pointing at the display case.

Kasem handed over some cash and settled back at his table, hoping the pastry would make him look less obvious. He studied his book and turned the pages to support the illusion that he was actually reading.

A few minutes later, he looked up and watched Saroyan as obviously as possible. He waved and then walked over to the table next to the window.

"Hi," Kasem said.

Saroyan's eyes narrowed. "Hi," he said tentatively.

"Sorry to disturb you. I just noticed that you were reading *The Glass Palace*. My niece really wants to read it and I haven't been able to find it anywhere in the city. Would you mind telling me where you bought it?"

"A friend gave it to me. I'm not sure where he bought it. Sorry."

"That's too bad. Well, look, here's my card. If you wouldn't mind asking him about it, I'd really appreciate it." He touched Adam's arm as he handed the card over and planted a small black bug on the back of his shoulder.

"Yeah, maybe."

"Thank you."

Kasem returned to his seat, finished his pastry, and then left to sit in his car and wait. He switched on the bug remotely and eavesdropped with his headphones while pretending to listen to music. About twenty minutes later, he saw Adam walk out of the café and head across the street to the park. Kasem followed on foot from a safe distance.

He watched Adam say hello to a short man outside the Shahr Theatre and listened.

"What took you so long?" a husky voice asked in Farsi.

"I thought I'd been made. I had to be sure."

"You weren't followed?"

"No. The guy disappeared. Just some weirdo bookworm," Adam replied.

"Let's go inside."

Kasem watched them enter the theater through a narrow side door. He would not be able to follow them inside without being seen, so he stepped away and focused on listening to the conversation.

"Do you have the information we need?"

"Yes. That should be everything."

Kasem frowned. *Is he some kind of spy?*

He reached into his pocket, searching for his phone to record the conversation until he realized that he had left it in the car. Grumbling to himself, he refocused on the conversation.

"You can take a look, if you'd like, but I still need protection, whether the information is enough or not," Adam continued. "He already had that commander killed."

"We'll see about that, but first, make yourself comfortable. You must be sweating buckets because it's so hot in here. Why don't you take off that ridiculous jacket?"

*Shit, no, don't take off that jacket.* A moment later, he heard muffled murmuring and then the feed went quiet. Kasem presumed that Adam must have shed the jacket before they went into another room.

He replayed the recording of the feed quickly, trying to decide if it was worth the risk to follow them inside. He elected to wait, listening intently and hoping the feed would come back to life.

Fifteen minutes later, Kasem heard rustling as Adam picked up the jacket.

"Go straight home," he heard the other man say. "We need the rest of that file."

*Another file?* Kasem thought, realizing he would have to wait to grab Saroyan. He watched as the two men exited, kissed on both cheeks in the traditional greeting, and parted ways.

Saroyan walked across the park toward his home in the Armenian quarter. Kasem followed slowly, glad that he knew where Saroyan was going so that he did not have to keep a closer tail.

When they reached Saroyan's house, Kasem crouched by the gate under the cover of darkness that had just set in. He took out his binoculars and trained them on the window of the study. Because of the light inside, he could see the target clearly.

Saroyan threw his jacket on the couch and started rummaging through items on his desk. He found what he was looking for and then went to stuff it in his jacket pocket. He paused, staring at his jacket.

Outside, Kasem knew that this time he definitely had been made. *Shit.*

"If you think I am going down without a fight, I will bury you," Kasem heard through his earpiece. Saroyan had pulled out two handguns from under the couch and was coming toward the window.

Kasem peered around the gate, looking for an opening. He briefly contemplated going over the wall to get a shot, but that would make him visible to Saroyan. If Saroyan had even moderate skill with those guns, Kasem would be dead before he even got over the wall. The best way would be through the back while keeping out of Saroyan's line of sight from the window. That would also obscure Kasem's view of what Saroyan was doing, though. Deciding quickly, he crept toward the back of the boundary wall.

He was still moving along the wall when an explosion went off behind him, ripping half of the wall open. It knocked him over and he landed hard on his back. Kasem fumbled for his gun, knowing that Saroyan was already a step ahead of him. He squinted to see through the smoke and dust and saw a shadow moving quickly across the front lawn. *He's getting away!* Kasem stumbled as he tried to get up and follow Saroyan. Then, acting completely on instinct, he raised his gun off the ground, squinted and closed one eye to take aim through the haze, and shot the man straight in the back of his neck.

The next few minutes felt like they happened in slow motion. Kasem pulled himself to his feet and limped over to the body. With the boundary wall explosion, he had to move fast to get out of there before the cops arrived. He reached into Saroyan's jacket, pulled out his wallet, and felt for anything else. There was a small metal business card holder wedged next to a Mont Blanc pen. Kasem grabbed them both.

He used his pocketknife to cut through the lining of the briefcase that Saroyan was carrying and whistled softly when he opened it. The briefcase contained two different kinds of explosives. Without wasting any time, he grabbed a small piece of plastic explosive and a detonator device. He positioned the explosive against the house wall directly underneath the study window and pushed the detonator in place on top.

He could hear the sirens as the police cars approached. He crept toward the other side of the boundary wall, which was still intact. Finding a dark spot, he forced himself to climb over it. His ears were still ringing from the explosion, but adrenaline kept him moving forward. He clenched his jaw to ignore the pain shooting through his body from the earlier impact. Safely on the other side, he braced himself for the second explosion.

*This is going to cause a scene,* he thought, looking back at the house.

When the blast went off, he used the chaos as cover to make his way across the street, and around the park's edge toward his car. He drove straight home without glancing at his phone. If he had looked at it, he would have seen the text message icon in the corner of the screen. The message was from an unknown number and read:

*"Emergency mission abort – LA."*

\*\*\*\*

Upon reaching his apartment, Kasem flopped onto the bed and slept for the next thirteen hours. When he finally woke up, the events of the past few days felt like a dream. He lazed around for an hour and then dozed off again.

Thirty minutes later, he woke up frantic with visions of the Suez Canal in flames haunting his dreams. He poured himself a drink from a bottle of scotch he had managed to sneak back from Jordan. Less than a week after returning, it was already almost empty.

He drank the scotch slowly, feeling numb as he gazed out the window. He dozed off and awoke starving with the morning sun streaming in through his window. After searching for food in his completely bare kitchen, he decided to enjoy one of his last meals out in Tehran.

Kasem got dressed quickly and grabbed his wallet and phone, which was dead. He plugged it into the charger and left without giving it another thought.

Fifteen minutes later, he was feasting on a real *nashtayi*—the Iranian term for breakfast. He ate several different *naans*, or flatbreads, coated with butter, Tabrizi and feta cheese, *sarshir* cream, and jam. Even though he was already stuffed, Kasem topped it off with a bowl of *aasheh mohshaalaah*, a thick soup with shredded lamb.

He was fuller than he'd felt in ages as he drove back to his apartment. Once there, Kasem just sat on his bed, staring at the wallet and business card holder he'd recovered from Saroyan's body. He scraped some of the ash off the business card holder and opened it to find a small USB key wedged inside. *Big surprise.*

He plugged the USB key into his computer and waited for it to boot up. When it opened, he frowned because the drive was full of pictures. *Why would Saroyan risk his life for this?* The other folders contained more of the same. *What was he up to?*

At the end of the list of folders, he found one labeled 'GM.' *General Majed?* Saroyan's words echoed in his mind. *He already had that commander killed.* He opened the folder to find a Word document and a series of pictures, many of which included the general. He clicked through them quickly until one in particular caught his eye. The picture was of General Majed with Khaled, along with several men he did not recognize. After staring at it for a moment, he moved on to the document.

His eyes widened as he read the document. He cried out and slammed his fist onto the desk, and then he leaned back in his chair in despair. "You set me up. You fuckers set me up."

He was still reeling when he heard a knock on his door. After grabbing a knife off the kitchen counter, he went to answer it.

Kasem felt his throat tighten as he stepped aside to let Lieutenant Afshar into his apartment, keeping the knife out of sight in his left hand.

"You. You set me up. You set me up!" In one fell swoop, Kasem shoved the lieutenant up against the wall, holding the blade at his throat. "You told me I could trust you, and all that time you were setting me up as the fall guy for the whole Suez Canal bombing. And then you had me kill the man investigating it, the man who had stumbled upon the truth. He could have proved my innocence. You turned me into a terrorist."

Lieutenant Afshar trembled as he spoke. "Kasem, I didn't know about this until yesterday. I didn't know why Majed wanted Saroyan dead. I sent you a message to abort."

268

"Stop lying to me. I never got a message. There was no message." Kasem moved the knife from Afshar's throat and stabbed it into his stomach.

Afshar's eyes glazed over as blood began to seep from the wound and drench his shirt. "I was coming to get you out," he choked. "I sent you a message."

Kasem fell back onto his bed as he watched the lieutenant die. He looked down at his hands now covered in the man's blood. Shaking, he made his way to the bathroom and washed his hands until the water ran clear in the sink. He walked unsteadily back to the main room and took his phone off the charger. It was still off.

He turned it on and waited while it booted. The first thing he noticed was the text message icon indicating that he had an unread message waiting for him. He opened the message, which read, *"Emergency mission abort – LA."*

He dropped his phone and slumped to the ground as his entire body felt numb. He erased the message from his phone and called Khaled Majed.

"Afshar and I got into a fight and I killed him."

"I'll send a cleaner. Come in and debrief."

Kasem pulled the USB key out of his computer and stashed it back in the business card holder. He hid it under a loose floor tile beneath his bed, where he had also stashed a couple of old photos from his time with Lila. He wiped his computer's temporary files to remove all traces of what he'd been looking at before the lieutenant arrived.

When the cleaner showed up, Kasem headed to the other side of the base to meet with Khaled.

"Kasem, tell me what happened," Khaled greeted him.

"The lieutenant came to see me. He was belligerent. We fought and I stabbed him with a kitchen knife."

"But why? Why did you fight?"

"I don't know. He was drunk and he attacked me. I was defending myself."

"I see," Khaled said as he made notes on a legal pad.

Kasem stared at him in silence.

"Okay. You're dismissed. We'll contact you about your next mission."

Kasem left quickly. He went through the motions of driving home, still feeling entirely numb.

****

Back in the conference room, Khaled waited for his uncle. He had already called to inform him of what had happened to Lieutenant Afshar. A few minutes after the call, the general arrived.

"Did you send a cleaner to take care of Afshar's body?" General Majed asked without any other greeting.

"Yes. It's taken care of."

The general looked out of the conference room window and mumbled an acknowledgement.

Khaled gave him a moment before asking, "What do you have planned for the boy, Uncle?"

"He will be an assassin to do our bidding. Circulate some fake intelligence about how instrumental one particular man was in the attacks on the Suez Canal. Make sure nothing can be traced back to him or us."

"Okay. I'll take care of it." Khaled paused as he was about to leave. "Who would you like me to credit the attacks to?"

The general tilted his head. "No normal man should be credited with such an attack."

"What do you mean?"

"Khaled, we must give him a new name—one that stretches beyond the fear of these attacks."

"I see. What sort of name were you thinking?"

"The name of a god, or a spirit."

Khaled bit his lip. "A spirit?"

"Yes, a spirit. He has become the Ahriman, our spirit of destruction."

****

# Chapter 21
## The Dewaniya

*Kuwait City, Kuwait – July 4, 2021*

The Ahriman passed through security without a hassle and proceeded straight into the dewaniya at Bayan Palace. Surprisingly, three people had arrived before him. Instead of being able to set his device before the evening's festivities, he realized that he would have to wait until afterward.

He took a seat in an effort to hide his mild frustration at the unexpected turn of events. The men began joking around as the first round of sheesha and coffee arrived. "Would anyone like a special coffee?" one of them asked, holding up a small flask.

Almost all of them held out their cups immediately, but the Ahriman held his back.

"Mustafa! You are not having any?"

"Not tonight unfortunately."

"Oh, come on!"

"Okay, okay! Hit me. Just a little, though." He handed over his cup and watched as a healthy portion of whiskey was doled into it.

"Thank you," he said with a smile. He took a slow sip, relishing the taste since he would be unable to drink more than one cup. His mission tonight would require him to have his full wits about him. He looked up as a couple of more men joined them.

"Aziz!" one of the seated men called out. "We haven't seen you in a few months."

They exchanged kisses on the cheek and the second man smiled at them shyly. "Salaam alaikum. My name is Henry Jones. I'm a good friend of Hamad's and he told me I should join you while I was visiting Kuwait."

"Welcome, Henry. We all miss Hamad, but it's good to have you regardless."

The second round of sheesha came around a few minutes later, and they all drank in its haze.

****

When Petra finally made her way through the entrance of the main palace, she was sweating profusely and breathing heavily. Even though she had kept her promise to Grant to be cautious, she was extremely nervous about the prospect of coming face to face with a nemesis as skilled as the Ahriman. Credited with the Suez Canal bombings, the Ahriman ranked at the top of the Agency and Interpol Watch Lists, as well as the most wanted lists of American, British, Arab, and French government agencies. Trying to apprehend him without any backup was preposterous, but she had no choice. Adding the president's visit on top was enough to increase her blood pressure by several notches in spite of the outward calm she had managed to project to Grant.

Petra followed the blueprints toward one of the entrances and then began searching for the attic entry she would use to reach the men's dewaniya. As she reviewed the plan multiple times in her mind, she knew how much could go wrong, but she forced herself to continue lest she freeze up completely. No matter how hard she tried to stop it, she just kept asking herself why she had decided to return to the field. Truth be told, up until now, she had been having a good time, but the Ahriman's involvement had transformed the romanticism of fieldwork back into its scary reality.

Instead of going directly to find the men's dewaniya, she moved across the courtyard toward the women's event. Confidently, she walked straight into the bathroom. The small, single bathroom was beautifully decorated in green and gold. She made her way over to the toilet and flushed it several times with her heel, slamming her foot down on the handle each time. After a number of tries, it broke. With the bathroom in the women's unit out of order, she now had a plausible excuse for needing to use the one in the palace's main building, which also housed the dewaniya.

She exited quietly. The event had just started, so no one paid any attention to her. She made her way back to the palace's main entrance and walked straight to the door.

One of the guards stopped her, pointing toward the women's event.

"The bathroom is out of order," she said in Arabic.

He nodded and let her through, pointing in the direction of the bathroom. She nodded and walked down the hallway. When she saw that he had turned back to watch the grounds, she crept around the stairwell. Looking back at the blueprints on her phone, she began searching for the doorway to the small storeroom she had seen on the map. On her left, she saw a plain door toward at the end of the corridor. *That must be it.*

She tapped her com link in her ear and whispered to Grant. "I've located the storeroom entrance. I should be at the dewaniya shortly, barring any unexpected developments."

In response, she heard a sharp tap to indicate his understanding. She reached underneath her burka and pulled out a slim white lock pick kit that was disguised as a small, innocuous makeup case. Using these tools, she began to fiddle with the lock, praying that it would work.

A moment later the door eased open and she crept inside, closing the door behind her. There, she shed her burka and tossed it onto a cardboard box. She then searched for the circuit breaker panel box on the wall. According to the blueprints, the access panel to the attic would be right above it. Once her eyes adjusted to the dim light, she could easily see the access point on the ceiling. Petra breathed a sigh of relief. She slung her purse across her chest and left shoulder, and fastened one strap to her belt so that she would have easy access to the rest of her supplies, including the pinhole camera kit.

"I'm heading into the attic now," she radioed to Grant. Communicating with him regularly made her feel less like she was on her own and helped to distract her from the impending meeting with the Ahriman.

She climbed onto a crate and hoisted herself up to reach the panel, which she slid back slowly before pulling herself into the attic. A moment later, she was belly crawling slowly through a crawl space in the attic. The blueprints did not make it entirely clear which direction would be the shortest route to the dewaniya, and the attic encompassed the entire palace. Either way would be a painful process given the number of boxes stored there and the thick layer of dust that covered the floor and everything around it. She focused on her instincts to choose the right direction to move toward the main dewaniya without disturbing any of the stored boxes and furniture jammed into the tight crawl space.

After slithering for some time, she pulled her phone out of her pocket and slowly slid it across the floor to a spot where she could both touch it and see the images on it. She scanned the blueprints quickly to confirm the distance based on the direction that she had crawled. *Almost there,* she thought as she continued to snake through the attic.

A few feet further, she noticed another access panel. She pressed her nose to the hinged joint. The first wafts of sheesha smoke began to filter into the crawl space. She wrinkled her nose and then let out a sigh of relief that she had managed to find the dewaniya.

She retrieved the pinhole camera kit from her purse and examined the access panel. The panel had warped from age and she could peek through one side and see the hinges on the other side that would have allowed it to open outward. She pulled out two pieces of structurally enhanced duct tape, which was standard Agency issue, and taped over the edge of the panel opposite to its hinges. Then, moving on to the hinged side, she used a small out-the-front switchblade to carefully scratch and chip away at the edge of the panel below the hinge. By doing so, the narrow gap between the panel and the attic floor widened to half an inch, just wide enough to push the pinhole camera through without having to open the panel. If she had been able to do recon before this mission, she would have gone ahead and drilled a hole in the middle of the panel for a better view without worrying about the access panel falling open or putting pressure on the artisanal grate underneath. With the dewaniya already taking place below, though, she had to make do with the tools she had.

Petra pushed the pinhole camera through the gap slowly while making slight adjustments until it cleared the access panel and touched the old vent grate below it. She let out a sigh of relief that she didn't seem to alert anyone at the gathering below. When the camera was in position, she connected the end of the camera's cable to her phone to use it as a view screen.

The screen flickered for a moment and the image sharpened. She saw the large artisanal grate in front of her and then much of the room beyond the grate. Although the grate itself did offer some camouflage, the camera would remain completely concealed as long as no one below looked directly up at it. She tilted the camera angle sideways and positioned herself to the left of the access panel. She could see a number of men, but only the tops of their heads. There were a few different colored gutra headpieces, but nothing easily identifiable about them. She did manage to recognize one of the men speaking awkwardly and uncomfortably in the corner. *That has to be Grant.*

Speaking into her com unit, she said, "Grant, do not look up. I'm in position above the dewaniya. Any word on who Mustafa is?"

After hearing no reply, Petra sighed. "I'll take your silence as a 'no.' Okay, just try to identify him if you can."

The conversation below was predominantly in Arabic as the men discussed vacation spots, the best beaches in the region, the economic situation in other parts of the world, increased investment in Africa—all most likely to avoid discussing the elections on the following day. Suddenly the conversation below grew louder.

"How many of us will be celebrating tomorrow after the elections?" one of the men asked.

"But the Emir will lose power."

"We should celebrate anyway. The Emir has made a strong power play by appointing the Crown Prince. The Assembly will be forced to concede to some more progressive measures, and they'll never be able to force him out as prime minister."

"Besides, we have this beautiful dewaniya and great sheesha."

"And don't forget about 'special' coffee."

Petra tried not to laugh as she remembered the black market liquor her parents would smuggle into Kuwait whenever they traveled.

"Mustafa, you are absolutely right. 'Special' coffee is the extra ingredient."

Then others began to jump into the conversation. "We should celebrate tomorrow. We cannot let them see that they got to us."

Petra listened to them drone on about the elections, trying to get a look at Mustafa's face. All she could see was a red gutra headpiece, which contrasted with the white ones most of other the men wore. It made it easy to identify him, but they still had to confirm that there was only one Mustafa in attendance that evening. "Looks like that's him in the red," she whispered into her com. "We have to confirm that it's him. There might be more than one Mustafa. Keep your ears open."

Over the next three hours, Petra almost fell asleep in the attic. She rubbed her eyes and wished she could have a "regular" coffee to help keep her awake. Her waiting was finally gratified when some of the men began to excuse themselves.

"It should clear out now," she said, tapping her earpiece. "Excuse yourself and wait for me at the car."

She reached down to her calf holster and pulled out her Colt pistol. With her other hand, she reached into her bra where she hid her silencer and attached it to her gun.

Fifteen minutes later, there were only a couple of men left. "Come, Mustafa," one of them said. "I'll walk you to your car."

"Oh, I'm okay. Actually, I need to use the bathroom before I leave, so please go ahead."

"Very well. I hope to see you tomorrow. The Emir has kicked us out of this place, but we will be right down the street."

"I probably can't make it tomorrow, Othman, but I will try. I'm sure the celebration will be great fun."

"Soon then? Maybe next week?"

"Definitely."

Petra watched the scene, now sure that this man had to be *the* Mustafa she needed to find. Something about his voice irked her, but she pushed it aside. She glared down at his head. *What a snake.*

She pulled the pinhole camera back and put it in her bag. Then she pulled the tape off the access panel and pushed it out slowly, trying to be as quiet as possible. Once the panel touched the grate, the pressure pushed them both open simultaneously. Both were hinged to the ceiling, so they fell open on the right side with a soft thud as they clanked together. The opening was just barely wide enough for her to fit through it.

Petra peered out of the opening and watched him walk away toward the bathroom. She then attempted to lower herself slowly from the ceiling. After descending about halfway, the grip of her right hand on the panel's interior hinge faltered and it slipped, so she abruptly fell straight down without enough time to adjust her landing. Pain seared through her right ankle and knee as she collapsed on the ground. Pushing her forehead into the carpet, she fisted her hands and bit back the urge to cry out in pain. Several deep breaths later, she forced herself up off the floor, thanking the decorators for the thickly padded carpeting because she could not imagine how painful it would feel to land on a ceramic floor. She wiped her nose and swallowed a sneeze from the dust that now covered her. Still crouching down on the ground, she maneuvered herself to hide behind one of the sofas, wincing in pain as she moved her right leg.

When he did not return after a few minutes, Petra began to doubt herself. Instinct told her that he would come back to set the charges in the main dewaniya. There was, of course, the small possibility that he would set the charges in the bathroom. It would be a much less foolproof system and would require a bigger charge, but it was still a distinct possibility.

Several moments passed and it felt like an eternity. She began to debate whether she should break cover and follow him to the bathroom. *What if he's already planted the charges?* The Ahriman would be able to get away long before she had the chance to follow since she and every other security officer would be occupied with trying to disarm the bomb.

After waiting another few moments, she moved quickly through the door toward the bathroom. "Grant, where are you?"

"I just got to the car."

"Can you meet me at the men's bathroom outside the dewaniya?"

"Babe, are you asking me to come and have some fun in there?"

"Not the time for jokes," she chastised. "I think he might be setting the charges there."

"Okay. What should I say to security?"

"I don't know, Grant. Say you forgot something. Make something up. Just get here."

"Okay, okay, babe. I'm on my way."

A few seconds later, Petra reached the bathroom. Luckily, it was not a single stall like the women's bathroom, so the main door wasn't locked and she was able to push it open a crack.

She could see a man with a bright red gutra crouching in front of the cabinet under a countertop with two sinks. From her vantage point, she was still unable to identify any discerning characteristics. She could not even estimate his height. Petra took a deep breath and planned her strategy. It would be a mistake for her to startle him if the bomb was already live.

She watched him pull a small panel out from inside the cabinet to access the bathroom's interior pipes. *Twisted genius. Instead of planting the bomb in the dewaniya, he's going to use the building's plumbing.* She kicked herself for not thinking of that. It would probably have been far more comfortable to monitor the bathrooms via video than to squeeze into the attic crawl space for several hours. *That might have been easier, but I still would have had to be on site to grab him.*

He removed a small device from underneath his dishdasha and began sliding it into the space. She closed her eyes and tried to remember the explosives training she had received many years earlier. Since leaving the field, she had paid little attention to refresher courses that her superiors recommended she attend, although never mandatory. Whenever bomb expertise was required, she had summoned an explosives expert to support her team. From what she remembered, most bombs could not be armed until they were fully in place, even when strapped to a moving device. While he was still trying to place the device, she decided to take the gamble.

As quietly as possible, she pushed open the door while reaching for her gun. "Stop," Petra yelled, pointing her gun straight at him. "Don't even think about doing anything with that bomb. Put your hands up and turn around, slowly."

He stood up and raised only his left hand overhead slowly. As he began to turn toward her, she saw him withdraw a small canister from his pocket with his right hand. A faint *whoosh* sound emerged from the canister before he had turned all the way around.

Even from the side, she could see a black piece of cloth covering half of his face. *Why is he wearing a mask?* She caught his eyes for a moment. *Those eyes are so familiar. I've seen them before. Who—?* As the room began to fill with halothane gas, Petra squinted as she fought the urge to pass out. Her vision grew hazy and she felt as if she had been transported into a hallucination from years earlier. He just stood there, motionless with eyes wide, gaping at her. Petra's hands began to shake as she attempted to hold her gun steady and tried desperately to comprehend the situation.

"Is, is that? Are y—?" she managed to utter as her vision clouded further. Her chest felt heavy as her breathing became more difficult. A moment later, the room went black as she passed out.

The Ahriman quickly shoved the panel back into the cabinet to cover his device, opened the window at the other end of the bathroom, and scrambled through it.

**\*\*\*\***

# Chapter 22
# The Manhunt

*Kuwait City, Kuwait – July 5, 2021*

"Hello? Where, where am I?" Petra said as she awoke at the hospital the next day. "Oh my God. My head feels like someone's playing the drums on top of it."

"You're awake!" Grant cried out, grabbing her hand. "Don't ever scare me like that again."

She squinted and shook her head. "I'm sorry. What happened?" She frowned and her vision began to clear. When his face finally came into focus, she could see the concern tattooed across it. "Tell me what happened. Everything feels so hazy."

"You told me you were following him into the bathroom and that you wanted me to meet you there. It took me a while to get past security. By the time I got there, I found you lying on the floor." He paused as his throat constricted. "I was so scared. I thought I might have lost you."

"But he got away? How long have I been out? How did you even get me out of there? Shit. Have the elections happened yet? He's going to set off the bomb!" She sat up abruptly. "Get them to take this drip out."

"Are you crazy? You almost died yesterday. Get someone else to take care of it!" He averted his eyes, his shoulders heaving. "I found you lying in a heap last night. At first, I thought you were dead."

"I'm so sorry, Grant." Petra touched her hand to his face. "I'm okay. This is something that I have to do."

He stared at her. "I don't want anything to happen to you. I feel so helpless."

"You said you understood why they called me back in. Now I need you to help me make sure that this bomb doesn't go off."

"Fine," he said, resigned. "I didn't tell them what happened, so they said once you woke up, they'd want to keep you for observation to determine why you passed out. I'll go talk them into starting the discharge papers."

"When this is over, I promise I'll take a long vacation."

He gave her a half smile and left the room.

Petra fell back against the pillow and she blinked tears away. *Did I really see—?* She closed her eyes and tried to remember what had happened the previous night. She recalled running into the bathroom and shouting with her gun raised. She remembered the *whoosh* sound coming from the canister in the Ahriman's hand as he turned around. Then everything became blurry. Her mind was foggy about those last moments before she passed out. For all she knew, it could have been a delusion brought on by the gas. She shivered, trying to divert her mind from all the memories associated with such a hallucination. She reached for the remote at the bedside seeking a distraction and turned on the news.

Grant walked in holding a sheaf of papers in his hand. "You just need to sign these discharge papers."

Petra barely heard him as she focused on the news. "We're too late."

Grant looked up at the television and they both watched the breaking news story.

*"The Kuwaiti royal family has postponed National Assembly elections for an undetermined period due to an emergency. We have reports of some kind of explosion at Bayan Palace, but we are still waiting for confirmation. The details behind these announcements are still unclear…"*

"Let's get out of here. We can call Chris and figure out what to do for damage control," he said, looking back at her.

She drew a sharp breath and nodded. *If that's even a possibility.*

\*\*\*\*

"Chris, have you heard? I just saw the news. What happened at Bayan Palace today?"

"Slow down, Petra. First, are you okay? Are you sure you should be up and running right now?"

"I'm fine. I just got knocked out."

"I was worried when Grant called last night. I'm glad that he was there to help you out. The cover story he told security about how you had passed out from a severe allergy was smart, fast thinking. Luckily, he managed to move you over to the entrance of the women's room before calling security for help. Since you were wearing a nice dress, they didn't ask any questions about what you were doing at the women's event."

Petra stole a glance across the room to the bathroom where Grant was taking a shower. She could hear him singing the Beach Boys. "Yeah, he does come in handy in a pinch. I was lucky he was there," she smiled. "I'm okay. It was just halothane gas. I remember that odor from some training course you sent me to years ago." She drew a long breath. "We can't waste any more time, Chris. Have you heard anything about what happened? Why did they call off the elections?"

"You're not going to like this."

She raised her eyebrows.

"It was the bomb scare. After Grant got you out safely, we had to inform palace security about it and they had some trouble disarming the device. He had already planted it when you found him."

"So he could have set it off anytime? Jesus..." She took a deep breath in relief. "At least they managed to disarm it."

From the on-screen image, she could see Chris tilt his head from side to side and purse his lips. "Well, they did, eventually, but one piece of the device detonated anyway. Two of the security guards are in the ICU, but it looks like they'll make it."

"So we were lucky." She exhaled loudly.

"Indeed," Chris concurred. "Now all we have to do is get this fucker."

*I don't know if I can,* she thought, but replied, "Consider it taken care of."

"The other problem is that we still don't have definitive proof to tie Fayed or Majed to this whole plot."

She nodded. "Definitive enough for everyone to know, but nothing that would hold up in court. Besides, we don't have any legal rights to most of our information."

"What leads do we have on this guy? Think you can track him down?"

"We have the name he's using—Mustafa Mubarak—but not much else. Unless," she said, but then paused. "Can you get us access to traffic camera and satellite feeds over Bayan Palace from last night? Maybe we can figure out where he went."

"Yeah, but it might take a while to get permission."

"No, it won't," Petra said, grinning. "Grant, think you can help with that?" she called out to her boyfriend who had just emerged from the shower.

Chris tilted his head to the side and frowned. "Hacking into the national database is not a good idea. We can make this work."

"Come on. This is the point of off-book missions."

He rolled his eyes. "Fine. Let's try to track down this asshole. He's spoiling my Fourth of July weekend."

"We'll find him. Go spend some time with your family."

"I will. Petra, I hate to add to all that you're juggling, but there's another problem."

"What do you mean?"

He sighed. "So you remember how Peter Reynolds was visiting the Emir?"

"How could I forget?"

"Yeah. Well, he's taken the explosion as an attempt on his life."

She raised her eyebrows. "And?"

"And he's even more trigger-happy than Arnold Schwarzenegger in the *Terminator* movies."

"Shit. What's he threatening to do? Who does he think is to blame?" She felt her blood pressure shoot up another notch.

"Thankfully, he believes that the Kuwaitis had nothing to do with it."

"As in the Kuwaiti government?" Her pulse was pounding in her ears.

"Yeah. Given that the Emir was obviously also a target—"

"So he's willing to give the oh-so-wonderful concession that he might not have been the only target of the damned explosion? He never should have been here in the first place! What the hell was he doing negotiating a private oil contract? And if he wasn't willing to give us that concession, then what was he going to do? Nuke the shit out of one of the United States' most important allies in the Middle East? Turn one of the largest global oil-exporting countries into a parking lot along with all of the other American interests here?" Her face had turned red and her ears felt like they were on fire.

Chris patiently waited for her to finish. "We would both have to agree that Peter Reynolds is a deeply flawed individual. Whatever our opinions are, though, he is still the president, and he's out for blood. We have to figure out who is to blame for all of this shit."

"I thought we already knew, even if it wouldn't hold up in court."

"You and I both know there has to be more to this than a politician who's pissed off at the king. The timing is way too coincidental."

Petra looked at the ground for a moment before finally managing to speak. Her face was no longer an angry red and had returned to its normal shade. "You're probably right. We'll get moving right away."

"Okay." He paused, considering. "Petra, are you sure you're all right? It seems like your mind is somewhere else. I wouldn't blame you if you needed to take a few hours off. I don't think we could find somebody else, unfortunately, or I would tell you to take a week."

"We can't afford a few hours off. Don't worry, I'm fine. I guess I'm just a bit spacey from that gas and waking up in the hospital."

"Okay, if you're sure. Keep me updated."

Chris hung up and she tried once again to decipher her hazy memory of the previous night. She was staring at the monitor when Grant touched her on the shoulder.

"Petra? You are okay, right?"

"I'm fine," she said, forcing a small smile. "It's just my knee. I thought I sprained it last night, but it's not as bad as I thought. I just need to rewrap the elastic bandage the nurse put on before I left because it's starting to slip."

She sat next to Grant and lifted up the end of her dress to unwind the bandage and examine her still slightly swollen knee. It was ginger to the touch and she grimaced while rewrapping it.

"Okay. Now let's get to it."

"I set my old hacking program up to access the traffic network. It's still uploading now."

He walked back over to his computer. "We're in. You called me back to the bathroom around 11:30." He keyed in a few strokes and the street outside of the Bayan Palace compound appeared on his screen with the time ticking in the bottom right corner.

Looking over his shoulder, Petra watched the image. "There shouldn't be too many cars exiting the compound at that hour."

"There," Grant cried out, pointing at a dark Toyota Yaris that had just turned onto the road after exiting the palace compound.

"Can you zoom in to be sure?"

"Already working on it."

He paused the image on screen and began zooming in to the front of the car. Slowly, the graininess cleared and the image sharpened.

"It's him," Grant said, squinting at the picture.

"What's the license plate number?"

"Hmm, let's see. B-4-5-3-5-7," he said after manipulating the image so that they could see the front of the car.

"It must be a rental. Can you trace it with the Agency's program? Maybe he's registered it to his hotel or office address."

"I hope so." Grant opened up a separate program and keyed in the plate number.

"Searching..." Petra fidgeted as she sat down next to him again.

"Got it. The car's registered to Mustafa Mubarak with *Total*."

"*Total*? Is there a contact number?"

"Yeah. It's 2572-0716."

"I really hope this is his hotel's number," Petra said as she dialed it. "If not, I'll have to come up with some reason to urgently see a *Total* executive."

"Seabank Hotel, how can I help you?"

"I'm calling to speak to one of your guests—Mustafa Mubarak."

"Mr. Mubarak is not in at the moment. Would you like to leave a message?"

"No, that's all right. I'll just stop by later. Where are you located?"

"In Salmiya, right behind Al-Bustan Mall."

"Thank you."

"You're welcome, ma'am. Is there anything else I can help you with today?"

"No, that's it. Have a wonderful day."

After hanging up, she typed a quick message to Chris. *"Seabank Hotel, Salmiya. Heading there now. His license plate number—B45357. Report location but do not apprehend."* She limped her way through a quick shower and change of clothes before heading to the Ahriman's hotel.

## *Shuwaikh, Kuwait – July 5, 2021*

The Ahriman sat in his car with the air conditioner blasting while parked in a shaded parking garage across the street from an abandoned construction site. The building was a fully built, small office complex that sat empty because no one had agreed to buy space in it. Several building projects around the region had been abandoned over the past few years because of the economic crisis, and the empty sites were perfect for his line of work.

He forced himself to concentrate on the list of tasks he knew he should be doing. He still had to go back and check out of his hotel before going to ground. After the events of the previous evening, he would have to hide out for a while before he could move around in the open again.

He looked down at the monitoring device on his ankle that he'd been wearing for years. *Could it really be her?* He leaned his head back against the headrest and tried to collect his thoughts. *How did this happen?*

Reaching over to the glove compartment, he pulled out his Leatherman multi-tool. *This ends now,* he thought. He held the knife over the anklet, hesitating. *And for what?*

He clenched his teeth and sliced through the anklet and dropped the tool to the side. He sat there for several moments staring at the now broken tracking device. *It's over.* His pulse was racing as he tossed the anklet out the window and ran over it several times with the car. When it was safely destroyed, he parked in the corner once again and gazed straight ahead, chest heaving with each breath. His hands were trembling as he tried to grip the steering wheel.

Finally, he managed to release the parking brake and grasp the steering wheel. He shifted into first gear and drove off, taking Fifth Ring Road toward Salmiya to check out of his hotel.

## *Surra, Kuwait – July 5, 2021*

"You mean to tell me that he didn't do anything? He set off the bomb on a couple of security guards?"

"He couldn't have planned it this way, sayeedi. They must have caught him in the act."

Fayed glared at his aide, Khaled Majed. "Did he get away?"

"Yes, but we don't know where he is." Khaled squirmed under his superior's gaze.

"You what? He could blow this entire operation wide open. We would be ruined! And we don't even know where he is?"

"No, sir, but we're working on it. Rest assured. We'll find him."

Fayed took a deep breath, still fuming. "The entire thing is still untraceable?"

"I am taking measures to ensure that."

"Don't give me that crap! If we don't even know where he is, how can we control him?"

"It's quite simple sir. We haven't paid him yet."

"You're still planning to *pay* him? He didn't do anything!" Fayed looked as if he could shoot daggers with his eyes.

"It would be wise to keep him on our side. We might even be able to get him to try again."

"Try again? Every investigator in the region is going to be searching for him in a matter of hours, if they aren't already!"

"Yes, sir, but that doesn't mean they'll find him."

Fayed was quiet for a few moments, considering the situation. "Fine. We'll go with your plan. If this doesn't work, I will make sure that you never set foot in any office in the Arab world again."

Khaled nodded and turned to leave Fayed's office.

"I have not dismissed you," Fayed growled.

"I'm sorry, sir. I didn't realize."

"Don't give me that shit. I gave you this job as a favor to your family, something I've regretted doing for a while now. So don't talk to me like I'm an idiot. I want you to take me through every part of this new plan. No more surprises; there have already been too many."

\*\*\*\*

A few minutes later, Khaled made another call while walking around outside to smoke a cigarette.

"We're in deep shit," he told his handler.

"Where is the boy?"

"I don't know. He's disappeared."

"What the hell went wrong? How could you let this happen?"

"I'm sorry, Uncle. I don't know. The anklet seems to be malfunctioning."

They were both silent for a moment. "Have they figured out the identity of the real target?" the general asked.

Khaled shook his head. "No one knew about the president's visit, so I can't see how they would."

"But Fayed is the one who paid for everything right?"

"Of course."

"Then he will take the blame for it, as we planned."

"Yes, Uncle."

"Very well. We'll have to devise another plan for that idiot Reynolds."

Khaled took a final drag from his cigarette, then threw it to the ground, and stomped it out with his shoe. "I'll get to work on it right away."

## *Salmiya, Kuwait – July 5, 2021*

Grant walked up to the concierge desk at the Seabank Hotel in Salmiya.

"How can I help you, sir?"

"I'm here to speak with one of your guests, Mr. Mustafa Mubarak. I told him I'd meet him here."

"Certainly, sir." The clerk glanced at the wall of keys behind him. "It appears that Mr. Mubarak is out at the moment."

"Could you call upstairs to make sure?"

"Of course, sir." Grant watched the clerk dial the number 240 on the phone at the desk.

"He's not answering."

"I'll wait for him here then."

"Please have a seat, sir."

As he sat down in the lobby, he pulled out his phone and texted Petra—*"Room 240."*

Waiting in the car outside, Petra heard her phone *beep* and read the incoming text from Grant. She tucked her shirt into her jeans and switched her flats for a pair of heels. Without showing any hesitation, she got out and walked to the entrance of the hotel. She strutted into the lobby and headed straight toward the elevators. It was all she could do to make it there without limping. Because of her jeans and heels, every clerk in the lobby ogled her ass rather than questioning who was walking through the lobby. She was her very own diversion.

She took the elevator to the second floor, thankful that no keycard was required, and glanced up and down the hallway to make sure she was alone. Once she reached the door for room 240, she knocked and listened for any noises on the other side of it. After a few moments, she was satisfied that no one was there and pulled out a small kit from her back pocket to pick the lock. It was much more complicated than the storeroom lock at the palace, but after considerable effort, the door popped open.

Petra closed the door behind her and began looking around. It was a small hotel room with a double bed, a television, a large closet area, a small bathroom, and a separate kitchen space. A number of pans were arranged on a drying rack next to the kitchen sink. She touched one of them with her finger; they had been dry for a while.

She took in the rest of the kitchen slowly. After noticing nothing out of the ordinary in the fridge or in the cabinets, she moved into the closet area. When she slid one of the closet doors open, several boxes tumbled out and landed at her feet. She opened a couple of them and found a wide array of *Total* paraphernalia.

The other closet contained several dishdashas, suits, and a set of shirts, undershirts, boxers, and socks. He had clearly been living there for some time. She went through the suit pockets to see if she could find any clues. Nothing she found either confirmed or refuted the hazy familiarity of that moment from the previous night. She also didn't find any hints as to the Ahriman's whereabouts. She walked over to the bed and sank down to clear her head. She closed her eyes, trying to push out the confusing memories.

*Could it really be?* She asked herself that question again, looking for anything in the room that might provide an answer.

After staring at the ceiling for a few moments to gather her thoughts, she decided to look through the trash for any more clues. She found a few receipts from different supermarkets and was about to give up when she pulled out another small piece of paper. It was a receipt for a parking garage in Shuwaikh on the other side of town. Grabbing her phone, she took a picture of the receipt, sent it to Grant, and then stuffed it into her jeans pocket.

She was still crouched on the floor next to the trashcan when she heard a key in the lock. *Shit. Why didn't Grant warn me?* She scrambled hastily for the nearest hiding place. She pulled herself under the bed, but there was barely enough space between the floor and the bed frame for her to maneuver. She was positioned parallel to the foot of the bed, with her feet precariously close to the other side. Before she had the chance to move her legs back toward the wall, she heard him step into the room. Straining, she tried in vain to reach for her gun holster on her calf without making a sound.

She heard noises coming from the closet, saw his feet approach the foot of the bed along with a wheeled suitcase, and then felt a thump as he threw the suitcase on the bed. She shifted further back, trying to distance herself from a pair of dress shoes next to her head.

A moment later, a hand reached down and grabbed the shoes. Petra froze. *Did he see?* She quietly exhaled in relief as she watched his feet move to the other side of the bed toward the window. She slid her legs together to move them away from that side.

*Damn,* she thought when she heard the click of a gun.

She screamed as she felt him grab her legs and pull her out from under the bed.

**** 

"Are you all right, sir?"

Grant stirred suddenly. For a moment, he had forgotten where he was until he noticed the Seabank Hotel logo embroidered on the clerk's shirt above his nametag.

"I'm, I'm sorry. I'm fine. I just dozed off. It must be the heat."

"Mr. Mubarak went up to his room a few minutes ago. He said he would be back down shortly."

Grant's eyes widened with surprise. *Oh my God. Petra!* "Oh, thanks. That's good to hear. Is there a bathroom I can use to freshen up?"

"Yes, sir. Straight down the hallway next to the staircase," the clerk replied, pointing to the hallway.

"Thanks."

He stood and walked down the hallway. Instead of turning to go into the bathroom, he ran straight up the staircase toward the second floor.

**** 

"Damn it, Lila. You're here again! Now stand up. Slowly."

Petra gathered her legs underneath her to stand. In one swift motion, she reached for her calf holster and realized that her gun was missing.

"Don't bother. I took it when I grabbed your leg to pull you out. Put your hands behind your head."

She placed her hands behind her head and turned around to face him. Her first glance confirmed her suspicions from the previous night. "Oh my God. It *was* you. I thought I was hallucinating. What happened to you, Kasem? Who the hell are you?" Her voice quivered as she spoke.

The Ahriman ignored the comment. "We're going to walk out of this hotel now. And don't try to escape. I really don't want to shoot you. Just keep quiet and pretend you're my girlfriend. You're good at pretending to be someone else, so it should be easy for you. Oh, and hand over your phone."

Petra stared at him, wide-eyed.

He could see a mix of emotions etched across her hazel eyes— fear, anger, confusion, disappointment, and maybe even the beginnings of hate. *Nothing I can do,* he told himself.

She handed over her phone and he pocketed it. He gestured toward the door with his gun. "Let's get going," he said. "Don't try anything because I will shoot you. I don't want to, but I will." He tightened his fingers, trying to hold the gun steady in spite of his emotions.

She nodded as the Ahriman slid the gun into his jacket pocket and pointed it toward her back. He grabbed the suitcase with his left hand and placed his right hand, still holding the gun in his pocket, at the small of her back. They walked out of the room and headed for the elevators. The door to the room swung back behind them, but did not click shut. A moment later, they stepped inside the elevator.

****

Grant heard the elevator door closing as he reached the second floor from the staircase. Moving quickly, he reached room 240. He tried the door handle, expecting it to be locked, when he noticed that the door wasn't even closed. Without a thought for his own safety, he swung it open and entered the room. "Petra? Petra?"

When he got no answer, he sank to his knees on the floor next to the closet area. *He took her.* Taking a few deep breaths, he looked around the room. *What would Petra do next?* Grant got to his feet and began to walk around the room, searching for signs of where they had gone. He even looked under the bed and found Petra's lock pick kit. Trying to stay focused, he put it in his jacket pocket.

He pulled out his phone to call Chris and noticed the message Petra had sent him with the parking garage receipt. He immediately sent a quick text message to Chris. *"P and A are missing. Tracing them to a parking garage in Shuwaikh. Will call you en route."*

**** ****

# Chapter 23
# The Ultimate Con

*Shuwaikh, Kuwait – July 5, 2021*

Petra watched the city pass by the car window in a daze, feeling unsteady and unsure. Her training had taught her a number of different options to get out of a situation like this one. She could try to knock out her captor, get the gun away from him, or steal her phone back, for starters. In that moment, though, all she could do was watch the world pass by outside the car window in a state of numb disbelief. She could not even summon tears because the situation felt so surreal. *They told me he was dead.* It was the only coherent thought she had been able to muster.

She realized how unaware she was when they stopped at an old parking garage in Shuwaikh. It took several moments for it to register that the garage was most likely the same one from the parking ticket she had found earlier.

"Lila, we're here," the Ahriman barked from the driver's seat. A moment later, he pulled her out of the car. "I'm still holding my gun. So don't try anything." His touch seemed gentle, but his tone was harsh and angry.

"I understand. I won't try to fight you," she said. *As if I could.*

They walked together across the street toward an old construction site. "What is this place?" she asked.

"No questions. Just walk."

When they got inside, he led her to a room in the back of the first floor.

"Here," he said, tossing her a zip tie. "Tie your hands. Use your teeth."

She got the zip tie around her wrists, tightened it with her teeth, and then lowered herself slowly to sit on the floor. "So, now what do we do?" she said, looking at him.

He shrugged his shoulders and sat on the floor as well. "We wait."

She stared at him for another second. Something in his eyes reminded her of the old Kasem.

"Kasem, what happened to you? I don't believe this is who you are," Petra finally managed to say. She needed to build a connection with her kidnapper the way she'd been trained to do. She told herself the question was for the sake of the mission, to try to change his mind, instead of acknowledging how much she needed him to answer honestly.

He looked back at her and his eyes moved from her face to her body and back to her eyes. Their eyes met for a moment, then he hesitated and diverted his gaze. "The people you work for abandoned us. So I made a bargain and I became their servant."

"What do you mean abandoned us? The people I work for?" She fought to keep her voice steady.

Bitterness seeped from his tone. "They wouldn't pay the ransom for you. So I paid it."

"What do you mean? You paid the ransom?" Her heart was racing. *What is he talking about? What ransom?*

"That's why General Majed let you go." He turned and glared at her. "Why the fuck would you go back to the same kind of life? How could you do that? You made my sacrifice worth nothing. I gave you a chance at a new life, and you gave your life back to that trash that you work for." She watched him stare steadfast at the floor, no longer able to hold her gaze as he started to tremble.

Petra shivered when she realized what he was saying. "Kasem, no one refused my ransom. There was no ransom demand."

He backed away, looking at her in shock.

Biting her lip, she continued, "I was never captured."

"That's not possible! You're lying."

"Why would I lie about that? We tried to get you out. Jamal was even willing to trade himself for you, but we couldn't get to you. No one knew where Majed had put you. We didn't have any information. Then a couple months later, we got word that you were killed by a Lieutenant Afshar."

"Lieutenant Afshar is dead!" he yelled.

She detected something in his voice, something about the way he spoke the name. "Was he your captor?"

"Captor, trainer, traitor—it's all the same. He's dead now, why does it matter?"

Petra caught something in his eyes that made her push further. "How did he die?"

"It doesn't matter. None of it does."

"I don't understand, Kasem. Why did they want to keep you? Why did they think you were so valuable?"

"What do you mean?" he growled. "Isn't it obvious? They thought that I was Nurah's handler. She didn't want to give you up, but they threatened her family. So she told them about me."

*So they thought he was the spy.* "What did you tell them?" she asked in a halting voice.

He kept his eyes fixated on the floor. "I never gave you up," he whispered. "I never told them anything."

She shut her eyes and drew in a long slow breath. Petra's voice wavered as she responded. "I know that's why they went after you, but there's no way they could have believed that after holding you prisoner. You didn't have any information to give them. They must have realized that Nurah lied."

His jaw set firmly as he continued his staring contest with the floor. "I don't know."

Looking at him now, Petra felt even more confused. *How could he do all this? Just to pay my ransom?*

"Kasem, did you agree to work for them so that they would let me go?"

"I already told you that I paid your ransom." His tone was harsh and cold.

"And what about last night? The Emir? The president?"

"The president? What president? What the hell are you talking about?" He was yelling again now. Petra could tell it wasn't out of anger from the range of emotions written on his face. Her mouth fell open as she watched him in shock. There was no way he was faking those emotions.

"You didn't know."

"Didn't know what?" He leaned back against the wall, panting.

"President Reynolds made an unscheduled visit to speak to the Emir before the elections."

His eyes narrowed. "What the fuck are you talking about? You're lying."

"I'm not lying. If you had set off that bomb on schedule, you would have killed both the Emir and the president of the United States."

"That's not possible. There was only supposed to be one target. I only had one target." He squeezed his eyes shut.

She tried to catch his eyes. "I don't know how this happened, but do you really believe that it's a coincidence that Reynolds was visiting the Emir on the same day you were supposed to set off a bomb?"

Kasem scowled at her in silence.

*He didn't know.* The thought comforted her slightly, but not when she remembered everything else that the Ahriman had done.

"What about everything else? The Emir? The Suez Canal?" Her voice cracked slightly; she wasn't sure she wanted to hear the answer.

"I sold my soul for you," he said in a soft whisper.

He stood up abruptly and headed for the door. "We're done talking about this, Lila. There's water and some chips in the cabinet. I'll deal with you later," he said as the door locked behind him.

**\*\*\*\***

The Ahriman sat down in the hideout he had created on the third floor of the office complex. The air in the small room was stale from the heat and lack of circulation, but his battery-powered fan helped a bit. He reached for the jug of water he'd brought in from the car and poured some water on his head. He felt a momentary cool pass over him. His pulse was still racing from their conversation, so he pulled out a cigar to calm himself. As he lit it, he remembered how much Lila had always hated cigars, and a painful smile crossed his face.

*She was never captured,* he thought, wishing that each puff would wake him from this nightmare. The radio news report about the Suez Canal from that morning in Aqaba popped into his mind. *A number of explosions in the Suez Canal...seven or eight freighters were consumed by fire...death toll is in the hundreds...*

His mind returned to the day he had stabbed Lieutenant Afshar, the only captor who'd been good to him. *That was my last chance and I ruined it.*

He felt under his shirt collar for the necklace that he'd worn for the past few years—the locket that General Majed had given him to prove that Lila had been captured. *If she was never captured, how did they get it?* He moved his thumb over the locket, trying to remember if she'd been wearing anything similar today. The general had conned him repeatedly, and yet he had stayed, continuing as his servant.

Through the window, he could see the last remnants of dusk lingering in the skyline. He waited for it to pass entirely and put out the cigar. He lay back on the yoga mat he had set up there a few days earlier. He stared at the ceiling as he tried to quiet his mind and he eventually allowed himself to sleep for a few hours.

****

Petra was asleep on the floor when she heard a sound at the door. It was still dark outside except for some ambient light from streetlights that filtered into the room. She opened her eyes and saw the door swing open. *He came back?* Before she could confirm her suspicions, he turned on a small portable halogen lantern like the one her family still used on camping trips. It blinded her momentarily, but when her eyes adjusted, she saw him take a seat on the floor in front of her. *Is it Kasem or the Ahriman?*

"Hello, Lila," he whispered. "I'm sorry to wake you."

She squinted and looked into his eyes. They were deep and dark, both in color and in spirit, but she saw him. The man before her was the one she used to know and love.

"Hi, Kasem."

He drew a loud breath. "Is Lila even your real name?"

"It's a nickname that I used to go by. My middle name is Jaleela."

"Used to?"

She looked down at the ground. "I stopped letting anyone call me Lila after I came back from Iran, but sometimes my dad still calls me Jaleela."

"How did you get out? Tell me what happened."

She swallowed slowly. "I'd just gotten home in Tehran when Jamal called me. He asked if you were with me because he was worried that he couldn't find you. He said that you sent him a text about an urgent errand that you had to run for me on the other side of town in the middle of the night." It took all of her energy to hold back tears. She had not faced the memory since the last time that she visited a psychiatrist in New York more than two years earlier.

"I was so scared. The only person I could think of who lived on that side of town was Nurah. So I went to her apartment. She'd left the signal to let me know that she thought she was being watched. I hadn't been by to check on her because I was away that week." She hung her head. "I broke into her apartment and I found your phone. There was nobody there and I knew you'd both been taken." Tears fell freely down her face now.

"What happened after that?"

"I picked up Jamal and took him to the embassy so that he'd be safe. They pulled me out right after that. I tried to use my other assets to find out what happened to you. I wanted to come back and get you, but my boss put me in emergency asylum and said he would send someone else in for you." She shook her head. "The next thing I heard was that you were dead."

"I see." He reached under his shirt collar, unhooked the clasp on the necklace, and placed it into her hands, still bound by the zip tie. "How did they get your locket?" he asked.

"I don't know." She held it close to her face to examine it and smiled grimly. "I had it with me when I went to Nurah's, but I think I dropped it when I was trying to charge your phone in my car." She tilted her head to the side. "We had to abandon the car at the airport. I didn't realize it was missing until I was on the plane."

"General Majed must have found it."

"Yeah."

Without saying anything, he touched her hands to retrieve the locket. Instead of relinquishing her hold on it, she clasped his hands softly. "Can I keep this?" she whispered.

He sighed. "I'd rather keep it. It's one of the few things I have left from that time."

She released his hands and gave it back to him. They were silent for a moment as she looked at him again, trying to read his emotions. "I'm so sorry, Kasem. This is my fault. I did this to you."

"Maybe you did." He stood up unsteadily.

She waited for him to say more as he made his way to the door. He was about to step out of the room when he turned back and spoke softly. "But there's no way you could have known." He reached back in and turned out the lantern.

"Good night, Lila."

## *The next morning – July 6, 2021*

"I found the parking garage, Chris."

"You are impressive with a computer."

"I'm impressive at a lot of things," Grant said in a feeble attempt to remain upbeat. "I just hope it's enough to find my girlfriend. I can't believe it took me this long to track down the place."

"Finding a random parking garage in Kuwait with only some old ticket as a clue isn't simple. She's lucky that you're there," Chris countered. "Besides, it's four thirty in the morning and you've been up all night. Are you sure you're in the right place?"

"It's a big industrial parking garage, so they have standard tickets. Since Petra thought it was important enough to send it to me, I think this should be the first step."

"I agree. What do you see around you?"

"I'm parked on the top floor of the parking garage. There's not much around other than industrial stuff." Grant scratched his head as he looked around. "A lot of factories, a couple of warehouses, that sort of thing. There are also two empty construction sites."

"Construction sites? At what stage?"

"The one across the street looks like a fully constructed building except for the missing windows on the top floors. The one next door isn't fully built. It's missing doors, windows, and a finished roof."

"Okay. Tell me more about the one that's fully constructed. What do you see?"

Grant pulled out the binoculars Petra kept in the car. "I can't see anything in either of them," he said, surveying both sites.

"Start with the one that's fully constructed. Go over there, but try not to be obvious."

"Go over there? In the dark and unarmed? Are you crazy? The freaking Ahriman is going to be armed!"

"Just go over there and check it out. Stay quiet and you'll be fine. You did go through Agency training once upon a time," Chris said, obviously attempting to placate him.

"Fine." Grant shook his head in annoyance. "Any updates from the Kuwaiti government?"

"The Crown Prince has sent out a team of investigators, but as far as I know, they're miles behind you."

"Okay. I'll message you with any developments."

"Grant, let me know if things go sour. I'll call in the cavalry."

\*\*\*\*

Petra was dozing off again while sitting up and leaning against the wall when she heard someone move by the door. She tried to force herself awake, expecting Kasem to walk in again. Her mind was still reeling from speaking to him earlier. Hastily, she took a swig from the water jug he had left for her. The taste of the warm water was so disgusting that she could barely stop herself from spitting it out.

"Petra, is that you?" she heard from outside the door.

"Grant?" She stood up frantically, almost losing her balance because of her zip tied hands. "Be quiet," she said as she reached the door. "Can you open it?" she whispered.

"I'm trying, but I don't really know my way around this lock pick kit."

Petra glanced around, trying to think. "Do the tools fit under the door?" she said.

"Never mind, I think I got it."

The lock clicked sharply and Grant pushed the door open.

"Petra," he exclaimed. He wrapped his arms around her, pulled her close, and kissed her on the forehead. "This is the second time in three days that you've given me a heart attack."

"I'm sorry." He took her face in his hands and kissed her.

She pulled away a moment later and gave him a tight smile. "We have to find him. I think he's in this building somewhere."

"You mean the Ahriman?"

"Yes." She reached out and touched his arm. "And Grant, we need him alive."

Grant pulled out his phone to send a message to Chris. *"I've found her. Send in the cavalry. She thinks the Ahriman is here."* He linked to his GPS to convey their coordinates, but she stopped him before he could send it.

"Don't send that yet."

He frowned. "Are you sure? I'll call it in and then we'll deal with him."

"Let's wait and make sure."

"Fine," Grant grumbled. "Let's get you out of this." He used the pocketknife on his keychain to saw through the cable tie holding her wrists together.

"Thanks," she said, shaking her wrists out. They had already turned red and sore and her hands tingled as full sensation returned.

"So now what do we do?"

"I saw some sort of utility room when he walked me down this hallway," she said, heading out the door. For the first time in the past twenty-four hours, she felt like she was thinking clearly.

"Utility room?"

"Yeah. We need to create a distraction."

Just off the corridor, Petra found the utility room she remembered seeing.

"Petra, I don't get it. What are we doing here?"

"We're going to build a bomb."

He threw his arms out to the sides. "A bomb? Are you crazy?"

"Didn't they teach you how to do this at Agency training?"

"Probably."

She grinned. "Don't worry. I'm crazy, not stupid."

"Did I ever tell you how much I love that you can quote *Speed*?"

She opened up a metal storage cabinet and pulled out a large plastic bottle of bleach, a bottle of chemical drain cleaner, duct tape, and four glass jars. After placing them on the ground, she grabbed a pair of utility gloves and then filled two of the jars with bleach and the other two with the drain cleaner.

"I haven't done this in a long time," she muttered. "This had better work."

"What exactly are you doing?"

"A bomb is just a corrosive chemical mixed with an oxidizing agent. Basically, bleach plus drain cleaner equals boom."

She screwed a lid onto each jar. Taking one pair of jars, she flipped one on top of the other so that their lids were touching and wrapped some duct tape around the joint. "So, here's a jar of each, the corrosive chemical is in the jar on top with something to keep it from mixing with the oxidizing agent long enough for us to get away." Petra handed it to Grant and looked around the room.

"Put it over by that window," she shouted at Grant, pointing to a window on the other side of the room. Once he had done so, she gestured toward the door. She grabbed the other two jars and tossed him the duct tape. "We'll need that. You already checked the rooms on this floor, right?"

"Yeah."

"Then let's get upstairs before this room burns red."

He nodded and they ran out of the room toward the staircase. They had just reached the second floor when they felt the floor shake.

"I can't believe you used to do this for a living."

Petra rolled her eyes. *Evidently, I still do.*

\*\*\*\*

The Ahriman was asleep when he felt the floor beneath him shake. He jumped up off the yoga mat and grabbed his gun. *Damn it, Lila.*

He sprinted down the staircase toward the first floor holding his gun in front of him.

\*\*\*\*

Petra heard footsteps coming down the stairs while she and Grant were still checking the rooms on the second floor. "Quiet," she mouthed and pointed to her ear.

She waited until the footsteps disappeared. "Let's go."

"I thought we were going to check each floor room by room?"

"He'll be heading downstairs to see what happened," she said, gesturing towards the stairs.

"Then let's get him and get out of here!"

"I want to find where he's been staying. He might have something we can use to tie this mess to Fayed."

"Damn it, Petra." Grant followed her reluctantly and the two of them crept quietly upstairs. They made their way up the stairwell until she stopped at the landing on the next floor.

She pointed at the ground and crept down the hallway. "There are prints in the dust here, which would mean that someone's been walking around. Let's check it out."

They moved slowly down the third floor hallway to a room in the back, trying to follow the faint path formed by the marks in the dust. Just before it ended, the hallway veered to the right.

"Looks clear," Petra whispered, straining to see around the bend. "Let's check it out."

She put the jars down and they approached the door slowly. "I wish I had my gun," she mumbled. *Even if I couldn't bring myself to fire it at him.*

Looking up, she noticed that Grant was watching her closely. "Don't give me that look. It would be useful for protection."

"I didn't say anything," he said, taken aback.

When she opened the door, she knew immediately that they had found the Ahriman's chambers. She recognized the suitcase he had taken from the hotel, and there was a tattered yoga mat lying on the floor next to a battery-powered fan and several large jugs of water. The room had one large window that led out to a fire escape and offered a view of the main approach to the building, likely why he had chosen to position himself there. She scanned the room quickly and moved toward the suitcase. "I'll check the suitcase," she said. "See if there's anything else here that might be useful."

Grant peered around the room unsure of what to look for as she rifled through the suitcase. "There's nothing here. Damn it!" she said, slamming her fist into the empty upper half of the suitcase. "Wait a second." She eyed the suitcase and pushed her open palm against the same spot. "Got you."

Turning toward Grant, Petra grinned. "Hand me your pocketknife."

"Here you go." He tossed it over to her. She took the knife out and sliced directly into the soft covering on the inside of the suitcase.

"There goes a $400 Samsonite," Grant muttered, watching her tear through the fabric and pull out a slim file. She opened it and found a document with some details about the Ahriman's accommodation in Kuwait and a picture of the Emir. "Better than nothing," she said. "Okay, radio it in and let's get out of here.

As they ran down the hallway with the file, Grant keyed in a message to Chris. "Found her." He connected to his phone's GPS to send over the exact coordinates. Chris's response arrived in a moment. "Cavalry's coming!" Grant cried out.

"Shh," Petra said. *I can't let them kill him.*

She grabbed the jars as they reached the stairwell and wrapped the duct tape around them, just as she had done with the other two jars. By holding it horizontally, she kept the fluids from mixing.

They made their way downstairs toward the site of the first explosion.

****

The Ahriman stood facing a burning room on the first floor. *She's gone.*

He rushed back up the stairs. As he passed the second floor, he heard noises coming from the floor above him. *Got you.* He moved back down to the first floor and settled at the base of the stairs with his gun trained upward.

A moment later, he had them in his sights. Lila was leading and carrying two jars wrapped together with some duct tape. A man was following her and the Ahriman recognized his familiar face. *The guy from the dewaniya?*

He aimed the gun and tried to pull the trigger. The possibility that the bullet might hit Lila made his trigger finger lock up. Even if the shot was not meant to kill, he realized that he would never be able to shoot her. Shutting his eyes for a moment, he made a decision.

His eyes opened abruptly when he heard sirens growing louder outside. *Shit.* When Lila reached the landing, he stood up and pointed the gun straight at them.

"Don't move."

Lila raised the device in her hand and he knew what it was immediately.

"Don't make me do this," she called out, turning the jars vertical. The fluids inside the jars would only take moments to mix.

"I'm not going to let you go," the Ahriman responded, keeping his gun level.

**** 

*I have to drop it.* Petra's hands felt frozen, unable to drop the bomb down the stairwell. She stared at her hands, wide-eyed and willing them to obey.

"Petra, what are you doing? Drop it." she heard Grant shout.

The stairwell around her felt as if it were spinning.

"Petra, it's going to explode, you have to let go!"

She only returned to the moment when Grant slammed into her hands and the bomb fell from her grip straight past the railing toward the first floor.

"Get down!" Grant bellowed as he pulled her to the floor.

Then everything went black.

****

# Epilogue

"So this guy was responsible for the Suez Canal bombings?"

"Yes, Mr. President." Tom Raver, director of the CIA, squirmed under the gaze of the commander-in-chief.

"And it's the same guy who tried to blow me up in Kuwait?"

"We're not sure, sir. Your visit was unscheduled, so we aren't sure if you were the intended target, especially since it was over the Fourth of July, which is an unexpected time for you to be there."

"I see. How did you collect this intelligence?"

"One of our partner agencies had someone on the ground who gathered the information from an asset."

"And you're sure that the source is credible?"

"Yes, sir. They've assured us that the intel is viable."

"What do you mean they've assured you that it's viable? You're the fucking head of the CIA. Is it viable or not?"

"It is, Mr. President."

"And this Agent Anahita, did you debrief her yourself?"

"No, sir. She's missing."

"Then who the fuck debriefed her?"

"Her agency did, sir."

"So you're telling me that up until two weeks ago, we thought this Ahriman guy was responsible for the Suez Canal bombings. Now you're saying that it's this crooked Iranian general, who was supposed to be dead. And the agent who told you this information is missing and no one in the CIA ever spoke to her?"

Raver swallowed loudly. "Yes, sir."

"Have you figured out if the Iranian government knew about this?"

"Not yet."

"What the fuck is wrong with you people? I've got President Safavi on the phone claiming that they will cooperate with us fully, and I don't know whether or not we can trust him on this."

"We just need some more time, sir."

"Now what the fuck am I supposed to do with this information?"

Raver pointed to a building on the map on screen in front of them. "We have reports that General Majed is staying in this building in Tehran. I'd like to send in a SEAL team to apprehend him."

"Goddamn it. That's where you think the guy who tried to kill me is hiding out and all you want to do is send in a team to apprehend him?"

"The building is located next to a hospital, sir. Sending in a SEAL team would minimize civilian casualties, while maximizing the likelihood of success."

The President frowned. "And how do we know they'll get to him before he realizes someone is coming for him?"

"We should be able to capture him with the element of surprise."

"Didn't the Brits try to apprehend him a few years ago?"

"Yes, Mr. President. They thought that he was killed in the attacks."

"But they were wrong, obviously."

"Yes, sir."

President Reynolds scrutinized Raver for a few moments and then shook his head. "I'm not letting this bastard have even the slightest chance of getting away again. No fucking way. We can't risk being duped like the Brits. We have to get this guy. I want to bomb the fuck out of that building."

"You can't mean air strikes, sir?" Raver's eyes had grown wide.

"I'm not talking about a full scale air assault, Raver. Your latest intel confirmed that they don't have any nukes, correct?"

"Yes, sir."

"So the potential retaliation is pretty minimal. Besides, I gave Safavi two weeks to turn the general over to us and he still hasn't done it."

"But, sir, the ramifications of an air strike in Ir—"

"Don't tell me about the ramifications. I'm the fucking commander-in-chief. I want you to move forward with a drone strike—not a full-on air assault—just a one-off drone strike. We can even let the Israelis take the punch if they want. I'll have Nina assemble the joint chiefs to prepare for war if Iran retaliates."

"But the hospital—?"

"That bastard is intentionally hiding out next to a hospital so that we won't strike. He's playing all of us, Tom. And if we know where he is in Tehran, you can bet Safavi does. He could have prevented a strike if he'd just given us the general. There's always going to be collateral damage when you eliminate a terrorist, and it's horribly unfortunate for the people of Tehran, but we have to stop this son of a bitch now. Order the strike. Have I made myself clear, Tom?"

"Yes, sir." Raver took a deep breath. "We'll have the area on screen for you shortly, so you can monitor the drone strike from here."

### New York City, United States – July, 2021

"Petra, I've got some bad news."

"What? Chris, can you speak up? The line is a little static-y."

"They're not going to send men in to capture General Majed."

"I'm sorry, now I know we have a bad connection. I could not have heard that correctly. Did you say they're *not* going to try to capture General Majed? He's a fucking terrorist! What are they going to do? Let him go?"

"No."

"Then what?" She clenched her fist to keep her tone under control. *President Reynolds, you are an absolute moron.*

"The president has ordered a drone strike on the building your source gave us."

She sank into a chair as if someone had punched her. "A drone strike, Chris? There are more than ten million people in Tehran and that building is in the middle of the city."

"I know. Raver tried to convince him that a drone strike is a bad idea, but he was adamant. Reynolds is still out for blood."

The line was silent for a moment. "Petra, are you there?"

"I'm here."

Chris waited for her to continue, but decided to change the subject. "Have you managed to recover the Ahriman's body?"

"No. We still haven't found it in the wreckage. We'll never know who he really was." She shut her eyes tightly, wishing she did not have to associate Kasem's handsome face with the hollow features of the Ahriman. *Maybe he survived?*

"When are you coming back?"

"I'm going to ground, Chris. I need some time."

"How can I reach you?"

Even though he couldn't see her, Petra replied with a noncommittal shrug before she cryptically said, "I'll check the Agency server from time to time."

"But that won't tell me where you are."

"If there's an emergency, talk to Carlos."

"Petra, I need to know where you are—"

The line clicked as she hung up.

****

A few hours later, Petra watched the news about the drone strike in Tehran. The first news report said that at least one hundred people had died and the body count was mounting with the local hospital and a number of buildings in flames. The broadcast showed photos of the city on fire with bodies scattered everywhere and people running in panic.

The picture was burned forever into her memory.

### *Paris, France – Six months later, January, 2022*

Ana Zagini smiled as she watched the Emir's speech on the evening news.

*"After the terrible accident that befell my home six months ago, I am proud to say that we stood strong. The elections held today are a statement to the strength and resilience of the Kuwaiti people."*

Turning off the TV, she picked up the small pile of letters she had taken from her mailbox earlier that day. One of the letters caught her eye. It was in a fat brown envelope addressed to "Ana Zagini" and she recognized the sender's address as she ripped it open. The letter was from Carlos, as she had expected.

Three smaller envelopes and a piece of paper fell to the ground. She picked up the lone page and began reading in silence.

*December 27, 2021*
*Dear Petra,*

*I hope you are enjoying your new solitude and time away from the Agency, especially now during the holiday season. I cannot agree with you more about needing to step away from it all.*

*Diane and I are both doing well. We look forward to welcoming you into our home whenever you are feeling up to it.*

*I am sending you this letter to forward several others that I think you should read. I hope my judgment is sound in sending them to you and that they can offer you some closure rather than further disrupting your life. Hang in there, Lockjaw, and happy New Year.*

*Love from both of us,*
*Carlos*

Petra frowned and reached for the three other envelopes. None of them had a sender's name on them. She leaned back in her chair, opened the first one, and read the note in silence.

*December 1, 2021*
*Dear Petra,*

*I've enclosed with this letter an official Agency commendation for your work in the field this year. I know how difficult it was for you to return to the field and we respect your need to take a leave of absence after everything that has happened. I look forward to seeing you back in your office in another few months.*

*I don't know if you've heard, but we had to ask Grant to resign his position with the Agency. After the court martial, he was sentenced to six months of house arrest. We were able to mitigate the sentence considerably since he was so instrumental in Kuwait. For your sake, I wish that we could have done more. I'm sure he will be very happy to see you once you return.*

*As you know, the elections in Kuwait will be held shortly. Because of your efforts, we were able to make sure that Marzouk Fayed resigned from the parliamentary race and will never return to Kuwaiti politics. The Emir preferred this solution over a public trial that would damage their national credibility.*

*Khaled Majed resigned his post as Fayed's senior aide and returned to Iran. We suspect that he is now working for his uncle, or rather that he always was. It appears that both our reports on General Majed were incorrect. He was never killed in the British raid, as you suspected, and I do not believe the US drone strike was successful in killing him either. If and when you return, we can devote some resources to exposing the numerous conspiracies he and his nephew have led together, and tracking them both down.*

*I hope you've come to terms with why I sent you on this mission. We miss you at the office.*

*Best wishes,*

*Chris*

Petra read through the letter a second time before putting it aside. *Three hundred people dead and General Majed might still be alive?* The thought made her cringe.

She pulled out the Agency commendation letter and snickered. "I guess this makes it all worth it," she said to her reflection in the mirror and tossed the pages aside.

She tore open the second envelope.

*December 5, 2021*

*My darling Petra,*

*If you are reading this then that means I successfully convinced Carlos to forward it. As he is the only one who knows your whereabouts, I will have to become a much closer friend of his.*

*I hope you are enjoying your time away from the Agency. I also hope that one day you can help me understand what happened after Kuwait and what you went through over the past few years.*

*I miss you and love you very much.*

*With all my heart, I remain your loving Grant.*

She smiled softly. It was amazing how he always knew the right thing to say even if he was still in the dark about so much that had happened.

*He didn't even mention being sentenced to house arrest or losing his job.*

She sat quietly for a few more minutes before venturing to open the third letter. When she recognized the handwriting, she could barely make herself read it.

*December 10, 2021*
*My dearest Lila,*

*I have spent the past few months trying to track you down. Since you have hidden yourself quite well, I had to follow your friend Grant to make it happen. Eventually, I managed to get this letter to your old mentor with a forwarding request. I hope that at some point this letter does actually get to you.*
*I was wrong to blame you for the path that I took years ago. I let myself become a pawn in a crazy man's game and I have done many terrible things. Thanks to the explosion your friend set off, I am finally free of him. I know that I can never make up for what I have done, but still, I wanted to say I'm sorry for everything that I put you through.*
*With all of my love,*
*Kasem*

Petra felt her eyes tear up slightly. *He's alive,* she thought, almost amused. They had never found a body in the building's wreckage, but she had not allowed herself to believe that he might have survived.

She stared at the letters for almost an hour before she picked them up and placed them at the bottom of one of her dresser drawers. After washing her face, she grabbed her purse and walked down the street toward the Seine.

When she reached the middle of the Pont au Change, she stopped and looked around. Paris was lit up all around her. The Palais de Justice stood out like a castle watching over the beautiful city. On the other side, she could see the steady figures of the Nôtre Dame de Paris and the Hôtel de Ville.

After taking in the scenery, she mustered a smile and then sauntered slowly over to a small café across the river. *It's time to start over. At least most of the memories are good here.* The few moments that she and Kasem had spent there were simple and fresh. She still felt guilty, she still felt betrayed, but in Paris, under a new name, she could distance herself from the Agency and the murkier parts of her past. Here, she could cherish the simplest things in life again, which mattered even more now. Here, she could focus on rebuilding her identity, one brick at a time. She took a seat at the bar and ordered a glass of Bourgogne red wine.

The bartender smiled at her. "Are you here alone?" he asked in French. He poured her a glass from the Chambertin vineyard. "It's quite a good one. First one's on the house."

Her face lit up. "Thank you. And yes, I just moved here. My name is Ana."

**\*\*\*\***

# THE END

Dear reader,

Thank you for reading my book. I do hope that you enjoyed *Ahriman: The Spirit of Destruction*. If you did, would you mind taking a moment to leave me a review at your favorite retailer?

Thank you in advance!

Puja Guha

# Acknowledgements

When I sat down to write my acknowledgments, I didn't know where to begin. There are so many people who have played such an important role in my writing, and particularly in *Ahriman: The Spirit of Destruction*. First, though, I'd like to thank you, the reader. Thank you for reading my book and participating in Petra and Kasem's story. You will meet them again in the near future in the second book of *The Ahriman Legacy*. As a writer, I am compelled to turn my thoughts and ideas into stories on the page, but that effort would be for naught without you.

My first idea came from the thrillers on my father's bookshelf—Tom Clancy, Frederick Forsyth, John Grisham, and countless others. I have to heartily thank all of those authors who have come before me. I never would have thought of starting down this path had it not been for you. Thank you, Dad, for exposing me to all of those books, starting when I was a little girl. My childhood would have been very different if I hadn't procrastinated studying by reading *Icon* and *The Pelican Brief*.

To my mother: the discipline that it took for me to start writing would have been completely impossible without your guidance and love as I grew up. You pushed me to be better, to be stronger, and to get through all of the distractions that would stand in my way.

I finished the first draft of *Ahriman: The Spirit of Destruction* while completing my master's by participating in the National Novel Writing Month (NaNoWriMo), which supports authors as they endeavor to write 50,000 words of a story in thirty days. Without their weekly pep talks and the NaNoWriMo community, getting here would have been much harder. Most importantly, though, I want to thank my longtime friend Anna Epshteyn Whitney for NaNoWriMo suggesting that I enroll in NaNoWriMo.

From the idea stage to the finished first draft, a number of my friends and family have supported me. I fielded so many requests to include individuals' names as characters in my book that I had to stop agreeing to them. Parshant Mittal, Viral Sarraf Mittal, Rajul

Gupta, Anahita Arora, Anton Leis Garcia, and Sophia Sen, thank you for believing in me to the extent that you wanted to see your names printed in my book. Some of them are already here, but for those of you who didn't make it into this one, I promise that you will see your names in my upcoming books.

One name is missing from that list so that I could give him a more extensive shout-out. Eric Sukumaran, I don't even know how many times you read different versions of *Ahriman: The Spirit of Destruction*. I may have fought you on some of your edits and pointers, but in sum, more than ninety percent of them have made it into this book.

Leigh Owen, my editor, has put so much of her energy and soul into this book. She has such an amazing grasp of literature as a whole and an ability to manipulate and analyze all of the details that comprise a story. *Ahriman: The Spirit of Destruction* is infinitely better because I found you.

My enduring gratitude and appreciation:

— To all of those who have read and edited *Ahriman: The Spirit of Destruction*, even in parts, although in particular, Lina Belosky and Susan Gleason, along with my late-stage beta reader, Merle Nygate.

— To Brian Elbogen and Hannah Messerli for their introductions to two recent authors who helped guide my revisions.

— To Trevor Weissman and Michael Pocalyko, fellow authors who gave me valuable intelligence on the publishing landscape.

— To Tatiana Villa for designing the perfect cover.

— To my friend Russell Saltz, whom I consider family, for sitting with me through countless questions and emotional days along the way.

— To Eneida Fernandes, Andres Garcia, Ganesh Rasagam, Francisco Campos, Leonardo Iacovone, Smita Kuriakose, Valeriya Goffe, and all of my other colleagues at the World Bank Group. Your support and even encouragement of my alternative schedule has been invaluable to my writing process.

— To my family in Kuwait, and by that I mean all of the residents of Durrar Complex, both past and present, for your loving support.

— To Dr. Arvind Raina, one of the most forward-thinking Indian philosophers I have ever met. You are one of the most enlightened and artistic individuals I've ever been lucky enough to speak with. Your wisdom has helped to inspire me to pursue a less traditional path, and to start and keep writing.

— To my deputy parents who have loved me through all of my tantrums and happiest moments: Anjna Sharma, Mohan Vatsa, Amit and Ana Ghosh, and Dib and Shampa Maitra.

— To Sujit and Runa Bhattacharya, Santa, Prasenjit, and Tapan Guha, and the rest of my family in India, for always being with me.

— To my numerous cousins and friends whom I am lucky enough to have as part of my extended family. Thank you, Sonia Bhattacharya, Pia Ghosh, David Ghosh, Kanika Khosla, Megha Raina, Amrita Sharma, Bakul Vatsa Stenning, and Kunal Vatsa for your relentless love and support.

I must end with the person to whom I owe the biggest thanks of all.

To my husband, Brendan Collins Snow: Thank you for supporting my writing every day of our relationship, even from the first time that we met to the week after our wedding. Your discipline and strength inspire me every day to pursue the inspiration that the muse has offered me and to not give up because some days the words come easily and some days they come only in sparse intervals. I love you more than anything.

# About the Author

Puja Guha began writing in 2010 by participating in the National Novel Writing Month (NanoWriMo). The idea for *The Ahriman Legacy* struck her during a family vacation shortly before that. She has lived in Kuwait, Toronto, Paris, London, and several American cities, including New York, Philadelphia, San Francisco, and Washington DC. She is a graduate of the University of Pennsylvania with work experience in finance and health care consulting. After completing a joint master's degree in public policy from London School of Economics and Sciences Po, she is now working as an independent consultant on international development programs, primarily in Africa and South Asia. *Ahriman: The Spirit of Destruction* is her first novel.

# Connect with Puja Guha

Email: pujaguha@pujaguha.com
Follow me on Twitter: http://twitter.com/guhapuja
Friend me on Facebook: http://facebook.com/puja.guha
Google plus: https://plus.google.com/106961837703326951468
Connect with me on Goodreads:
http://www.goodreads.com/user/show/21394716-puja-guha
Connect with me on Linkedin:
http://www.linkedin.com/in/pujaguha
Webpage: www.pujaguha.com

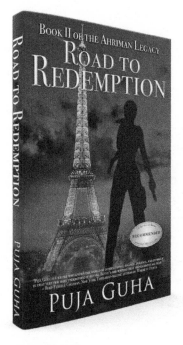

After the events of *Ahriman: The Spirit of Destruction,* Petra Shirazi settles into a life in Paris under the alias of Ana Zagini. Her new world comes crashing down after a visit from a former Agency colleague forces her back into fieldwork. As they race to stop a mole that has infiltrated the Agency, they uncover an insidious plot to destroy the leadership of the International Monetary Fund and place it in the control of a corrupt nuclear power. The investigation spirals downward and she is forced to enlist the help of the Ahriman, now in hiding and presumed dead by most intelligence sources. Together they must face their demons to stop a conspiracy that threatens to bring the world's financial infrastructure to its knees.

# The Ahriman Legacy Book III

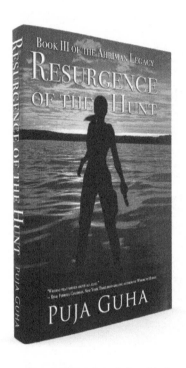

Former spy Petra Shirazi and the Ahriman, a retired Iranian assassin, work together to bring down an illegal arms trader who has eluded international authorities for decades and propped up conflict zones around the world.

Nine years ago, Agency operative Vik Jennings was brutally gunned down after he infiltrated the inner circles of illicit arms dealer Duc Nguyen, responsible for aggravating numerous conflicts around the world. Seeking justice for Vik, his former colleague Carlos engages the help of retired spy Petra Shirazi and the Ahriman, a retired Iranian assassin. Along with two CIA operatives, the team sets up an operation to gather the evidence to take Nguyen down, first at his country home outside of London, and then later during the celebration of his son's marriage in Madagascar. The investigation leads them into a labyrinth of deception implicating intelligence agencies all over the world. As the operation unfolds, Petra must keep her relationship with Vik a secret to hide her culpability in his murder from the rest of the team.

Made in the USA
Monee, IL
09 October 2022

15487357R00198